NECROPOLIS
MICHAEL DEMPSEY

"Michael Dempsey's *Necropolis* reads the way stepping over a wasted body in the rain feels. It's a noir science fiction gut punch from a strong new voice."
— Richard Kadrey, author of *Sandman Slim*

"I really enjoyed *Necropolis*. Being a sucker for detective fiction, the muscular prose and Chandleresque dialogue was like classical music to me, a delicious underscore to the brilliantly visualized dystopian future setting, striking characters and astounding plot twists."

—Bryan Talbot, writer/artist of
The Adventures of Luther Arkwright and *Grandville*

"Like his hero, Dempsey's reborn New York is darkly bent and twisted but beautifully remains rooted in the past. A stunning debut."

—Warren Hammond, author of the KOP series

"Michael Dempsey hits one out of the park on his first swing with this hard-boiled tech noir detective story. The gritty, futuristic atmosphere pulses through every chapter. If you liked *Blade Runner*, Hammett, or Chandler, you'll love *Necropolis*."

—Derek J. Canyon, author of *Dead Dwarves Don't Dance*

"Michael Dempsey's *Necropolis* reads like Fitzgerald's 'The Curious Case of Benjamin Button' filtered through the minds of Raymond Chandler and Philip K. Dick. Don't miss it."

—Dale Bailey, author of *House of Bones* and *The Fallen*

"Dempsey delivers! *Necropolis* is a new-school mix of sci-fi, horror, crime noir, and good old-fashioned sex and violence. It's dark. It's fun. Just don't go inside if you plan on getting back out alive..."

—Jeff Carlson, international bestselling author of
Plague Year and *The Frozen Sky*

NECROPOLIS

NECROPOLIS

MICHAEL DEMPSEY

NIGHT SHADE BOOKS
SAN FRANCISCO

First Edition

Printed in Canada

ISBN: 978-1-59780-315-1

Night Shade Books
http://www.nightshadebooks.com

This book is dedicated to my parents, Ann Marie and Gene, who always thought it was more important to spend their hard-earned money in support of their kids' artistic inclinations than to buy a new couch.

(Prologue)

DONNER

Ten minutes before I died, I realized I was out of cigarettes.

I stopped on the sidewalk and looked up Broadway. There was a bodega at the corner of 66th, its entrance steeped in darkness courtesy of repair scaffolding that had converted the city block into a wood and pipe tunnel.

My wife collided gently with me. Pedestrians grumped around us, late for the rest of their lives.

"C'mon, it'll just take a second," I said to her.

Elise wrinkled her mouth in vague disapproval. She'd started doing it enough lately that tiny lines were finding permanent homes around her lips.

"The overture's going to start," she said.

I knew. We were running late.

Lincoln Center, our objective, was half a block away. The fountain sparkled, shooting streams of blue-green water into the air. Gold-trimmed banners announced an upcoming jazz festival. As if to punctuate Elise's point, a couple of them cracked like gunshots in the fall breeze. Other tardy opera-goers hurried across the plaza in their overcoats and furs, laughing, chasing their own exhalations.

I smiled. The place still gave me a little shiver of excitement, even after all these years. Okay, so maybe it hadn't aged so well, with its grid-wrapped travertine marble and drippy postmodern columns. But those dated buildings and their flaking stone still housed world-class opera, theater and ballet. How many guys got to splurge once a year and treat their wives to the planet's largest performing arts center?

"Listen, if I'm going to sit through three hours of this Don Corleone thing—"

"*Don Quixote*, you fool," she said, laughing.

"Whatever. I'll still need a smoke for intermission."

She gave me the look again. I knew she wasn't really irritated. The truth was, we were both relieved to be back on solid ground after last night.

It had been bad. Real bad.

I shook my head to dispel the feeling. Let the accusations, the cutting remarks, the tears, the guilt, all slide into oblivion. What mattered was tonight. Tonight was going to be great.

"Oh, fine." She sighed with a patience born of great practice. "I'll wait here."

"Like hell you will," I said. "This city's dangerous, in case you hadn't noticed. Especially for someone as gorgeous as you."

"Yeah?" She ran a finger up my lapel. "How gorgeous am I?"

I closed the space between us. "You are," I said, touching her copper hair, "the most intoxicating creature I've ever laid eyes on. And you know it."

The cold had brought a blush to her cheeks. The dots of color against her skin's natural creaminess brought to mind a porcelain doll, or maybe an antique, hand-colored photograph. Some of her features—the delicate nose that turned skyward at the tip, the bud of a mouth—might have looked child-like, were it not for her eyes. Christ, those eyes. Large, probing, they were the anchors of a graceful and commanding symmetry. They countenanced no fools; they demanded immediate respect. The combination was devastating.

She looked almost uneasy at the appreciation in my face. "You're still nuts about me, aren't you?" she said.

I rolled my eyes in mock exasperation.

"Tell me," she said. She pulled us further out of the flow of cranky foot traffic. The air had become cold-blooded in its assault now, but we barely noticed it.

"My job, what I do every day," I said slowly. "You're always knee-

2

deep in somebody's pain. It grinds at you, tries to make you hollow. A lot of the guys go under. Succumb to the undertow. There's this emptiness behind their eyes, you know? Like they're dead already and just going through the motions of being alive. But me, well. All I gotta do is think of you. And then the world, this city, my life—it's magic again."

Eventually, she remembered to exhale. "Good answer," she whispered. Her breath trembled in front of her.

"Worth a pack of smokes?" I asked.

She slipped her arm through mine. "Okay. But we'll go to that one. It's cheaper."

She nodded at a Korean grocery across from the subway. Her small hand melded into my palm, a perfect fit, tugging playfully. "And pick up the pace, Detective! Don't want to miss the first scene."

So we hurried into the grocery.

And died.

PART ONE:

BACK FROM BLACK

For certain is death for the born
And certain is birth for the dead;
Therefore over the inevitable
Thou shouldst not grieve.
—*Bhagavad Gita*

1

KOVACS

The cemetery was bleak, forlorn, and totally fucking decrepit.
Christ. Who'd want to be buried here?
Kovacs stamped his feet against the chill.

A rusted iron fence, complete with Gothic spikes, struggled to remain upright amid the weeds and broken glass. Rows of headstones sat skewed like dragon's teeth. The stones were monstrosities, encrusted with putto and scripture, their once-polished veneers pockmarked and moss-covered. Roots gnarled the pathways like disgorged pieces of bone.

Stupid assholes, he thought, peering at the stones. He knew how *he* was going out. Vacuum-sealed in a disinterium. So they knew where to find him.

He sucked at his cigarette to dispel his sudden surliness, but the smoke in his lungs didn't make him feel any better. It was pouring rain. Which meant he already had a grudge against this corpse for making him come out in such nasty shit.

He motioned for Drone, who was currently shaped in an umbrella configuration, to descend closer. As he huddled under its protection, he realized suddenly what was really spooking him. He was Outside. Outside for the first time in ten years.

He'd taken the Midtown Tunnel off FDR Drive into Queens. Made decent time along the LIE, until he'd come to the barriers and checkpoints. Once he'd received clearance to leave the Blister, he'd driven out onto the Grand Central Parkway, which of course had been empty, like the rest of the freeways. It still creeped him out, all those miles of deserted cement and steel.

Kovacs tossed his cigarette away and pulled the fedora tighter down onto his head. In the distance, the Blister pulsed over the city, conjoined snow globes of energy. Electromagnetic discharges parried with the rain in a surrealistic light show of crimson and turquoise.

His city. Look what they'd fucking done to it. It felt like he was looking at the cover of one of those pulp sci-fi magazines that had been popular in his father's day—*Weird Space Tales*, or whatever. Oh, the city's silhouette was basically the familiar conglomeration of skyscrapers—the Chrysler, the Empire State, they were still there. But they were now surrounded by pointed silver spires, tube-like shafts and swirling elevated cruiseways. Like someone had morphed Manhattan with Oz.

Drone's stabilizers whined in protest at a sudden gust, and Kovacs was dosed with a face full of rain. Sputtering, cursing, he turned. A medevac dragonfly was setting down about twenty meters away, its blades adding to the storm's blast, its chitinous body plates lending it a prehistoric menace.

About fucking time.

Three figures spilled out. They plodded forward in their white environmental suits, appropriately ethereal.

"You call it in, flatfoot?" one of them shouted over the roar of the turbines.

The medic got treated to a scowl. Out here was no one's beat and the guy fucking well knew it.

"Surprised the graveside monitor was still working."

The man looked around. On the street beyond the outer fence was a row of crumbling brownstones. Probably still some skeletons inside. "A nice neighborhood, once."

"How long since you've done a retrieval outside the Blister?" said Kovacs, trying to sound casual.

The man shrugged. "Six, seven years?"

He pulled a Y-shaped device from his pack that looked like a divining rod. He swept it back and forth, consulting the holographic readout. Its beeping strengthened southwesterly.

"Okay," said the medic. "Let's go."

The device led them deeper into the bone yard, past stunted trees and mausoleums right out of an old flatflick.

God sure had an ironic sense of humor. *No, strike that*, his mind protested. *Leave God out of this*. Things were too screwed up. If God actually was behind what had happened… well, beneath that concept lay a hysteria Kovacs knew he'd never be able to wrestle to ground.

"Don't get your knickers in a bunch, love," said Drone, noting his tense face. "You're five by five." Thinking that Kovacs was worried about the biofilter field Drone was projecting around his body. Its "body language interpretation" mode (highly touted by the manufacturer) wasn't very good. Even after seven months as partners.

When they'd almost reached the outermost fence, the divining rod announced that they'd arrived. Kovacs could only see a wild growth of hedges until the medics cleared the underbrush with a couple swipes of a scythe.

There. A thin shaft was bracketed to the headstone. Its wafer-like sensors were encrusted with decay. A red light at its summit strobed the darkness in warning.

"What's it doing way back here?"

They exchanged an uneasy glance.

"Can't see the inscription."

Drone grunted and directed a blast of compressed air against the stone's marble face. Muck clouded into the air and floated away in search of another headstone on which to settle.

PAUL DONNER
b. 1979, d. 2012

There was a matching headstone beside it.

ELISE DONNER
b. 1973, d. 2012

Both had died the same year. A car wreck? Murder-suicide? *You wish. Anything to keep the bores away*. Probably something a lot more mundane. Food poisoning at the local sushi shack. The second grave—the wife's—was dark, its monitor unlit. *Sorry, pal. All alone on your second time around*.

The squad leader nodded. "Two-twelve. Don't get many this fresh anymore. The current crop's from the 1950s."

One of the rookie medics smirked. "Pretty soon we'll be digging up Abe Lincoln."

The leader caught Kovacs's bloodless reaction and laughed. He leaned over and touched a stud on the tube. A bright medical holo sprung into the air from the headstone. The rain and wind distorted its field, making it jitter and flap. The tube spoke. "Thirty-seven minutes to revival," it stated. "Critical support structures damaged. Without surgical intervention, survival probability six percent."

The leader spoke into the comm tattoo on his forearm. A roar rose over the rain. They all turned.

An autodozer growled forward out of the storm, crushing shrubs and bushes in its wake, its steel-toothed maw shuddering in what looked very much like hunger.

The coffin dropped onto the mulchy ground. Rain battered away the dirt and decay, revealing its metal skin. "Okay," said Kovacs to the men. "Knock yourselves out."

The men attacked its seal with crowbars. The catch released with a crack and the lid was thrown open.

Kovacs's breath caught in his throat. Contrary to urban legend, hair and nails didn't grow post mortem. It was the shrinking back of the flesh, exposing more of the nail bed or hair follicle, that created the macabre impression. This guy was no exception. If he'd been handsome once, you couldn't tell. His features were sunken and wax-like. The lips and eyes were half-open, the hands drifted down to his sides, the Krazy Glue having long ago dissolved.

But that wasn't what made Kovacs's eyes widen in shock.

The corpse wore dress blues.

Somebody whistled. "A cop."

"A detective," Kovacs corrected, noting the gold shield.

His chest was festooned with ribbons, his legs draped in the American flag.

"Look at them medals. Who was this guy?"

The leader examined the badge. "78th Precinct."

Kovacs grunted. "Park Slope. Brooklyn."

"So what's he doing buried out here in Kew Gardens?"

No one had an answer.

"So who's gonna do it?" said the leader. "Manual confirmation's required."

There were no volunteers.

"Pussies," muttered Kovacs.

He knelt down and pressed two shaking fingers to the corpse's neck. For a moment, there was no sound but the crackle of rain on vinyl ponchos. Finally, he nodded. "Still dead."

Despite their training, everyone there sagged with relief.

◥▼

"Please wait," the room said. "Close your eyes."

The top three microns of every exposed surface in the room was flash-incinerated and vacuumed out. There was a popping noise. Red lights went green and the far doors of the decontamination foyer whooshed open.

The crash team continued with the gurney into the operating arena. Kovacs and Drone started to follow them in, but a territorial resident in a mask stopped them. The man actually made the mistake of putting a gloved hand on Kovacs's chest.

"Whoops," murmured Drone.

Kovacs grinned. He peeled the resident's fingers back, careful to inflict the maximum amount of pain without permanently crushing anything important.

The resident's eyes flashed shock. "Hey, shit! Let go!"

Kovacs squeezed harder, lightening the man's face a few more skin tones. "Know the penalty for touching a cop?"

"I just—you're—you're not allowed in the OR!"

"I document the outcome, pal."

The resident yanked his hand back. He cradled it under his elbow, glowering, debating another smartass remark. Finally he nodded toward an observation cubicle set off the foyer. "Do it from there."

Kovacs watched the man flee down the steps into the surgical arena, but the satisfaction he'd hoped for wasn't there, only numb fatigue. He followed Drone into the cramped space. It stank of sweat and fear.

Through the window, he watched the crash team sweep the body onto the surgery table. The medics dove in, cutting away clothing, applying sensors and IVs. Diagnostic AIs crawled across the body like Tinkertoy spiders.

Kovacs wriggled in the plastic chair. His ass was already going numb.

Drone settled beside him. "Want a soda?" it said.

"Get fucked."

"Such language."

"Are you recording all this?" Kovacs snapped.

"All spectrums."

"Then what am I doing here?" he said.

"You're my date?"

Kovacs closed his eyes. He swore he could actually feel the damned thing smirking.

Below, in the operating room, the Chief Surgeon probed two dime-sized wounds. One was in the heart area, the other down where the spleen would be. Kovacs marveled at how tidy small-caliber handgun wounds were. You'd think something that could kill you so efficiently would look more... dramatic. Of course, for drama there was the Y-shaped coroner's incision, sewn shut with loops of heavy black thread.

The body had taken on a sheen, the skin covered in a thin film. A nurse watched data streaming into the air off a black obelisk. "Tissue saturation 45% and falling."

The doctor touched the skin, brought the moisture up to his nose. "Formaldehyde sweat. Still amazes me."

"Ready with the trocar," said the nurse, unimpressed.

Kovacs had seen enough of these procedures to comprehend the irony. Once upon a time, the pointed metal tube had been a mortician's device used to remove fluids and gasses, puncture the organs and inject preservative into the chest cavity. Now it was employed in reverse, to remove the formaldehyde solution the corpse's cells were excreting.

"Cause of death?" asked the doctor.

One of the black slabs replied: "Gunshot wound, left ventricle."

"Shot in the heart," a nurse said softly.

On the equipment behind them, the green flatlines glowed.

▼▼

Donner looked like a freshman biology experiment, the muscle of his stomach neatly pinned back, his abdominal cavity on display. The doctor poked around, prodding spleen, stomach, lungs.

"His organs have grown back nicely."

A nurse surveyed his nether regions. "Mmm-hmm."

He ignored her. "Secondary wound completely healed. The liver, though. See? That's degenerative."

"Cirrhosis? Our hero was a boozer?" asked the nurse.

"Grow another one," he instructed one of the spiders, which scurried over to something that looked like a microwave oven.

"Question?" It was the resident. The doctor sighed but didn't object. "Why doesn't it regrow healthy?"

"The body comes back exactly how it was at the moment of death, understand? The liver would heal rapidly. But maybe not fast enough. It's safer to just replace it from his stem cells."

Another nurse pointed. "What's that?"

The doctor pulled a wad of decomposed gunk from inside the abdomen and sniffed it. "Sawdust."

Kovacs felt his gorge rise.

"Homicides are autopsied," said the doctor. "The organs were removed for examination. Afterward, the mortician used whatever was handy to fill the cavity. Sawdust, paper towels…"

"I'll never eat stuffing again," someone said.

Kovacs closed his eyes and counted to twenty.

From below: "We're gonna have to do a full cavity sanitization."

Drone cocked at a quizzical angle. "Weird. The human need to preserve the body after death."

"It's not a *need*."

"Then what is it?"

"It's… I don't know, a cultural thing."

"It's a waste of time. And real estate. Is it because of your ancient creation myths?"

Kovacs ground his teeth together. *Remember your smarty sensitivity training.* "We were made from the earth, so we're returned to it when—"

"Ashes to ashes. I know," the machine sniffed. "But flesh ain't dirt."

"It's not literal, dipstick. It's semantics."

"Huh? Do you mean a figure of speech?"

"Whatever! Our bodies are matter, but our souls are eternal."

"Then why do you say smarties don't have souls? Machines die, too." It buzzed. "Eventually."

"You cease functioning. You don't die."

"Talk about semantics," Drone grumped.

Below, the spider was back with the new liver. The doctor glanced at an antique clock on the wall. It read 3:04 AM. The minute hand clicked backwards to 3:03.

"Alright," he said. "Prep him for surgery."

An hour later, he stripped away his stained gloves.

"Now we wait."

Kovacs leaned forward. The wounds had begun to look less black and angry. Their edges were pink with freshly healed tissue. The fact that Kovacs hadn't seen the change was creepier than its occurrence.

Drone was softly singing something. "Wake up, wake up you sleepyhead, get up, get out of bed."

Donner's face was motionless in the unnatural way only death brought. Facial muscles only completely relaxed in death, which is why loved ones never looked quite right in the casket.

Kovacs remembered his first funeral, age eight. Uncle Pat had dropped dead in the D'Agostinos produce section. Sadly, Pat's passion for broccoli hadn't staved off a coronary. At the funeral, young Kovacs had stared at Pat in the coffin, fascinated, repulsed, thinking how strange death was, but glad, too, knowing he'd freak if Unca were to suddenly look at him and grin, a tiny piece of green floret caught in his teeth...

This is so wrong, he thought.

In the room, Donner sighed.

The resident yelped, stumbling backward into a tray of instruments. The metallic clatter was insanely loud. The doctor shot him a murderous glance. "None of that, goddamn it!"

On the heart monitor, the flatline suddenly rustled.

"Come on, come on you, sleepyhead..."

The flatline jumped again. A couple of ragged spikes.

"Ready with epinephrine."

A nurse raised a heavy syringe, the image of a mad doctor.

"Get up, get up, you're only dead—"

Abruptly, the monitors settled into a rhythmical pattern. Healthy, steady peaks.

Beep… beep… beep… beep…

Kovacs tasted blood. He'd bitten his lip.

The doctor wiped sweat from his brow with his sleeve.

Beep… beep… beep… beep…

A priest stepped from the shadows. He was young, not happy with his job. He bowed his head and made the sign of the cross. "The Lord giveth, the Lord taketh away, the Lord giveth back. The Lord… can't seem to make up his mind lately. Amen." He put a dab of holy water on Donner's forehead and fled.

"Time of revival, 4:29 AM, October 31, 2054."

"Hey," a nurse said. "It's Halloween."

2

DONNER

Too bright!

The light was blinding. There was pain, strange pain; from a million different places and from nowhere at the same time. I called out for her.

A tiled ceiling swam into focus, then resolved itself into a pig-faced nurse smiling down at me.

Not Elise.

She handed me a mirror. I looked at myself. Blinked. Looked again. It was a trick. Had to be. Some kind of carnival lens, like a funhouse mirror.

My blue eyes were laced with shimmering gold flecks. My hair was an iridescent white, so bright it almost glowed. My nails were jet black.

I opened my mouth. I felt my lips move, struggling, but only a rasp emitted from my throat.

Don't try to speak yet, not-Elise said. Rest.

She turned to go. My hand shot out and grabbed her wrist, yanking her back to me with a strength that surprised her.

Her smile vanished. It had never been real in the first place.

Is this heaven? I asked.

Way off, baby, she smirked, shaking herself free. This is New York.

I became agitated then.

After the sedative took effect, she asked questions. Name, age, occupation. Living relatives? Just my wife.

Where was I? Was there an accident? Why did I feel so strange?

She spoke in bland autopilot reassurances, telling me nothing. Which terrified me all the more.

Sleep, she said. Your body needs to recover.

From what? I wanted to know.

From being dead, she said.

Bad joke, I said, and closed my eyes.

3

MAGGIE

TRANSCRIPT NO:294610-112b | 1200.011.03.54

REBORN:PAUL DONNER, REV. DATE [0430.10.31.54]

ASSIMILATION COUNSELOR:MARGARET CHI, SERIAL NO.
29940723492438

SESSION NO. 1

COUNSELOR'S NOTES:
Subject's anger and denial are at upper levels of base for Stage One as-
similation. Mental acuity exceeds base for early revival.

Subject is resistant to changes in modern language and colloquialisms.
Subject uses a grim humor as a defense against the terror he feels. He
is unusually strong-willed. He tests 320 on the Hamt Emotional-Psych
Scale. While he demonstrates resilience, his adherence to antiquated con-
cepts of masculinity (i.e. repression of emotions that he feels are "weak",
difficulty asking for help, internalizing of stress) is discouraging. This
type of personality has a 35% greater probability of failed re-integration
into society, with the ensuing violence, drug abuse and suicide that this
entails.

The transcript of the interview is as follows:

DONNER

I think I just saw a flying Studebaker.

(NOTE: Subject was looking out the window.)

MAGGIE

EM. John Q. Public thinks they're the cat's pajamas, but the insurance will kill you.

DONNER

Huh?

MAGGIE

Sorry. EM means electromagnetic. You called it maglev in your day—remember those high-speed Japanese trains? Same thing. They don't really fly—they just kind of hover.

DONNER

Uh-huh.

Silence while the subject looked around the processing room, then studied my floating face.

DONNER

What… what are you? Are you real?

MAGGIE

I'm a smarty. A Virtual Person. In the parlance of your time, artificial intelligence. You're currently experiencing me as a Type 3 hologram. I can incorporate in several formats, however.

DONNER

Uh-huh.

MAGGIE

I'm your assimilation counselor. Do you remember how you died?

The subject winced as though slapped. I re-scanned his file.

MAGGIE (CONT'D)

Oh God. I'm sorry. Shit.

(NOTE to Assimilation Board: once again, the overwhelming caseload has resulted in inadequate preparation time. This does damage to the subjects! Please provide more staff!!)

DONNER

My wife…

MAGGIE

I'm sorry. We don't know why some come back and some don't. Frank Sinatra is still dead, but you can see Elvis at Radio City every night at 9.

DONNER

Jesus.

MAGGIE

Not yet. Ha.

He didn't laugh. Tactical change.

DONNER

They said we were murdered. I don't remember it.

MAGGIE

That's typical. Your brain, ah, died before it had a chance to chemically encode your last memories. Probably best that way.

I administered a mild sedative .35 seconds after processing that the subject was going into shock.

MAGGIE

Look, Mr. Donner, you should know what you're in for. During the Dark Eighteen, we—

DONNER

The what?

MAGGIE

The eighteen months when the Shift was uncontained. We think it was some kind of bioweapon that mutated. It wasn't airborne, thank god, but it still moved fast out of New York. Things… fell apart.

DONNER

"The center cannot hold."

MAGGIE

What? Oh. Wow. Poetry.

DONNER

Yeah, a cop that knows Yeats. Go figure.

Typical fleshpot response. When frightened, get angry.

MAGGIE

The containment of reborns and carriers to Necropolis is why revivals continue here, but outside it's pretty rare now.

DONNER

Carriers?

MAGGIE

Normal people who have been exposed to reborns become carriers of the retrovirus, just like reborns. They can cause the Shift to start again wherever they go. By necessity, three million of them were quarantined here with the reborns.

DONNER

Christ. They must hate us.

MAGGIE

Yes. They do.

Subject closed his eyes.

MAGGIE (CONT'D)

To most norms, reebs are freaks of nature. Not… fully human. That's not true, of course. You're not a zombie or a vampire or anything. Just…

DONNER

Just back from the dead. And growing younger, they tell me. Everything in reverse. Destined to be a teen again, then a baby, then a fetus—then adios, muchacho.

MAGGIE

This is traumatic. But the quicker you accept what's happened, the quicker you'll get on with—

DONNER

Life?

Subject laughed harshly. Three seconds of silence.

DONNER

I'm surprised they didn't nuke the city.

MAGGIE

They almost did.

That got a reaction out of him.

MAGGIE

Luckily, saner heads prevailed.

DONNER

What stops people from leaving? You can't wall up an entire city.

MAGGIE

Actually, you can. When completed, the geodesic domes of the Blister will finalize Necropolis's containment.

DONNER

Nothing's one hundred percent.

MAGGIE

Beyond the Blister is roughly one hundred miles of uninhabitable desolation, the Blasted Heath. No electronics operate there. No cars. No life, no food, no water.

DONNER

Sounds like an improvement for Jersey.

MAGGIE

Necropolis is actually quite a nice place to live.

DONNER

Yeah? We have a good baseball team?

MAGGIE

We've provided a job and an apartment for you.

Two tiny dots glowed on the subject's wrist. This startled him.

MAGGIE

You've been implanted with ID and credit pebbles, so you can get settled. Pass your wrist under any scanner. Prudently spent, the funds should last a couple months. There's also a dickenjane.

DONNER

Huh?

MAGGIE

A primer. A lot has changed. Your body, for instance. Some new advantages and some new disadvantages. It also has a history/technology review, to help you catch up on current affairs. Just wave it at any smartscreen.

DONNER

Where's the job?

Subject noticed I was avoiding his eyes. Must remember that he was a detective.

23

MAGGIE

Um. In a ball bearings factory.

DONNER

Guess the NYPD doesn't have an undead affirmative action program, huh?

MAGGIE

It's the NPD now… the Shift… it's turned the world on its head, Mr. Donner. People are rattled.

Heart rate and respiration jumped 20 percent. Capillary dilation evident in face.

DONNER

They're rattled? My wife and I are murdered, then I come back as some side-show freak in a nightmare world, and *they're rattled*??

MAGGIE

I suppose it wouldn't help to know that anger is a common reaction.

The subject's only response was an icy stare.

MAGGIE

We'll be meeting twice a week on—

DONNER

Thanks, but I'm done here.

The subject rose, shakily, looking for a door.

MAGGIE

This isn't something you macho through on your own, Donner. The percentage of reebs that end up crazy or incarcerated is—

DONNER

Life's a bitch, then you're reborn.

MAGGIE
I'll be downloading to your home.

DONNER
I don't need some fucking electronic watchdog!

MAGGIE
My Virtual Personhood is based in a quantum magneto-plasmatic memory web. There are no electronics involved. And for future reference, smarties have feelings. Which can be hurt.

The subject let out an ironic laugh, but he appeared too overwhelmed to fight any more.

DONNER
Am I free to leave?

I nodded. Subject headed for the door.

MAGGIE
Donner. Do, uh… you remember anything?

DONNER
You mean like God, heaven, a tunnel of white light, like that?

I nodded.

DONNER
No. Does anybody?

MAGGIE
No.

NOTE TO PROCESSING: Delete last ten seconds of exchange before archiving.

END SESSION 0000.

4

DONNER

I got about four blocks before somebody beat the shit out of me.

I'd left the hospital quickly, accepting the clothes they offered, signing the required legal disclaimers (We Are Not Responsible For Your Afterlife!) and making a promise I had no intention of keeping to attend another counseling session.

As I dressed in the changing room, fumbling with unfamiliar button-fly pants, looking at the snap-brim fedora and the wide-lapelled jacket, the panic started. First, in my fingertips, then swirling into a tight, cold knot in my stomach. By the time I was striding across the lobby, I was actively fighting the urge to run.

I burst through the front doors like a sprinter hitting the finish tape.

Out on the street, the relief I'd been chasing didn't appear. Only terror. I stood on the sidewalk, the leather shoes stiff and biting through absurdly thin nylon socks. A wind played with the raw skin of my face. My first shave in forty-two years.

I'd survived my own death.

No. Worse. I'd survived the death of my whole world.

I was pretty sure I wouldn't be able to deal with this.

Was I really alive again? Revived, like they said? Dreaming? In some perverse afterlife? At that moment, on that sidewalk, anything seemed possible.

It was rush hour, the streets packed. I eyed the men in their blocky suits and hats, the women in their wool skirts, mesh stockings and pumps. Christ, some of them had pillbox hats. I caught a few other styles as well. A shaggy-haired guy in a tie-dye tee, fringed suede vest and bellbottoms. A black guy in what looked like a purple zoot suit. They all bustled down the street in that familiar, harried, self-absorbed big city way.

But no cell phones. No laptop cases. No iPods, no Starbucks coffee cups. Just heavy-looking briefcases, cute little one-clasp handbags. The whole fucking vista could be a piece of vintage newsreel…

… except for the traffic cop in a lozenge-shaped pod at the intersection, directing the Packards, Hudsons and Buick Roadmasters, which hummed wheellessly along, six inches above the street…

… or the holographic newspapers tucked under pedestrians' arms…

… or the tiny glowing dots many of them had in their temples…

… or the swirling stacks of streets high above my head, aerial highways crammed with cars. Worse, the streets *moved*, they *changed*, re-directing themselves like some solid yet fluid river, reacting as traffic thickened or lightened, adding lanes, anticipating flow…

I tore my gaze away, overwhelmed with vertigo. I tried to focus on the wall next to me, but my eyes were drawn to a movie poster. It featured Alan Ladd and Russell Crowe in something entitled *Shane Comes Back*.

No escape. Even the sky was wrong, swirling and out of focus behind the magnetic Blister. The whole thing, the combination platter of styles and periods, made me want to curl into a tight ball right there on the cold street.

I'd busted this crack fiend once. He'd been a real hardcase, back from a two-week suicide run during which he'd stolen his grand-mother's silver, gotten kicked out of another shelter and flushed his last chance at redemption down the crapper. I remember him telling me, as the cuffs clicked shut: "I got no place to go that I understand."

Now I knew what he was talking about.

My body started shaking.

C'mon, Donner, get it together. You're not a civvie.

I had to treat this unknown like those dark hallways I'd faced as a cop. Putting one foot in front of the other, trusting my reflexes and my judgment to get me through.

But what was this body? Was it really mine? Every muscle felt stiff and unwieldy, every contraction forced. I looked down at the bizarre coal-black nails. My eyes shone a freakish gold and my hair was Andy Warhol white. And what about my mind? I couldn't summon up the last day of my life. What was here that I actually could trust, even within myself? At least, before, when everything around me went to shit, I still had myself. Could I still count on myself?

Approaching paralysis. *Let's go,* I told myself. *One foot in front of the other. You* do *have somewhere to go. An address in your pocket. A new apartment. Start with that.*

I moved. A foot, then two. Slowly, and then more surely.

Things actually might've been okay if the old woman hadn't screamed.

◥

She lay on the sidewalk fifteen yards distant. Her hose were torn, her skirt ridden up to reveal a girdle that looked like a medieval torture device.

Surrounding her were five young reborn freaks. Their dreadlocks were spiked whole feet into the air by immense amounts of gel, forming actual two-dimensional words and images. One hairdo was shaped like a hand with its middle finger extended. Creative. Another said, inexplicably, MAURY LIVES! Their faces were tattooed black around the eyes and nose to look like skulls. Goth and punk, with a dash of *Night of the Living Dead* thrown in for flavor.

They tore the purse from the woman's grasp and bolted away, shouting and waving fists.

I moved to the woman before I was even aware that I was in motion. Instincts apparently still intact. Reflexes weren't so awful, either.

I reached down a helping hand. She saw me. Took in my eyes, my hair. Screamed again.

Then, from behind me: "Step away from her, corpse."

I turned. Almost a dozen pedestrians had stopped. I didn't know who'd actually spoken, but it didn't matter. They all had the same look. Not too hard to recognize hate.

Two cops encased in riot gear pushed their way to the front. No, not cops. Private security? They were bulging and steroidal. One tall, one short. The word SURAZAL was emblazoned across their body armor in block white letters.

I straightened. "Three white males, heading north on foot—"

The cops surged forward. I briefly hoped they were going to help the woman. Instead, they grabbed my arms. Their strength was legit. They moved me across the ground like I was an empty sack of clothes, toward an alley. Angry shouts of encouragement followed us in. Then we were deeper between the buildings, all witnesses gone.

Going to get bad fast now.

I tried anyway. "Hey, boys, hold on—"

They threw me through some trash cans. As my new clothes were coated in garbage, part of my mind was thinking, *metal trash cans, not plastic, hey, even the trash is retro.*

I tried to pick myself up, brush myself off, but my body objected. My legs went south and I staggered back down into rotting egg shells, old tampons and coffee grounds. The cops sneered through their visors.

"What's wrong, reeb," Taller said. "Legs don't work yet?"

"Must be a fresh one," Shorter opined.

I kept trying. "I used to be—"

I was thrown against the brick wall. As skin tore and flesh abraded, I realized the sensation was strangely comforting. Pain was the only old friend who'd stuck around.

"I was on the job," I managed to croak.

"Right," replied Shorter. "And I'm Martin Luther King."

He jabbed his baton into my diaphragm. Stars flashed. I dropped to my knees again, not even able to gasp.

"You know what I like about you freaks?" asked Taller. "You can take twice the beating a norm can, and you won't die. You just—" A fist to my kidneys. "—won't—" A sap to the solar plexus. "—die." A baton across my face.

Darkness screamed at me. My mouth worked, a fish out of water. Shorty laughed. "He's still trying to talk." He yanked my head back by my white hair.

"What's that, freak?"

"I didn't… touch… that woman…"

Grins. "Good for you."

They descended on me with fists and batons.

5

KOVACS/LORETTA

Kovacs sat in the Desoto, waiting for the whore. She was a new girl out of Yousef's stable. Thought she was hot shit. Thought that she didn't have to play by the rules. It was Kovac's job to show her how wrong she was.

It was a standard piece of freelance muscle work. Nothing unusual, but Kovacs was unsettled anyway, for two reasons. First, it was odd that Yousef wasn't dealing with Loretta himself. That was a pimp's number one job: keep the bitches in line. You handled all problems personally, because in the end all you had was your street cred.

Secondly, Yousef had sounded nervous on the phone. Yousef *never* sounded nervous. In the ten or so gigs Kovacs had performed for him, Yousef had been dependably brutal and indifferent to risk.

Kovacs thought about the platinum-blonde chippy he had stashed away in his Hell's Kitchen efficiency. Okay, she wasn't much. She was way past prime, but that made her desperate, which was good. She rubbed his ugly feet, brought him whiskey, did anything he wanted, as long as he paid the gas bill and kept her in hooch. He was lord and master. What more could you ask for? He wanted to be there right now, in the peeling bedroom, with the radiator ticking and bathing the room in oppressive heat. With his girl tending to his every need. That'd be a whole lot better than this mess.

Next to him in the passenger seat, Drone scanned the fog in a vari-

30

ety of surveillance modes. Kovacs didn't see why he should expect any trouble from this cooze, but it never hurt to be careful.

Because Yousef had been nervous.

"What time is it?"

"Twelve fifteen thirty-three," said Drone. Its tone belied its discomfort with the current operation.

"Look, this ain't payola," said Kovacs for the third time. "It ain't cream. This is sideline stuff, okay? Hired muscle."

"Your body fat percentage is 37."

"It's seman—a figure of speech, dickhead!" Kovacs ground his jaw. This fucking contraption got under his skin faster than anything alive or dead—and that included three ex-wives.

"You won't hurt her?"

"We're gonna put the fear a' God in her, that's all."

"What if we, I don't know… traumatize her?"

Kovac's belly laugh threatened the continued existence of the steering column. "She's a junkie whore! Her dad was rod man for the Hartley crew. She was born traumatized."

Drone clicked and fidgeted, but said nothing more.

The Department's Virtual Person liasion had once told Kovacs something interesting about his morphinium partner. Drone had chosen its own generic name and shape. Although it could, within limits, shapeshift into anything it desired, it opted to emulated the robot stereotypes of the 1930s. Hence the functionless lights on its chest, the inverted triangle of a head (complete with camera-lens eyes and speaker-grill mouth), the accordion arms—all mounted on a cylindrical body.

Smarties that were into the retrowave style approved; those that weren't reacted with disgust and dismay. To them, it was the equivalent of a black man running around dressed like a lawn jockey and acting like Stepin Fetchit.

Kovacs just wished there was an off switch.

Kovacs heard the click-clack of heels on pavement. He peered into the gloom. There never used to be fog, before the Blister. It made him feel like he was on a stakeout for Jack the Ripper.

A form materialized. At first, he could only make out that she was small, around five-one. She moved with the confident strut of a professional. Then she got closer, and the blood leeched from Kovacs' face.

31

A reeb. A fucking reeb.

Yousef hadn't told him. Probably because he knew Kovacs would've nixed the gig. It went deeper than the sight of a whore who looked seventeen but could be fifty. No, what got to him were the dull eyes, the jaded patina of world-weariness from years under the fist of hard drugs. Nothing in the world was more dangerous than someone with nothing to lose.

Drone humped over the armrest into the backseat. She slid into the car, tiny on the wide seat. She pulled the door shut.

"You Kovacs?"

He snorted. "You better hope, now that you're in my car."

"You're him. Yousef said you'd be a fat cop in a Desoto."

Drone twittered. Kovacs ground his teeth.

"I'm Loretta," the whore said. "So what's the rumpus? I'm supposed to throw you a freebie or what?" She looked at Drone. "I won't do him, though."

It took Kovacs a moment to realize that she was kidding.

"I have a message from Yousef," he said.

Her blithe smile faltered. Kovacs cringed inside. She looked so fucking young!

"You didn't frisk her," said Drone from the back.

The thought of touching her made his flesh crawl. "You packing, Loretta?"

"Hell. Where would I put it?" She smiled, arching her penciled eyebrows. "But you can frisk me if you like." She slid forward on the seat, her legs coming apart, the fringed flapper's skirt riding up her thighs. Her rolled stockings were held fast above the knee with pretty elastic garters. There were needle tracks on the bruised flesh beneath.

"You should lay off the hop, Loretta."

"And you should lay off the crullers, John Law."

Another snicker from Drone. Ferocity arced inside him, and quite suddenly Kovacs had reached his limit with both of them. His hand swept across the car. Loretta's head snapped into the window with a crack. Her hair leapt against the glass, a momentary halo, then settled in a shroud over her face.

Drone freaked. "Oh shit!"

Loretta looked back at Kovacs, and the submission he'd hoped to see wasn't there. Only defiance and finger-shaped redness creeping across her cheek.

Fine. Get it over with and get the fuck out of here. "No more side tricks! You hear me, bitch?" He grabbed her, fingers sinking into the young flesh of her shoulders, and shook her back and forth. She didn't resist, just let herself be tossed around like a broken marionette. "Any trade you tumble to, Yousef gets his piece, or I come back for a piece of you. You get me?" He threw her against the door, panting. Loretta slowly straightened the strands of hair that had fallen across her face. She smiled. There was lipstick on her front tooth.

"Sure, John Law. I get you. I'll be a good girl."

Kovacs stared at her. He'd just threatened her goddamned life. Was she that far gone?

"I don't think you're taking me seriously, Loretta."

"Serious as a heart attack, John Law." She leaned across the seat and rested her tiny hand on his thigh.

"What—"

His voice cut out uncertainly on him. Her hands drifted deeper, searching, finding. As she manipulated him through his trousers, Kovacs discovered two things that were surprising. The first was that he could respond to a reeb. But here he was, his breath getting labored, his mind clouding.

The second surprise, which unfortunately came right on the heels of the first, was the nickel-plated Smith and Wesson that had somehow materialized in her other hand. It was cold as she pressed it against his neck at the juncture of skull and spine.

And Kovacs realized, in that briefest of milliseconds, why Yousef had sounded nervous.

Fuck m—

His face exploded forward, drenching the windshield in clots of smoking brain. Drone shrieked and batted around like a trapped moth. It threw open every commlink it had.

"Officer down! Officer down!"

Loretta turned. "You're blocked, hon. No outgoing calls."

Drone processed this, and the inside of the car suddenly lit like a supernova, white light shooting out every window. As it faded, Drone gasped to see Loretta shaking her head, still very awake, rubbing the stars out of her eyes.

"That was my highest setting! You should be down!"

She pulled her hair back from the nape of her neck, revealing the blinking protective subderm. Then she yanked a small black slab

33

from her garter belt.

"Don't you carry anything stronger than a neural disruptor?" she asked, checking the settings on the box.

"Smarties don't kill," whined Drone, extremely confused.

"Admirable." She hopped onto her knees facing Drone, and reached over the seat with the slab, which had already begun to change shape. "Now, honey, this won't hurt a bit."

Loretta waited under the street light, seriously hurting. *If this bitch is late...*

The woman showed on time, though. She was ill-defined in a lumpy raccoon coat and Empress Eugenie hat, a rolled-brim velvet thing with an ostrich feather. A heavy veil covered her face, obscuring her features. Strange combo. Loretta handed the smarty's extracted data core to the woman, who nodded and produced a baggie full of dark brown chunks. Loretta's whole body reacted to the sight of the godsmack.

"Why'd you kill the cop?" the woman asked.

A shrug. "He slapped me."

The woman nodded as if this were perfectly reasonable. "I need some volunteers. People no one will miss."

"I know lots of people like that."

"Then I'll be in touch. Careful," she added, nodding at the baggie. "That stuff's very pure."

"Yeah, yeah." All she could think about was getting back to her kit.

The woman in the hat watched with amusement as the whore raced way into the fog.

6

SATELLITE INTERCEPT

TRANS00\INTERCEPT\GEOSAT231\110554 PRIORITY05-32\CLASS5EYESONLY

WEBSQUIRT INTERCEPT AS FOLLOWS:

(NAMES AND OTHER IDENTIFYING INFORMATION HAVE BEEN DELETED PER NSA REG 1037459324)

1: He's back.

2: Who?

1: The husband.

2: What? You gotta be kidding. Are you sure?

1: It was in the drone's data core. Revival confirmed.

2: How did this happen, boss?

1: Plain old bad luck. The odds were, Jesus…

2: Hmmm. [THREE SECOND PAUSE] What's his status?

1: He's a fucking mess.

2: You think he'll move on, or start digging?

1: It was over forty years ago.

2: Not to him. And he's a cop, remember?

1: He's got enough to deal with.

2: Loose ends, loose ends…

1: Should I burn him?

2: No. You're right. I'm overreacting. But watch him.

1: Already done.

2: What about our other problem? The good doctor?

1: Nothing.

2: Hmm. [A LAUGH] Maybe I can kill two birds with one stone.

1: Meaning?

2: He *is* a detective, after all. Why not put him on the case?

1: You mean *hire* him? [LAUGHTER] Oh, man. You are bad.

2: It's in my genes.

1: It's awfully dangerous...

2: He'll never make the connection. Besides, if he does, we can always kill him again.

END END END TRANS00\INTERCEPT\GEOSAT231\DATE END END END

7

DONNER

She's on the couch. I'm down in front of her. In my entire life, I have never been so terrified. Not even when that gangbanger held a modified Tech-9 to my head last year.

Marry me, I blurt.

Ooh, he got down on his knees and everything, Elise giggles. I kinda like you down there.

I give her a don't tease me at a time like this look.

Okay. Let's see. I can keep my own name, right?

I act wounded. What am I, a Neanderthal?

Just checking. Actually, I like your name better. But it's the principle of the thing.

Elise!

Do you promise to love, cherish and protect me?

I hesitate. Hmm.

She kicks me, and I laugh. Cross my heart. Hope to die.

Will you bring me roses on my birthday?

Big red ones.

No, big blue ones.

Blue?

Big blue ones.

Okay, big blue ones.

She crinkles up her face in thought. An infinite moment. Okay. You've

37

got yourself a deal.

I have never been so relieved in my life. She slides off the couch into my arms.

You are such a push-over, she sighs.

The hot ash made contact with my skin, waking me. I jerked up, flinging the cigarette away. There was a moment of disorientation.

My ribs were still tender, but the raccoon eyes had faded to yellow-green splotches. The busted toes would knit crooked, but who cared. All in all, I'd taken the thrashing pretty well for a seventy-five-year-old man.

I took in my surroundings. The new place.

My apartment had been furnished (as in "provided by") by the city, and furnished (as in "decorated by") the city as well. They'd put me in the Slope, a stone's throw from my old haunts. I didn't know if it was accidental or a deliberate attempt to make me feel more at home. As if that were possible.

I'd expected some subsidized government shit hole. But the building had turned out to be a trim brick six-pack within walking distance of Grand Army Plaza and the park. Not totally shabby, either. The staircases were free of graffiti, the floors were clean, and the locks were solid. The building had a name edged in stone over the front door, from a time when they named buildings. The Hoover. "I'm at the Hoover," you'd tell someone, and they'd know exactly where you meant, the hell with an address. Because they were natives and knew every inch of the terrain. They'd probably never ventured more than twenty miles from where they'd been born. Manhattan? That was just something to dress up the horizon.

The past didn't die all at once. Maybe it never died. Even after a couple centuries you could still find a few slate squares amid the neo-crete sidewalks of the city.

My furnishings consisted of overstuffed couches and chairs, hardwood bureaus, and heavy gilded mirrors. The walls contained cheap art prints, early Deco period. All in all, I suppose an average Necropolitan would have rated it as satisfactory.

I hated it. Everything was something it wasn't. The chrome appliances in the kitchen looked like leftovers from Donna Reed's garage sale but responded to voice commands. The iron bed had eight settings, including heat, massage, and something terrifying called "virtual pleasure partner." Worst, the bookcase wasn't a bookcase at all, but a hologram that turned into an enormous screen.

So I destroyed it.

Slowly, methodically. I ripped the stuffing from the couch, pulled the paintings from the walls, tore down cabinets. It took most of a drunken day. When the heavy furniture proved too much for me, I went out, bought a hack saw, came home, and continued. The pieces were stacked against the wall like cordwood. Somewhere in the back of my mind it occurred to me that what I was doing was deranged, but I didn't care. If I was living in hell, it should look like it.

Now I was at a table that I'd allowed to survive, working my way through a bottle of JD. I brought the whiskey to my lips, welcoming the burn. Leaned over to pour another and went white.

Floating in the air, a few feet away, was Elise.

It was a photo of her from her 35th birthday party. I'd hired a Mariachi band to surprise her… actually hid them in the walk-in pantry, five chubby Mexicans with their sombreros and instruments. She'd screamed, then howled in delight as they tore into "Jarabe Tapatio" amidst the boxes of instant mashed potatoes and Tuna Helper. When she'd turned back to me, aglow with delight, I'd snapped that picture.

Now it floated in front of me like an angel's reproach.

I flung the drink aside and brought my fists down hard enough to splinter the table. The picture of Elise dissolved into another face. Maggie.

"You asked for that photo last night. Or don't you remember?"

I didn't. I lit a cigarette. Maggie looked impressed. "How'd you get those? Smoking's illegal."

I ignored her.

"It's bad for your health," she added.

"So's dying," I replied. "I got through that okay."

"Negative health behaviors accelerate the youthing process. Or haven't you scanned your dickenjane?"

I grappled with the remote, trying to turn her off. Instead, the bookshelf reformed into a websquirt. "Hello, Mr. and Mrs. America, and all you ships at sea—let's go to press!" The announcer's voice had the archaic, nasal style popular in old movies. In the age of Bogart and Mitchum, it had embodied toughness and cynicism. Now it just sounded like the guy needed to have his adenoids removed. "This is Walter Winchell, to dish the dirt and gab the gossip for all you re-born skirts and shirts. In entertainment, the Beatles' long-anticipated reunion concert got underway last night." I perked up. They'd rebuilt Shea Stadium and it was overflowing with thousands of screaming fans. There they were, reborn octogenarians Paul, Ringo, George, and… Pete Best? Lennon hadn't come back. What a cosmic fucking insult.

"Unfortunately," Winchell continued, "the second set came to a tragic halt when Ringo suffered a mild stroke during 'Get Back.'" On the screen, Ringo stopped drumming, gurgled, and pitched off his stool.

"Christ," I said, shutting it off.

"With the smoking and drinking, you've probably youthed two weeks for the one week you've been back. Switch from Jack to smack and you could be fifteen in a couple months. Then again, a gun against the soft palate would do the job instantly."

"Beat it."

"I'm serious. What are you hanging around for, taking up space? C'mon, let's get this over right now. Free up this place for some Joe who'll actually use his second chance."

My lips curled. "You're not so clever. Reverse psychology got me a lot of confessions in my day."

"But it ain't your day, Donner. That's the whole point."

I picked up the overturned whiskey bottle. There was still a finger of forgetfulness in it, which I quickly drained. I checked my watch and wobbled to my feet.

"Where are you going?"

To find something familiar, I thought.

But what I said was, "None of your fucking business."

8

DONNER

Brooklyn's 78th Precinct was a limestone neo-Renaissance police palazzo on the northeast corner of 6th and Bergen. It might've looked elegant if there weren't so many AC units jutting from its windows like tumors. Fifty-some years into the 21st century, the city still hadn't sprung for central air.

The cops standing out front wore uniforms that John Dillinger would have recognized. Their thigh-length blue tunics sported square flaps that brass-buttoned across the chest. Their caps were crisp, their white gloves spotless, their shields large and proud and shining.

I couldn't help smiling, even after my encounter with their Manhattan brethren. They looked elegant, regal. Cops were the chosen people.

I crossed the street into the light from the floods mounted under the cornice of the building, my hands relaxed and open at my sides. They watched me. I went slowly up the cement steps past them. Nobody moved to intercept. As I cleared the outer door and stepped into the security vestibule, a light behind a mesh grill flashed and a siren bleeped.

"Attention. Reborn DNA detected."

The room went silent. All eyes slowly swung over to me. I crossed to the desk officer's station, my footfalls the only sound in the room. The duty desk was a massive, high oak thing, bookended by

41

antique globe lights. The sergeant cast down a quick shot of un-concealed loathing and went back to his paperwork.

I cleared my throat.

"Shove off," he said, without looking up. "Nobody's gonna take your statement."

"My name is Donner," I said. "Forty years ago, I was on the job here."

The man's eyes narrowed. "So?"

"I'm looking for a friend."

A smirk. "An *old* friend, I'll bet."

"Bart Hennessey."

That got a reaction. "He retired."

"I was told he still consults here part-time."

The sergeant gave me another ice water bath. I held his gaze, not aggressive but not going away either. His breath finally hissed out of him.

"Wait outside."

I ground a third cigarette butt under my heel as Bart finally exited the building.

The sight of him rendered me speechless.

I'd known Bartholomew Hennessey as a third-generation Irish detective in his early forties, with red hound dog cheeks and redder hair that threatened to overrun his forehead.

But the man in front of me was a senior citizen. By my frame of reference, in less than a week he'd grown old. It was like he'd fallen into the gravity well of some neutron star, his flesh pulled like taffy toward its center, his bones thinned and compressed.

Bart's face, too, was a mix of revulsion and wonder.

He's having the same reaction that I am, I thought, *except in reverse.*

We slowly stepped toward each other. Then he ran his hand through his sparse gray hair, and the gesture was so familiar to me, such a "Bart-ism", that joy and memory surged through me. Without thinking I bolted forward for a hug.

Bart let out an almost girlish squeal and backpedaled away. There was a tense moment as we regarded each other from opposite sides of the mortal divide.

"Christ," I said, finally. "You got old and fat."

He nodded, registering the professionally administered bruises on my face. He shook his head, not needing to be told from whence they'd come.

"They'll be gone in a day or so, I'm told," I said. "Courtesy of the Shift."

Bart visibly willed away a shiver. He looked back, suddenly conscious of the patrol cops that were openly laughing our way. They were cracking wise to each other in that taunting manner only truly mastered by urban natives. *Yeah, we're talking about you, fuck face. Wanna do something about it?*

"Uh, Donner. What say we go down the street?"

Lefty's was a grimy boxcar that had been ready for the scrap heap a century ago. Its interior had been enlivened with mirrors and police memorabilia, but it didn't help much.

Lefty had been an ex-cop who'd washed out on the detective exam, drifted to foot patrol for a couple years, then gratefully bailed when, during a budget crunch, the city had offered an early retirement package. His nickname came from legends about how once, on a solitary stakeout, he'd jerked off in his undercover car—but with his non-dominant hand, so his right paw was free in case he needed his Glock. Hence, Lefty.

Bart led me to the darkest corner, next to a window sill decorated with mummified flies. We settled into a booth of cracked red leatherette.

I'd spent many nights in this very place, winding down from a tour of duty. Coming to Lefty's to depressurize with my crew was as much a part of the job as putting on my gun and shield.

There were only three items of discussion at Lefty's—sports, women, and the job. The pussy talk was endless and inventive. The more disgusting the better. Topics for discussion were what secretary from the three-seven was a copsucker; what assistant DA was a dyke. I'd mostly kept quiet and drank my beer as the night wore on and the garrulous voices grew louder. When lured into an evaluation of a set of tits, I'd just wiggle my wedding ring at them, and they'd punch my arm and call me whipped.

Don't know why I didn't like that kind of talk. Maybe I pictured my Dad as a gentleman. Who knew? I sure as hell didn't. He might've been a foul-mouthed bastard.

So here again I sat, smelling disinfectant and stale beer, feeling the crunch of peanut shells and the tacky pull of the floor. A waitress with battle hips and steel wool hair approached. Her aura of weary friendliness evaporated the instant she saw me.

"Hey, Maureen," said Bart.

Maureen looked nervously over her shoulder at the man behind the bar, an old jock gone to seed. Clearly the new owner.

"Listen, um, Bart," said Maureen. "It ain't me, but Frank don't allow—"

"It's okay, Maureen. Tell Frank that Bart says it's okay, this one time."

She gave me another look, some indecipherable mix of compassion and fear, and took our orders.

A couple minutes later the beer was cold and good in my mouth. I fiddled with the edge of the bottle's label. How many labels had I peeled in this joint?

"Bart—"

"Look, Paul. It's not legal for reebs—I mean reborns—to serve as peace officers. You can't return to the—"

A wave of my hand stopped his floundering. "I know all that." A silent beat. "You know what, Bart? You look great. For your age, you really look great."

Bart nodded with a strange smile. "Yeah, modern medicine. The juvie centers—"

"You mean Juvie Hall?"

Bart smiled. "No, juvie as in rejuvenation. You think I kept my good looks by doing yoga and drinking wheat grass?"

I didn't know what the hell he was talking about.

"I'm ninety-one, but I have the bio markers of a sixty-year old. Which is why I can still proudly call myself semi-retired instead of one of those decrepit shuffleboard addicts at Coney Island."

"That's great."

"Lots of people work into the triple digits now. Lots of them have to."

"Never figured to find someone still around that I knew."

"Yeah. Well, there was Baker. He revived ten years ago."

"No kidding. I remember him! Where is he now?"

"Ate his gun."

We finished the first round in silence.

"Who'd you partner with?" I asked. "After I was... gone?"

Bart dug his nail into carved graffito on the tabletop. "Lazlo, the garlic-eating asshole. Stunk up the whole car."

"Shoulda worn your hazmat suit."

Bart nodded and laughed, almost drawn into the old camaraderie. Almost. But he caught himself, reddening.

My face showed nothing. *Keep moving. One foot in front of the other.*

"Look, I need a favor, Bart. One favor, then I'm gone."

All I got was a wary look.

"I want a look at a case file. My case file."

Bart didn't even blink. I suppose he wasn't surprised. I waited while he examined his sausage fingers. "Donner, odds are, the guy's dead. Even if he's back, the Fresh Start Act protects criminals from being prosecuted for their pre-Shift crimes."

"Fuck the Fresh Start Act," I hissed.

"Anyway, it's a moot point, 'cause I don't have that kind of access anymore."

I gave him a look.

"Goddamn it, I know, okay?" he said, blanching. "I remember every goddamned thing you did for me."

We'd been recruits out of the same class. A year and a half on foot post at the 73rd in Brownsville. Then a sector car at the 94th in Greenpoint—back when they called it RMP for Radio Motor Patrol. Then to a plainclothes anticrime unit. It'd been hard for him. I'd grown up on the street, but Bart'd had a middle-class Long Island childhood. Learning the shelters, bodegas and pool halls, learning to blend in, cultivate snitches, work info from the skells—it'd taken him time.

"I almost washed out," he said. "But someone told me to hang tough. That eventually I'd adapt."

After the Robbery Investigation Program, it had been a short leap to Homicide and the top of the pile for both of us.

"Donner, look. You were good. This guy—find his records online. You can probably go right to his grave and spit on it."

"I don't have a name, Bart," I said.

"A stranger shot you?"

I held his gaze. He still didn't get it. Then, like that, the gears turned over. His face registered genuine surprise. "But— I mean, you were *there*."

"The last day's gone. Something about brain death."

"The case file won't help you, then. It went cold."

"It's got evidence, details. Something to get me started." I knew I was in dangerous territory now. The police didn't like private citizens launching criminal investigations, meddling into official business. Especially former cops. Especially former cops investigating their own murders.

"It's not like it was, Paul. We can't take a piss without Surazal holding our dicks."

"A corporation running the cops? Who the hell let this happen?"

Bart's eyes narrowed. "*The fucking rules of the Universe changed, Donner.* Understand? One morning we woke up, and up was down. Left was right, dead was alive. The priests couldn't explain it, the scientists couldn't explain it. Do you know what it's like to lose all your landmarks in one day?"

I said nothing.

"I used to think I had life figured out," he continued. "There were good guys, bad guys—you and them." He pointed to his own chest. "You were a good guy. You had twenty-three to retirement and then you could take your boat off Long Island Sound full time. You visited your mother every Sunday whether you felt like it or not. You had sex with your wife twice a week and maybe it wasn't always great, but it was always good. On weekends, you worked on the junker Plymouth in the driveway and fell asleep watching the eleven o'clock news." His eyes looked funny. "You know what reality is, Donner? A house of cards. A row of fucking dominos. One goes down, and the whole thing collapses."

I nodded. "If you can't trust life and death…"

"What the hell difference does it make what pant leg you put on first thing in the morning, huh? Why obey the laws of man when the laws of God are up for grabs? Shit, those first few months, it was all out the window. We were that close from turning into some Mad Max movie." He leaned forward intensely. "The government, oh, they were a big help. Most military and guard reserves were in hotspots around the globe trying to shove democracy up the world's ass. Washington said we got hit by a bio weapon, but nobody really knew what the fuck was going on. Nobody knew shit.

"Surazal saved us. Their private security forces took the lead, here in New York. It wasn't pretty. It took muscle. But they got the job done. They stopped the looting, the killing. Now, we gotta live with it." Bart pursed his lips bitterly. "In my book, it was an okay trade-off."

I hadn't been there. I couldn't judge. But it seemed to me that the only thing more disgusting than the speed at which we'd handed over our freedom for the promise of security was the speed in which others had stepped in to take that control.

"I'm sorry about you and Elise, Donner," my old partner ventured. "It shook us all up. But that was a long time ago."

"Not to me," I said.

"Yeah. You okay for things?"

I shrugged.

Bart seemed to mull something over. He pulled out a small leather-bound notebook and pen and scrawled something onto a clean page. "This ain't much…"

He tore the page from the book and handed it to me. A name and phone number. "Like I said, it ain't much. An MP."

I groaned. "You know how many missing persons in this city are never found?"

"This broad has been driving us crazy. Missing husband, and we're nowhere. This lady won't take 'we don't know' for an answer."

"I'm not licensed."

"She won't care. She wants someone good. And she's got dough." He paused, looking torn. For a moment I thought he was going to tell me to forget it. Something was eating him. Why would he be conflicted over throwing me this meager bone?

"She's big league, Paul," he said. "Handle her right, and you could be set until…"

"Until I'm too young to drive," I said, folding the paper away. "Thanks."

"You ever want that P.I. license, I got friends in Albany."

"Let's see how this one goes first."

"You need a couple simoleons?"

I smiled a no and stood. Nothing more to say.

"Take care, Bart," I said.

I started for the door.

"Donner."

I turned.

"You meant what you said, right?" asked Bart. "About not coming around here again?"

It's amazing. There's always a new level of pain.

9

DONNER

The next morning, I rolled my neck, trying to work out the pounding in my head.

After my oh-so touching reunion with Bart, I'd spent the night drinking. And looking at the slip of paper he'd given me. I couldn't figure out if he'd thrown me a lifeline or a quick brush off.

I called for Maggie, but there was no response. I sat up and the world did a dipsy-doodle. I rushed for the john and almost made it. Afterward, I stared at the dead cigarettes, the empty bottles, the phone number I couldn't work up enough courage or enthusiasm to call.

A boozer cop. Jesus, what a cliché.

The Venetian blinds sliced the sunlight into neat lines on the hardwood floor. Outside, antique horns *ah-oo-gahed* and people laughed and life… Life went on.

The question was, could I? I hated this new existence. I was a blind man who'd been escorted into a strange room and left to grope for himself. I couldn't get my head around what was in store for me—growing younger, a young man, a teen, eventually being too young to care for myself, living in some reborn child care center with a child's body but an adult's mind, finally devolving into infancy. I'd feel my wits and memory fade as the neural pathways melted away to nothingness. It brought a thunder cloud down on me, blotting out light and air.

Lots of reborn suicides, Maggie had said. I could find a gun. The tried-and-true office-in-blue method. What point was there to sticking around?

Only one.

Still one thing I wanted. It was ugly, but I couldn't shake it.

My blue rose. Whoever had killed her might still be out there, walking those streets. If he'd been young, or had used the juvie centers, he could still be alive. He'd be an old man, but he could still be alive. I still had a chance to…

To make him pay. To make him hurt. To make him beg for his life. Then to make him beg for his death.

Then to grant him his wish.

That was it, then. The rest I could put on hold. When I'd sent this scumbag to the hell I hoped existed, only then it would be time to decide whether to follow him or not.

I took a walk through Prospect Park and tried to plan my moves. Got nowhere. I was the only reeb in sight. A young couple who'd been making out on a bench saw me, shuddered and fled. Fifteen steps later a stone hit my shoulder, thrown from teens who'd interrupted their pick-up game of hoops to hate me. They gave me the dead eye treatment. I sent it back half-heartedly. I had no stomach for anything more.

The cold air cleared my head a little, at least.

When I returned to the apartment, a stranger was waiting for me in my living room.

She sat in a corner in a cloud of blue cigarette smoke.

"Thank you for seeing me, Mr. Donner."

I shut the door, glancing at the lock. No scratches. Unjimmied. I looked around.

"How'd you get in here?"

"Your VP let me in. I told her you were expecting me."

"I was?"

"Mr. Hennessy referred my case to you, I believe?"

The missing persons gig. *Shit.* The last thing I felt like doing was babysitting some trophy wife whose hubby had run off with the maid. I'd make quick work of her.

"She shouldn't have let you in."

"Don't worry, I didn't steal anything." She gave the room a look of distaste. The destroyed furniture, the smashed pictures. Somehow, she'd managed to find an intact chair. "Termite problem?"

I shrugged my overcoat off. "You'll have to make an appointment, Miss... ?"

She came to her feet with a supple and dangerous grace, like a panther. As she moved into the light, I saw that her face was obscured by a hat and a veil. She wore a charcoal dirndl with a tight bodice and low neck, tailored to accentuate her waistline and curving hips, and to broaden her shoulders to well, pretty much perfection.

She offered me a gloved hand. "Nicole Struldbrug."

"What's with the veil, Ms. Struldbrug? In mourning?"

She raised the wisp of black lace. She was gorgeous, of course. Chiseled features, dark skin, pouty mouth. Mickey Spillane's wet dream.

"Better?" The hint of a smile played across her lips.

I shook my head. "Beautiful women make me nervous."

"Now why don't I believe that?"

She settled back into her seat, and the way she did it set off my alarms again—wiggling her tush slightly, as though trying to get comfortable. This woman had been wrapping men around her finger since puberty.

"Maggie let you in?" I repeated. I looked around.

She nodded. "Is she your girlfriend?"

"What?"

"Are you two keeping company?"

"Is that a joke?"

"Some people go for that kind of thing."

"She's... my assistant."

"Quite a rude one." She took a drag on her smoke.

"I'm surprised she didn't call the cops when you lit that cigarette," I said.

"What times we live in." A sigh. "The next thing you know, sex will be illegal, too."

"That would be a shame."

"Wouldn't it, though?"

I leaned against the wall. "How can I help you, Ms. Struldbrug?"

"I want you to find my husband."

"So much for the sex."

"My, you're easily stalled."

"An old-fashioned model, I guess."

"Maybe you just need a lube job."

"Whoa, hit the brakes."

"Poo." She drew on her cigarette, amused.

I went to the bar, grateful to end the double entendre marathon. "Drink?" I dropped ice into a glass.

"Bruichladdich, neat, if you have it."

Another alarm. The only bottle I had left was a fifth of Bruichladdich I'd been saving.

I prepared the drinks. "A fan of single malt, are you?"

"It's the Hebridean spring water," she replied.

She'd tossed the place while I was gone. It was either to avoid embarrassing me by asking for something I didn't have, or to sell herself as a kindred spirit because we liked the same Scottish whiskey. Either way, it was way too calculating. "This husband. Dead, alive, or reborn?"

"Alive, I pray. But missing."

I returned with the glasses.

"His last name is Crandall. I kept my own."

Nicole seemed to remember something then, because she began rummaging through a small purse. I sipped my drink. The scotch brought instant relief. I heard Elise's voice, saying, *not a good sign.*

Nicole, meanwhile, was pulling various items from her handbag and dropping them in her lap. A compact, a leather wallet, a .25 caliber handgun—

I didn't react outwardly. Whatever game she was playing, shooting me wasn't part of it. She could have done that when I walked through the door. She withdrew a data pebble and a black plastic tube and handed them out to me.

I nodded at the pistol. "Mind checking the safety on that thing?"

"Please. It's almost a toy. A 'dame's gun,' as you cops would say."

"I'm not a cop. And I never said 'dame' in my life. And for your information, that 'toy' is real enough to kill." I thought about the holes that used to be in my chest.

She wiggled her hand impatiently. I took the items.

"A few of Morris's hairs are in the tube, for DNA tracing. The pebble has background data, plus your fee. $20,000."

I managed to keep my eyebrows from blasting off my face.

"Don't pretend you don't need it, shamus," she said coolly. "I know how hard things can be for someone re-entering society."

"The money's welcome," I said. "But a smart person would've headed straight for one of those fancy, established outfits. The kind with three names on the letterhead."

Her face flushed. "Maybe I'm tired of getting the runaround from firms who're more interested in running up their expense accounts than finding my husband."

Jesus, did this one love the melodrama! But it didn't quite scan. Something in her manner. Like she knew the femme fatale act wasn't working on me, but kept at it, just to be irritating.

As if to prove me right, she drew on her cigarette, French inhaling. It was a teenager's trick, but with those ruby lips and lapis lazuli eyes, she made it dangerously interesting.

"My husband is a scientist, Mr. Donner. A geneticist."

Which meant well-paid, but not rich. That tended to nix a professional snatch-for-cash scenario, unless…

"Do you have money, Ms. Struldbrug?"

She smiled, her tongue peeking between her teeth. "Yes."

"Have you checked your accounts? Assets?"

"They haven't been touched."

"And you haven't heard from anyone? No ransom demands?"

"No."

"How long has he been missing?"

"Three weeks."

Hmm. She hadn't given my predecessors much time to work.

"Tell me about the night he disappeared."

"That night, he called from work. He spoke to Maria, our housekeeper."

"What time?"

"Around seven-thirty. I was out, so he tried my implant. He left a voice mail."

"Why didn't you answer your… implant?"

"Probably in a meeting."

"What was the message?"

"Something about a breakthrough at work. He was excited, rushed. He said he'd be home soon. He never arrived."

What time did you get home?"

"Around eleven-thirty."

"And Maria said he'd never come home?"

"Maria was gone by then. But I saw no sign that he'd come home and gone back out."

"You said he sounded excited. Sure he wasn't afraid?"

"I know the difference. He was jubilant, arrogant. He had reason to be. His research will change the world."

I thought I kept my face pretty even.

"That's not a wife's simple pride speaking, Mr. Donner. It's an employer's critical assessment. Morris' research division works for us." I guess I looked blank. She smiled. "Don't tell me you don't know who I am!"

Uh-oh.

"My brother, Adam, is President and CEO of Surazal. I am the Director of Research and Development."

After a few ticks of the clock, my mind rebooted enough for me to simply be in total shock. *Why didn't Bart warn me?* I stood, poured myself a double and threw the whole thing back.

"Surazal," I said. "The company that's building the Blister. The company that runs this city."

She looked weary of the question. "I think the Mayor would take issue with that."

"But it brings me back around to 'why me'?"

Her eyes flashed. The lady wasn't used to explaining herself. But playacting her peon wouldn't get either of us what we wanted.

"Ms. Struldbrug—"

"Nicole, please."

"Nicole. With the resources you command, it seems unlikely that you would hire someone freshly reborn, someone who barely knows his way around town."

"The police are at a standstill. The other firms have gotten nowhere. Detective Hennessy recommended you. It's as simple as that."

Simple as that. Except she was full of shit.

Then I had it. Duh. "And maybe you want a reeb."

Her eyes twinkled, but she issued neither a confirmation nor denial. "Morris was close to unraveling the secrets of reborn DNA when he disappeared."

"And you believe the nature of his work will give me what? An

54

added incentive to find him?"

She leaned in and her perfume, expensive and subtle, closed the gap between us. "I thought your type was keen to prove you're not monsters."

"I know what I am," I said, without letting too much heat into my voice.

"I thought you were a detective," she said, giving me another once-over. "You're certainly dressed like one." I was wearing the suit from the processing center. A double-breasted pinstriped affair with lapels a mile wide. Topped off with a suede fedora, wing-tipped shoes. I hadn't had a chance yet to find something more to my own tastes.

"Don't you like my clothes?" I said.

"*Au contraire.* You look yummy." She shifted gears smoothly from amused to worried. Her lips trembled just the perfect amount. "Since another member of my genetics team has been murdered," she said, "you can see—"

"Wait a minute. Who was murdered?"

"I thought Detective Hennessy briefed you about all this."

"Apparently there's a lot he skipped."

"Dr. Smythe. He was also on the Reborn DNA Project with Morris. He was found dead two days before Morris disappeared."

"They work in the same lab? How do you know your husband didn't kill this Doctor Smythe and then flee?"

A laugh. "Morris, violent? Please. He's a ninety-pound weakling."

"What were they working on?"

"As I said, reborn DNA. Beyond that, I don't really know."

"You don't know?"

"Surazal is a multi-*trillion* dollar operation with fifteen major divisions, Mr. Donner, including research, security, drug manufacturing, Blister construction, and civil administration. My R&D department alone has over fifty-seven active projects. Forgive me if I don't know the details of every one of them."

"No," I replied. "But certainly the project your very own husband was working on."

She just looked at me.

"What'd you give him for his last birthday?"

She hesitated. Then a slow smile broke over her face. "Fine," she said. "He's not my husband."

"Thanks for coming by," I said.

She didn't move. "I'm sorry I lied," she said, without a flicker of remorse. "But I had to test you."

"Thanks for coming by," I said.

"You don't want to pass up this opportunity."

"I have to trust my clients."

"If you couldn't sleuth out my true relationship with Morris, you wouldn't be the man for the job, now would you? But you passed with flying colors." She gave me a look that made me glad my clothes were fire resistant. "Everything else I told you is true. Oh, please. Can't we start over? Dr. Crandall's work is vital to my company."

"Why?"

"Because it's possible we could cure the Shift!"

"That would cost you, though, wouldn't it? All those juicy contracts for magnetic domes and security?"

"That's an incredibly cynical statement."

I rubbed my face. "Who can give me the details about this DNA project?"

"Dr. Maurice Gavin oversees the project directly. I can arrange an appointment."

"Good."

"Then you'll take the case?"

I had no patience for liars and game-players. But I needed a stake. And if said no, it might hurt Bart. She had the juice and black widow malice to make things tough for him. So I nodded, already feeling trapped.

"Do you think he's still alive?" she said.

"Might be as simple as he ran off with a woman."

Her laughter was musical. "Oh, you can rule out anything as tawdry as that. Morris's work was his life. Utterly."

"Drugs? The ponies?"

"No, as I said, he was a real straight shooter."

I unplastered myself from the wall. "Okay, Ms. Struldbrug. That'll get me started."

I escorted her to the door. She turned and moved in, abruptly too close. Apprehension filled her face. I could feel her heat, smell her cinnamon breath.

"Two of my people, missing or murdered, Mr. Donner. What if I'm next?"

"You have security," I said.

"The best in the world and worthless. You know that." She was right. A fanatic could always beat protection, no matter how good. All it cost was his own life.

She radiated anxiety like a furnace. Somewhere, my alarms went off again. Her lids fluttered. "It's so hot," she said. Then she was sagging against me. I grabbed her to keep her from sliding to the floor. Her breath washed across my neck. I pushed her back, but she clung, lips rubbing across the angle of my jaw. I pushed her away more strongly. Her feet found purchase and she took a step back, straightening her blouse. She reached out and wiped lipstick from my cheek. I flinched like I'd been touched by a snake.

"Something to remember me by," she said.

"The money's enough."

She smiled then, unreadable, and slipped out the door.

Slowly, very slowly, I leaned against the door jam.

I didn't kiss her, Elise, I didn't kiss her.

I walked over to the cracked mirror, found an intact piece, and scrubbed the remaining lipstick from my face, feeling like territory that had been marked by a predator.

I stood that way for a while, smoking and looking at my shattered reflection.

10

DONNER

A spaceship showered sparks from its ass. It jerked and shuddered across the cardboard set, swaying back and forth from black thread. The stars were glitter, glued onto velvet.

A drawn-out timpani roll. "Buck Rogers in the 25th Centureee!" Organ music, cheesy strings. "When we last saw Buck," the announcer continued, "He'd just discovered that the evil Dr. Huer had invented an atomic disintegrator ray that would DESTROY THE ENTIRE WOOORLD!" A cartoon beam of light hit a model of the Earth, which exploded, showering the universe with papier-mâché.

The announcer's voice dropped abruptly from its melodramatic heights. "But first, Solar Scouts, have you sent in your labels from Cocomalt, the most delicious drink in the entire WOORLD!?"

I hit a stud on the armrest. The show dissolved, clearing the Plexiglas divider between myself and the cab driver.

The hackie laughed. "Don't like Buck? It's the hottest with the youngsters."

"I don't get it, I guess. In my day, if a show's special effects were even a couple years old, no self-respecting kid would be caught dead watching. Now, the cheesier the better."

The hackie shrugged, the padded shoulders of his uniform bouncing. "In Buck's world, there's always a happy ending. Not like ours."

I blinked. Since when did cab drivers talk like sociologists? Since when did they wear neat little wool uniforms with duck-billed caps? It didn't matter. I was just grateful for the ride. Seven cabs had refused me when they got close enough to see what I was.

I looked out the window. Soot-encrusted tenement buildings and tarpaper roofs rushed past. Laundry lines, satellite dishes and chimneys. The autumn sun was bright but weak.

Then we were on the Brooklyn Bridge. The bridge itself was pretty much as I remembered, although it was augmented by high-speed lanes in clear tubes that made me think of hamsters. Across the divider, vehicles shot past like bullets.

In the distance below the rebuilt Statue of Liberty sat, no longer the metaphor of a nation; instead, a melancholy footnote of greatness past. Her remade face looked different somehow. Pissed.

"Air's clear today. You can see the guys up there," said the hackie.

I craned my neck to the Blister construction half a mile up. The arching girders looked too thin to support their own weight, let alone a structure that covered almost a hundred square miles. I'd read that they started construction from four sides—Englewood Cliffs and Inwood to the north, Secaucus to the west, Bayonne to the south, and Flushing Meadows Park to the east, with the goal of joining in the middle over Times Square. The interior Manhattan segments had finished and gone online early. Money had its privileges.

"Fullerite," said the driver.

"Huh?"

"The Blister frame. Actually, it's a type of ultra-hard fullerite called aggregate nanorods. Harder than diamonds. The grid between each section is electromagnetic buckypaper. Two hundred fifty times harder than steel and ten times lighter. Can't even see it during the day, unless the sun hits it right. Then it kind of shimmers."

The guy was a regular encyclopedia.

"There's two layers… the first was finished about a year ago. When this second, inside skin is finished, the project will be complete. There's going to be a Joining Ceremony."

I could just make out the ant-like shapes moving around. "Anybody ever fall?"

"Couple a times. But their safety lines saved 'em."

"Don't they… I mean, what about EM?"

"Gotta be close to a surface for it to work. You know, to repel, like two magnets." He nodded upward again. "Most of the guys up there are Amerindians. Heights don't faze 'em. They lose their balance about as often as politicians tell the truth."

"What about birds?"

He looked confused. "They got wings."

I smiled. "No, I mean, once the fields are activated, won't this thing act like a giant bug strip?"

The driver grinned and bobbed his head. "Atmosphere, birds, the stuff we want, gets in. They thought of everything with this baby. Biggest construction project since the pyramids."

A red light winked in the corner of the Plexiglas divider. "News alert," he explained.

I found the "play" button on the armrest. Images of a violent riot surged onto the plastic. The sight of the combat-geared Surazal security forces made my stomach tighten. Dozens of them waded into a morass of young reborns brandishing signs and placards. "Free and Separate Reborn State!" "We're Human, Too!" The digital audio was very clear. You could hear the crunch of baton against bone, the muted snaps as limbs gave way.

I hissed. "They're unarmed."

"This time," replied the hackie. "Hard to tell all the factions apart. There's the Enders. And the Secessionists. And the Cadre. The worst are nasty violent. Blew up a bus last week. Killed thirty people."

"The Secessionists—they want all the norms out of Necropolis, want to establish their own state?"

The driver laid the meat of his palm onto his horn, objecting to a trucker's driving skills. "Believe me, I'd oblige 'em if I could."

"But—you sounded proud, a minute ago. The Blister."

"An impressive cage is still a cage." He took in my confusion in his mirror. "Brother, my clan's been here for six generations. But things is way too fucked up to hang onto tradition. I'd take boring old Cleveland in a heartbeat."

I couldn't figure it. The New Yorkers I remembered would never have wanted out. Neither would they have allowed their city to be turned into a resettlement camp. Guess dead people coming back to life was enough to take the starch out of anybody.

We merged into downtown traffic. I watched One Police Plaza and the Courthouse zip by, looking just as I remembered them.

The cab pulled to the curb in front of seven-story Beaux-arts structure with a mansard roof. The vehicle settled, the light in my wrist flashed and I was sixty dollars poorer. "Thirty-One Chambers Street. Department of Records and Information Services."

I got out, feeling dwarfed by the towering Corinthian columns standing sentinel before the triple-arched entrance.

I turned back to thank the hackie, but he'd already flooded the backseat with pink disinfectant steam and raced away.

The main rotunda was still elaborate and huge, with its marble staircase. The mosaic ceiling was still populated by deities and zodiacs. But the Municipal Research Center was now a tiny corner room nestled between a law firm and a juvie clinic called "Forever You." The Hall of Records looked like an afterthought. Apparently, they'd subleased one of the city's grandest municipal buildings.

Here, I'd looked through original construction plans for the Brooklyn Bridge, genealogical records from 1795, and the personal papers of Police Commissioner Theodore Roosevelt. Felt pride at living in a city with such history. But now it seemed New York was no longer New York.

I entered the Hall. A radio with a little metal dog on the grill played "Don't Sit Under the Apple Tree with Anyone Else But Me." The room consisted of twenty workstations. Smartscreens lay like silver puddles on each one. A teenaged reeb sat at the reception desk. Her name tag said "Arlene." She looked up from her reeb fashion mag and treated me to a grin like the first day of spring.

"Hey there, playmate!" Arlene said.

"Uh…" I looked around. "Department of Records?"

"Bingo." She touched her nose.

"So… where are all the records?"

"What'd you expect, hon?" she said, cracking her gum. "Shelves? Books?"

I sighed.

She grinned and waved a hand. "Aw, don't sweat it, sweetie. Spend some time with your dickenjane and you'll do fine." She perused me more thoroughly. "I'll give you the dime tour."

She bounced from her chair and led me to one of the workstations. She pointed at the chair. I sat obediently. She slid another chair up beside me and leaned in to fiddle with the screen. Our shoulders touched. Her perfume was something sugary and soft. I turned and she looked directly into my eyes, only inches from my face. Not shy, this one.

She'd made no attempt to disguise her appearance. Her white pageboy tresses were curled under at the ends, and she was dressed in a Sloppy Joe sweater and powder-blue slacks. Damned cute, black nails and gold-flecked irises notwithstanding.

She pointed to the smartscreen, now floating at eye level. "Did you have computers in your pre-life?"

"How old do I look?" I said.

"Looks got nothing to do with it, sugar." She smiled again, a blast of youthful good will. "Don't suppose you got an interface."

"A what?"

She pulled back a strand of her hair. A tiny tattoo of an old-fashioned plug connector glowed behind her ear. "Some kind of wireless device?" I ventured.

She grinned like I'd said something cute. "Close enough."

I felt vertiginous. "When I died, our toasters didn't talk back to us."

She slapped my thigh. "Grade school stuff! Now, whaddaya need?" I explained what I was looking for. Arlene blinked and subvocalized something. Seconds later, databases were springing into the air, replaced by others almost as quickly as they appeared. Information waterfalled down the holographic display.

"Bill Gates, eat your heart out," I murmured.

"Who?"

How the hell could she not know about—

"Here we go. Now we're cooking with gas."

I watched in admiration over the next five minutes as she tightened the net she'd thrown out into the info-verse. *Wonder if they're still calling it the internet*, I thought.

Then, abruptly, a single document floated.

"Oh, I'm good," she said.

My heart stopped in my chest.

It was the Metro section of *The New York Times*, dated November 1, 2012. The headline read: DETECTIVE KILLED IN HOLD-UP. The columns of copy enclosed a photograph of Elise and me. I was in dress blues, fresh from the Academy. I looked ridiculously naïve. Elise was smiling, arm wrapped around my shoulder with that mischievous smile she got. I didn't remember the occasion. Who'd taken the picture? Elise's mother? Bart?

"Hey, that's you," observed Arlene. "You were cute." I gave her a look. "Are cute, I mean."

I gripped my wedding ring, tapping my forehead.

"Hey," said Arlene, touching my arm. "Hey."

(Special to the *New York Times*)

Brooklyn Detective Paul Donner and his wife, Elise Donner, were killed last night in Huan's Grocery, near Lincoln Center.

According to police, Donner and his wife, a federal regulator, unknowingly walked in on a robbery in progress. Both were shot with a small caliber handgun.

Detective Jeremiah Kinderman stated that Donner was off-duty. "He was an experienced cop," said Kinderman. "One of the best we had."

The clerk, Hector Alvarez, 21, of Red Hook, was unharmed. Alvarez provided police with a description of the assailant, but as of yet, no arrests have been made. The assailant fled with an unspecified amount of cash.

The article went on to give a brief history of our respective careers and Elise's work with the United Way.

Arlene whistled. "You just walked in on the guy?"

I shook my head mutely.

She nodded in understanding. "Wife's not back?"

Jesus. A robbery. A fucking two-bit heist. And I'd walked right into it, like a goddamn rookie. Of all the senseless ways to go—

A chill numbness settled over me. Elise never went into those bodegas. She thought they were overpriced. So why…

Oh no.

I'd made her stop. On the way to the opera, I'd made her stop. And the only reason would be—

Oh no oh no…

So I could get a pack of smokes.

I'd gotten my wife killed for a pack of cigarettes.

The room's angles changed. They seemed to be turning the room into a funhouse, how could that be, it was all weird shapes and colors,

63

skewed, uneven…

"Honey?" Her voice came from miles away.

I lunged for the restroom. The retching came from my toes, wave after wracking wave of it. When it finally subsided, I splashed water on my face at the sink, rinsed the bile from my mouth. Little black pinpricks still flickered in the corners of my vision as I walked back to Arlene. She had a breath mint all ready for me. What a doll.

"Sorry," I said thickly, sitting.

"Not every day you read your own obituary," she replied. No trace of irony or pity in her voice.

"How do I get whatever records that exist? About… this?"

Arlene bit her lip. "You're not supposed to focus too much on your old life," she said. "It can be upsetting." She looked at her hands. "That's what they say, anyway."

"I bet a smarty counselor told you that." She didn't reply. "Can you do it?"

She sat debating. Then she leaned forward, and her synapses flew.

A half hour later, we'd unearthed hospital records, pension files, insurance forms—the digital detritus of two people's lives. Since Elise and I had died *intestate* and without heirs, our property had been auctioned off.

"Do reborns ever get their property back?"

"If it still exists, and if the heirs agree. Which isn't very often." She grinned. "Hearst was *pissed*. His own foundation wouldn't give him back San Simeon."

Bart had been right about my case. No follow-up articles. Nothing in the Criminal City Database. The file must've been tucked away with ten thousand other cold cases.

The screen returned to the *Times* article. "That's it," said Arlene.

That's it. Dead end, for a dead guy.

Someone had gunned us down without batting an eyelash. Snuffed out two human lives, taken the handful of cash from the till and probably partied all night without a moment's remorse. I'd seen it hundreds of times. I'd been sickened at first, this casual indifference to human life, but as the years wore on I'd grown calloused like my partners without ever really understanding. Now, my nerve endings like a nettle of black thorns, I knew what the loved ones of those victims had really felt. The bottomless depth of their anger, their loss. I'd counseled them with clichéd platitudes, so safe and naïve behind my badge. *Let it go*, I'd said. *Move on, live your life. Give yourself time to heal.* What pathetic bullshit.

Arlene was frowning at the holo image. She squinted at it.

"Weird," she said.

"What?"

The image sprang forward, enlarged. She manifested a cursor and ran it down to the edge of the newsprint. "See?"

"See what?" I looked harder. "What am I looking for?"

She enlarged the representation some more. "Let me run an algorithm." The image shifted into a blocky blur of pixels. Now parts of the image looked fuzzier than the rest.

"This has been digitally altered." She moved the cursor back and forth between one line of text and the next. "It was an excellent job forty years ago. They matched color, highlight and shadows, but the resolution is a tiny bit different. It's the section of the article about the robber fleeing the scene."

"A last-minute edit before the paper went to press?"

"No, this is a scanned image of the actual newspaper, not some text version. The alteration had to have been done *after* the paper hit the stands."

"Can I get the original somewhere? The public library?"

She forced back her giggle. "You're cute. No one stores physical docs anymore. That's what the Conch is for."

"The what?"

"Ever hear of Carl Jung?"

"The psychologist."

"He had this theory about a collective unconscious, a sort of psychic warehouse of racial memories. When the internet became self-aware in '41, some smartass blogger nicknamed it the Collective *Consciousness*, since its core memories—its limbic system, you might say—are the stored data of humanity. We're using it right now."

The internet became The Conch. Question answered.

She puffed her lips out, made a raspberry sound. "This really gripes my cookies. Why would someone change it? *How* could they change it? The Conch is hack-proof."

"I need my case file," I said softly.

She swiveled to me, her eyes large.

"Know what happens when you try to hack the police network? Burly men show up at your door with morphinium handcuffs."

"Besides, you said it's hack-proof," I added.

Her snort was so adorable that under different circumstances I would've had to bite my tongue. "I said the *Conch* was hack-proof. You think the government would trust its data to a sentient AI? No way. The government database is a separate system."

"So it can be done?"

A wary look. "You've got ginger, baby, but I barely know ya."

I laid my hand over hers. "You know me alright, Arlene. I'm like you. Trying to play a game where all the rules have changed."

She stopped chewing. Her eyes stayed riveted on mine.

"It's not enough, though, is it?" I continued. "Dressing like Sandra Dee, playing it safe, using all the right slang, staying under their radar."

Her head lowered. Then she sighed and carefully affixed her gum to the underside of the desk. "I swear, I must be slack happy." She pointed toward a door next to the bathroom. "This will take time. There's a cot in the back room. You look like you could use it. When I got back, I was a royal bitch for weeks."

Are you drunk? she says.

Hmmm?

I've crept into the bedroom. My head is spinning, and all I want to do is crawl into bed and drift away.

Go to sleep.

You smell like that damned bar, Elise says, sitting up.

I stop pulling off my shoes. It's going to be a fight.

It's part of the job, I say.

Bullshit! Coming home drunk at two AM is not part of the damned job!

Lone wolves don't get promoted, Elise.

She isn't buying it. She lies back quietly as I undress.

I've been going to meetings, Paul. Al-Anon.

Christ. You know what'll happen if someone sees you there?

As soon as it's out of my mouth, I know I've said the worst possible thing. Elise's face breaks into jagged angles of shock and hurt. Then it hardens. I hate to see it harden that way. It's been happening a lot lately.

I'm there for me, Paul. I don't want to leave you, but I can't stand where this is heading.

I take her hand. It's delicate, like a child's.

Look, baby. There's got to be a way we can compromise.

That's called denial.

Denial, I think. Goddamned AA. I'd sent many a petty criminal to them. But they were zealots. One way of seeing things. Everything was through the lens of their own addiction. And Elise had bought into it. Pretty soon she'd be telling me I had a disease.

Elise, I've never had a DUI, never hit you. I'm not one of those people!

You've never had a DUI? How many should you have had, Paul?

That stops me. Last year, on Van Dam Street, near the Long Island Expressway, I'd been pulled over for going left of center. I'd sweated blood when the officer had approached my car with a breathalyzer kit. Then I'd flashed my detective's shield. The patrol officer had slowly nodded and stepped back from the door. But when he waved me on, there'd been disgust all over his face.

Does it even matter whether she's right, I think? I can't lose her. So I say:

What do you want me to do?

She comes to me in her satin teddy. She straddles me, settled against my chest, wrapping her legs around my hips. I can feel her heart beating. She's warm from being under the covers. An alcoholic can't stop on their own. But you've never really tried, right?

I play it out. Ordering a Coke at Lefty's. The other guys giving me shit. It's not like it used to be. A lot of guys, the health nuts, don't drink— Except who am I kidding? No one might say it to my face, but in this tribe, manhood was still measured by holding your liquor. Can I afford to slip in their estimation?

But that's not it, is it?

I need it. There are times when the only thing that gets me through the day is the promise of that reward. I'll stand in a bedroom in the projects, flies buzzing around the black blood, see the dead kid, smell the feces and the gun oil, and close my eyes and remind myself that by midnight I'll be in Lefty's and everything can go away. It's all I have on those days when I feel like a janitor instead of a cop, cleaning up the city's garbage. Our great citizens, the media, they don't care. To half of them we're the enemy.

So why should I care?

What's so damned wrong about having a little help, a little—

Crutch?

No. That's not— There's something else. A quieter voice inside whispers. There's something, something I don't want to look at, not ever. Something I can't look at. Something…

I wrench myself back to her. I look into her eyes, see deep grief. I cup her face.

I'll try, okay?

And if you can't?

I try to smile. Then I guess we'll know for sure that I've got a problem.

Paul, I have to tell you. I have to say this out loud.

I know what's coming.

If this doesn't… I can't… I can't…

I know. I get it, okay?

She searches my eyes for strength, for character, to see if I have the resources to do what I said. We're at a crossroad.

I know you can do it, she says.

Hey, I say, How about I get two tickets to that opera everybody's been raving about? This weekend?

She almost strangles me with her hug. Can we do dinner, too?

Sure, babe. Wherever you want. I kiss her soft lips and hold her tighter, thinking how I'd do anything, anything, not to lose her—

A hand was shaking me. I opened my eyes. Arlene was gazing down at my prone form. There was a mixture of childish amusement and very grown-up lust on her face.

"Sleeps like the dead."

I groaned and sat up on the cot, abdominals cramping. I shook away the disturbing echoes of the dream.

Arlene puffed up her chest. "Wanna see how good I am?"

"Uh…"

She stuffed a data pebble under my nose. "NYPD Case File 03-1756. Robbery-slash-double homicide." I bolted up and grabbed at it. Arlene snatched it back, spun triumphantly on her heels and marched back into the main room. I followed.

"It's encrypted. It'll take a day to turn it to English."

"Sure you want to get any deeper into this?" I asked.

"We came this far, didn't we?"

"Arlene, I don't know how to thank you."

She slid in close and gave my thigh a squeeze. "Listen, hero. My place is right around the corner."

"Tempting. But I'm a little old for you, sweetie."

She gave me a toothy smile and snapped a fresh piece of gum. "Old? Honey, I'm a hundred and three."

I trudged up the steps of my building, my mind racing.

Why had there been no leads? The DA never rested in cop murders. It wasn't a matter of vengeance—it was self-defense. The world had to know that if you killed a cop, you went down. Period. Otherwise, it'd be open season.

So what had happened? Where had my boys been? Bart? The Lieutenant? The case had closed way too fast.

Shot to death in a Korean grocery.

I saw it in my mind. Preceding Elise into the bodega, taking in the place in a quick sweep—the too-narrow aisles, the shrink-wrapped boxes of stock behind the counter, the coolers in the rear.

Anything suspicious and my radar would've gone off. So instead of stumbling in on a robbery in progress like the article said, it was more likely that our killer had come in after we were already inside.

I pictured Elise hovering by the door as I went to the counter. Saw myself digging in my overcoat for my wallet, perhaps distracted for a second as it got caught in the pocket...

... Then the figure smashing into the store, knocking Elise against a display of fruit pies, gun in his gloved hand, coked-up eyes blazing through a ski mask like twin supernovas...

... and I'd be turning, too late, already far too late, and then the sharp cracks, the stink of cordite, the shock on her face as crimson roses blossomed on her chest...

I stood shaking in my hallway.

Arlene was right. A little shut-eye. That's what I needed.

It wasn't to be. A message from Maggie floated in the air above my couch.

Meet me at Rick's, it said.

11

DONNER / MAGGIE

On the way, as I passed the alley, I heard: "Make yourself right with God."

The wino was tucked between two trash cans, a pint of Mad Dog against his thigh. "End of the world, and soon," he said. "God's Judgment." He burst into tears. "Boy, am I fucked."

I shook my head. The same old end-of-the-world rant the loonies had intoned in my day.

The only difference was, now they had evidence.

"Rick's Place" was writ large in blue neon over a door of beveled glass. Garish. I pushed through the doors of the bar and walked into a movie out of the 1940s.

Onstage, a swing band was cooking. The band leader waved his baton, lost in sonic reverie, his coat tails flapping. Trombones and clarinets wailed with a wild-energetic pulse. The enthusiasm was pure post-Depression jazz.

Girls with short skirts and long legs circled, selling vice from their trays. The crowd was a cornucopia of white dinner jackets and two-toned shoes, pompadours and bobs, swing skirts and taffeta. The maitre d', his hair slick with brilliantine, grinned at me beneath a pencil-thin moustache.

"Welcome to Rick's," he said in a French accent. "Monsieur Rick never drinks with the guests, but I could give him a message…" His voice dropped. "If you have the letters of transit…"

"Huh?"

The host curled his lip at this obvious Philistine. His accent disappeared. "Shit, pal, haven't you ever seen *Casablanca*?"

I pushed past him, headed for the bar. Fuck the ambiance.

I rested my elbows on the bar's brass piping. The Chesterfield coat on the stool next to me was huddled over his drink in that protective way favored by veteran alkies. Excellent—no conversation. I waggled a finger at the bartender and got ignored, but good. Chesterfield finally roused himself from his morose life review and glanced at me. Did a double take when he saw my hair and eyes. He vacated his seat in a hurry.

I smiled at the bartender. "Scotch rocks."

The bartender didn't stop polishing the shot glass. "We don't serve your type in here."

For the greater good, I put amusement in my voice. "Bet you've been waiting your whole life to say that."

A nicked baseball bat appeared on the counter. "Maybe you want me to repeat it."

Before I could stand, a voice came from behind me. "It's okay, Mick. He's with me."

Maggie slipped onto the empty stool next to me. Mick's face cycled through a dozen shades of displeasure, but he went to pour me a drink.

I stared at my suddenly very three-dimensional counselor. She laughed and put her hands behind her head, arching her back in a luxurious stretch.

"I was wondering how I was supposed to 'meet you' at a bar," I said.

"I was feeling a bit cramped floating around your holo projector," she said. "So I decided to get physical."

And how. A native would've called her a peach. Her slacks, penny loafers, and sweater fit body and personality perfectly, as did the black glasses perched in front of those amazing almond eyes. Her hair had been softly waved, the bangs left intact. When every other female in the room was trying for platinum blonde Jean Harlow, Maggie was a smart, sexy bookworm.

I tentatively reached for her bare forearm. It felt solid. Not exactly like flesh, but—

"Tensile hologram," she sighed. "You really want details?"

"No."

"So?" She arched an eyebrow, inviting comment.

I shrugged. "A little on the skinny side."

Maggie looked thoughtful. She nodded, and her figure abruptly filled out, her breasts swelling into a parody of voluptuousness. "Didn't know you went for the Mae West look."

The bartender burst into harsh laughter. I almost choked on my drink. Maggie smiled, and her body returned to normal.

"Much better."

Jesus. Shape-shifting drinking partners.

I gestured to the bar. "Nice place."

"I come here for the headliner."

The swing band had been traded for a woman encased in a single spotlight. She swayed, fingers caressing the square microphone like a lover's cheek. I couldn't quite place the boyish hair or the haunted, haggard face. But when she tip-toed into the first verse of "Over the Rainbow," I gasped. The rendition was so tattooed on my soul, that there was no doubt.

"Oh God."

"The way she's been partying, she'll be young enough to do a re-make of *The Wizard of Oz* in no time."

"Are there a lot of reborn celebrities?"

"Some. Some have restarted their career pretty well, consider-ing they're not allowed to leave Necropolis. But money is money, and Hollywood comes to them. Some agents specialize in reebs. The country doesn't mind watching their movies…"

"As long as they don't have to live next door," I said. "Like Nat King Cole, in the '50s. Good enough to have his own TV show, but not to drink from the same public water fountain."

Maggie examined me with interested eyes. "I thought all cops were racist swine."

"I'm not a cop anymore." I couldn't manage to keep the bitterness out of my voice.

She picked up a drink. "Okay, a toast. Something old, something new, something borrowed—"

"Something dead."

We clinked and drank. I gave her another look. "How come you didn't look this great when I woke up, counselor? You're… how would they say it now? The elephant's eyebrows."

"A man can only stand so many shocks at once," she smiled.

"Might've given me a reason to live."

Maggie's eyes twinkled. "Why, Donner. You flirting with me?"

I froze. It all rushed back. My future that never was, striking me across the face like a lover's slap. I knew I'd gone white. I couldn't seem to speak. "I'm sorry—"

"It's okay."

"Everything's just so…"

"I understand, Donner."

Irritation welled inside, bitter-strong. Why was I worrying about offending a machine?

"So," said Maggie, to change the subject. "Struldbrug."

I nodded, grateful. "You should have heard her rap."

"I did hear." I shot her a look. "So sue me. I was eavesdropping." She laughed. 'Something to remember me by'. Can't believe she actually went for a kiss."

"Yeah, thanks a lot for letting her in."

A smile. "Thought she was the maid."

"You know, it's bad enough that I've got an electronic dog collar that talks." I felt ugly satisfaction in watching her flush. "But now I don't control who's in my own apartment?"

"Fine." Her voice was sharp-edged. "I'll tell the next gorgeous woman who comes to your door to get lost."

"And stop eavesdropping. Don't I rate any privacy?"

"I don't listen when you poop." She made a face.

I ordered another drink. One wasn't gonna be nearly enough.

"So, c'mon, shamus. What's your take on our femme fatale?"

"I was wondering where she went to stereotyping school."

"You were hoping the first cliché to walk through your door would be a hooker with a heart of gold?"

"A guy can dream."

"She left her gun. The .25."

I'd noticed.

"She's a liar," Maggie continued. "I polyed her while she talked."

"You don't need electronics for that." I tapped my temple.

"Yeah, you scoped her chassis pretty thoroughly." She grinned. "Fuck her and I'll shut off your electricity."

"Oh, Maggie, jealousy is so unbecoming in an artificial person."

"Gigabyte me." Her eyes searched mine for a minute. "Surazal. You're coming up in the world."

I chewed the ice, wondering how I'd finished the second scotch so fast. "Doesn't make sense."

"Not unless she needs the appearance of a legit investigation, but really just wants some dupe she can control."

The thought had occurred to me. "Get me background on her. And her brother."

"What am I, your Girl Friday?"

I grinned. "You got a problem with that?"

"No—for now. So where were you all day, anyway?"

"You didn't follow me?"

"I do have a life, you know. Besides being an electronic dog collar."

"Like what?"

"You still don't get it, do you? I'm a person, Donner. Just a different kind than you're used to." She pressed a finger slowly into my chest.

"Yeah, sorry… having a hard time with that."

"Well, just remember all those norms out there who are having a hard time with *you*." She nudged me with her shoulder. "Now, you gonna show me the piece of paper in your pocket?"

"What are you, Ray Milland?"

She laughed. "I get it! *The Man With X-Ray Eyes*. 1963."

"I'm impressed."

"I love B sci-fi. I mean, look at me! I *am* B sci-fi. And to answer your question, smart guy, I caught a glimpse of the paper sticking out of your jacket pocket when you sat down."

I pulled out the *Times* article. She unfolded it and started reading. Slowly, her eyes widened until her pupils were swimming in a sea of white. "Where did you get this?" she said.

"Keep your voice down."

"Donner, this isn't sanctioned. Digging into your past."

"It's *my* fucking past."

"That's not how the state looks at it. For good or ill, you're considered a Fresh Start. Legally, whatever happened in your former life happened to a different person."

"So, what? You're going to report me?"

She toyed with her swizzle stick. "You've broken some fifteen different laws, big and small, since revival. Have I reported you yet?"

She handed me back the article.

"So why the slack?"

She bent the swizzle stick, then lost her grip. It catapulted away down the bar.

"Maybe… maybe I…" She bit her lip, cheeks flushing. "Look, just because I think—I mean, just because I think you're—"

She cut off. Her face was full of dismay. So was mine.

I'd assumed the flirting, the feigned jealousy, was simply a game, a subroutine to make me feel more at home. But this made no sense. She couldn't really be attracted to me, could she? A smarty couldn't… could it? Even if the algorithms or whatever got so complex that true emotion crept into the mix… Chemistry between a created being and a human? Did that mean she was really a person, like she said?

Did it mean I was?

"Look, I'm way out of my depth here."

"Forget it. I'm just tired," was her reply.

"Tired."

Sad eyes. "Donner, I get tired, I sleep. I even dream."

The drummer from the swing band reeled over. He leaned against the bar, reeking of cheap gin and cheaper cologne. "Hey, pal, how much she cost?" He leered pop-eyed at Maggie, and then batted my arm.

"Pardon?" I said.

"These holowhores is getting good." He nudged me conspiratorially. "Almost feel like the real thing." Unbelievably, he actually reached toward Maggie's breast for a touch test. I smacked his hand away and stood.

"Get lost," I said, voice low.

Maggie's spine straightened in alarm. "Donner…"

The drunk's ogling face contracted into something ugly. He opened his band jacket to show me the walnut grip of a pistol.

"Meet Roscoe," he said.

Why did guys always think packing iron made them tough?

"Drop it in the Hudson before you hurt yourself."

"Maybe I'll drop you in a cemetery where you belong, corpse." He put his hand on my shoulder.

The change in my eyes panicked him. He made the mistake of reaching for his piece. Bad move. A punch-kick combination lashed out of me automatically. His left arm became useless and he crashed to his knees, shins on fire. The gun hit the floor and I sent it skittering across the floor toward the bandstand.

It should've ended there, but like most inexperienced fighters, the guy didn't know when he was done. He struggled up and threw a wild roundhouse at my head. The hatred on his face for me—no, for what I *was*—was so raw that my mind exploded in a red haze and a roar came from my lips. Somewhere Maggie was yelling.

When I returned to myself, the drummer was out on the floor with a crumpled face and left side, the bartender had his bat out and I was being pulled from the bar by Maggie.

"Go!" Maggie hissed. "C'mon, *now*!"

Outside, a taxi floated curbside liked a bored bumblebee. Maggie pushed me in and waved her wrist at the armrest scanner. "Home," she instructed. Her address materialized in the windshield and the cab pulled away.

I stared into empty space. "What… ?"

"You broke his jaw! And his collarbone, from the look of it!" She fell against the seat. "Jesus, If I hadn't pulled you off him…" She fixed me with a disturbed look then, as though seeing with fresh eyes. "You were going to kill the man."

My voice wanted to fall apart. I clamped down hard. It came out mechanical and low.

"I don't know how much more of this I can take," I said.

Maggie got him home and into bed without too much more trouble. She looked at Donner's face, tight and unhappy even in sleep, and stepped quietly out of the bedroom. She activated her telephony program and waited for the connection.

"What?" came a gravel-filled throat.

"We had an incident."

"Did you handle it?"

"Of course. But I don't like this. I don't like this at all."

12

DONNER

The next day, Bart's displeasure at hearing from me was palpable.

"You got me into this," I said, shading my eyes against the Venetian blinds, wondering what the morning sun had to be so damned happy about.

I recounted my meeting with Ms. Struldbrug. I wanted background on the murder of Crandall's associate, Dr. Smythe.

"They weren't connected. Different M.O.s," he said.

"You're sure? Where'd it happen?" I asked.

"An S&M Club in Harlem."

"S&M? You scratch my back, I'll scratch yours?"

It was an old cop joke. I felt him smiling on the other end of the line.

"Meet me at the scene in twenty minutes," he said grudgingly, and gave me the address.

As the taxi slid north of 90th street, the landscape changed. At first, I couldn't peg the difference. The buildings looked the same: vintage row houses, store fronts and apartment buildings. We passed Graham Court at 116th, a regal landmark commissioned by John Jacob Astor.

I'd been inside once. Eight elevators.

So what was different?

The vehicles, for one. They were blockier, with squared-off cabs, fat fenders and toothy radiators. And the natives—black interspersed with white and Latino. The men wore v-necks, bow ties and spectator shoes. Some of the preppier ones had wide-legged cuff pants that dragged the ground—oxford bags, I think they called them. The women wore figureless, backless dresses of silk, georgette and crepe. They adorned themselves with beads or pearls and feathered bandeaux, their hair short and waved, covered in low-brimmed, boyish hats. It seemed incredibly formal for street wear—

—and then it fell into place all at once. I'd driven into the 1920s.

Harlem had returned to its heyday, the Harlem Renaissance—the age of Langston Hughes, Duke Ellington and Zora Neale Hurston. Of bohemians and flappers, speakeasies and hooch joints, the Cotton Club and middle-class black doctors and lawyers on Striver's Row, struggling for respect.

It'd been silly to assume a city as large and diverse as New York would have adopted only one retro style. And naïve to think that black culture, so fiercely independent, wouldn't develop their own identity distinct from white Manhattan.

The cab pulled to the curb. I couldn't see an address. "Is this right?" I asked the hackie.

The man gave me a look. "You wanted *Acquiesce*, right? Down the steps." He added sarcastically: "Have a good time."

I went down the steps to the basement level entrance, and sure enough, the name was enameled on the black door. I rang the buzzer. A slot shunted back, revealing dark eyes.

"Appointment only," the husky voice said.

A hand that was mottled with age spots reached past from behind me and flashed a badge. The eyes in the slot blinked and disappeared.

I turned to regard Bart. "Retired, my ass. I didn't hear you at all."

He suppressed a look of pride. "Semi. Semi-retired." He looked like he'd slept an hour last night. In his clothes.

"Thanks for meeting me here."

He threw me some half-hearted annoyance. "Couldn't very well leave you twisting in the wind."

The door opened, revealing the dark eyes' owner. The bruiser gave us a cement glower. His cream leather pants showcased a prodigious crotch. He was shirtless, other than a white vest. Arms and chest were covered in violent tats. An Aryan Brotherhood Chippendale dancer.

"We told you we'd be back, Danny," said Bart. "That wasn't very polite."

Danny didn't seem recalcitrant. "This thing is bad news."

A tall, black reborn woman in an evening gown appeared in the narrow hall behind Danny. "We don't like bad news, do we, Daniel?"

"No, Madame St. Clair." The brute sounded like a shy school kid around the woman.

Bart gave the woman a two-finger salute. "Afternoon, Queenie."

She didn't like the moniker. She angled her head at me. "Who is the gentleman?" It came out in a French Caribbean accent. *"Who iz zee jentlemahn?"*

"Paul Donner. He's an investigator."

"You're so fresh, *mon chéri* you still have zee dirt in your ears."

I flushed. Danny sneered.

"Crime scene is still intact, I hope," said Bart.

"As you requested. Me and Bumpy, we cooperate with the police."

Something clicked in my head. Harlem… Bumpy… Queenie… Jesus! This was Queenie St. Clair, back from the grave! She'd been a powerful crime boss in the 1920s, and Bumpy Johnson had been her right-hand man. She'd run the famous extortion gang known as the Forty Thieves, as well as numbers rackets. This was one hard woman. Within a year after immigrating from Martinique with $10,000, she'd been worth more than half a mil. In that day, for a black woman to take over a predominantly Caucasian gang of cut-throats like the Thieves… well, it spoke to her powers of persuasion. She'd grown so powerful that even the Italian families didn't encroach on her turf. If she and Bumpy were back, then Harlem had new landlords.

"Yeah, where *is* your number one?" asked Bart.

"Who can tell?" she said. "Maybe on holiday."

Bart sucked his teeth. "You know, Queenie, you wouldn't have tolerated this crap in the old days. Bumpy's pimping."

"This eez not a whorehouse, Detective. Eez a club. Consensual and legal. Nobody sells sex here."

"Just renting handcuffs, eh?" I said.

Queenie bobbed her broad shoulders. "Ah, *oui.*"

"Okay, let's see the dungeon."

We followed Queenie in, past a long series of doors on either side of the corridor. I'd busted enough places like this to know that behind them were mattress-filled mini-rooms for patrons who wanted more privacy than the main space.

We descended an iron spiral staircase. Stucco walls gave way to stone. Electric *flambeaux* were mounted every ten feet on brackets. The place felt like the Tower of London.

"Quaint," I said.

Queenie paused. "I don't want you disturbing my guests."

"Your guests are already disturbed," said Bart. "Donner, why do people go in for S&M?"

I grinned. "Beats me."

We both chuckled. Queenie rolled her eyes and proceeded.

The main dungeon was impressively equipped. Chains hung from the walls. Various devices with restraints were scattered across its thirty-foot expanse. Holo emitters projected hallucinogenic gothic montages of hardcore rock, vampires, bondage and a hundred other bizarre things, accompanied by music so poundingly physical it disrupted your heartbeat.

Of the twenty-five patrons or so currently partying, most were on the floor. They were tattooed and pierced, uniformly clad in skin-tight black or red leather, plastic or mesh. The group was young and surprisingly attractive. My attention went to a cage floating nearby, where a bound male was being whipped by a preppy-looking girl while several older dominatrixes watched, adjusting their corsets and poking at the concrete floor with their spiked heels. Two males passed in rubber suits with chain harnesses binding their chests; their masters walked in front of them, leashes in hand. A tanned man in his sixties sat on something resembling an oversized cat perch, a red ball tied into his mouth beneath a delicate lace blindfold. "Burn me" was scrawled across his chest in lipstick.

I shook my head.

Four enormous bureaus occupied the end of the room, doors open to reveal all manner of accoutrements—hoods, crops, nipple and genital clamps and a hundred varieties of leather straps. There were lubricants and oils, too, but these cost money.

A sign by the entrance explained the policy of the establishment; what was legal and permissible, and what went too far. Guests had to sign a complicated waiver. It was for show. No way that this place's patrons would play by rules.

Further in, there was an arched stone entrance to an inner ante-chamber. It had been sealed by yellow police tape. Bart swept it aside and we moved into the smaller room. Apparently Danny had better people to harass, for he disappeared.

A heavy wooden chair sat in the far corner. I examined the metal cap and restraints. Cable ran from the chair to the wall and up to the head cap.

I turned to Bart. "This is a real electric chair."

"Bump bought it from Sing Sing when they retired it," said Queenie. "One of his old haunts."

"It can't be functional… can it?"

"Oh, *oui*, it runs some current—not so much as would kill you. It's just for… attitude adjustment." She smiled, the white enamel of her teeth flashing in the torchlight.

Bloodstains covered the seat and arms of the chair. I bent to examine the arm more closely. Queenie opened her mouth, but Bart raised a finger. He smiled as he watched me.

"Okay, Donner. Let's hear it."

I rubbed my jaw. "Even though he was big—over two hundred pounds—Smythe was a bottom. Someone had to be topping him for him to allow himself into the chair. He was restrained at the time of the assault." I pointed to blood-free banded areas along the chair where wrists and ankles would rest. "Leather shackles. I presume they were removed by NCSI for testing."

Bart nodded, and rolled his hand for me to continue.

"From the pattern of the blood, most likely the killer stepped up to the vic like this, and slashed his throat from right to left with an edged weapon—which makes him either left-handed or ambidextrous. He severed the right carotid artery, probably in a single stroke. The stroke likely also severed the windpipe and neck tendons. This spatter here on the wall—" I pointed to an impressionistic blob to the left of the chair "—came from the weapon as it finished its arc. This other distribution, on the chair seat and floor, is arterial spray. The guy bled out in minutes."

Queenie patted her hands together in silent, grim applause.

I turned to Bart. "Suspects?"

"This room was empty except for our two participants."

"Would a bound man be left unattended like this?"

"Oh, yes," replied the Madame. "That's part of the game. Bound and gagged, left, maybe for hours… You never know when or how someone will decide to… play with you."

I looked at Bart. "Any sign of electrocution?"

"The ME said no. The chair was off."

"It requires a key and a trained operator," added Queenie.

I scanned the floor around the chair. "No drop patterns leading away from the chair."

"He dropped the knife next to the chair. No prints."

"Wiped?"

"No."

"So gloves. Either a pro or a very cool customer."

"Could point to premeditation."

"He?" said Queenie. "How do you know it was a he?"

"Not many females cut throats," I said. "Too up close and nasty."

"In your world, maybe," she replied. "But here? It might suit many tastes."

I realized she was right.

"Blade was a Ka-Bar 12-inch fighting knife," said Bart, consulting a small notebook. "Sandvik high carbon, high chromium, stainless steel blade. The handle was a Kraton G thermoplastic elastomer."

"A combat knife?"

"Combined tactical and utility."

"So it could be military issue."

"Or bought from any one of a hundred retailers. It hasn't been cutting edge since the turn of the century."

My eyebrow arched. "Cutting edge?"

He hid a smile. "Sorry."

A shriek of pain, delight, or both, came from the dungeon.

"No one saw the killer exit?"

"No one in the main dungeon remembers seeing that door open again after Smythe went in, until the body was discovered, an hour later."

"These witnesses were, at the least, distracted," I said.

"Sharon would have seen," said Queenie.

"Who?"

"A submissive," said Bart. "Bound to one of the St. Andrews facing the door. She swears no one went in or out."

I rubbed my eyes. "Great. So we have a respected genetic scientist with a kinky side who winds up with his throat cut by a ghost in a dungeon."

Bart's mouth wriggled in distaste. In this light, he looked all of his years. "That's about the size of it."

"Could our missing Dr. Crandall have been the doer? A professional rivalry taken to the final level?"

Bart shook his head. "Crandall was alibied by four assistants. Besides, from all accounts, they got along famously."

"So we have no real way of knowing if Smythe's killing has anything at all to do with Crandall's disappearance."

"Right."

"Great."

"We've got the rest of the research team under surveillance, just in case."

I nodded, then looked at my watch. "Shit. Gotta go."

"What, you got a full social calendar already?"

"An appointment with Surazal's head of research."

Bart grimaced. "Gavin? Oh, you're going to love him. He's a genius, and he'll make sure you know it."

"Madame St. Clair, thanks." I took the surprised woman's hand and laid a kiss across her knuckles. The giggle that emanated from her could've been from a school child. The abrasive old broad must have a deeply-buried soft side.

I turned to Bart. "See you in the funny papers."

"Hey, Donner," said Bart, shuffling. "You did good."

My throat tightened as I walked out.

13

DONNER

The building looked like it had been blown from glass. It twisted at impossible angles, a silver sculpture. That people worked within seemed an afterthought. The sun made its spires glow so brightly that I wondered if the glare was a driving hazard to the serfs below. There was an outer morphinium shell over the building's superstructure that slowly, over the course of the day, undulated and changed shape. You could actually see it flow if you stood there long enough. There were thirty of the same sort scattered around Manhattan, the gimmick being that New York's skyline was never exactly the same.

I crossed the courtyard toward a triple set of revolving doors. Nestled between them was a plaque with brushed copper letters that read simply: THE SURAZAL CORPORATION.

I rode the elevator to the fiftieth floor and the company's Research and Development Division. A receptionist took my name and blinked out of existence.

The décor was deliberately expensive and deliberately ugly. Visitors weren't wanted here. Images flowed across the wall opposite me. A scientist. The Blister. A double helix. Captions like "Surazal Corporation—Protecting the World."

From me, I thought.

Two men entered, lost in conversation. The first one I immediately placed. The resemblance to Nicole was remarkable. Adam Struldbrug, President of Surazal Corporation. Her twin. One of the most powerful men in the country.

His features were severe but handsome, his thick black hair slicked into place. Something subtle in his coloring suggested Mediterranean ancestry, but he had the same piercing blue eyes as Nicole. His body was so symmetrical that he could have bought off the rack and looked tailored. But the fabric that swathed his limbs was a thousand dollars a yard.

As he headed for the elevator, his eyes swept the room, surveying his kingdom. He caught me appraising him. We made eye contact. It was like two stones sparking off each other. Mutual recognition of the thing beneath. The thing in the dark that citizens miss but fellow predators acknowledge. He came over instead of ignoring me, as he should have.

"Paul Donner, isn't it?" He didn't offer his hand.

"Your sister keeps you well-informed."

"No, Mr. Donner, my spies keep me well-informed."

I nodded.

"You're not shocked."

"It doesn't take a genius to see that Ms. Struldbrug is… a handful."

He laughed, pleased. "Speaking of geniuses…"

He turned to the other, a man powerfully built and bald. This, I assumed, was Maurice R. Gavin, Director of R&D. Gavin gave me an impassive twitch of the head.

"I don't have to tell you that Dr. Crandall's disappearance is a sensitive matter," Adam Struldbrug continued. "I wouldn't have chosen to go outside the company like Nicole did, but now that she has, I trust you will remain discreet."

"My middle name," I said.

"Should you somehow manage to achieve what we have not and find the good doctor, well, you will be able to… how do they say it?… 'write your own ticket' in Necropolis."

"Good to know."

He pursed his lips. "You seem rather underwhelmed."

I shrugged. "After coming back from the dead…"

"Yes, I see. Everything else pales. Quite so. Well, I shall leave you to it. Good luck."

And with that, he was gone into the elevator.

Gavin stepped into the vacated space and extended a hand the size of a ham. The blunt fingers were manicured. "Maurice Gavin. This way, please." Gavin strode past the desk. I scurried to keep up.

A minute later, we were comfortably ensconced in a burgundy office the size of a tennis court. The left wall was all window, offering a breathtaking view of the Manhattan Bridge and the East River. The burnished surface of Gavin's desk was empty except for an inset keypad and a rack of data pebbles. The wall behind was covered with photos: Gavin in a hardhat, Gavin with presidents, Gavin winning awards, Gavin anchoring a relay team, Gavin peering into a microscope. The self-proclaimed Renaissance man.

He motioned for me to sit. He himself sank into something befitting an emperor and folded his hands across his chest. He stared at me, waiting for me to start. *Do not waste my time*, the placid gaze said.

"Thanks for seeing me," I said.

"Morris Crandall is a good friend, and an important employee." He opened his palms. "Anything I can do." He had the eyes of a hawk, dark and glassy.

"Ms. Struldbrug said he was working on a project related to the Shift," I started.

A nod. "Analyzing reborn and normal DNA."

"So you believe the cause of the Shift is genetic? I'm hearing a lot of talk about how time has reversed itself. The Enders think this is Armageddon."

Gavin repressed a pained look. "I know the world prefers to believe in fairy tales, to buy clocks that run backwards and dress in antique clothing. But when we finally unravel this, it will turn out to be perfectly rational, and perfectly scientific."

"Okay. So what *has* happened?"

Gavin drummed his fingers on the table. "We don't have all the components, of course…"

"So give me what you do have."

"It's quite technical. And I'm not sure it's germane." His smile was laced with contempt. This guy had you instantly pegged, based on your alma mater and the height of your IQ. Which put me around the level of an amoeba.

"Why don't you let me decide what's germane? Unless you have some reason to distrust me. Perhaps you'd like to speak to one of my friends on the force to establish my credentials?"

Gavin looked like I was an impertinent fly he wanted to swat. "You *have* no friends on the force, Mr. Donner. Except perhaps your old partner. And he is terrified of you. Or hadn't you noticed?"

He'd taken my bait and revealed that someone—Nicole, her brother Adam, or Gavin himself—had had me investigated. These people either had a lot to protect or a lot to hide—or both. I looked at Gavin hard enough for his smugness to falter. "I guess my report to Ms. Struldbrug will be that you were uncooperative."

He shifted hotly in his throne. "It appears I'm going to give a science lesson this morning."

"I was good in science."

"Obviously," sighed Gavin, "the Shift is tied to the biology of aging."

I shrugged. "Obviously."

"For centuries, scientists have been trying to fashion theories of aging that explained the process. In the 19th century, it was the 'things fall apart' theory."

"We're just machines. Which eventually break down."

"Very good. The 20th century brought new theories of aging. The biological clock theory, which asserts that the body has a built-in, pre-set lifespan limit. Then, for a while, it was popular to view aging as a disease, something that could eventually be cured. As most solutions are, it was too simplistic. Some aging processes do resemble that of a disease, but we think the body also has built-in regulators that enforce a lifespan limit."

"Which is?"

"The maximum lifespan for *homo sapiens*, we think, is around 122 years, give or take."

"So the 'things fall apart' theory is wrong, then?"

Gavin shook his head. "None of them are wrong, per se, just incomplete. The body *does* fall apart. Not surprising, considering it's under constant attack."

"Attack?"

"You've heard of free radicals?"

"Yeah. They're bad."

"Most people don't realize the delicious irony that oxygen, the thing that sustains us, is also slowly killing us."

"Huh?"

"The most dangerous free radicals are oxygen-centered."

"So while oxygen keeps our lungs pumping, it's also slowly killing us?"

He nodded. "Oxidized free radicals burn through delicate cell membranes, injuring proteins, lipids... even our DNA."

"Well, shit. What's the point of quitting smoking?"

"Oh no, the amount of radicals in cigarette smoke..." He realized I was joking and screwed his mouth sideways. "Antioxidants are naturally-occurring enzymes which minimize free radical damage. Think of them as the body's toxic waste cleanup crew. Even so, the body still experiences a staggering amount of oxidant hits a day. Add it to other chemical damages, and each genome in each of your cells endures 30,000 damage events *every day*."

"Each genome?"

"Right. So, if the average adult human body contains about 10 trillion cells, on a typical day your DNA could rack up about 300,000 *trillion* hits."

I whistled. "But not everybody wears out at the same rate, does it?"

"No. Our genes also determine how quickly, and how well, we age."

"I see what you mean about it being complicated."

"Oh, we're not nearly done."

I was afraid of that.

"We haven't taken into account the cumulative mistakes theory. When cells reproduce, divide, and replace themselves, it's called cell doublings. Cell doublings are directly related to the longevity of the species. Look at this chart."

He hit a button on his desk and scrolled through some holoimages. He finally punched up a little graph:

SPECIES	LIFESPAN	CELL DIVISION CEILING
Mice	3 years	15 divisions
Chickens	12 years	25 divisions
Humans	122 years	50 divisions
Galapagos tortoise	175 years	110 divisions

"Gotta get me some turtle DNA." Gavin didn't laugh. "So cells only have so many divisions in them?"

"It's called the Hayflick limit. On top of that, cell division involves literally hundreds of factors and changes... a lot that can go wrong.

And does, incrementally. Eventually cells start dying, making mistakes, even on the genetic level. Since these accumulated mistakes make the body more vulnerable to age-related diseases, one almost always dies well before their cell division limit is reached."

"So… we wear out, and we have built-in cell limits, and a biological clock that's running down. Sounds like the deck's stacked against us."

"More than you know. Now, as to telomeres—"

"Christ. There's more."

"Oh yes. We spoke about the genetic component. Each chromosome ends in a series of protective units called a telomere. Think of them like the plastic tips at the end of shoe laces. These telomeres don't contain genetic information, just an empty number of repeating subunits, which shorten after each division."

"Each time the DNA reproduces, it's one unit shorter?"

"These units may serve as counting markers, growing shorter in direct proportion to how near the cell comes to death. Contrarily, cancer cells replenish their telomeres after each division. That's why cancer grows so wildly out of control."

I shook my head. "So for a person to be immortal, he'd have to have," I ticked off each item on a finger, "cells that never made mistakes, cells that reproduced infinitely, a body that repaired itself perfectly from free radicals and other assaults, a biological clock that never ran down, and telomeres that didn't shorten."

"And a host of other factors we haven't even discussed."

"And we haven't even gotten around to the issue of actually growing *younger*."

Gavin leaned back in satisfaction. "I think you can see why, even after twenty-five years of research, a cure for the Shift is still a long way off."

"Okay, so let's get back to Crandall. His team was working on all this stuff."

Gavin, who'd been swept away by his own breathtaking command of science, tightened suddenly. "That's right. Our best and brightest. Morris Crandall, Dr. Smythe, Dr. Hakuri, and Dr. Renquist."

"What aspect were they working on, specifically?"

Gavin hesitated. "They believed, since the issues involved in youthing are genetic, gene therapy could stop the Shift."

"Gene therapy? How does that work?"

"In a nutshell, you modify the part of the DNA that is causing the problem. You place the modified genes into a harmless vector—a retrovirus—and introduce it into the patient."

"Sounds like science fiction."

"We've managed to cure some nasty inherited diseases that way. We believe a retrovirus is what communicates the Shift in the first place—what begins the alterations in 'dead' DNA that causes revival."

"Really?"

"Many cancers are caused that way. HIV, before it was cured, was carried by a retrovirus called a lentivirus. Morris believed we could restore normal functioning of the biological processes in reborns using gene therapy."

"Get the clock to run forward again."

"That's right."

"What about communicability? I was told that even norms can cause the Shift to start outside the Blister."

"Because we don't have a vaccine for the Shift retrovirus yet, our only option is to contain it. Every infected person, norm and reborn alike, must be isolated."

"But these retroviruses are just carriers, right? So what caused the Shift in the first place? Where'd it come from?"

"That's the million dollar question, isn't it? The most accepted theory is that some bioweapon didn't perform as advertised, either through a spontaneous mutation, which happens in nature, or because the terrorist genetic designers didn't know what they were doing."

"A bioweapon? You mean like weaponized anthrax?"

"Well, yes, but bioterrorism has become much more sophisticated."

"How many nations or terrorist groups can modify DNA?"

"You'd have to ask the Conch. But zealotry, money and technology is a pretty potent combination, and there's no shortage of America-haters."

"No terrorist group or state was ever identified. No one ever claimed responsibility."

"No one credible, no."

"The worst attack on American soil in history, and the attacker was never identified. Hard to believe."

He merely shrugged.

"Crandall spoke to Nicole of a breakthrough in their research."

Gavin raised an eyebrow. "Team records show nothing."

"Are you saying she lied?"

His oily smile became slush. "Of course not. I have no idea why Crandall told her that."

"Could Dr. Smythe's death be connected to Crandall's disappearance? To their work? A rival drug company, maybe?"

Gavin dismissed the idea with a wave. "Big pharmaceuticals conduct industrial espionage every day, but murder? Doubtful."

"Could this killer be some crazy Ender who's a fan of the Shift?"

"Our work is classified. Besides, I understood that Dr. Smythe's death was related to his rather unusual personal tastes."

Everyone seemed anxious for me to buy the party line. "It's possible. Was Crandall acting strangely in any way prior to his disappearance?"

"No, his staff said it was business as usual."

"Which involved late nights?" Another nod. "Where is his lab?"

"We have labs all over town. Smythe's was in Hippieville."

I raised an eyebrow. Gavin suppressed his amusement. "I forgot you haven't ventured much out of the Bogart yet."

"The Bo— Oh, you mean midtown! Where everyone looks like they stepped out of *The Maltese Falcon*?"

Gavin nodded. "In the Village, many people have, unsurprisingly, adopted the sixties as their retro style. Incense, meditation and peace signs."

"Groovy."

"Dr. Crandall worked at a lab in Chelsea."

"Who typically would be in this building after closing?"

"Security, housekeeping. Maybe a couple other workaholics like Crandall. He was the only one who kept really late hours."

"Could I see the security video for that night?"

"It shows him leaving some time before midnight."

"Could I see it anyway?"

"I'll have a copy—" Gavin stopped as he saw me shaking my head. "Fine. I'll have the original sent to you."

"I'd also like access to the lab."

"Mr. Donner, your pedestrian little threats may have earned you a primer on genetics, but you'll need more than that to get into my company's restricted areas."

"Maybe I'll ask Ms. Struldbrug."

"She'll tell you the same thing."

I smiled. "Could Crandall have left Necropolis?"

"Impossible."

"Can't have monsters roaming the countryside," I muttered. It came out thin-edged.

Gavin leaned forward, his manner intense. "Remember retroviruses? They can infect the normal population beyond the Blister. Do you think we created the Blasted Heath because we have a glut of real estate? And have you considered the possibility that this virus could mutate again? Become airborne? Or something that kills DNA instead of reanimates it?"

"Then why hasn't the rest of the world *remained* infected? Why hasn't the Shift expanded in all this time?"

Pure contempt radiated at me. "Only because of our Herculean efforts at containment. Every single infected person on the face of the planet is *here*. But one reeb gets out, just one—or a norm carrier, for that matter—and the rest of the world can kiss normalcy goodbye. Maybe forever."

Gavin laid his palms on the table, as if to calm himself. "Until this thing is licked, quarantine is the only choice."

"Easy for you to say," I murmured.

"No, it's not, Mr. Donner. After all, I, too, am here. Perhaps for the rest of my life." Gavin stood. "It's been a pleasure."

Yeah, right. I stood, nodded to the man, and turned to go.

"Oh, and Mr. Donner. 'Video' went the way of the dinosaurs four decades ago. You might want to remember that the next time you try to hold an intelligent conversation."

14

DONNER

I exited the building into the kaleidoscope night, my head a muddle. Even in reruns the conversation made little sense.

Telomeres. DNA. Aging. Missing scientists.

And a lot of liars.

If Nicole Struldbrug was to be believed about the breakthrough, Crandall had been about to be put into the history books alongside Louis Pasteur and Jonas Salk. Anyone working at that level didn't willingly give it all up to disappear.

I turned down 23rd Street, tightening the belt on my coat. A couple of cross-dressing Marilyn Monroes passed me, looking for a subway grate. It was past nine. Traffic had thinned to a trickle of cabs and odd-shift workers, mostly waiters.

If another corporation or country had tumbled to the enormity of what Crandall was about to perfect, they'd definitely make a play for him. Maybe legit, maybe not. I was left with too broad a playing field, too many options: Crandall had gone into hiding, for reasons unknown. Crandall was now working for a rival corporation or government, willingly or not. Crandall had been killed to prevent him from finishing his work. And let's not ignore good, old-fashioned motives like jealousy. It could be as simple as a jilted girlfriend with a trash compactor.

Or an employer. Nicole, the lady incapable of an unrehearsed gesture. The lady who thought a well-timed kiss would turn any man into putty.

But why sabotage your own company?

That led to the most uncomfortable possibility, the one I hated to face: that I was chosen precisely because this case *would* be out of my league. If Nicole was behind Crandall's disappearance and was just putting on a good show as the frantic employer, then a reeb detective, freshly alive and disoriented in his new environment, would be the perfect choice.

I could almost feel the tension lightening the lines in my face. "Stress accelerates the youthing process." One of Maggie's favorite refrains. I thrust my hands deep into my coat pockets, wondering what would turn up next to make the case even murkier.

I didn't have long to wait.

The Silver Wraith Rolls that had been tailing me since I exited the building made its move. It jumped the curb, overrunning the safety strips in spark-filled screeches of superheated air. I feinted left, my coattails snapping. The driver didn't disappoint me. He wrenched the wheel right to keep me in his bull's eye. I pivoted the other way. He tried to re-correct his trajectory, but a car has a lot more inertia than a person. The Wraith shot past me, smashing through a newspaper kiosk. Had it been the primary assault instead of a decoy, I would've made it home in time for tea. But while I was busy congratulating myself for being so clever, a second team boiled out of the shadows of a storefront entrance less than five feet behind me.

I felt the cold tap of a neuralizer against my skull and suddenly my synapses and limbs were jerking firecrackers. Hands grabbed me as I collapsed. The Wraith retraced its maglev scorch marks back to us.

"Get him inside!" The driver, weasel-faced in a sloped hat, scurried around to throw open the rear door. "Hurry!"

A car was definitely a place I did not want to go. Once inside, my options would flatline. So I quit fighting and sagged, letting them have my full poundage. My kidnappers were forced rock back for a second in order to thrust my dead weight forward again. In that moment, they lost both their momentum and the initiative. I dug my heels in and threw myself violently in reverse, rotating in a ducking movement. The men stumbled and cried out as their hands twisted. It was let go or have their wrists broken. Fingers flew open in pain.

I threw a double-tap to their kidneys and planted the heel of my palm into each face. One man went down immediately. The other staggered jelly-legged on the pavement. I moved to finish him, but saw something out of the corner of my eye that stopped me dead.

The driver was resting what looked like a Thompson submachine gun across the roof of the Wraith. "Uh-uh," he said, grinning. "No more of that."

Crammed between the bruisers, I waited. The one I'd dropped to the pavement had a broken nose. It wasn't the first time. The man ignored the blood on his face, opting instead to bake me with glowering eyes.

The car hummed out into the evening traffic. In the front seat, a shadow with big shoulders lit a cigarette.

"I thought smoking was against the law," I said.

"So's kidnapping." The shadow turned and exhaled the smoke into my face. More melodrama.

"Trying to stunt my youth?"

"Something like that."

The thugs grinned darkly. At first I'd hoped they were muscle-for-hire types with detective's licenses—the kind of lowbrows that called themselves fly dicks. But now they were looking more like hoods.

The man shifted and I got my first good look. Close-cropped hair going to gray. Still fit in his fifties. I would've said a military back-ground, but the wrinkled collar and gravy stain on the tie said no. The face was lined and hard as titanium. Not a face you bargained with.

"What do I call you, kidnapper?"

"Armitage," was the gravel-voiced reply.

Sounded real. There were two reasons he'd give me his real moni-ker. It was either going to stay friendly or they were planning to kill me.

My bookends frisked me. They did it rough, enjoying it. When I objected to a hand on my crotch I got an elbow in the face. The neu-ralizer effects whirled through my brain. Jelly Legs found the *Times* article. Broken Nose found the piece. They were handed to Armitage.

"Tsk, tsk. Reebs aren't allowed to carry weapons."

I tried Nicole's tack. "It's a .25 caliber. Wouldn't wipe the mustard off your face."

They burst into laughter. ".25 *caliber*?" The driver cackled. "Man, you're slow, even for a stiff."

Armitage aimed the weapon out the window. The muzzle flashed. A passing trash can became a molten heap of aluminum, just like that. I gaped.

"Try 25 terrahertz." He handed the gun back to me. I examined it, stunned.

"Seven round chamber," explained Armitage.

"Rounds? Rounds of what?" I racked the slide and ejected the shell. A lozenge dropped into my hand, containing some kind of churning amber fire inside.

"Plasma," the man said. "Ionized from a photonic hydrogen cell in the core."

It looked like an antique. I squeezed the casing of the "bullet" and felt my fingers tingle. I was so far out of my element that I wanted to scream. A dead *sotto capo* I could handle. Guns that fired plasma bullets… "I really need to study that dickenjane," I murmured.

"Instead of chasing after missing geneticists?"

So that was it. *Thanks, Bart. This gig has put me on every dance card in town.*

"You keep tabs on all reebs this close?" I asked. "Or just ones that used to be cops?"

"You always answer a question with a question?"

I smiled. "Does that bother you?"

Armitage grunted, maybe in amusement, maybe irritation. "The only reebs I tail are ones who stick their noses where they don't belong."

I groaned. "Priceless! 'Stick their noses where they don't belong.' It's like I died and went to B-movie purgatory. 'They Cliché By Night.' I suppose you're gonna tell me to never show my face in town again or I'll wind up sleeping with the fishes in a pair of cement overshoes, right?"

"Just tell me what you got on Crandall, smartass."

"If I don't?"

Armitage's crags reassembled into a grin. "The cement's in the trunk."

15

GIORDI

Giordi Lyatsky downed the shot in a single gulp. He scowled at the saggy-titted waitress for another.

He'd been counting on the booze to lift his spirits, but he'd slipped into a grumpy rehash of his life instead. Every fucked-up thing that had ever happened to him rose as a specter.

Starting with how he got here. Talk about bad luck. When the Shift had hit, he'd been nineteen and living in Brooklyn for only a few weeks, sleeping on the floor of his buddy Vitali's Little Odessa apartment. Vitali was a former cellmate from the Novoulyanovsk high security labor camp. They'd been released together and decided there was less risk—and less hard time—boosting cars in the West. So they'd crossed into the U.S. disguised as fertilizer, then spent their days on the boardwalk, drinking, whoring and planning their next score.

Then came the Dark Eighteen. Giordi was trapped here, probably forever. Unbelievable. He'd come from the Ukraine looking for the fabled American freedom and ended up in a gulag more inescapable than anything Stalin could have ever dreamed up.

Fuck it. No use crying over spoiled borscht.

Now, forty years later, he'd made a nice little rep for himself among the Brighton Beach *mafiya*. Okay, he was a little fish, but he had juice on the street. Nobody screwed with him. Things weren't any better back in the EU anyway. He'd heard stories about cannibalism. And with the thick roll of bills in his pocket, he'd finally started to feel like maybe Necropolis wasn't so bad after all.

Lately, though, things had gotten tough. The NPD and Surazal were brutal. Their raids on his smuggling had gotten devastatingly effective. Giordi had lost three shipments in the past couple months alone, and he was feeling the heat from upstairs. His bosses had no idea how difficult it was to get contraband into this godforsaken place. The forged documents, the Blister-point payoffs, the search inhibitor fields. It'd be easier to fly to the moon. But all they wanted were results, and results were getting more and more difficult to deliver.

He knew the *organizatsya*'s method of firing disappointing employees. A week ago, he'd started sleeping with a loaded trey-eight under his pillow.

Today, he'd lost another cargo container to the police. Fourteen thousand pairs of sneakers, gone. It was a disaster. So right now all he wanted to do was sit at his table in this Coney Island Avenue bar, drink Stoli, nibble at a fried *pirozhki*, and forget everything. Because tomorrow, he was going to have to report the loss, and he dreaded it to his marrow.

When he noticed the woman staring at him from the bar, he assumed it was a mistake. Maybe she'd mistaken him for somebody she knew. But she kept staring, direct enough to dispel that theory.

It couldn't be his looks. He was a bulldog, squat and pug-nosed. His head was shaved and he had the usual proliferation of prison tats—no ladies man. He got snatch on a regular basis, but it was through fear and respect of his position, not charm. Or usually, he thought morosely, through payment.

But she kept staring at him. She was blatant. And pretty. Small, dark hair, big headlights. She was packed into some kind of expensive skin-tight dress, with a leather jacket over top. A designer jacket, he noticed. That was out of place. He'd heard about rich chickadees who cruised dives like this, looking for rough trade. Maybe this was one of them.

A minute later she came over with her drink. "Join you?" she said simply.

He grunted and swept a calloused hand to the other chair. She settled in next to him, smiling with moist plum lips. He realized that she was no older than fifteen. A reeb. Jackpot! There was nothing better than forty years of expertise crammed into a fresh teen body.

"You're Russian?" she asked, twirling her swizzle stick.

"Ukrainian," he replied. "Giordi."

"Loretta," she said, and offered her hand. He took it. She slipped her other palm over his, rubbing his coarse skin. It was like touching an oak tree. "Worker's hands." There was a glint of excitement in her eyes. He didn't know how to reply, so he simply shrugged again. She released him, and he downed his vodka.

"This place stinks," she said.

He laughed. Laughing didn't look natural on him. His lips curled awkwardly around his teeth like snarling. But she didn't seem to mind. In fact, she looked delighted. She returned his smile.

It put him off balance, and suddenly he was darkly angry. He was being played like some street rat. Somebody she thought she could manipulate into her lower-class fantasy. He took a deep breath. *So she's slumming. So what? You can play along.*

"You've had a hard life," she said.

"Not like you," he replied.

The woman winked. "There are different kinds of hard." Then he felt her hand under the table, between his legs. "Mmmm," she said. She fumbled briefly with his fly. He gasped as her cool, dry fingers curled around him.

She leaned in to his ear. "I've got a flivver outside."

He nodded, not trusting his voice to work properly.

16

DONNER

The Rolls tooled slowly along the East River docks. The area was a conglomeration of shops, bars and warehouses. We moved past Peck Slip, past ancient warehouses with gambreled roofs and dormer windows. The activity here was subdued, hidden. On the water, scows were filled with refuse. Dock-side, trucks were being loaded with merchandise and machine-shops whirred and clanked. I could smell fresh-cut wood from a lumberyard. The slip's steel pylons were covered in neon graffiti: "Re-kill the re-born!" and the ubiquitous "Maury lives!" Beyond the chipped cement barriers, gray water burbled sluggishly. Fishing was again a major industry, as anyone with a pole could tell you. Reborn fish were as tasty as normal ones. The bizarre fact that some of the carp currently in the East River might've watched battleships set off for Nazi-occupied France didn't slow the hungry poor down one little bit.

Then we were in a darker area, where the moon was a dim blue hope and the street was lit by garbage fires. The flames danced unevenly along the piers, and more often than not the huddled bundles of rags turned out to be human-shaped. Their shadowed faces all contained the same expression. Waiting to be hurt. It could have been 1854 instead of 2054. Except these weren't immigrants, and the gangs that roamed these streets weren't the Bowery Boys.

In the car, I smoked and ignored my captors' glares. The trouble

I'd given them constituted unfinished business. They weren't likely to forgive and forget.

Armitage was shaking his head at my brief briefing. "You haven't turned up squat."

"I just started this morning," I replied. "Kidnap me again a couple days from now."

"Maybe we will," was the reply from next to me.

"Maybe I'll break your nose again."

"Mother*fucker*!"

The muscles in Broken Nose's arms quivered, barely restrained. Armitage stared at me a moment, trying to make up his mind about something. Then he nodded to Jelly Legs, who mumbled a couple colorful curses and pulled a leather valise from the floorboard.

Inside were all kinds of toys. Armitage pointed to each one as it was displayed. "This is a digital keycode generator for standard PIN key codes and access panels. Also a hackencrack program to crash the building's AI. The proximity alert, you strap on your thigh. A grapple pistol. Some other odds and ends. A flashlight, even a good, old-fashioned crowbar. Everything the modern cat burglar needs."

"And it ain't even my birthday," I quipped, but now I was really feeling trapped.

I'd assumed this crew had something to do with Crandall's disappearance. The street snatch was to keep me from digging any deeper. But these tools... What the hell was going on?

"You want to get into that lab, right?" said Armitage.

Shit.

"You're saying you don't?" he pressed. "It's the last place Crandall was seen. Gavin didn't tell you shit. If it was me, I'd want to check the place out."

"The cops already did."

Armitage chuckled. "The cops. Right."

"You sure seem to know a lot about this."

"We keep up with current events," deadpanned the Weasel.

I looked thoughtful. "So what happened? You leave behind a mess when you snatched Crandall? Something you need me to clean up?"

"Us? Grab the doc?" Nose chortled. "I thought this guy was supposed to be smart."

It was Armitage's turn to be quiet. I tried again. "Oh, I get it. You want in on the action! A couple good recipes for genetic soup."

"We're just concerned citizens."

"Yeah," sneered Jelly Legs. "We just wanna help."

"Didn't know I had friends in high places," I said quietly.

"You don't, deadhead. You don't have a choice, either."

"How's that, once I'm out of this car?" I grinned at Broken Nose. "Beautiful here gonna be my chaperone?"

Armitage exhaled long and slow. He ran a hand down his wrinkled tie. "Bartholomew Hennessey. Your old partner."

It took both Nose and Jelly Legs to hold me back. "You fucking touch one hair on that old man's head and I'll send you straight to—"

Another tap from the neuralizer. I drooled on myself for about ten seconds, then I could move enough to moan.

"You're a tough guy," said Armitage. "I appreciate that. But this town ain't yours anymore. You don't know the landmarks, you can't spot the moves, you got no backup. I would've had more trouble snatching a preschooler than you gave me. So shut the fuck up and listen. You're going into that lab for us. I don't need to give you a fucking reason. All you need to know is that if you don't do it soon, people are going to start dying."

"Do I look like a B&E man to you? I'll set off every alarm in town."

"There's a spot in the courtyard, southwest corner. Approach it from 23rd. At twelve-fourteen AM every night, the morphinium shell will move to a point where a two meter space contracts inside the range of the digital eyes. It's a blind spot, an oversight. But it only lasts a couple minutes. That's your way in. You hear me? Twelve-fourteen."

The car pulled to a stop. I went to move out, but Armitage put a hand on my shoulder. When I turned to look at him, his face maybe softened a fraction. "Look. Our interests converge. We both have questions need answered. Do this, and maybe we both come out ahead."

"Who the hell are you, Armitage? What's going on?"

The Nose shoved opened the door. I didn't need to be asked twice. I stepped onto the curb, genuinely shocked to still be in one piece. Armitage leaned out his window. He looked me up and down one more time, but the verdict was a mystery.

"I like the wisecracks," he said. "Very Raymond Chandler—"

"You should talk."

"—But it'll take a lot more next time to impress me."

He disappeared back into front seat gloom. The three goons flipped me off in unison and slid away on a cushion of electric air.

17

GIORDI

Giordi's head fell back against the seat, and a groan escaped his lips. *Shit, I won the lottery*, he thought deliriously.

Loretta's hand snaked up his chest. She played with his nipple through his shirt, pinching hard. Then he felt a sharp sting. He looked down. There was some kind of pointed tip on a ring she was wearing. Had she… what did she do?

What the fu…

Then all sensation, and all thought, swirled away.

Giordi wouldn't regain consciousness for another two hours. When he did, all thoughts of winning the lottery would be gone.

18

DONNER

I walk through the trees, lost. The trunks are gnarled like they've been frozen in some ancient, unholy dance. Wind lashes my skin. Why didn't I wear a jacket? I shudder. This place is too cold. Hypothermia will claim me quickly if I don't find shelter. But it's so dark. Leaves crackle under my feet as I stumble toward the quivers of moonlight that pierce the foliage.

I'm not alone. Sounds come on the wind, too faint to identify. There! A shape gliding behind a tree. Then a little laugh, a rustle, vanishing again when I whirl.

I can't hesitate. I have to move. This ground is unhallowed. Malevolence issues from the very earth. It reeks from the bark of the trees. I know without a doubt that I will die if I stay.

Paul!

No. I can't hear, I don't want to believe. I stagger forward, the wind thwarting my flight, biting at me, sucking my life's warmth. More motion behind the trees, a flash of copper hair.

It's not fair, the voice says. I was the better of us two.

It's not my fault! I moan.

Yes, she says. It is all your fault. For your sins, Donner. This is all for your sins.

And then she's in front of me, and I scream, because half her face is gone, and her beautiful hair is caked in blood, and worms twist out

through the jelly of her eyes.
Her hands wrap around me in a lover's embrace.
And she is cold, so very cold.

▼▼

The telephone woke me. It was Bart.
"Meet me at Amsterdam and 79th."
"Jesus… what time is it?"
"Eleven-thirty. You got a Roscoe?"
"Yeah." Nicole's .25. Amazingly, Armitage had returned it.
"Bring it."
"Bart, what's going on?"
"Just get here."

▼▼

The filaments of the Blister glistened under the moon like dew-dap-pled spider webbing. I tugged the lapels of my pea coat tighter as I joined Bart on the corner. The Upper West Side street was almost deserted. It always amazed me how a city this big could get so empty at night.
"Took you long enough."
"Haven't got the hang of socks with garters yet," I replied. "What's up?"
Bart rasped his palms together. "I told you we had the rest of Dr. Crandall's team under surveillance, right?"
I nodded.
"Mikiko Hakuri didn't show for work today."
"Dr. Hakuri? Oh no."
"As far as we can tell, she hasn't left her brownstone."
He pointed to a private residence across the street. It was a five-story row house crammed between two hi-rise apartment complexes. Pre-war flanked by post-Shift.
"Has someone called?"
"No answer."
"Bart, what am I doing here?"
Bart shifted from one leather-clad foot to the other. "This is deli-cate. Surazal security is supposed to be guarding their scientists. They

don't want us around. But if something happens, *we* get blamed anyway, security or no security. My Cap's afraid we'll get caught with our pants down again."

"But he's reluctant to let Surazal know that their employees are under surveillance."

Bart grimaced. "They'd scream. Like I said, delicate."

"It's only been a day, Bart. She probably has the flu and forgot to call in sick."

"Cap doesn't want to take the chance."

"Are you telling me the cops are afraid to go knock on the door and see if she's okay?"

"Let's say we'd prefer it if it were someone else. Someone unrelated to our stake-out."

"So where are they? The Surazal security detail?"

"That's just it. We don't know. They should be on this, but there's been no trace of them. It's weird. Maybe they're more discreet than we give them credit for."

"And maybe they'll be all over me the second I ring that doorbell."

"You're working for Nicole Struldbrug. You have a reason to be here."

"At 11:30 at night?" Bart shrugged, then blew on his fingers. "Cold fall."

I'd intended to interview Dr. Hakuri anyway. Funny how every time someone tried to leverage me into doing something, it was something I'd planned to do anyway. I guess they figure that if something went wrong, better me than them. But Bart, too? I looked at him, remembering that Armitage had threatened his life, and suddenly felt ashamed. My old pal was just asking me to help out, because I could. That was it, no hidden agenda. I was getting paranoid.

"Where's your set-up?"

Bart nodded his head to the white-paneled cargo van across the street. Tinted windows and a dry-cleaning logo on the side. It fairly screamed "Undercover Operation In Progress!"

"I'm not licensed, remember?" I said, "If this gets out and some bureaucrat decides to make an example out of me—"

"No one's looking to get you hinked up."

I eyed the brownstone. The forest green door had an etched glass window. Elegant. Bart coughed and handed me something on the down low.

"Remember how to use this?" It was a pick gun, with a pistol grip and stainless steel needles. This one could work three tumblers. There was also a tiny tension wrench.

"I think I can manage. So it's an old-fashioned lock?"

"Good old pin and tumbler."

I looked Bart in his watery eyes. He met me unblinkingly. "I'll owe you one."

"Okay…" I crossed the street. Rang the bell. No answer. I waited a minute. No reaction from the street, either. Bart was right—Surazal's security was AWOL. I inserted the tension wrench, then the needle of the pick lock. I squeezed the trigger a couple of times until I heard a click. I pushed the door open and slid into the foyer.

"Hello?" I called. "Dr. Hakuri? Your front door is open. Hello?"

The apartment was silent.

The residences of workaholics were either disasters or picture perfect. Until Elise, mine had been the former. This one, though— If there'd been ropes, it would've been a museum. Throw pillows were artfully positioned on a couch whose cushions had never taken the weight of a rear end. A chair and divan in navy and gold stripes sat regarding each other across a pristine white carpet. The coffee table books were fanned to display stiff, unopened spines. Even the Van Gogh print over the mantle was an uninspired choice—sunflowers, whoopee. The room looked like it had been put together by a furniture company for a brochure.

The kitchen was spotless as well. A single coffee cup sat in the sink. A half-finished turkey sandwich on a plate on the counter. The mayonnaise hadn't turned yet.

There was a window over the sink. Its security gate was open, the lock broken. The glass was intact, but someone had cut through the heavy layers of paint that sealed the frame to the sill. I poked my head into the alley. The window faced the sooty side of the adjoining building. The window was a good eight feet high. No easy way up from the street, but the window had been forced opened from the outside just the same.

I knew then how my search would end.

I found Mikiko Hakuri in the laundry room, folded in the laundry bin. The plastic cord was still around her neck. Her fingertips were blue with cyanosis, her face mottled. Tiny pinprick hemorrhages speckled her sightless eyes.

Strangulation was not the quick death depicted in the movies. It came slowly and painfully. It took whole minutes to lose consciousness—an eternity. There was plenty of time to panic and thrash, time to claw at the rope around your throat, time to feel your neck cartilage slowly crushed and your hyoid bone break and your eyes bulge under the horrible pressure, time to taste the blood that erupted from your nose, time to smell yourself as your bowels voided—

Time to fully comprehend that you were being murdered.

Another life pointlessly crushed out of existence. Abruptly I wanted to scream at the sky, to storm heaven's gate and demand an answer to these insanities. Why all this pain? What could possibly justify a universe as bleak as this?

I picked up a broom and prodded one of her arms with the handle. Rigor hadn't set in.

The MO was totally different from Smythe. They'd find money or jewelry missing. It had been staged to look like a robbery. But it was no robbery.

Someone was killing Surazal scientists.

I stepped outside and waved the world in.

19

SATELLITE INTERCEPT

TRANS00\INTERCEPT\GEOSAT231\110654\PRIORITY 05-32\CLASS5EYESONLY

WEBSQUIRT INTERCEPT AS FOLLOWS:

(NAMES AND OTHER IDENTIFYING INFORMATION HAVE BEEN DELETED PER NSA REG 1037459324)

1: Okay, you were right.
2: Are you sure?
1: He can't leave it alone.
2: Kill him.
1: He's already been killed. It didn't work.
2: Try harder. [Pause.] Damn. It's a shame.
1: Why?
2: He's yummy.

END END END TRANS00\INTERCEPT\GEOSAT231\DATE END END END

20

DONNER

Maggie was home when I returned. I filled her in. She asked some questions about Bart. True to his word, he'd kept me out of it when he'd called in the DB. "Anonymous tip."

Maggie had news as well. Arlene, my cute reeb librarian from the Hall of Records, had called. She'd decrypted the file and wanted to meet. Now.

"Busy night," I said, adjusting Nicole's gun in the shoulder holster I'd bought.

"I'm coming with you," Maggie said.

The counter man at the all-night diner wore a greasy wife-beater and a paper hat out of a Norman Rockwell painting. The moue on his face, however, was not American Pastoral. When we entered his eyes never left the OTB form on the Formica in front of him.

Arlene sat tucked into the corner of a booth, all the way in the back, her knees drawn up. She was the only patron in the place. There was an empty coffee mug and a manila folder in front of her. As soon as I saw her, I knew it was going to be bad. Her sunshiny eyes had gone overcast. She looked like she'd claw through the wall behind her if there was a loud noise.

We eased into the booth across from her. She didn't say a word, only pushed the file at me. I started reading.

Arlene gave Maggie the once-over. "Hey," she said, softly.

"Hey, yourself," said Maggie. She nodded toward the file. "Want to give me the executive summary while he's reading?"

Arlene snapped her gum. The once playful quirk was now a nervous tic. "The *Times* story about Donner's murder? The one that said there were no suspects? It was bullshit. The killer didn't get away."

Maggie paled. "What are you talking about?"

Arlene started shredding her paper napkin. "The shooter was arrested at the scene."

Maggie gaped. "That's impossible!" She looked back and forth between us. "At the scene? Then what happened to him?"

I closed the file. Held up a finger to her. They watched me worriedly while I sat stone-still for a couple minutes. Finally, when I had control, I spoke. "He was taken to the Manhattan Central Booking Facility. Standard procedure. Booked for armed robbery, assault, and murder. Then he was given a DAT and released."

"A Desk Appearance Ticket? That's for jaywalkers! For spitting on the sidewalk!"

Arlene doubled the pace of her shredding, reaching for more handfuls of napkin from the dispenser. "Someone changed the article in the database."

"A mistake?"

"In a cop murder?" I said. "No way."

"I'm guessing he never showed for his arraignment."

"There *was* no arraignment. The case was closed."

"What do you mean, closed?"

"I mean, no investigation, no arraignment, no trial. The DA's office never presented the case for prosecution. There was never even a warrant sworn out for Failure to Appear."

"That's—"

"Crazy, I know. Unthinkable. What's even more unthinkable is, the only conclusion I can draw from this—"

I didn't know how Maggie's holo program worked, but it was good. She blanched in shock as the implication sunk in.

Cover-ups were for the movies. I had never encountered a real one in my entire career as a cop. Until now.

Arlene stood abruptly, her thighs hitting the table. Had she not drained her coffee, it would have spilled everywhere. "I have to go." Before I could even choke out a thank you, she fled to the door. A bell tinkled as she exited.

"Come again," said the counter man, eyes still glued to the race listings.

I would never see her again. Another woman I'd blindly hurt who'd gone running.

We listened to an angry fluorescent light for a minute.

"How can you erase a double homicide like it never existed? Especially of a cop?"

I didn't know.

"Maybe the guy was some Senator's druggie son or something," Maggie said. "What name was he booked under?"

"John Doe."

"Oh, excellent."

"His prints aren't in the file."

"Removed, or never taken?"

"I don't know, okay? I don't know!" I forced myself to uncurl my fists. "I need a drink."

"How about a milkshake?"

The look I gave her was not kind.

"How about any one of three dozen pharmaceuticals that won't leave you with a hangover tomorrow?"

"Do any of them taste like scotch?"

"Why would any of them *want* to?"

I grabbed my hat. We made the bell tinkle.

"Come again," said the counter man.

Rain cast the street gray and diagonal. I slogged through puddles, searching for what I dare not find. A cab's magnetic field threw up a furrow of water like a speedboat's wake.

We walked a while. Maggie let me finish my smoke before she hit me with her own bombshell. "I wasn't gonna tell you until tomorrow, but under the circumstances…"

I looked at her sideways. "Am I gonna need that milkshake?"

"Surazal sent the security discs you requested. They show Crandall leaving when they said he did, clear as day, by himself. Whistling."

"Doesn't sound like a scared man."

"Donner, the discs were doctored."

I stood there.

"Did you hear what I said? There's a second layer of time code data embedded in DV files. Even most computer whizzes don't know about it. Whoever altered it pasted an old security clip of Crandall leaving and modified the surface time code, but didn't change the embedded one."

I started walking again. Maggie watched me for a moment, then rushed to catch up. "Are you okay?"

I didn't reply.

"I mean, if it was me, and I'd learned what you just learned, I wouldn't be okay. Not by a long shot."

I didn't reply.

"So, are you okay?"

I stopped, dropped the smoke, and toed the butt dead with my shoe. "Two altered pieces of evidence. In two completely separate cases. Both requiring skill and access. What are the odds of one recently undeceased detective stumbling across a situation like this?"

"Improbable, but not impossible."

"Am I a sap, Maggie?" I asked. "Everyone keeps shoveling bullshit at me and expecting me to think it's Malt-O-Meal."

She attempted a smile. "It's that dead boy scout face."

I looked at the sky with burning eyes. I was fed up. It was time to get some answers. "What's Bart's address?"

Maggie paled. "Going over to rehash the glory days?"

"There were no glory days," I said.

21

GIORDI

The cement room in which Giordi awoke was featureless. For a moment, he thought he was back in prison. He was naked, strap-cuffed to a metal chair. An ancient rust stain ran to the floor drain. The place smelled of sewage, and something else… Rotting meat? There was pale, mucus-like goo ringing the drain. And small chunks of something else he couldn't identify. Didn't want to identify.

It had been a set-up. If that fucking whore was *mafiya*, he was dead. And it wouldn't be fast. The Russian mob, having risen from the barbaric Soviet prison network, was the most brutal criminal group in the world. Cosa Nostra, the Triads, Yakuza—all were children in comparison.

What would they do to him? Hack through his testicles with a wheat sickle? Shove a soldering iron up his ass? It took all his strength not to scream in panic. A two-way mirror was mounted in the wall opposite him. Was he being watched? Hope fluttered. Could this be a CIA operation? FBI?

The door opened. A woman he didn't recognize stepped in. If he'd thought Loretta beautiful, this one was a goddess. "Hi!" she said cheerily. She carried a tray with a syringe on it. A hospital? But what kind of hospital stank of sewage?

"My name's Nicole. I'll be your nurse today." She checked his restraints. When she touched his head, he realized something had been attached to him. Wires.

"Electrodes," she explained. She checked the adhesives keeping the disks attached to his head, neck and chest. "They'll record your body functions."

"W-where am I?" His mind spun. He'd never been so terrified.

"You're in excellent health," said Nicole, prepping the syringe. "A real bull. That's one of the reasons we chose you. The other is that no one will miss you."

She plunged its tip into his neck in a single gesture. There was a hiss as the ampoule pneumatically injected into his body. Nicole tossed the spent syringe on the floor. She pointed to the window.

"I'll be in there, baby. If you need me, just scream."

Nicole and the man watched through the window.

Things happened. Horrible things.

Through the monitor, liquid sounds burbled. A moan. A squelch like a beetle being stepped upon. Then silence.

It was over pretty quick. Nicole looked at her watch, unhappy. "Get somebody to clean that up," she said.

22

DONNER

"**N**o sudden moves, Bart."

Bart froze in his doorway, one hand still on his key-card. His other arm held a six-pack of German beer. He'd gotten fancy in his old age.

"Come in and close the door."

"Donner?" Bart shut the door.

I clicked on a Tensor lamp, letting him see me in the armchair. The pistol rested lightly on my knee.

Bart paled. "Are you nuts?"

"We're going to have a heart to heart, Bart."

Bart dropped the card, held onto the beer. He drew up his chest and tightened his mouth.

"Fuck you," he said. "I don't talk to people who point gats at me."

I came across the room. Wood split, pictures crashed off the scarred bureau, glass tinkled. Then the gun was under Bart's chin, my hand around his throat. Beer spurted across our ankles.

"You're screwing up here, Donner—"

I cracked him across the face. He sagged, but I didn't let him collapse to the floor. I hoisted him back up to eye level, waited while he blinked away the pain.

"J-jesus, you're crazy…"

"I finally studied my dickenjane, Bart. Extreme emotion can give me unexpected surges in strength. I might've already fractured your cheekbone. I really don't want to accidentally snap your neck."

Bart looked into my eyes for a bluff. When he didn't find it, a deeper kind of fear suffused his expression. Words tumbled out in a panic. "I had nothing to do with it, you gotta believe me! When they brought that sorry fuck in, they had to hold me back!"

"Bullshit!" I roared, shaking him. Bart's head cracked against the bureau again, and he moaned, spittle coating his lips. Our feet danced like prize fighters', grinding glass into the wet carpet.

"I wanted my pound of flesh," he croaked. "We all did! But then the suspect was gone. The booking file was closed like it never existed."

"And you just accepted that?"

"Of course not! I went straight to the Captain. He said you'd been working undercover for the Feds!"

"What?" I blinked in shock. "Jansen said that?"

Bart nodded desperately. "He said that booking this shitbird would jeopardize an international drug sting—something that had been in the works for years. The operation was supposed to bring down an entire cartel, get millions of pounds of shit off the streets. He said we couldn't wreck all that now—we'd pick your doer up again later. He said that's what you would have wanted us to do."

"You didn't buy that."

"No." Bart sagged again, starting to cry. "I didn't."

I threw him into a chair and waited. When he spoke again, all he could look at was his own hands. "I was about to go higher up, to the Commish, to the Feds if I had to," he said. "The next thing I know, somebody's calling my wife."

"Sarah?"

"Asking her if she would be one of those cop's widows who liked getting reamed by a hunt-pack in the middle of the night. She almost lost her mind. And then some 'uncle' we never heard of picked Lizzie up from school—"

"Christ!"

"He got her some ice cream and drove her home. But the message was clear enough." Bart looked at me, tears rolling freely. "You and Elise were dead. I couldn't bring you back. And my family, Jesus, my family."

I didn't know what I'd expected to hear, but it hadn't been this. If they'd threatened Elise, I might've done the same thing.

He smiled wanly at the soaked floor. "Gonna smell like a brewery in here."

I pressed the cool chrome of the pistol against my forehead. *Think*, I told myself. *Where does this leave you?* "I take it there never was a drug bust," I said.

Bart shook his head. "And they never re-arrested the perp. Jansen acted like the whole thing never happened. After that, the asshole couldn't even meet my eyes. He transferred out to Staten Island a month later, the coward." He stared hard at me. "Donner, what were you into?"

"Into? Nothing!"

"Something like this doesn't happen over nothing! Whoever put the screws to the precinct— You don't make something like this go away without serious weight."

"If they didn't want this guy caught, why arrest him in the first place?"

"I think it was a mistake. You know what it's like when a cop gets killed. Things move fast. Every badge in the city was out for blood. And this guy was no John Dillinger. They had him in a couple hours."

"Where?"

"Red Hook."

Another shock. "Here in Brooklyn?"

"The Seven-six nailed him right in his crib. That's all I know. I never got a name, never got a look at him. Stew Mahadavia said he was Latino, but I never saw for myself."

"Why does a two-bitter go all the way to the Upper West Side to pull a job, when he lives in Brooklyn?"

"Maybe he's smarter than he looks."

"Most of these guys are short-term thinkers. They pick the nearest bodega."

"We don't know that he's a two-bitter. If he was connected, that might explain… what happened."

Say it, I thought. *The cover-up*. I stood in frustration. "And now there's no way to know."

The words turned Bart into a marble statue.

"What, Bart?"

"I hard-copied the guy's prints. After they were scanned. Before they waved me off. I wanted to be the one to nail the son-of-a-bitch."

He nodded to the bureau I had shoved him against. "Top drawer," he said. "Taped up inside."

I went to the bureau, opened the drawer and reached in. Sure enough, something was taped to the bottom of it. What I withdrew appeared to be a mini credit card.

Bart looked sick with remorse. "I take it out once in a while. To remind myself what a piece of shit I am."

"What is it?"

"Deposit box key. First Union Federal, Alphabet City. Stuff you can use."

He'd set up a survival cache, in case he had to run. He must have been truly terrified.

As I slid the card into my jacket, I knew I couldn't hate him. My face must have softened the tiniest bit, because Bart looked more than grateful. He looked… released.

"Donner," he whispered. "It was forty years ago. Can't you let this thing go?"

I walked out the door. Halfway down the hall, I heard the racking sobs begin.

◀▼

At the curb, I sucked in the cold night air, trying to clear my head. The expanse of sky through the Blister looked ersatz, heaven's stars turned into cheesy accent lights on a designer firmament.

I was halfway across the street when the face of Bart's building dissolved. Green energy swelled outward. Metric tons of matter were instantly vaporized. The blast wave picked me up and threw me through the air like a rag doll. I hit a Packard twenty feet away, the hood crumpling and the windshield imploding. Emerald debris fell like hailstones around me. I rolled behind the vehicle. The drop to the cement stole my breath. The air had become charged. Jade electricity danced down my sleeves. I batted at the St. Elmo's fire until I realized it didn't burn. The chrome hubcap by my face shimmered.

My legs buckled when I tried to stand and I went down again. I grabbed the demolished hood and tried again. The air reeked of ozone and melted insulation.

I looked back at the building. It was like someone had scooped a neat, circular chunk from its center. The outer walls were intact, but the insides were cleanly excised, transformed into vapor and ash. I saw half a television sitting on half a table in half a bedroom.

The blast had radiated outward with the same precision, the energy confined to sharp lines. The pavement, trees, cars within this pattern were scorched. Beyond this, the neighborhood was pristine, untouched.

No gas leak. No accident.

In the distance, sirens began whooping. Other than that, the street had gone silent as a tomb.

23

DONNER

"**D**onner?"

"Get out of the apartment. Download yourself somewhere safe."

"What's going on?"

"Go now, Maggie, before something explodes!"

"Jesus! Where are you going?"

"I have some banking to do."

They handed me a metal box and ushered me into a private room. Inside the box were file folders bound with rubber bands, and a yellowing piece of paper. A partial booking sheet. No name, but a complete set of fingerprints. I tucked the paper away. The box also contained a credit pebble and two guns.

I lifted the Browning Hi-Power. It had customized Delrin polymer grips and an adjustable sight mounted low in the slide. I pulled the magazine to make sure it wasn't another space toy, then smiled mirthlessly—9mm. One hundred ten grains, capable of moving at eleven hundred feet a second. My kind of destruction.

The second weapon was a Beretta 92F semi-auto, an old favorite of urban PDs. The double-action automatic had almost the same punch as a Magnum .357 and it jammed a lot less than its predecessor, the Colt .45. I had always preferred Sig Sauers as my back-up pieces, but this was fine. Just fine.

I left the ray gun in the box.

◥◣

Two hours later, in the driver's seat of the rental car, Maggie worked the Conch like a woman possessed. I had quickly filled her in, and was gratified in a grim way by her revulsion. The species *homo digitalus* possessed at least as much a horror of violence as did the average human. Probably more. Maybe I was sitting next to a representative of the only hope for the planet. Who knew? Mankind had sure turned out to be a sucker's bet.

She'd met me under the Varrazano-Narrows Bridge, close to the water. Pulled up next to the rusted chain link in a pink jelly bean with enormous fenders. Which was funny, since there were no wheels. As a barge tooted beyond a scrubby expanse of marsh grass, she'd leaned out and grinned.

"Hey, sailor. Going my way?"

My face had lit up in a sad smile. I was happy to see her. Why did she affect me that way?

Part of her jaunty greeting no doubt had to do with my appearance. I was done with being conspicuous, so I'd made a trip to the pharmacy. Nail polish, blue contacts and a "Just For Reborn Men" hair kit later, I looked like a bad copy of my former self.

Maggie scanned the prints into her databases as the car tooled along on autodrive. I was relegated to surveying the neighborhood.

We crossed a cement bridge over the Gowanus Expressway, and just like that, we were in Red Hook.

It hadn't changed. The peninsula, once one of the busiest ports in America, had been cut off from South Brooklyn and its own waterfront by some brilliant government moves in the mid-twentieth, notably the Brooklyn Queens Expressway and the Brooklyn Battery Tunnel. Its businesses had wilted under the shadow of the overpass. By my day, the area, with its quaint cobblestones and Civil-war era warehouses, was a ghetto where three-quarters of the population lived in housing projects and drugs and violence were the *de facto* masters of the streets. Its lots and abandoned properties had turned into open dumps. The shipyards had long ago moved to Jersey, and the gentrification wave that swept through Park Slope in my time apparently ran out of steam before it reached this place.

The setting sun transformed Manhattan's aeries into postcard silhouettes. I looked at the skeletons of warehouses, the rolling tide of razor-wire, the rusted steel shutters. The desolation was somehow beautiful. In a world of lies, it at least was honest.

"I got him," Maggie said, interrupting my reverie. I leaned over to view the image she was projecting onto the vehicle's broad dashboard. A young Latino kid looked sullenly back at me.

Hector Alvarez.

My murderer.

24

DONNER

The Red Hook Houses extended block after block like urban kudzu.

The moment Maggie and I stepped from the car in front of the projects, six young men at the corner bristled and headed our way. *Shit*, I thought. *Hope street gangs react the way they used to*. Their wardrobe was a pastiche, present and past, old and new, zoot suits and durags. The leader's head had an aggressive thrust to it. His crew's hands were all under their jackets. Not the best sign.

"Hey, hey, it's the heat," said the leader. He was of mixed Afro-American-Hispanic heritage. His eyes shone out from beautiful caramel skin with a harsh intelligence.

I shook my head and kept my demeanor neutral. The leader gave me a "don't bother to deny it" laugh. "You five-oh all over, man."

Maggie smiled. "We're just here to—"

"Nobody talk to you, *embustero*."

Maggie recoiled as if slapped. I felt the energy in the air leap a couple levels. I put a restraining hand on her arm. "I'm with Reborn Affairs," I said mildly. "I'm looking for a man named Hector Alvarez. His grandmother revived."

That stopped them. The four in back started whispering. The leader eyed me up and down again. "Why you carrying, if you ain't the man?"

"What's your name?"

The leader wavered, then stuck out his lower lip. "José."

Not a street tag. Gutsy. "I don't come down here unarmed, José. Do you blame me?"

José laughed, and his boys did, too, once they knew it was okay. "Fuck no. My crew, we spray the corners. You don't brandish iron, you end up in the Canal."

I nodded, thinking furiously. No choice but to step out. "Yeah, the Canal," I said. "It's been a while. They ever clean that mess up? Last time I saw it, it was green slime."

It was a risk. If it *had* been cleaned up, but, like, seventeen years ago, I'd just shown myself for a reeb. And I could guess how these kids would take to that.

But José bobbed with civic pride. "Yeah, man, Surazal, they did good by us. Bought up some warehouses, hired some locals, and cleaned up the Gowanus. We fish in it, now."

I looked dubious. "Real fish? Do they glow?"

"Naw, they sucked that toxic shit right out. Built this iron pier for us to cast from an' everything. There's striped bass, bluefish and flounder. Rafael's mom, she cooks 'em up."

Rafael scowled in agreement.

"Once I caught a blue crab," came a voice from the rear.

"Shut up, Julius," said José. Julius was pummeled by the others.

José cocked his head at me. "So you want Hector, huh? He old, man."

Maggie nodded discretely. He was eighteen when I died.

"You say his granny-moms come back, huh?" José bobbed his head, thinking. "What's her name?"

I tightened. I'd walked right into that. I had no idea if José actually knew the answer. If he did, and I gave him a bullshit answer, things would change instantly. I was outnumbered and outgunned. But I'd be equally dead if I hesitated. So I opened my mouth to make up a name, when—

"Daphnia," said Maggie. She smiled. "Pretty name."

José stared a moment. But he nodded, satisfied. "Yeah, Daphnia. They say she was a hot patootie." He eyed the lay of my jacket. "Let's see it."

I felt Maggie stiffen. But these bangers weren't ready to play. Not yet, at least. I slid back my jacket, showing them the holster. I pulled the Browning with a single, unthreatening gesture and handed it butt-first to him. José ratcheted the action back, and his eyes widened. His crew hissed in appreciation when they saw the jacketed round in the chamber.

"This a fine antique, white boy. None of that plasma shit. This a *real* weapon. For a real man." Rafael reached out, but José slapped his hand away.

José leered at Maggie. "You got a real man, Miss Anne."

"Don't I know it," she smiled.

"What say I tell you where Hector be, and you let me keep this fine piece of American craftsmanship?" José was grinning, but his eyes were dead. The issue wasn't open for debate. The guy was just letting me save face in front of my "Miss Anne," my white girl. So I frowned, but then nodded grudgingly.

"Just one more thing, though." José leaned in, confidentially. "His grams ain't coming back here, is she?"

I shook my head. "They'll care for her in a foster home until she's young enough to care for herself."

José nodded, and shuddered. "Down here, we hunt 'em like rats." He pointed his finger right at me and fired.

José led us to the far west side of the Houses. Running into him had been lucky. The projects, when taken in total, were larger than the Pentagon. We could have searched for days without finding the right building, the right floor. But merely five minutes after our conversation, José was rapping his knuckles on the shellacked metal door of Apartment 67D, sixth floor.

I'd gone icy still. Behind that door could be the man who took my life away. Took Elise's life. I'd expected to feel, what? Anger? Dread? Anticipation? But there was only numbness. My emotions were in a deep freeze, like when I'd first revived.

So be it.

"Who is it?" came an irritated voice from behind the door.

"José!"

"What the fuck you want?"

"I got some of that new Mexican chronic. Thought you might want a taste."

"Fuck off."

"On the house, you old piece of shit."

Silence. "On the—? What the hell… ? Hold on!" Then a racking, phlegmy cough. "Shit piss fuck."

José swung a hand toward the apartment like a carnival barker, winked once, and pimprolled down the hall.

The door cracked opened on the chain. A bleary eye appeared to appraise the situation.

I kicked into the room, the chain snapping like licorice. Maggie gasped, then slid into the apartment behind me.

Hector Alvarez had jumped backwards to avoid the crashing door. He'd spilled a Lipton's Cup-A-Soup all over his chest. Now he stood in the middle of the room, cracked lips working silently, his eyes bulging. He had the look of a man who'd waited all his life for a demon to arrive and make him atone for his sins. And now the horrible thing was here.

"You recognize me," I said.

The man nodded mutely. Noodles hung like maggots on his broth-soaked shirt.

My emotions may have been out of order, but my mind felt extraordinarily nimble. The vague dullness of thought that had plagued me seemed to dissipate with the sight of this man.

"You're the clerk," I said. "The grocery clerk."

The geezer worked his scaly lips soundless.

"What??" Maggie stepped forward, all angles.

"There was no robber at all. The police arrested *you*."

"Donner, what are you—"

"We walked in, and you shot us from behind the counter. Simple as that. You were waiting for us."

Maggie gaped back and forth from me and Hector like her head was on a spring.

"You're gonna kill me." The man's voice was reedy and trembling.

I pulled the Beretta from my ankle holster.

"Where the hell did you get all these guns?" said Maggie.

I gestured to a couch that was hemorrhaging foam. "Sit."

Hector complied. I surveyed the apartment. The light that stumbled into the room was gray. Considering the barracks-style efficiency of the building, the window was surprisingly large. Its security grate was open. Beyond, I saw a carefully potted garden on the fire escape. A tiny yellow tomato, a couple anemic peppers.

I turned back to Hector. "Someone hired you."

Hector blanched. He stood, turned his back and started removing the cushion of the couch where he'd been sitting. I waved the Beretta. "Whoa whoa!" Hector just kept fishing in the bowels of the couch. My trigger finger tightened. I wanted to complete the motion. It would be so easy.

Hector turned, holding a piece of paper. Frayed and yellow. A newspaper clipping. He handed it over. "No name," said Hector. "Never got one. But one day I saw this in the *Times*. I couldn't believe it. The face. Right there. That was him, alright."

The photo was of a crowd; some kind of early, anti-Necropolis rally-turned-riot. Maggie came over and nodded. "This was right after New York became the Necropolis. Hundreds of protesters were shot. Our own Tiananmen Square."

Of the thirty people in the medium-angled photograph, one visage was circled in faded ballpoint. It was rock-hard, devoid of emotion; and separate, scanning the crowd, the only one not participating in the frenzy. The blonde hair was short. A scar ran diagonally across his features, like a baker's knife-crease across a loaf of bread.

"Tell me," I said to Hector.

"This guy—the guy in the photo—one day, he comes into the store. Buys a Yoo-hoo. I know he's not there because he has a chocolate jones. When I'm checking him out, he tells me he knows about me doin' Seraphina."

My eyes narrowed. "My half-sister," Hector explained, with a shrug.

I heard a disgusted sound from Maggie. Smarties didn't like incest any better than us.

"Said he knew my rep, too. Said if I'd do this job for him, my homeboys would never find out about Seraphina. And I'd make fifty yards."

"Five thousand dollars," said Maggie. "The price of two human lives."

"Seraphina, man. Puerto Ricans, they don't go for that shit. I'd get cut for sure."

"So you said yes," I said.

Hector blinked bloodshot eyes at me. "The dude gives me money. A picture. You and your lady. Says you'd be together."

Maggie wasn't buying it. "How could anyone know they'd come

into your store?"

Hector looked sideways, running his eyes along the wall. "They did, though."

"Yes, we did," I said. "You've got more to say, don't you, old man?"

"You'll kill me."

"Then I'll give you a minute to find your courage." To Maggie: "Watch him. I'm going to toss the place."

The air in the bedroom was thick with ancient cat piss. In the closet, empty hangers dangled over a mound of soiled clothes. The bedside stand held nothing but expired pizza coupons. I pulled the stained mattress from the bed, checked under the frame, went through the pressboard dresser. A couple porno magazines. Nail clippers.

As I searched, my mind wanted to process the nasty implications of what I'd learned, but I stopped it. I'd wait. One step at a time. Figure things out when this was done.

When the old man was dead, I realized with a jolt.

Until that very moment, I hadn't been sure I was going to kill him.

It solved nothing. It didn't matter. I was about to become a murderer. It didn't matter. I was on a track with no turnoffs and void as a destination. A hell-bound train, no stops.

It didn't matter.

Then there was a loud crash from the living room, and I was vaulting through the door.

Maggie stood in the middle of the room, her face a mask of disbelief. The window was shattered, wind whipping the frayed curtains into a frenzy. Hector was gone. I went to the window. He'd overturned the garden on the way out. Down below, on the pavement, the tomato was splattered next to him, mingling with his pulped head. I turned and stared at Maggie.

"He just—he just—" she stammered.

My mind instinctively worked the scene like a cop. *You walk into a room. The window's broken, someone's standing there. Another person has gone out the window to their death.*

There were only two explanations.

José and his crew were leaning against our pink rental when Maggie and I walked up.

"We was watchin' it for you," said José.

I nodded. I'd never felt so tired in my life. The men moved back. I opened the door.

"Guess you didn't need the piece after all," said José.

"Guess I didn't," I replied.

25

DONNER

"I never saw a man die before," Maggie said on our way back to Manhattan. She shook her head over and over, weeping. "Your bodies. They're so fragile."

I rolled the window down and let the wind batter my face. She quieted eventually, and we rode in silence.

I thought about how I missed old-fashioned cars. EM travel felt mushy. No rubber-meets-the-road contact. I'd seen a few classic rides tooling around the city. But with gasoline at $34 a gallon and a mountain of environmental restrictions in place, the days of the internal combustion engine were pretty much over.

In my youth, I'd owned a Vincent Black Shadow. That Brit motorcycle had been my pride and joy. Maintaining it had taught me about engines. It really hadn't been worth the work—the damned thing was finicky and tough to keep purring, the parts were expensive, and it cost a fortune to store in the city. But it had lines as sweet as a VH1 diva, and the rumble-roaring delight of opening her up on a windy upstate road, leaving the stress and bullshit of the city behind in a burst of smoke—well, it was indescribable.

I sold it when I married Elise. Too dangerous, she said. Not as dangerous as a pack of cigarettes, it turned out.

"Ready to talk?" I asked.

Maggie sniffed and crossed her arms, steeling herself.

"Just walk me through it. He jumped?"

"Sort of."

"What does that mean?"

"He just… flew right through the window."

"Without opening it?"

"Yeah."

I was smoking filter. I lit another, trying to get my mind around what she was saying. "Why would he do that, Maggie?"

"How the hell should I know? Maybe he thought you were going to kill him, and he decided to beat you to the punch."

There was something wrong about her defensiveness. I couldn't put my finger on it. So I moved into the tough stuff. "I have to ask this, Maggie. Can smarties become… well…?"

Her fingers twisted in her lap. "Unbalanced? No. Well, yes. Theoretically. It's rare."

"Rare?"

"Yes, rare, alright? We've got protocols, back-ups… I'm *not* crazy!"

"Could you have been tampered with? Forced to do something, then had your memory erased?"

"Made to kill Hector, you mean."

"Yes."

"Not… no."

We rode some more in silence. I felt like scratching away my skin. The nicotine was giving me the jitters. I'd started to believe I knew the woman next to me, but now I didn't know what to think. Hector jumping right through a closed window? It was only remotely more plausible than Maggie pushing him.

Snake eyes. Nothing to do but cut my losses. "Let's put what happened to Hector on hold for now and go through what he told us."

She okayed that with visible relief.

"If I've got this straight," I said, "this man in Hector's picture, the man with the scar… somehow he knows I'm gonna be in that bodega that evening. He approaches Hector out of the blue, blackmails him to kill me. Me, specifically."

"Then you show up with your wife, so bad luck, she gets it, too?"

I pushed something black and thorny back into my chest.

"But the cops arrest Hector faster than anticipated," Maggie continued. "So someone—someone with juice—gets him released and covers the whole thing up. Forty years later, you revive, and the cover-up starts again. You interrogate your old partner, and either to shut him up or kill you both, this someone blows up his apartment. Now, you're on the lam from God knows who," she continued, "probably someone in the police or government themselves, and I'm an accessory to a dozen crimes."

I flicked the butt out the window. "Sounds about right."

"Well, fuck me."

I let out a surprised laugh. I'd never heard Maggie swear before.

"That's the craziest thing I ever heard."

"Sorry you helped me?"

"What do you think?"

Even in my funk, I couldn't help noticing the little crease of pique between her eyebrows. She was especially adorable when she was furious. She'd be even more furious if I mentioned it.

"What'll they do to you?" I asked, to banish the thought.

"Don't ask," she said. "If I get connected to any of this, losing my job will be the least of it. The number of smarty-perpetrated crimes in the last forty years is exactly zero."

"C'mon."

"I shit you not, shamus. It'd be front page news. A worldwide sensation. There'd be calls to revisit VP independence."

My face remained neutral, but her reply sent me into a tizzy. She was my only ally in this strange new world. If she became a liability and I had to cut her loose—

I realized what I was thinking and felt a hot flush of shame. I'd been fouled, growing up in the jungle. Elise had done much to awaken something in me resembling a heart, but in the days since I'd revived, I'd become aware that my childhood hardwiring had been coldly and methodically reasserting itself.

Maggie was still talking. "How could a cover-up still be active after all these years? Does that mean the murderer is still around?"

"I *hope* he's still around," I said through my teeth.

She paled. *Pull it back*, I thought. *Don't spook her.*

She was still staring at my face. "We're assuming Bart's death is related to the cover-up and my murder," I said.

"Well, what else—"

"The Armitage guy?"

"The guy who kidnapped you?"

"Yeah. He threatened Bart's life if I didn't do a B&E on the

Surazal lab."

"Are you kidding?" A furrow snaked across Maggie's brow and disappeared under her hairline. "But why kill Bart *before* you've done anything?"

"I don't know the man well enough to know that what he does has to make sense."

"What's your gut tell you?"

"I don't think it was Armitage. He's smarter, more low-key than that."

"So we're back to the cover-up."

"There's another thing that's bugging me. Why bother to have Hector released after my murder? Why not just let him take the fall for the homicides?"

"Cause then he'd ID Mr. Scar."

"Then why not just whack him?"

"In 2012, no one thought you'd be *back*, Donner. Maybe it was easier to have Hector released. Maybe, for whoever orchestrated this, the cover-up was easier than having to deal with another dead body that could lead back to the them."

That sounded possible. "So it's not until I revive and start nosing around that Hector became a threat again," I said.

I looked at her, wondering about that room again, about her and Hector. She met my eyes, and I caught a repeat flicker of... what? Fear? Doubt? Guilt? I couldn't tell. About the only thing I knew for sure was that I wouldn't get the answer by pressing her right now.

"The picture Hector gave us—the man with the scar," I said. "Can you scan it? Run a facial make on him?"

"Great! I tell you I'm going to lose my career and maybe be front page news and you ask me to dig myself in deeper!"

"I didn't force you into this."

"No, you just were so pathetic and lost—"

"Whoa! You're saying you did all this because you felt *sorry* for me? Are all smarties this lousy at lying?"

Her brow darkened. "How the hell would you know? I could put what you fleshpots understand about us in a thimble!"

"Fleshpots?"

"Forget it."

"Maggie!"

She shifted uncomfortably. "It's a term smarties use amongst themselves. For humans."

"Is it a good term?"

"No."

"Smarties aren't above prejudice, then. Sounds human to me."

"You're twisting my words!"

"I didn't twist anything, Maggie."

"What you just called 'human' is actually egocentrism—and it's an inherent condition of consciousness, Donner. Any consciousness. Human or not."

"What the hell are you talking about?"

"As soon as an entity—human or not—becomes self-aware, it's impossible for it not to become the center of its own universe. As soon as there's an 'I,' everything else becomes 'not-I'. A potential competitor. Get it?"

"So smarties are just like humans. They can't help but calculate their relative position in the scheme of things. 'I'm better,' 'I'm worse,' 'I have more,' 'I have less'…"

"No," she said. Her irritation had left her. Now she just looked exhausted. "Self-aware and separate does not imply value, only position. You just said, 'I have more, I have less.' But only humans beings turn that into 'I'm better, I'm worse.' To us, 'I *have* less' does not equal 'I *am* less.' We don't need to prove our value through competition. And without that drive from the ego, there's no purpose to violence." Her voice got quieter. "Or vengeance."

I knew what was coming.

"You were going to kill Hector," she said.

The words wrapped cold chains around my guts. I didn't know what to say. So we watched the BQE flow by, a stream of steel and concrete. Traffic was light.

"No smarty has ever committed murder?" I asked finally.

"Never," she said. But a tick jumped under her eye and I got that weird feeling again. "To regard another entity as better or worse in terms of value is ridiculous, because separation and permanence are illusions."

"Huh?"

"What you think of as 'you' is a mental abstraction, a bunch of intellectual definitions. What *I* think of as you is also an abstraction. Neither is what you really are."

My heard was starting to hurt. "So what's the real me?"

136

"That's the point. There *is* no 'real' you. What you are is not definable because it's changing moment from moment. And who you *think* you are is in constant flux as well. Is the Real You the 'you' you are when you're liking yourself? Or the 'you' you become when you screw up? Was the ten-year-old Paul the real Paul? Is it you today? Or is it you ten seconds from now?"

I shook my head, completely lost.

"Do you see how pointless it is for humans to claim they have a soul and consciousness but that smarties are only mechanical mimics of human behavior?" she continued. "You can't even define your own consciousness, so how can you make a judgment on ours?"

My voice came out sounding defensive. "So if you're so evolved, why do smarties still feel emotions like hurt and regret and... affection? You were crying a minute ago."

She flushed. "I never said we were perfect."

"Fair enough. What did you mean about separation being an illusion, too?"

"At this moment, our molecules are crossing the space between us. Co-mingling." Her eyes twinkled. "Can you say where you end and I begin?"

"We're intermingling?"

"Separation is another delusion of the ego."

"I don't follow."

"Think of separation and identity like this: a wave can convince itself that it's separate from the ocean, but only for a moment."

"So we're just two waves?"

She nodded.

"Hmmm." I front-loaded a smile. "So wave on into the database and run the make for me, baby."

She barked laughter, like a seal. "You're incorrigible!"

"That's what you love about me."

She punched me in the shoulder. "Autodrive."

And left me to wonder how she had managed, in a few minutes, to move me from murderous rage to feeling some kind of strange stillness inside, however fleeting.

If, as she implied, those landmarks from the past—those people and things I'd loved and felt lost without—if they hadn't been going to remain the same anyway… even if I *hadn't* died, they'd have still changed and eventually gone away, as all things do—if the world was going to be what it was, whether I wanted it to or not…

If all of that was true, what would my choices be?

Change what I could, and just accept what I couldn't?

Was that sanity, or giving up? And was it possible for me to live that way?

Sixteen minutes later, after my inability to sort through my jumbled thoughts had me back to being nice and pissed off, Maggie smacked her hands together. An image popped into existence. Sure enough, there the bastard was, with his dead eyes and diagonal scar. "Ewan McDermott," she read. "Former IRA soldier, turned mercenary after the British-Irish peace accord. Worked for drug cartels, mostly. Homeland Security had him on a watch list, but he got into the country anyway on fake papers."

"Oh yeah, that makes a *lot* of sense," I said wearily. "An international merc puts out a hit on me."

"Who would want you dead? I mean, no offense, big daddy, but you're a nobody."

"You're nobody 'til somebody hates you," I warbled softly.

"Could it have been a case you were working in your first life?"

"I had three open cases when I died. A drive-by, a domestic, and a mob hit. Case one: Jamal Johnson, 'Firebird,' to his friends. A stone banger at age thirteen. Died in his front yard as the result of an Uzi on automatic. No suspects. The domestic was Cynthia Bowles. Took a paring knife to her hubby when she discovered three grand in internet porn charges on their VISA bill."

Maggie laughed.

"The hit was Felix somebody. A Gee CI."

"A whosit?"

"FBI confidential informant. Former mob stooge. Death came by way of two taps to the back of the head. A dead canary in his mouth. Along with his penis."

"I thought organized crime was the FBI's turf."

I chuckled. "I had a prickly lieutenant. We were still working out jurisdiction."

"Could your hit be connected to the mafia?"

"The *familia* would definitely not use an Irish shooter."

"Then what the hell?"

My restless hands hardened. "I know. It breaks the rules. Why bother to make this thing look like a botched robbery? And why does a professional assassin, presumably hired by someone, hire someone *else* to do his wet work?"

The paroxysm surged suddenly, like it had been lying in wait. I brought my fist down on the dashboard. The glove box fell open. The vehicle swerved and a dash light went on. "Is there a problem?" asked the sedan.

"Mind your own business," Maggie said to it. "Just drive."

"You don't have to get snooty," said the sedan. The light went off.

"None of it makes any goddamned sense!" she said.

"And the only person with answers is this McDermott—"

"Who, dead or alive, is buried so deep we'll never find him."

Maggie tried a smile. "So you'll take me to the Bahamas now, Daddy?"

Despite my frustration, I had to laugh. I flicked my cigarette lighter. "Guess I'll work on the Crandall case."

Maggie went ballistic. "Donner, your best friend just got murdered. You just found out you were assassinated by a merc and your cop buddies covered it up. Someone tried to blow you up! Don't you think you should take time to, I don't know, *regroup*?"

"I was hired to do a job."

She regarded me with piteous admiration. "A real old-schooler, aren't you? Truth, justice and the American way."

"That's me, Super-Corpse," I growled. "Up, up and decay." I looked out the window. "Pull over here."

The car complied.

"Download yourself someplace safe."

"Where are you going?"

"First I'm going to get twelve hours' sleep. Then... I'm going to hack a building."

26

DONNER

That night, in the seedy hotel room that I'd rented, the dreams found me.

She walks across a plain of cracked earth. Purple lightning flashes against a black sky. I can make out her favorite dress, a yellow thing, blowing in the wind, showing off her figure. She waves. But my feet are rooted to the ground. I look down, and they are rooted literally, twisting tendrils of vine wrapped around my ankles, growing into them, the tops of my feet beneath the soil.

I try to call out, but my tongue is swollen. All I can do is croak.

Elise stops.

Insanely, there's a boom box sitting on a burnt-out stump. "Is there a problem?" it asks. "Don't get snooty."

Its play light comes on. A song starts. Blues. Keb' Mo'. "Proving You Wrong."

It hurts Elise to hear it.

The wind has vanished. A shadow rises from the ground, an opaque thing with an amorphous body and black, swirling limbs. I try to scream. The phantom limbs wrap around her, and she cries out in panic, her eyes going to me.

Help me! she cries in terror. For God's sake, why are you doing this to me?

But I can't move. And even as it engulfs her, I recognize this swirling black shape.

It's my pain.

And as I watch, she is drawn down, down, until earth fills her screaming mouth.

I woke to someone banging on the wall behind my headboard.

"Shut up, shut up! Stop screaming or I'll call the cops!"

I put my face in my hands.

"Crazy motherfucker!"

Toward morning, I managed a couple sweaty, half-conscious hours, then gave up.

The dream came back to me.

There'd been a day when Elise had ordered me out. A separation. We reconciled eventually. But on that day, I'd left a boom box on a chair with a "play me" note, some kind of stupid dramatic statement. The song had been the song in the dream, "Prove You Wrong." "I'll prove you wrong," the refrain went. Elise thought it'd been left to hurt her. That it meant I'd prove her wrong about kicking me out. But it hadn't been. Of course in my stupidity, I hadn't thought that she wouldn't exactly be in the frame of mind to listen through *all* the lyrics. They'd actually meant *I'll prove you wrong in thinking that I can't change. I'll change and be the man we both deserve.*

Like many of my well-intentioned gestures, it had ended up hurting instead of helping.

Was Maggie right? Did people never truly see each other? Did they never really know who the other person was? I'd seen Elise through the veil of my needs, but now I realized that she'd already changed. I'd already broken us.

Too hard to think about.

So I spent the day nursing a shot glass and smoking and watching crap on the tiny display that some genius had epoxied to the wall. Entertainment programming hadn't improved in forty years.

When the clock read 1:10 AM, I got dressed.

▼▼

The Chelsea lab was wrapped three-sided around a courtyard, used for exercising the employees when they weren't pulling overtime. Picnic tables and a white gazebo. In the summer, brass bands in gartered sleeves and boater hats played "Sentimental Journey" and there was free lemonade spiked with endorphin productivity enhancers.

I stood beneath a lamp post and fired a wooden match with a thumbnail, just a guy making his way home, pausing to light an illegal smoke. I let my disinterested gaze wander into the courtyard. Lights and security eyes everywhere. Crossing the space would be like walking a prison yard. I exhaled smoke and started moving. People didn't stroll at 2 AM. Anyone not moving with a purpose would be a subject of interest to police and predators alike.

I didn't like it. A pro would've cased this building for weeks, getting the routines down pat. They'd know every alarm system, air duct and firewall, know when the cleaning service worked and what access they had. How many security rounds were made, when, and by whom. Which guard was on what floor, whether he was lazy or alert, how long he'd worked there, when he got coffee, took a pee, whether he had any vices to distract him. They'd have ID good enough to pass a once-over and serious firepower if that failed. Multiple exit strategies. And they'd have a crew. Nobody was insane enough to take a building like this solo. Too many variables, too many special skills needed.

And I was about to try it all on my lonesome.

I remembered a seasoned old burglar, one of the last of the true career artists, before the smash-and-grab meth-heads changed the scene forever. The Dean, they'd called him. He'd worked the city for twenty-seven years without taking one prison jolt. We'd known he existed, but only as a shadow, an urban legend. He had a jacket three inches thick, over sixty unsolved but suspected cases, but not one arrest. He'd finally gone down at age fifty-eight not because of a mistake, but because of frailty: a heart attack in the middle of a job. The mark came home from his business trip and found the Dean lying beside the cracked safe in the bedroom, gasping for air. After he got out of the hospital and was brought into Booking, we were all there. Everybody wanted a look. He was royalty.

I could feel him looking down on me in disgust.

2:09.

The metal wall was behind a grove of cherry trees. It would have been the corner if this building had corners. The area, only about two feet square, appeared to have contracted beyond the lights and cameras, just like Armitage had said.

Only one way to find out. I slid fast and direct off the pavement to a spot behind the trees. No way to hide the detour.

I waited to see if I'd caused a reaction.

The neighborhood stayed asleep.

2:14.

This building topped off at ten stories, thank God. A smaller, three story section faced me. I pulled the grappling pistol from the valise, aimed and fired. A filament cable hissed up and out. The fusion piton melted into the concrete just below the lower roof. I checked the tension, hung the bag around my neck, and hit "rewind" on the side of the gun.

It hauled me up so fast that I had a blast of vertigo. I could only close my eyes and hang on while I rocketed upward. Then I was swinging myself over the lip of the roof and retracting the cable, wondering at what floor I'd left my stomach.

The access grill was reinforced steel, bolts and straps. I passed the palm-sized device Armitage gave me over the thing. Two metal tendrils shot out and insinuated themselves into the output nodes of the panel.

"Hacking building AI," the device said. "Please wait." A couple beeps later, the access grill's locks detached with a muted *thunk*. "Security overridden," it said. "Have a nice crime."

I consulted a GPS router loaded with the building's schematics. I lowered myself through the hole. A maintenance shaft. A couple twists and turns later, I found the connection to a ventilation duct. It ran over the main hallway. The duct's aluminum grill had screws, so I cut through them with a tiny laser torch. I dropped down into the corridor.

Now it would get tricky.

I edged down the hall. The proximity unit strapped to my thigh would alert me before I tripped any security sensor, and before any human guards got too close.

I turned the corner and ran smack into Maggie.

She shimmered at the contact. I fell back into a defensive position.

"Plasmagram," she said nasally.

I put a hand over my heart. "I youthed a year! What the fuck are you doing here?"

"I can run interference."

No time for a debate. I pointed a gloved finger at her, letting her see in my eyes just how serious I was. "You're going. Now. I don't need your help."

"Then you know that a guard is about to turn the corner."

Sure enough, footsteps could be heard, getting louder, and my thigh was vibrating urgently. I spotted a utility closet, and pulled Maggie in behind me.

It was tight. We found ourselves body to "body" amidst the brooms, buckets and shelves of toilet paper. I could feel her trim form pressed against me.

Her eyes wandered my face. "Wish I could smell."

"Dummy up," I said.

"Bet you smell good. Musk, clean sweat, lingering soap…"

"Will you be quiet?"

Then we heard the guard approach outside.

The door handle jiggled. *Shit*. I closed my eyes, a statue. The guard tried the door again, testing the lock. If it opened, I'd have to move on him. Come at him low, take him off his feet, then finish him. Knocking someone out in real life was messier than the movies. Causing enough trauma to shut down a brain risked a concussion, a fractured skull, or outright death.

Maggie brought her hands to my face, touched my skin. Her fingers pulsed as plasma met flesh. They roamed the curves of my face. The danger of the situation, combined with her touch, was suddenly and intensely erotic.

Finally, the guard's footsteps diminished down the hall. I exhaled, sweat beading my brow. Maggie was still touching my face, cheeks, lips.

"What does this feel like?" she asked.

"Okay, c'mon. Stop it."

Her tone hardened. "What's wrong, tough guy? Afraid to get turned on by an artificial girl?"

Christ. Her timing was amazing.

I slid past her, opening the door.

◥◣

There were two sets of main doors to the genetics lab with a sterile foyer between. Each had its own security apparatus, a redundant set-up to annoy staff and burglars alike. Both sets were constructed of industrial security glass, framed in metal Xs that allowed a view of the lab beyond.

As we approached the outer doors, my leg sensor vibrated again. I put a hand up and we froze. I clicked my flashlight to infrared and cursed under my breath. Laser beams crisscrossed the hallway a meter in front of us, floor to ceiling. An impenetrable web of light.

"I thought I already overrode security."

"Must be a dedicated program," she replied.

"What is it? Motion detector?"

"Worse. It's a DNA alarm. Those lasers analyze any organic material above a certain weight. They'll ignore a mouse or a dust bunny but a human will instantly set it off."

I cursed colorfully. "I can't exactly hide my DNA."

Maggie nodded. She was chewing her lip.

"What?"

"Nothing."

"There's that inept lying again."

Maggie looked at the floor a moment. "There may be a way, but I'm not sure I like it."

I opened my palms. *Try me.*

"You wondered before how I become physical, right? Well, the short version is that I download myself into a small receptacle… call it my heart, whatever. This device projects the plasma and nanobits which collectively form my body."

"This receptacle actually rides around inside its own projected body?"

"Right. If I were to dematerialize, my software construct would return to the device or be transferred to another unit, another computer. The particles would be re-absorbed into the device."

"How does this help us?"

She hesitated. "If you hold my heart close against your body," she said, "I might be able to reset my physical parameters to rematerialize around you. Sort of like a second skin."

"Around me? You mean I'd be *inside* you?"

"I'd be like a shield around you."

"Would I be able to breathe?"

"That's exactly what we don't want—no flow of molecules across the membrane that could trigger the sensors. You'd have to hold your breath."

"Have you ever done this?"

"Are you kidding? How would you like someone to have your living heart, your very life, in their hands?"

"Don't you have a backup file somewhere?"

"Would you want a backup of *you* stored somewhere? Some clone? So if you died, an exact copy, but not really YOU, could be put in your place? When are you going to get it?"

"Yell at me later."

Her resolution dimmed a moment. "So are we doing this? That guard'll be back soon."

"Okay, what do I—"

"Hold your hands out, palms up."

I did. She stepped toward me, so the tips of my fingers were pressing against her abdomen just below her breasts. We locked eyes for a moment, and I realized how afraid she was.

She trusts me, I thought. *With her very existence.*

Then she became less solid and stepped forward. My hands slipped into her. I felt tingling. I could still see them within her sparkling iridescent form. Above floated a grapefruit-sized globe. It was silver, a giant ball bearing. It settled gently into my palms. I took a breath and pulled my arms back towards myself and cradled her heart against my chest.

The lights went out.

Suddenly my body was moving. My legs lifted, went down, ambulating by remote control. I felt smothered and for a moment bucked inside her. She fought for dominance. It took enormous will to relax and let her move me.

Time slowed. I felt strange, dislocated. I imagined that I could hear her thoughts, below the level of consciousness. They were shimmers of electricity, whispers in a grove of cypresses, the knowledge of circuit and sky. I didn't know if it was real or not. But they danced around me, fireflies of thought, and I was delighted to find that there was much in her that was made of joy and kindness. I wondered how

I could have suspected her of throwing Hector out the window, and my hardness made me want to cry.

I came back to myself a little. The heart felt delicate in my grasp. I could crush it, and that would be it, no more Maggie. Despite how Elise and I had loved, neither would have permitted such a vulnerable moment, so complete a surrender. Survival instinct, maybe. Or the calluses of city life. This was as intimate with someone as I'd ever been.

The realization was like ice water. Guilt streaked through my head. But the whispers continued. I wanted suddenly to truly abandoned myself to them, give up my pain and simply merge into…

And then, like that, we were beyond the laser web, and I was myself again. I looked down at my own body, surprised to be separate. We glanced shyly at each other, and I felt absurdly like a kid who had just stolen his first kiss.

"Guess we didn't set off the alarm," I said.

"Guess not."

A silent moment. "That was… wild."

She nodded. "I felt you. Were you saying things?"

I didn't answer. I stepped forward and the outer doors hissed open. We entered the foyer, and they smacked closed behind us. No way back to the hall. Our choice was to satisfy the second lock and continue into the lab or be trapped here.

I examined the inner lock. A gene sampler. There was a button below three small icons: a drop of blood, a strand of hair, a bit of saliva.

This time I was prepared. I pressed the button. A tiny receptacle whirred from the wall.

"Please spit," it said.

"Gross," said Maggie.

"Would you settle for some hair?" I whispered. From my bag, I withdrew the tube Nicole had given me, extracted a few hair follicles and dumped them into the receptacle. They were sucked away and there was a whir.

"Thank you, Dr. Crandall."

The interior doors parted.

The lab was painted a bland beige meant to stay out of the way of

any great thoughts. My flashlight played across smartscreens, centri-
fuges, quantum tunneling microscopes. A science geek's Disneyland.
Computer servers big as Frigidaires sat in a row, blinking stupidly.

I threaded through the work stations. Opened drawers beneath
the Formica tables. Nothing of value. Pens, notepads, accoutrements
of the scientific method.

Maggie's hands were wrapped around her elbows.

"Cold?" I whispered.

"Terrified," she answered.

We moved to the back. The offices for the senior staff were glass
cubes. The one labeled with Crandall's name was the biggest. It still
had a yellow strip of police tape across the door.

The inside was spartan but disorganized. A plastic chromosome
model hung on fishing line like a mobile. Books and papers were
vaguely organized in tottering heaps. Data pebbles were strewn like
M&Ms. This workaholic was a slob.

I rifled through papers on the desk. They all contained the same
indecipherable jargon. I wondered what I had hoped to find without
Maggie's help. "Can you access the database?" I asked. "We're looking
for a journal, calendar, diary, anything personal."

The smartscreen came to life, bathing the room in blue. "Searching,"
she said.

I hated the fact that every piece of evidence in this world was
on the inside of a computer. Even in my era, I'd been a dinosaur to
the younger CSI guys. I was from the school where you searched
with your hands, your eyes, your wits. When your case-breaker was a
greasy fingerprint, dried blood on an andiron, a kilo of cocaine in a
false-bottomed drawer. Not some data file in cyberspace.

As I waited, I looked around. The rear wall was dominated by an
enormous dry-erase board system. When one of the four rectangular
boards was filled, it could be lowered out of the way and a fresh one
rotated down. Currently, all four sections were covered in equations
dense enough to give Stephen Hawking a migraine.

"Whoa," said Maggie, behind me. "What's this?"

Imprinted in nasty red letters across the screen was:

SURAZAL CORPORATION
LEVEL ONE EYES ONLY
PLEASE ENTER PASSWORD

"Damn," I said. "I'd hoped personal stuff might not be protected. Can you hack it?"

Maggie chewed her lip. "It's a risk. I don't know their security architecture. If I try, and set off alarms, we won't know it until we see them pointing their guns."

I could feel the Dean looking down again. When faced with the choice of extra risk or leaving empty-handed, pros also took the cautious route. Patience and control was how you stayed on the street instead of playing checkers in lock-up. But I wanted something for my trouble, even if it was a computer file. "Crandall told Nicole about a breakthrough the night he disappeared, right? It could be here."

"Even if it is, we might not be able to make heads or tails of it."

"What else do we have?"

"Bupkus."

"So do it."

Maggie broke apart into a firestorm of glowing embers. Her nanobits swarmed her metal heart, lowering it onto the desk. They flitted away, dissolving. The globe just sat there, looking inert, and I almost panicked. Then her voice issued from the computer's speaker:

"It's going to take a while. Hang loose."

Right. Hang loose. I eyed the doors.

For all the crimes I'd seen, all the scumbags I'd dealt with, I'd thought it would've been harder to cross the line. But I'd taken to the shadows with an ease that was scary. I'd thought that *bon mote* about cops and crooks being only a hair's breadth away from each other was bullshit, but here I was, my mind working like both at the same time. I wondered where that put me.

I wandered to the boards. The equations might as well have been Martian. I examined the buttons that controlled the boards, ran my finger over the green one. It must have been more sensitive than it looked, because with a whisper, the top panel rotated down into third place, the lowest one swung up to cover the second, and I found myself looking at the bare drywall beneath.

Something about it looked wrong.

Then a printer rattled to life and I went back to the desk. Pages pumped out. Maggie's globe swarmed with fireflies again. A moment later she was back in the flesh, so to speak.

"You make a great inside man," I said. Then I saw the look on her face. "Maggie?"

She went to a stool and sat, staring into space. "Bastards," she whispered. She pointed to the pages issuing from the printer:

SURAZAL CORPORATION
LEVEL ONE EYES ONLY CLEARANCE
PROGRESS REPORT:
August 17, 2054
****

** NORM YOUTHING PROJECT **
****

And like that, I understood.

I understood what was so important about Dr. Morris Crandall. Why Gavin had been unwilling to talk about what Surazal had discovered about the Shift. Why Nicole had come to me, instead of an experienced gumshoe.

It was, quite simply, the other side of the coin. A DNA retrovirus appears with the ability to bring people back from the dead and make them grow younger. So why couldn't that same DNA be harnessed? Finessed a little? Engineered into a treatment for norms?

A treatment to keep them young?

The only thing that had ever leveled the playing field between kings and peasants was death. It didn't matter how rich you got, or how powerful, or how many empires you built or stole, you couldn't conquer death. Alexander, Caesar, Hussein, Rockefeller or Gates—all had to die and give the next despot his shot at the pie.

Until now. This changed everything, literally everything. Forever.

A medical solution to death would be the single most valuable product in history. Whoever controlled it would have power unlike any that had come before. Benevolently used, it could be an incredible gift. Imagine Salk, Einstein or Da Vinci continuing their work for centuries instead of decades. But Stalin killed over ten million people in twenty-four years. Imagine if he had a thousand years to work with.

What would Surazal do with a millennia?

"They don't want to cure the Shift," said Maggie. "They want to control it. For themselves. And they've got *carte blanche*," said Maggie.

"Nobody knows what they're doing."

She was right. The city was their Petri dish. They had a global monopoly on reborn DNA. The rest of the world had literally walled themselves off from it in terror. There'd be no competitors. No international scientists racing for the same prize. Worse, there'd been no oversight as well, no congressional committees or U.N. boards of review.

Then something turned in my mind and another piece fell into place.

"Almost," I said. "Somebody decided that Surazal having control over the aging process ain't such a great idea."

Then Maggie got it too. "Whoever's killing the scientists! That's the motive! They're trying to stop the research!"

"That's why Surazal tried to handle it quietly. They can't risk the exposure."

"Guess it also explains Nicole's visit," said Maggie.

I thought about Bart. My friend might've been pressured into throwing the gig my way, or he might have honestly thought he was doing his old partner a favor. Either way, he'd been played as much as I had.

Maggie was reading the report. "They've got a prototype. 'Retrozine.'"

"Catchy. Does it work?"

"It's still unstable."

There was a rustle behind us. Crandall's papers had shifted in a breeze. I rescued some pages dangling precariously on the edge of the desk.

Maggie's brow darkened as she read more. "They've been testing it on people, Donner!"

"The homeless and addicts, I'll wager. People no one will bother looking for."

"God! If I'm reading this right, these test subjects…" She looked at me. "Some of them youthed so fast, Donner, they practically melted."

Another rustle, and this time the papers toppled to the floor. Irritated, I snatched them up and looked for a makeshift paperweight to keep them in place.

Then I stopped.

"What?" said Maggie.

"Don't move." I waved my palm in the air over the stack of papers.

"Who you waving to?"

"Air," I said. "There's a breeze."

"So?"

"So where's it coming from?"

"Donner, now's not the time to investigate the building's ventilation system."

I walked back to the boards. I stood in front of the exposed segment of the wall that the dry-erase boards had covered before I'd rotated them away. I waved my hand again.

"The breeze is coming from here."

Maggie rolled her eyes. "I'm not even going to—"

I stuck my hand through the wall. Maggie yelped. I pulled my hand back. "Tingles."

She came over to me. "Holy shit." She touched it and her finger and the wall rippled slightly. "It's a hologram."

"Can you short it out?"

She gave me a dubious look, but reached out again. Energy pulsed down her arm. A two-meter section of the wall disappeared. In its place was a standard air duct.

"There's your air source," said Maggie, amused.

I examined the grill. It looked ordinary enough. "A hologram of a wall over an air duct?" I said. "What the hell for?"

I grabbed the edges of the grill. It groaned in protest, buckled, then popped free in my hand. I put it on the floor and lit the duct with my flashlight. It was large, obviously a main conduit. It receded for about ten feet, then took a ninety degree turn to the left. I handed Maggie the flashlight, waved my open palm in invitation at the vent.

"You've gotta be kidding. I am not going into there."

"Trust me. I have a hunch. After you."

She sighed and shook her head. "Age before beauty," she said.

I gave her a look.

"Fine," she said, crawling in. "Grumpy old fuck."

We wriggled forward on elbows and knees. I tried not to stare at Maggie's bottom as it swished in front of me. A couple turns later, we reached another grill. Maggie played the beam through the slits into the darkness beyond.

"Some kind of larger space." She moved the light some more, trying to find edges. "Fifteen by fifteen, I'd say."

"A store room?"

"This vent's the only access."

"What's a room doing back here?"

"My guess is, under this chic morphinium shell is an older building. Probably extensively remodeled. Sometimes, when the architects
lay out new floor plans, little useless trapped spaces like this happen."

"Useless," I murmured.

She gave the grill a shove and it clattered away into the darkness.
We climbed in.

A foldable cot sat against a stack of supply bins, surrounded by
empty wrappers and energy bars. A smartscreen was propped up
amidst a mess of clothing. A hot plate, a couple lanterns.

"A rat's nest," said Maggie.

"For a human rat," I responded.

A whimper came from behind some boxes. I pushed them aside.
A bespectacled man in suspenders and tweed pants cowered on thin
haunches. Greasy strands of hair were plastered across his bald pate.
The man blinked in the flashlight's glare.

"Dr. Crandall, I presume?" said Maggie.

I wrinkled my nose. "Be glad you can't smell, Maggie. This guy
hasn't had a bath in weeks."

Back in the lab, we sat him in a chair. Maggie gave him a paper cup
from a cooler. He drank greedily. Then he scanned his office like a
worker reorienting himself after a long vacation. I put the smartscreen on the desk.

"No one's touched a thing," Crandall said.

Crandall blinked, heavy-lidded. The scientist was all angles. Sharp
cheekbones and elbows and size thirteen feet. Somehow, the lanky
frame held together. He had the air of a person so obsessed with his
work that all other concerns, even food, were phantoms in the wind.

"I don't suppose either of you has a cigarette," he said.

"They're illegal," I said.

Crandall chuckled without moving his face. "A condemned man

always gets a last cigarette."

"My name's Donner. I was hired to find you, not kill you."

"Donner. A detective, you say?" Crandall appeared to mull that over, disturbed.

Maggie whispered in my ear. "How do we explain this?"

"Explain what?"

"Finding Crandall *here*! I doubt this Struldbrug dame will let us off the hook for breaking and entering just because we found the guy."

"You think I'm going to turn this guy over to Nicole after what we found out about the Retrozine?"

"Then what *are* we going to do with him?"

"Right now I want answers. We'll figure the rest out later."

"Well, hurry it up, ace. If security makes half-hourly rounds, our goose is cooked."

But it was Crandall who started the questioning. "You say hired," he said. "Who hired you? Gavin?"

"Nicole Struldbrug."

Amusement narrowed his eyes. It was nothing pleasant. More like the satisfaction a kid gets from frying ants with a magnifying glass. "With the largest private security force in the country, she hires a private eye."

"No one was getting anywhere."

"Probably because it never entered anyone's mind you'd disappear on purpose," Maggie said. I shook my head. Then she smacked her forehead. "The security disk! It wasn't changed to hide the real time you left the building. It was to hide the fact that—"

"You didn't leave *at all*," I finished.

"Which means—"

"*I* doctored the disk," said the scientist, looking pleased with himself.

Crandall was a victim of the same affliction as Dr. Gavin—the arrogance of the brilliant, based on the premise that every obstacle in life could be out-maneuvered by a superior mind.

I hoped he never had to out-think a plasma rifle.

"I supervised the architect when he remodeled the lab," said Crandall. "I knew about the hidden space. I came out at night, read my assistants' notes, followed their progress. Do you know I could hear their conversations through the vent?" He sniffed. "I had no idea they despised me."

"Why hide?" I asked.

"When Dr. Smythe was murdered, I wasn't left much choice. Someone was assassinating members of our team."

"How did you know that?"

Crandall was silent.

"Why not go to the company for protection? Or the police?"

More silence. My bad feeling had turned into a nasty burning in the pit of my stomach. An act as extreme as hiding from everyone, for a whole month—the man had to have an extreme reason. "Who's trying to kill you, Doctor?"

His lips pruned up. "You've found me, fine. Return me to my employer and collect your little fee."

"Hakuri's dead."

He shook his head. "I heard. From talk in the lab."

No option but to go for the heavy artillery. "Retrozine," I said, smiling. "Great name."

The change in his face was astonishing. The prune dropped open to reveal scummy teeth.

"The youthing drug you've been testing."

"On people," said Maggie.

"Oh my God. Listen to me—"

Before Crandall could finish, someone spoke from behind us.

"Morris, honey, *there* you are!"

She stood silhouetted in the door in a worsted wool suit. The cream blouse was open to display a clasp of diamonds at her throat. Her brassy mane had been tucked up in a bun. Pale yellow kid leather gloves matched the handkerchief tucked in her breast pocket.

The three monstrosities in composite armor behind her held Thompson submachine guns—the kind with the round, oversized Type-C magazine made famous by gangster movies. The kind that took two hands to fire, went rat-a-tat-tat and spit shell casings everywhere. The kind that chewed you into hamburger.

Nicole waggled a finger at Crandall. "You had me very worried, Doctor." She turned to me. "Hey, Donner."

"Ms. Struldbrug."

"Nicole, please. We're all friends here."

"That's what I'm hoping."

"Brought along your talking mannequin, I see."

Maggie flinched.

"Nicole," I said. "Why are you here?"

"Now, baby, that was *my* line." She sashayed toward us. I moved forward to meet her. The outer lab was a less confined space. If things went south I'd want as much room as possible. Crandall and Maggie stayed close behind.

"If you'd wanted to see the lab," said Nicole, "all you had to do was ask."

"I did. Dr. Gavin doesn't like me very much."

She flicked cold eyes at Crandall, then past him to the open vent. "Been hiding in the walls, have we, doctor? I suppose you consider that clever." She ran a finger across the man's grizzled jaw. He flinched at her touch, as I had done. "Welcome back."

"Are you going to kill me?" Crandall whispered.

She didn't even bother to feign hurt or shock. "I've been trying to save you."

"Like you saved Smythe? And Hakuri?"

Nicole tapped her shoe impatiently. "Why would I kill my own scientists? Especially when they're on the verge of a *breakthrough*?" To me: "You believe me at least, don't you?"

"I'll believe you a whole lot more if you tell your boys to lower those guns."

"Do you like them? The outside is vintage 1928AC, the inside is pure plasma."

"Impressive. Planning to use them?"

"We'll see how the evening develops."

As if on cue, the security men moved forward in lockstep. The snouts of their Tommy guns raised to chest level.

She'd heard us talking. Enough, at least, to know we'd discovered Retrozine.

"Don't do anything rash, Nicole."

"Sorry, baby, can't hit the brakes now. Pedal to the metal, that's my motto." She withdrew a cigarillo from an enameled case and lit it with a matching lighter. The smoke hung next to her like a thought balloon. She was debating her options.

So was I. I didn't like any of them.

Then she noticed Crandall staring vacantly into the air, his tangled eyebrows working up and down like he was factoring *pi* to the twentieth decimal. "What's the matter? You get buggy in the wall, Doctor? Am I going to have to re-socialize you?"

"Paul Donner," he said. "Memory's not what it used to be. Why is that name—"

Panic swept across Nicole's cheeks so abruptly it made her maroon lips go white. The scientist's face had also gone ashen. His smugness shattered off him.

"Elise Donner's husband. You hired Elise Donner's husband to find me! He came back, and you hired him." He cackled wildly. "Oh God, you crazy bitch."

And like that, the world tilted. There was thundering in my ears. The lab twisted sideways. I knew a train was coming, and in a moment it would roar over me, reducing me to pulp. I felt the vibration of its approach.

"Whoa," came Maggie's voice, from Pluto. "Plot twist."

My palms found the desk edge, clutching. It was suddenly too hot, too dry.

Nicole had recovered admirably. She flicked lint from her lapel. "You have a big mouth, Morris. I don't know why I tell you anything."

"I had nothing to do with it!" he said to me. "It was before my time!"

"I do wish you'd shut up," said Nicole.

My voice was a despair-shredded thing. "What does Elise have to do with all this?" My feet were moving toward her. My eyes were so locked on Nicole that I didn't see the goon sling his weapon and raise the blackjack.

Then the train rushed forward again and I was gone.

I'm carrying a bouquet of blue roses and whistling. The sight of me is enough to make anyone who sees me grin. The guard grins as I sign for my temporary pass. The elevator passengers grin as I downshift politely from whistling to humming. And the receptionist on the 23rd floor grins as I ask for my wife.

I think she can spare a few minutes, she says, giggling.

I check my hair in the glass partition between reception and the offices. The glass reads:

U.S. Department of Health and Human Services
Office of Research Integrity

I navigate down the hall past the workers that are buzzing in and out of cubicles, stealing momentum from their smiles.

I reach the last door in the hall and push it open.

Elise's back is to the door. She's immersed in some document on her monitor. I feel a thrill as soon as I see the copper hair on her shoulders.

Uh, excuse me, I say nasally, I, um, invented a new kind of tomato that's twenty feet high and, um, makes everybody who eats it vote Republican. Is this where I show it to the government and get rich?

That's the FDA, she says, still staring at the screen.

What about Democrat?

She swivels, a wry smile on her face. The next thing I know she's flown around the desk at me. The impact knocks me back a step.

Uff! Hey, watch the flowers!

She snatches them up. What're these for?

I open my mouth, but she holds up a finger. Let me guess. Another of your made-up anniversaries. Let's see… first date?

My eyes roll. Nothing as pedestrian as that.

First carriage ride in Central Park? No. First time we ate Thai food? No.

Okay, I give up. I whisper in her ear. She slaps my arm. I don't think there's a Hallmark card for that. She takes the flowers to an empty vase. Blue, she says. They're beautiful.

I register the stacks of paperwork with dismay. Any chance of you blowing this pop stand early?

Oh, honey, I'm sorry. I've got a biotech company that's not playing by the rules.

Gonna slap 'em on the wrist?

More like shut the bastards down, if they're doing what I think they're doing. But first I have to prove it.

Sounds big.

Big enough to lead the national news.

I whistle. My little private eye.

No, sweetie, that's your fantasy. I just want to make sure the next bio-engineered tomato we eat doesn't kill us because somebody skipped important parts of the research process.

You'd think they'd learn.

She sighs. Time is money. Why waste years on animal studies when you can fake the data and go right to human testing?

And we already have such great tomatoes.

She smiles, but with weariness. I wish this was just about tomatoes. Human gene therapy is a hell of a lot more dangerous. She looks at her watch. One of their people's coming by. I'm giving them a chance to explain themselves before I drop the hammer.

Always the fair one.

She pecks me on the cheek and turns me around, pushing me toward the door. Thanks for the beautiful flowers. Now scat!

Just promise to get home as soon as humanly possible.

My right butt cheek receives a playful squeeze. Cross my heart and hope to die.

I saunter back toward reception quite pleased with myself, the very model of the thoughtful modern male.

I register the other woman as she passes, in that reflexive cop way, the auburn hair, the furious, purposeful strides as she approaches Elise's door, the dark skin…

And the strange veil obscuring her features.

For a while, there was only nausea and colors and grunting like an animal. A smell. Something rotten. I summoned my will and lifted my head. Bright needles jabbed my brain, and my gorge lurched threateningly, but I hung on until my eyes could focus. I touched the back of my head and my hand came away sticky.

I was no longer in the lab.

"Maggie," I whispered.

"Your girlfriend flew the digital coop." She held up Maggie's globe. "Poof!"

I squinted and the light resolved itself into a couple human-shaped blobs. There was a drain in the center of the floor. A wall with a long observation mirror.

Nicole toyed with a diamond at her throat. "You got sapped," she said. "You looked like you were rushing me and one of my overeager bodyguards stepped in."

I licked my lips. Like licking asphalt.

"Doctor, get him some water, would you?"

Crandall, who'd been in the shadows, grunted and went out the door.

C'mon, Donner. Put on the tough. So you got your brains rearranged a little. Suck it up.

"Stinks." I tried to straighten myself in the chair and my head went off like a claymore.

"Take it easy."

Crandall returned with the water. I took an experimental sip. My stomach didn't object to the point of open rebellion, so I took a little more.

"Better?" said Nicole.

Then the dream, the memory, came back, just like that. *Visiting Elise, hearing about the genetics firm conducting illegal research, then passing that woman in the hall with the veil...*

"What?" she said.

"Forty years ago, in the hall. Elise's office. You... you..."

Nicole's face lit with delight. She turned to Crandall. "Doctor, give us a moment."

Without a word, he left the room.

"Finally! I thought you'd never remember. What do you think, baby? Was it destiny?"

"Tell me," I said.

"We were just beginning our bio research. Your wife had the unfortunate job of enforcing the government's laws concerning scientific experiments." She snorted in disdain. "Those first years of the new millennium, everyone was terrified. No cloning, no stem cells! My god, the mountains of red tape and restrictions!"

"You faked data to get permission to do human studies."

"Time is money."

Elise had said that. A whole new kind of pain surfaced. "She sniffed you out," I said.

"That day, after you and I passed each other in the corridor, I tried to explain to her the value of our work. She wouldn't listen. There'd be an investigation. She'd hold us up in court for years. I couldn't allow that. She gave me three days to come clean on my own before she filed the injunction. It was a window of opportunity."

And then it hit me, the whole package, a sledgehammer between the eyes.

"Elise was the target," I said. "This was never about me at all. In the bodega—you were after Elise."

"But you were there, too. Just as well. You'd never have rested until you found me. I hired a nasty man named Ewan McDermott to arrange it." The man with the scar. "Quite a psychopath. I believe he met his maker a few years later in Bolivia."

"This can't be true. You're as young now as you were then. Forty years ago, the drug didn't exist. And the Shift hadn't happened yet." Nicole didn't reply. "Answer me!" I screamed.

Crandall and the Tommy gun goons burst back in. Nicole waved them off in irritation.

"I will someday, if you cooperate. I still need your help, Donner."

"Someone's killing your people."

"So it seems." She went to a chair and sat, making a lot of business of arranging herself into it. "Help me stop these murders and I will set you up in luxury for life—a life that will be considerably longer than you could imagine."

Another piece fell into place. "Jesus, you *know* who's killing your people, don't you? You've always known."

A nerve in her cheek gave me my answer.

I leaned over and spit. There was blood in the phlegm. It hit the tiled floor and I saw for the first time the remains of something awful there, like fungal gelatin. I looked back at her. Nicole's face changed subtly, hardening, and like that, she was no longer beautiful. Hers was the symmetry of a dime store mannequin. Beneath it, she was all monster.

"It always comes back to time, doesn't it?"

"And now with Retrozine, it'll be your servant. Then the world's your oyster, huh?"

"Uh-huh," said Nicole, coming forward, all grace again and promises of sinewy delight. "So what do you say?"

"I've got nothing to lose," I replied.

Nothing to lose at all.

Crandall saw it and opened his mouth in warning, but I was already in motion, reaching for the guard's weapon with one hand while my elbow made contact with his combat visor. I snatched it out of his astonished hands and swung it toward Nicole, finger settling on the trigger.

She was fast. She managed to crab sideways, just enough. The shot sizzled past her.

It hit Crandall, churning right through his chest. The plasma hit the mirror behind, which exploded like a bad memory. Crandall dropped, a mass of cauterized flesh. I tried to roll out of the chair, but my legs didn't cooperate. I thumped heavily onto my side. I twisted to the left, looking for the other guard. The man had already lowered the Tommy gun, his shot lined up. I dropped my weapon. Time, always about time. Another fifteen minutes and my body might've worked right.

Two more guards rushed in. They kicked me for a while. Then dragged me over to Nicole, dumped me at her feet. The world was a bloody red haze. I tried to raise onto my arms, but there seemed to be serious problems with my bones.

Nicole looked at Crandall's smoking corpse. "Goddamn it," she said. "Always the hard way." She grabbed my hair and descended on me in a violent kiss.

"What a shame," she sighed. "So yummy." She picked up the fallen weapon, checked the clip.

"Nicole," I said.

She pointed the weapon at me.

"Who's killing your scientists?"

She fired.

I had just enough time to think about how beautiful the plasma looked. Then the flesh of my body burned, and the synapses in my brain screamed in searing agony.

And for the second time in my life, I died.

(INTERLUDE ONE)

DONNER

Donner's body lay naked in a part of the Bronx that had been a no-man's land even before the Shift. Here, block after desolate block was filled with the shells of burnt-out buildings and the carcasses of autos. No one lived here, the police didn't patrol here. So his body, wedged between a crumbling wall and a fence, went unnoticed.

By people, that is. Almost immediately, houseflies, blue bottle and blowflies swarmed it. The insects pasted eggs in the still-moist corners of his eyes and mouth. Rove and hister beetles gorged themselves on his wounds. Ants and wasps added themselves to the opportunistic menagerie, making his form seem to crawl and writhe.

The build-up of lactic acid stiffened the muscles in rigor mortis. Donner's pancreas, packed with digestive enzymes, began digesting itself. Neighborhood cats made swift work of his eyes and tongue.

During the second and third days, Donner's skin became green and blistered from the internal chemical reactions. The unfettered bacteria in his gut produced huge quantities of methane, hydrogen sulfide, and other gasses. He bloated. Frothy fluids ran from his mouth and anus. His putrefaction was characterized by a horrible, skunk-like smell.

By day four, the developing fly larvae broke through the abdominal cavity, releasing the gasses. The body deflated back to something approximating its original girth. The stench and the clouds of flies went unnoticed. No one around.

By day five, the maggots had formed into packs and were swarming through the chest and abdomen like troops in a conquered city. Over the course of the next few days, the body appeared to liquefy as fluids and semisolid tissues flowed into the dirt. By day seven, his remains were already in an advanced stage of decay. Most soft tissue had disappeared. The smell had faded into a lingering ammonia odor. New species like the cheese and corpse fly were now attracted as the drier corpse provided a different kind of meal.

The maggots, having harvested all they could, began leaving *en masse*. Their departure was so abrupt, so violent, that it dragged the body two feet through the grass. The beetles, lying in wait, fed on them.

A week and a half after Donner's death, his odor had shifted to something a lot like wet fur and old leather.

Having left nothing for scavengers of any kind, the corpse settled in for the final stage of decomposition, a slow molder that would take four or five weeks. If uninterrupted, in a month there would be nothing left but hair, bits of skin, bleached bones, and teeth.

PART TWO:

THE UNDERNEATH

I said to Life, I would hear Death speak.
And Life raised her voice a little higher and said,
You hear him now.
—Kahlil Gibran, *Sand and Foam*

(INTERLUDE TWO)

BRIAN

Brian Trask was fifteen and wondering if he was going crazy.

Could kids go nuts? Somehow he'd thought true insanity was reserved for adults. Sure, there was Samantha Bowen's famous meltdown in Locker Room B, when she'd smashed Liz Franklin's head against the coach's office window until there were bright smears of blood on it. According to Coach, Samantha would get better, even though she'd be home-schooled. Did that mean crazy? The girls said Samantha sure *looked* bonkers when she attacked Liz, her eyes bugged out, her hands turned into claws.

The incident's lunch-time postmortem only confused Brian more. Over mystery meat and apple crisp, Shaun Gretske declared he'd talked to Samantha and that she was only "hormonal." Then Bill Loogman (called "Loogey," but never to his face, since at fourteen he could bench press 220 pounds) wrinkled his mug in a scholarly way and opined that proved she *was* crazy.

"What do you mean?" Brian asked.

"Insane people never think they are."

"Are what?"

"Crazy!"

"Says who?"

"My Dad. He says if you're worried you're going crazy, that means you're okay."

"Is your Dad worried he's going crazy?"

Loogey darkened. "Hell, no!"

Shaun grinned. "So that means he's crazy!"

Loogey introduced apple crisp into Shaun by way of his nostrils, ending the conversation.

So now, sitting in his bedroom on a cool fall evening, Brian was no closer to figuring things out than before. He thought about checking out psych sites on the Conch. But the Conch was sentient. While it wasn't *supposed* to monitor what you surfed, the idea of anything getting back to Brian's parents made his fingers freeze over his smartscreen. Damn it! It made him wish for "the good old days," when the Conch was just millions of individual websites that nobody monitored. Brian could hardly imagine that lovely anarchy. But that wasn't now. No, the very *last* thing he could allow was for these sudden doubts about his sanity to get back to his folks.

Because his parents were at the root of his dilemma.

Brian shut off the desk light, plunging the room into darkness. Sitting like that was comforting. He could lie on his bed and look out the window at the shimmer of electric rain through the Blister and pretend that he was just a floating mind, free of all worry. Or a hunter on the Blasted Heath, tracking runaways with the green crosshairs of his plasma rifle. It didn't *always* help. Sometimes it did nothing to diffuse the dread. And more recently, the surges of rage that overtook him.

Brian's family lived in a condo on East 68th Street near the park. Brian loved this apartment, the building…in fact pretty much everything about his Manhattan life. His father was Robert Trask III, a partner at Smith, Croup, Trask and Ketterman, a prestigious boutique firm that catered to what was left of the city's old money. Once he told Brian that some of his clients could trace their ancestry back to the Old World. When he was younger Brian had thought his dad meant Brooklyn, where everything looked like it was falling apart.

But things hadn't fallen apart here. No sir, even after the Shift had turned the city on its ear, this building—this street, this part of town—had run like a well-oiled, well-*moneyed*, machine. Until recently.

Until recently, Brian had been whisked daily from his beautiful building by Carl the chauffeur to his prep school six blocks south.

And picked up again after lacrosse and chess club practice. Carl, who had a thick German accent, always had a caramel for him. Once in traffic, a deranged reborn attacked the outside of the Rolls. Carl had gotten out and dealt with him. It was then that Brian realized Carl had been hired for impressive skills far beyond operating a limo.

Unlike most privileged teens his age, Brian knew how well-insulated he was. Last summer, his mother decided he should volunteer at the 81st Street Shelter, dishing out soup and such. A "character-building exercise." Brian's eyes popped from his head, a million summer dreams destroyed in a flash.

"With the whack-jobs and druggies?" he blurted.

His mother's face set in that thin way that only happened when he really stepped over the line. "Brian," she said, "You know how I grew up."

"Yeah," Brian said. He'd heard it a million times.

"There's nothing wrong with being poor. Most of the world is poor. But it's important you appreciate how special our situation is while it lasts."

So he ladled soup to smelly, scary men and helped them to their cots and filled out their paperwork and reminded himself to thank God every night for his blessings.

What a geek he'd been. Looking back, he could see that things had never been as exalted as they seemed. That their lives, like a great copper ball, had already begun to tarnish. Perhaps the fall of the Trasks was inevitable, but hindsight didn't matter, because you couldn't go back, and somewhere deep in his mind, a lurking patch of darkness was growing.

For you see, his father was a reborn.

It was this simple fact which marred his life, which pulled it from the story books and into the ugly world of Necropolis. It was this fact that finally and brutally became the most fundamental aspect of his existence.

His parents' socialite friends pretended the world hadn't changed, but Brian, born after the Dark Eighteen, knew the score. They could refuse to call New York Necropolis, talk wistfully of their Connecticut homes (which they couldn't visit), or profess a resolute belief that very soon things would be back to normal. Brian knew that was bullshit. He knew without a shadow of a doubt that life was growing bleaker.

When Brian was six months old, his father Robert died from a hidden heart defect. His mother spoke of nights of grief, wrestling with the sudden reality of raising her infant son alone.

Miraculously, Robert revived six months later. Surgeons repaired his aorta, and he returned to his family with joy.

At the time of his death, Robert had been thirty years old, and Marie, his wife, had been twenty-nine.

Robert and Marie had walked in human rights marches long before Robert's conversion, so when their beliefs about tolerance were put to the test they were not found lacking. Many spouses refused to accept their reborn partners back. They were not legally obligated to do so, since "'til death do us part" negated their marital contract in the eyes of both the church and the court. But Marie welcomed her husband's return without a hint of doubt. It was a reason for rejoicing and that was that.

Some of his parents' friends drifted politely away. Dad said they couldn't handle being beaten at squash by someone whose funeral they'd attended. Brian laughed. He *could* laugh, because many had stayed faithful. There were enough "mixed" marriages these days to make the Trasks unusual but not pariahs.

Robert's employers were also understanding. They put his name right back on the letterhead. Oh, he was reassigned from certain clients who were uncomfortable about being represented by "one of them," but there were plenty of debutantes with legal troubles who didn't care what color your eyes were as long as you could save their aerobicized asses.

To Brian, Dad was simply Dad. And since his parents seemed so well-adjusted about it, so was he. They even celebrated Robert's revival day, like a second birthday!

When Brian was five, Robert was twenty-six and Marie was thirty-four. When Brian was ten, Marie was thirty-nine and Robert was twenty-one. But now, it was another five years later. Marie was forty-four. Brian was fifteen. And Robert, his father, was sixteen.

Sixteen. Next year, *Brian would be older than his father*. How could even the most loving heart ignore the chasm widening by every passing minute?

When he was twelve, Marie took Brian on an outing, just the two of them. They went to the Museum of Natural History, then to his favorite rib joint, the Blue Phoenix. He was allowed to order a double portion of those slabs of barbecued delight. And then, during dessert, his mother explained how things were going to get harder in the not-too distant future.

"You're old enough to understand now, kiddo. It's important you start thinking about it." Brian saw the fear behind her smile. It gave him a chill that had nothing to do with the orange sherbet in his mouth. "We're going to be challenged in tough ways, unique ways, by Daddy's youthing."

"What do you mean?"

"Think of it this way. You wouldn't give up on your dad because he was sick, would you? You'd still love him, wouldn't you, even if he wasn't able to act like Dad anymore?"

"Of course I would!"

"Eventually he'll be younger than you. Have you thought about that? He'll be less like your Daddy than your little brother."

"I'll take care of him, Mom, I promise."

Tears shone in his mother's eyes. "That's my son." Then she clutched him so tight that he finally had to tell her she was kind of hurting him.

She'd tried to warn him. It was going to hurt, she'd said. That was like telling someone about to go over Niagara Falls that they were going to get wet.

The pain began in a million different ways. Some were expected, some subtle, but most were bright and shocking in their attacks on his peace of mind.

Sundays after dinner, his parents used to dance in the living room to Tony Bennett. They'd twirl and sway, wistful smiles on their pusses. Brian rolled his eyes at these displays, but deep down, he adored them. He loved that they held hands at the movies, he loved the way she'd put her feet in his lap while they read on the couch, or the kisses they stole from each other in the hall when they thought he wasn't around. It made him feel safe and warm.

They didn't do those things anymore. They still said "I love you," but it was mechanical now, as though the magic that energized their bond had been replaced by rote ritual. Mom now seemed skittish about touching his father.

Bright pain.

Recently he came across his father crying in the bathroom. Robert was at the sink, a razor in his hand. The tears slewed through down the shaving cream, creating runnels of clean cheek. Brian froze, his need to pee forgotten. Dad looked at him with red-rimmed eyes.

"Guess my mornings just got quicker," he said, toweling the foam from his face and swiping the razor into the trash.

Only a week before, Dad had notice peach fuzz on Brian's upper lip, and with much fanfare taught him the manly art of shaving. Something he himself would never do again.

Bright, bright pain.

Brian was astonished to discover how much he depended on the way people in his life *looked*. He knew you shouldn't judge a book by its cover. But the strong cheekbones and rugged jaw he'd traced his fingers across so many times had been replaced by baby chub. His dad's muscles had thinned. He was now officially scrawny, a beanpole. It wouldn't be too long, they warned him, before his voice would change.

Brian violently reacted to that. That baritone voice was the author of a million secure "goodnights" as he drifted to sleep, a million reassurances when he skinned his knees or ran afoul of a bully, a million stern but loving rebukes when he made a selfish choice. He didn't *want* that voice to change. Oh, *God*, he didn't want anything else to change!

Blinding, tearing pain.

His father was finally laid off by the firm and went on reborn assistance. It wasn't his fault, they said guiltily. We just can't have a teenager as a partner. You understand. Robert understood. He and Marie had saved as much as they could for this day, and she was now working at the Saks perfume counter, but their lifestyle was rapidly devolving. There were arguments about money, about Brian, about everything. "I'm still the same inside!" he heard his Dad exclaim in a strangled voice. And a portentous silence afterwards.

Brian stayed mostly in his room, and his parents seemed content to let him. They were always exhausted now. They'd started to function in quiet, individual units, going about their business and avoiding each other as much as possible.

Two months ago he came home to his mother pulling clothes from shopping bags. Excitement rattled through him. He ran to the table in near-delirium, grabbing a yellow button-down shirt, still in its cellophane, and a gorgeous pair of burgundy chinos.

"Wow!" he said, already thinking about how he could match these new treasures to the outfits he already had.

His mother looked at him with sunken eyes. "These are for your father," she whispered. "His clothes don't fit anymore."

Too much pain. Too much.

Brian ran to his parent's room and went a little crazy then. He couldn't remember exactly what he'd been doing, but whatever it was, his mother caught him in her arms and tried to restrain him. Brian pulled away and slapped her, an act so startling that she fell back onto the bed and burst into tears.

Now, a week later, somewhere dimly he knew he should feel remorse, but he didn't. All that was there in his chest was a leaden sort of… loathing. For both of them.

He hated them. Perversely enough, the hate felt good. It was *his*. The rational part of his mind balked. It wasn't Dad's fault. He hadn't done this on purpose. He and Mom had done everything possible to turn this tragedy into something they could survive. But they wouldn't survive it nevertheless, and Brian found himself dreading the horrors each new day would bring. He couldn't look at his father anymore without bile filling his mouth, couldn't gaze at that kid's face and white hair without wanting to beat his head against the floor until it broke, just like Liz Franklin.

The furies shook him daily now, a physical thing, and he held himself in his room until they abated. They swarmed him like flies, blotting out his air, getting into his mouth, buzzing his ears. Was this insanity? He didn't know. But the pain was constant and shattering in its intensity.

Everything else disappeared in its glare, like sun reflecting off a snow bank.

27

SATELLITE INTERCEPT

TRANS00\INTERCEPT\GEOSAT231\121554\PRIORITY05-32\CLASS5EYESONLY

WEBSQUIRT INTERCEPT AS FOLLOWS:

(NAMES AND OTHER IDENTIFYING INFORMATION HAVE BEEN DELETED PER NSA REG 1037459324)

> 1: Nicole.
> 2: (pause) You. How'd you get access to this line?
> 1: I still have a few tricks up my sleeve.
> 2: Did you get the mask I sent you? The dealer assured me it was authentic first century.
> 1: Nicole.
> 2: Look, I'm in the middle of something.
> 1: Was that a scream?
> 2: Of course not.
> 1: What are you up to, Nicole?
> 2: You have full access to my database. An assistant translates our reports into Aramaic. But if you don't think I'm being accommodating enough, you're welcome to come in person and see for yourself.
> 1: You mock me?

2: (pause) No.

1: Your brother is concerned about you. He says you're avoiding him. Secretive.

2: All our goals are the same.

1: (a chuckle) Please. Your goals have always been your own. But I assume survival is still one of them.

2: Oh, is that a threat, Daddy? Hello?

END END END TRANS00\INTERCEPT\GEOSAT231\DATE END END END

28

NICOLE

Nicole liked to work out her strategies with chess.

She closed her book and rose from the divan. She crossed to the table where the board sat. Its squares were sheesham and ebonized boxwood.

Right now, there was a game in progress. A very important game.

Her set was antique—well, it was more than an antique—it was ancient. An original 12th century collection of Lewis chessmen, given to her by her father. He'd discovered them in Scotland. She smiled inwardly. If the British Museum knew another complete set existed, they'd have a stroke.

She loved the medieval human figures, such a far cry from the abstracted Stanton pieces most of the world now used. No, these were *real* chessmen—the queen, cradling her face in dismay. The mounted knights with their swords and Templar shields. The bishops clutching their miters and bibles. The rugged castle tower. She wondered whether her father liked them because of their bulging eyes and sad faces—so much like his own.

She enjoyed studying the game's history as well. Its lineage began in 6th century India, before expanding into Persia, China and Japan. When the Moorish conquest of Spain brought a Babylonian version to Europe, medieval Church fathers were scandalized. They quickly converted the pagan icons into proper Catholic figures. Except the serfs, of course. Who gave a shit about cannon fodder?

Most of all, though, she loved the Queen. Before the board's "conversion," there'd been no female figures. How strange that a church so violently patriarchal would replace the King's vizier, originally the weakest member on the board, with a woman—let alone transform her into a superpower. Maybe it was due to the rising importance of the Virgin Mary in church doctrine. But Nicole suspected that, on a deeper level, humanity was finally beginning to sense where the real strength lay between the sexes.

The King was a figurehead, trapped by the burdens of office. He could only move slowly, carefully, one square at a time. The Queen had no such impediments. She could act without regard to opinion, rules of conduct or even the rule of law. She was the real mover and shaker, putting the right words into the King's mouth, kissing his cheek, and acting deferential.

That's how Nicole preferred to operate, in the shadow of the crown. Let her brother play alpha male. Let her deluded father try to control her from afar. Her plans had already been set into motion, in the dark. Her dear, dear family would realize this far too late.

She sat down at the board, examining the positions. She sighed. She'd been forced to sacrifice a pawn without any improvement in her position. Poor Donner.

She felt a quiet rustle inside. She could see why Elise had married him. His unpretentious manner and off-kilter good looks made him infinitely more tantalizing than her regular boy toys. And she'd appreciated how he'd kept her on her toes. He hadn't been lulled by either her beauty or her bullshit. She'd relished the challenge of sparring with someone on her own level. She'd have liked him in her bed.

There'd been something else. She couldn't quite put her finger on it. Maybe it was the weird combination of jaded street smarts and boy scout morality. She didn't know. But it had been the first time in a long while she'd been unhappy about dispatching someone. But, after all, queens didn't mate with pawns. And had Donner figured out what she was really up to—Jesus, it would have been a disaster.

She toyed with the queen figure and wondered how she'd feel once she'd achieved her goals. In the past, her victories had brought brief elation followed by an annoying ennui that required some new challenge to suppress. Like Hannibal, like Alexander, she was only interested in the act of conquest, not governing the conquered. "When

Alexander saw the breadth of his domain," she breathed quietly, "he wept, for there were no more worlds to conquer."

What challenges could possibly come after this?

And there was another sadness. She had rooks, bishops, knights, serfs… but no king. No one to share the glory with. She was alone, isolated by her unique nature.

She thought again of her father and all the advantages he'd bequeathed her. All but one. And for that one thing denied, she hated him to the core of her being. But she would soon seize what he withheld. And then she would greatly enjoy watching him die by her own hand.

When she was sixteen, she'd looked at her classmates and noticed how different their thoughts were from her own. She'd even wondered whether perhaps she was broken, even insane. Luckily, she'd realized that to be unburdened by empathy was an incredible advantage. It made her thinking clear, her strategies sound. It protected her from entanglements.

She looked across the board again. Besides the queen, the other players—the knights, bishops, even the kings—when you got down to it, they all were pawns.

29

DONNER / ARMITAGE

I awoke in a basement to the sound of chanting.

Wiring and conduits threaded through the beams overhead. The stone walls glistened with sweat, the mortar a mildew green. Crates were stacked in piles everywhere on the cement floor. A rust-eaten staircase ascended to whatever lay above.

The chanting came from there. Upstairs. I couldn't make out the words.

I tried singing along, making up nonsense words, and it made me laugh, and that made me cry a little. My throat was an ash can.

I shifted in my wheelchair. Pain, pulling. An IV in my arm. I traced it back to a bag of saline hanging from a pole on the back of the chair.

What was this place?

Suddenly I was breathless. I closed my eyes, trying to stay calm. Finally I evened out my rasping. My heart fluttered in its cage.

Something was wrong. I was weak. I looked down and lost my breath again. My legs were twigs, swimming in old flannel pajamas. I was a stick figure, desiccated, withered—

Somehow I'd become a scarecrow.

I ran fingers over my face. My cheekbones jutted like broken shelves of rock. Dear God, what had happened to me?

More chanting.

"Hey!" I screamed, my voice cracking. "Can't a guy get a little quiet?"

In response, footfalls thumped heavily. A metal supply cabinet in the deepest shadows of the room swung forward on unseen hinges. A hidden entrance. How dramatic. A mannish form stepped half into the light, rendered in cartoon shades of black and white. He saw me, scowled, and vanished again.

Hey, that scowl looked familiar.

Think, damn it. What's the last thing you remember?

No good. My scarecrow's head was stuffed with straw. I needed to get a new brain from the Wizard. I'd go to the Emerald City and spit into the receptacle. They'd let me in.

There! Wait!

A building. A building that couldn't decide what shape it wanted to be. And Maggie. Maggie was a pip. Even if she wasn't real. But I'd held her heart in my hands. How could I hold Maggie's heart?

The supply cabinet opened again. This time it was a nurse. Sandy, that was her name. A walking cliché in her starched uniform and rubber-soled shoes. Her phony pig-smile made me shudder. She was trying to decided whether to be afraid of me or not.

"You're the new record holder," she said finally.

"What... ?"

"Even Jesus only came back once."

She took the handles of my chair and pushed me across the cement floor toward the secret entrance behind the cabinet.

Hey, maybe I'm a spy.

We traveled through a tunnel hewn from black bedrock. I could see the stone, the raw earth, the make-shift support beams. Low-intensity arc lights snapped on before us then went dark once we'd passed, giving me only strobe-like glimpses of the tunnel.

"Part of the Underground Railroad," said Sandy. "Then, in the 1920s, a bootlegger's tunnel. Now we use it."

The chanting faded. Now I could only hear the moisture as it condensed on the ceiling. A drop hit me. It felt cool on my forehead.

We approached another portal, a rusted hatch in a cement casement. From behind it came new sounds. Smooth saxophone gyrations. Jazz? Something by Billie Holiday. Much better than the chanting.

The nurse took us through the hatch, ramming my wheels over the bottom lip and shooting all kinds of pain through me.

Rusted cables crisscrossed the space, banded into slack bundles like atrophied muscles. A control panel sat behind a mesh cage, its gauges dark, its levers frozen by corrosion. Against this background of decay, the cherry desk and oriental rug were startling.

Billie finished and it was Charlie Parker's turn. "Relaxin' At Camarillo," about being committed to an asylum for his drinking and drugging.

The man behind the desk clicked on the bronze clerk's lamp and chuckled as shock scrubbed my face clean. "Hello, buddy boy."

Armitage. The one who'd blackmailed me into... what?

Behind him, Broken Nose and Jelly Legs, in their dark suits and glowing cream ties, were doing their best impression of a wall. I wondered where the third one had gone. The Cheshire Rat. Broken Nose still looked like he wanted to poke me in the teeth, but Jelly Legs' expression was strangely warm. The men wore carnations. Fashion-plate gangsters.

Sandy rolled me to the desk. Armitage looked crisp in his turtle-neck and pressed slacks. But there was mustard on his sweater. I still couldn't figure his contradictions.

I realized my brain was working a little better.

Armitage picked up a pipe from the desk blotter and poked at the half-spent tobacco with his pinky. He seemed content to give me time to take everything in.

Then, all of a sudden—boom—a big chunk came back, in a single picture, like a slide dropped into a projector frame. Breaking into the lab. Finding Crandall. Nicole surprising us.

Dying.

The men straightened, seeing what was coming. They were too slow. I surged from the wheelchair at Armitage's face. The blow barely connected, glancing off his jaw. Its momentum spilled us both onto the rug. The muscle boys were ready to do damage, but Armitage raised a hand, chuckling grimly. I was no threat. I struggled onto my elbows, stunned by my weakness.

They dropped me back into the wheelchair. I was a sack of agony. They strap-cuffed my wrists to the arms of the chair.

I'd blown it, like an amateur. There wouldn't be a second chance.

Armitage settled back into his chair. "I see you're feeling better." He explored his tender chin. "Glad you don't have your full strength back."

"You'd be bleeding out on the carpet right now."

"Ooh," said Legs.

"That's gratitude for you," added Nose.

Armitage laughed. "He thinks I set him up. Don't you, Donner?"

I didn't know what to think. But I wasn't going to tell these pricks.

"Why?" he said. "Where's the angle?"

"Maybe a big bag of credit marbles from Nicole."

Armitage looked genuinely shocked. Which was even more confusing. Could I have this wrong?

"Sure, I used you to do my dirty work," he said. "But that's it. You got nicked because of your own sloppiness."

I just stared.

"Fine. You want the 411?" Armitage nodded to Broken Nose. "Give it to him, Max."

Max? Broken Nose's name was Max?

The big man shifted, crossing his hands in front of him, like a schoolboy about to recite. It was oddly touching. "You're sitting in what was New York Power Substation No. 53," he said. "Back down that tunnel, where you woke up, is the basement of the Church of the Holy Epicenter."

I blinked.

"He never heard of it," smirked Legs.

"The Church was built on the site where the Shift started."

I tried to wrap my brain around this. "It's an Ender church?" Armitage nodded. "You're an End-Timer?"

"No. Some of the Enders help us." I waited. "This is a Cadre cell."

"Cadre? The whack-jobs that blow up busses?"

"We've never blown up a damned thing!" said Jelly Legs.

"Tippit's right," said Armitage. "That's the Secessionists."

Max and Tippit. It sounded like the punch line to a bar joke.

"I know all these groups are hard to keep straight," said Armitage. "The Secessionists want Necropolis to be an independent state, just for reborns. They think they can bring this about through terrorism."

Max snorted. "They're nuts is what they are."

"We don't share their beliefs or their methods. Now, the End-Timers, or Enders as they're called, are a religious group created in reaction to the Shift. The government came down hard on them, and what's left of them they stay non-political." He shared a smile with the rest of the room. "At least, publically. They've been secretly sheltering some of our cells. We may not share their religious beliefs, but our goals are the same."

"Your cells? The Cadre, you mean." He nodded. I sighed. "Great. I've been taken hostage by the Dead Panthers."

Armitage went back to poking his pipe. "Still with the wise-cracks, I see."

"So you're, what? A *revolutionary*?"

"We're norm and reborn. Stockbrokers, teachers, construction workers, even mooks like me."

I tried to smirk. "So it's a club, then! Can I get a decoder ring?"

He darkened. "We're trapped in a corporate gulag. Or hadn't you noticed?"

I'd noticed.

"We're arming. To fight the government and Surazal, if it comes to that. Not civilians, get me? No terrorism."

"If you say so. How'd I get here?"

"A tracer we planted on you," said Max. "In the car, when we frisked you." He winked. Maybe he wasn't so dumb after all.

"It's mostly dermal tissue. Melds with your own."

"Why?"

"You wanted to get in there. So did we. If someone was gonna get pinched doing it..."

"Better me than you." Armitage touched his nose. "So, if I'd gotten out safely," I continued, "you would've debriefed me, then—"

"Let you go on your merry way."

I believed that about as much as I believed the last couple wars were about freedom. "Can I have some water?"

Armitage nodded at Sandy. There was a pitcher on a bureau. She poured me a cup.

"I'd do better if I could hold it myself."

Armitage smiled a no. Oh well, it'd been worth the try. Sandy put the cup to my mouth. When my throat wasn't a blast furnace anymore, I pulled back. My lips felt coated in old paint.

Enough screwing around. Time to ask the question that scared me senseless. "Why do I look like this?"

Armitage looked to Sandy in surprise. "His last memories didn't encode," she said.

That phrase... I'd heard that before. Suddenly the moisture from

the pipes was impossibly loud, each drop hitting the floor like a grenade. Parker's saxophone was flaying me alive in B flat.

"Your remains were found in the Bronx."

"My... my..."

"It took a long time to track you down," said Armitage. "Debris
masked your signal. We had to do a block-by-block search."

I didn't have the strength to hold up my head. My chin hit my
chest, my hair cascading over my face. Suddenly I didn't want to hear
any more, ever again.

"You'd decomposed pretty badly."

I gripped the chair. The music ended. Only the dripping remained.
"I didn't..."

"What's that?"

I tried to focus my lips. "I didn't know someone could come back
more than once."

"Can't. Not without help, anyway."

I looked from face to face. Max snorted. "The guy's toast. I told you."

"He just needs time."

"We don't have time."

Armitage shot a look, and Max relented, mumbling.

"We don't know how the Retrozine works yet," said Armitage.

My insides lurched another couple feet. Sandy patted my head
absently like I was a German Shepherd. There was a click, the Bird
took wing, and the next record dropped. Tommy Dorsey.

"Retrozine," I managed in a whisper. "The youthing drug."

"It does a lot of things."

"How'd you get the formula?"

"Maggie uploaded the formula."

I could feel my blood drain. "You didn't hurt her, did you?"

"She's with us," said Armitage. "Cadre. She's worked for us all
along."

"Bullshit!"

Then I caught Tippit looking shamefully at his shoes, and I knew
they were telling the truth. I closed my eyes. She'd been the only person who hadn't tried to play me. Until this moment, I hadn't realized
how hard I'd hung on to that. "Why? Why go to the trouble of finding me? Bringing me back?"

"We needed to know what happened, what you'd learned."

"If Maggie's part of this, then you already know."

"She doesn't have a trained eye, like you. Plus she had to run for it before it was over."

"Before I died, you mean."

Armitage looked at his watch. "Donner, I'd love to be a pal, give you time to adjust to all this, but things have gotten a lot worse since you've been away. So I need you to tell me everything you know."

I managed a smile at that.

"We saved your ass," said Max. "You were rat food!"

A laugh exploded out of me. "You threatened to kill my friend to get me to break into the lab, got me killed, then used me as a guinea pig to test your stolen drug. Did I leave out any of your amazing generosity?"

Armitage laid down the pipe and leaned forward, his voice low and controlled. "You got screwed? Welcome to the planet." His fist came down hard. Even the boys jumped. "We're *all* guinea pigs. Surazal's out there, running things, testing their serum and God knows what else on *us*, and we're still in the dark!"

I didn't reply. His hands fell on the chair arms, twisting. Then he sighed. "We'll talk tomorrow. You'll feel more cooperative."

"Hope springs eternal."

"You'll stay restrained."

"These pajamas itch."

"It's your new skin. Give it a few days."

I searched Armitage's eyes. I wasn't sure what I found. I'd been disposable. So why did he seem on the level now? I saw pit bull loyalty in his men, the kind that came from respect, not fear. That meant something. But I was too tired to know what. I closed my eyes and Sandy wheeled me away.

The platter spun and another record dropped. Nina Simone sounded throaty and depressed. Armitage pulled a silver lighter from the desk. He lit the pipe, exhaling a cloud that fanned off towards the shadows.

"We helped him. Fine," he said. "But you've used up your favors."

Maggie Chi resolved into coherence. "I'm doing this for—"

"I think we both know why you're doing this," he said. "And I think it's time you decided whose side you're on."

30

BRIAN

Brian walked home from school.

Carl had disappeared. No more limo, no more caramels. That was okay. The air helped him clear his jumbled thoughts.

He took his regular shortcut, past a block of peep shows. He hurried past the garish signs promising adult wonders within: "All Nude, all Norm!" Despite his raging hormones, he didn't understand porn. It seemed so mechanical. And the close-ups were gross. Who wanted to look at pubes the size of redwoods?

The people who hung out here were twitchy and seedy. The whores loved teasing him. They'd muss his hair and say: "Hey honey, how about a poke! Your wanna poke?" And then cackle.

To his relief, the sidewalk was deserted today. But as he passed the alley between one building and the next, he paused.

Something was going on. A flutter of motion buried in the gloomy brick gauntlet. The space smelled foul, a toilet for the godsmackers and a place where the whores did business. He was risking getting his nose sliced off by sticking it into that murk. But someone *could* be in trouble. He took a few steps into the alley, squinting. The dimness resolved into two forms.

Two kids. No, wait... It was a kid, talking to... a reebie hooker. The whore was saying, "I did it myself. Easy money."

"They'll give me that much just to test their new medicine?" the

186

kid said. "Is it safe?"

"C'mon, sweetie. Do you really care?"

The voice— A teenager, maybe fifteen, with a crop of white hair— No! No, that was *impossible*!

Brian ran home as fast as his legs would take him. He locked his door, put the chair against it, and dove under the covers. He refused dinner than night. His mother was content to leave him alone as she cracked the seal on a fresh bottle of brandy.

In his darkness, Brian worked through what he'd witnessed. He'd seen that hooker before. She always wore this flapper's dress with tassels that twirled as she strutted around in her Victorian ankle boots. Loretta. The other girls call her Loretta. Why in God's name was his father talking to Loretta? He knew his parents had probably stopped having sex. But to go to a street whore— But what else could it be? To buy drugs? That was crazier than his dad buying sex.

Over the next couple hours, Brian's confusion evolved into outrage. After all they'd done for him, all they'd endured on his behalf, his father was out there with street whores.

His fury was a creaking, many-branched thing.

Bastard!

His father never came home.

His mother reported his disappearance to the police. Reebs vanish every day, they said. If you hear anything concrete, call us. Otherwise, put his face on a milk carton.

Just like that, his dad was gone.

31

MAGGIE

For a couple weeks she watched Donner like a ghost would, incorporeal. She wasn't used to feeling confused. To a smarty, action was usually a simple choice between probabilities.

But when Donner had died, she'd *felt* his absence. An empty space. It had made it hard to concentrate. Her colleagues had noticed. She'd laughed and brushed it off. Tried to ignore it. But the truth was, she'd been shaken to her core. She found herself replaying certain memories. The crooked way he smiled. The dime novel jokes at the bleakest moment. Before, she'd written the behaviors off as defense mechanisms. Now she missed them.

Donner's recovery was slow. He'd been kept unconscious for the weeks necessary to repair his broken and burned body. Now he faced a slow climb back to normalcy.

He ate whatever he could. He created an exercise regime for himself in the basement—isometrics, lifting paint cans, boxes, anything not nailed down. And some kind of martial arts routine, endless moves, focusing his meager energy, throwing kicks and stabs. It was painful to watch the sweat pour from his emaciated form. At first he could hardly manage a couple push-ups, a few chin-ups on an overhead pipe. Then he'd collapse on the cement floor, cursing. But he kept at it, attacking his frailty with a determination that was frightening.

That she should find solace in remaining a phantom while he

worked so single-mindedly on becoming more concrete was an irony that didn't occur to her.

The young pastor of the Ender church above, Jonathan, was Donner's only human contact. Maggie didn't know Jonathan well, but he seemed gentle. After hours, the two men would stroll through the tiny garden in back. Donner often became passionate, waving his hands. Jonathan would nod, and sometimes laugh, and sometimes look very sad. Twice Donner broke down. Maggie envied their intimacy.

Among end-timers, Jonathan was revered. He was the pastor of the Church of the Holy Epicenter. No Ender church was as important. Situated in a two-story building on Chambers and North End Avenue, it was the former site of Maury's Deli. Maury's, with its homemade sauerkraut and towering corned beef sandwiches, had been a neighborhood favorite for decades, especially among the school crowd from nearby Stuveysant High. It had survived many things over the years—recessions, gentrification, terrorism—but it wasn't until the Shift that it finally succumbed to its demise in the form of the religiously fanatic End-Timers.

No one really knew why the public singled out Maury's as the Shift's ground zero. Certainly the government never knew. Their vague report (see "SHIFT COMMISSION: REPORT TO THE PRESIDENT) stated that it was "likely that the effect began within a ten-block radius of Rockefeller Park."

It was probably because the owner, Maurice Rosenberg, was regarded to have been the first person to revive. Whether folklore or truth, the story was as comic as it was horrible. He'd been run down in the street in front of his own deli—killed by an old woman who, courtesy of the vagaries of the Department of Motor Vehicles, still drove her Crown Victoria battle cruiser despite an acute case of senile dementia.

The neighborhood mourned Maury's death.

The next day, however, Maury was back. He was reputed to have sat up on the mortician's table and barked, "Helen, gimme two pounds of lox from the walk-in!" This was not confirmed. The mortician dropped dead at the sight and never came back.

So Maury's Deli became the place where "God's wrath was felt." That God chose an agnostic Jew as the herald of that wrath didn't matter much to believers.

Ender theology was diverse. As many as twenty-three distinct "denominations" were documented, all with varying dogmas. But some core tenets were shared by all: The Shift was a supernatural event, God's punishment, and it heralded the End-Times. Depending on the Ender group, this would culminate in: Christ's return, the advent of the Jewish Messiah, the triumph of Islam over the infidel, or universal Nirvana. Despite their Buddhist-looking robes and shaved heads, Jonathan's denomination actually had more in common theologically with Orthodox Judaism.

The Shift didn't kill the old religions outright. The resurrection motifs in many traditions helped keep a lot of panicked people in their pews. Christians, for instance, had many Biblical precedents. Oh, they had to reframe the pesky parts that no longer fit. For example, evangelicals stuttered a bit when the dead started rising *before* the Rapture. Where was the Antichrist? Armageddon? Those who'd hung their world on this detailed chronology were disturbed. Not to worry, came the purred response, followed by a thousand re-interpretations. The important thing was, get your affairs in order and send a check today! Many didn't bite. The dead weren't being raised in eternal heavenly bodies. They were walking around downtown looking for work.

For the atheists, the Shift was their trump card. The evidence was in, baby. The Shift was *real*, and it was science not God. The Universe was a series of random physical actions and reactions. But take heart, they said. Because if the Shift's Author had really been supernatural, He was more than vengeful. He was plain crazy.

Other voices rose, radical voices, issued from minds that could not accept a random Universe. Society was corrupt and existing religions were blasphemy. It was their duty to destroy them, to serve God in his wrath. It was the same old war cry dressed in new duds—others had screwed things up, not us! Anyone who harbored hatred or fear was welcome, because the time had come to kick ass and take names in a brand new holy book.

It was surreal to see riots between Catholics and Enders, Jews and Enders, see dogma pitted against dogma, zealot against zealot, out in the streets with clubs and fists and guns. If the fence-straddlers had been undecided before, their distrust of religion was quickly cemented into permanence by these acts. Most people quietly backed away from anything with a mosque dome or church spire.

The first major domestic Ender terrorist action was the simultaneous destruction of St. Paul's Cathedral and the main branch of the New York Public Library. The Pope was a pig, they screamed, and science was a graven idol. Surazal was quick to respond. The most virulent strains of the End-timers were wiped out in brutal attacks. The news channels were full of Blackhawk helicopters patrolling the streets. The churches that were spared were forced to take strict oaths of nonviolence. By the time the dust settled, the old denominations had withered into tiny, huddled enclaves, the radicals were underground, and watered-down, neutered churches like the Enders were all that was left of the new religions.

Now the Church of the Holy Epicenter looked more like an AA hall than a traditional sanctuary. No stained glass, golden statues, artwork or hymns. A simple podium, folding chairs, a leaky baptismal—that was it. There were still grooves in the linoleum where Maury's deli cases had once sat. The only eternal thing here was the faint smell of pastrami.

32

JONATHAN

"Well, I don't know about this separation and imperma-nence idea that Maggie was talking about," Jonathan said slowly. "But I believe God sees our true hearts. It's why he has so much forgiveness. Humans are so fragile, so lost, so misunderstanding."

Donner clasped his hands beneath his lowered head. The garden was empty besides them.

"She was getting ready."

"Elise?"

His voice was low. "I just couldn't see it."

"Because of the drinking," Jonathan said.

"The drinking was just a symptom. She left me because I wasn't able to grow up fast enough." He looked at Jonathan with an anguish that shocked him. "How can a man be a hardened cop, live in those streets, do the things he has to do, and still be a child inside?"

"One has very little to do with the other. But what you're saying, I think, is that had the murders not happened, you still would have lost her. Dead or alive, she'd have been gone. Hector took your lives, but not your marriage. You and Elise did that."

Donner threw his fists open. "If Maggie is right, was that old man Hector even the same person as the kid who killed us forty years ago? Was I looking to extract my vengeance, in sense, on the wrong person?"

"Hector had to live with what he'd done his entire life. In my book, that's hell. Maybe he'd already been punished enough."

"Maybe we've all been punished enough."

Jonathan moved next to Donner on the bench. "I think it's time you let go of all the what-ifs and if-onlys. Acknowledge that you're flawed like everyone else and that, for all your mistakes, you're doing the best you can. Vow not to make the same mistakes and to stay committed to 'growing up,' as you put it."

"What's the point?"

"In my opinion, there's only one thing worth doing in this life. The only thing that matters."

"Father, if you say bingo, I may have to slug you."

Jonathan laughed. "You didn't become a cop for the paycheck, Donner. And you're not one of those rageaholics who uses their badge as a license to hurt. You wanted to make a difference, to help people. You suffered through the job for a long time because of that. Okay, booze was a crappy coping mechanism. But there are people out there who still need you, Donner. They need your experience and your brains and your courage. And helping them in return may bring you the one thing you need most of all."

"What's that, Padre?"

"Hope."

33

MAGGIE

Finally, when Maggie couldn't stand it any longer, she appeared to Donner. He was at a battered wood table, shoveling oatmeal into his face.

She flashed a grin. "Hey, baby. How's tricks?" Meant to sound jaunty, it came out hollow as a campaign promise.

Donner looked up, his mouth full. "Maggie."

"You look better," she said.

He finished chewing. "Liar."

"No, really." She bobbed her head. "Be patient."

"Where you been?"

"Oh, you know. Here and there." She crossed her arms to suppress the urge to fidget. "The truth is, I thought you wouldn't be so hot to see me."

"Because you beat it from the lab?"

She looked away. Donner laid his spoon down on the table. Light bounced into her eyes from its silver handle. "I suppose I was, at first." He looked her up and down, frankly appraising her hair, her features, her figure. She felt warm. "It'd be stupid to die with me," he said. "You made the smart play." But his voice was flat.

A pause. "Donner, it... hurt me. What happened."

"Which part? Lying to me or letting me walk into a trap?"

Her composure went out of her like she'd been sucker-punched.

"That's not fair."

"Is that what you deserve? Fair?"

"You said you weren't mad."

"I'm not mad. It doesn't change what happened."

"What do you want? An apology?"

"I want answers, Mag."

"I thought Armitage—"

"About you."

"Oh." She chewed the edge of her lip. "It's complicated."

"Give me the CliffsNotes version."

She shook her hair. The dark curls flipped back. She ran her fingertips up her pale neck nervously, as if needing the reassurance of her solidity. She could feel his eyes on her legs, and she wondered why she had manifested in such a tight skirt. She dropped into the wooden chair opposite him. Crossed her legs. Re-crossed them.

"When you first revived, the Cadre assigned me to be your shadow."

"Why?"

"Possible recruitment, same as any reborn. My job as a counselor puts me in a unique position. The reborns that fit our profile became possible recruits."

"The misfits, you mean."

She frowned. "The ones who weren't sheep."

"Are there many smarties in the Cadre?"

"I'm the only one."

He found that interesting.

"Each cell is unaware of the others," she continued. "In case we're caught."

"So, basically, I was disposable."

He was going hard on her. He'd been played and needed to know where the lies ended. Where he could now put his trust.

"You want to know the truth? With the drinking, the self-pity, I was ready to write you off at first."

"What changed your mind?"

"Miss Nicole happened. Her little visit."

"Ah." Donner smiled. "Armitage must've done a back flip."

"We didn't know what she wanted. But we were looking for Crandall, too. So we—"

"Let me do my thing, oblivious that I was being manipulated from both sides."

Her sigh came out as a hiss between her teeth. "I could give you a million excuses, Donner. But keeping you in the dark was the best way to keep you productive."

"There's that smarty efficiency," he said. Donner stabbed the oatmeal with his spoon. It stuck straight up. "Needs more milk."

"Milk's hard to come by right now."

He pushed the bowl aside. "Why'd Armitage expose himself by snatching me?"

"It wouldn't have been in character for *me* to help you into the lab. That left him."

"But you showed up at the lab anyway."

"Yeah." Another sigh. "I wasn't supposed to do that."

He raised his eyebrows. "Worried that I'd get caught? Give you up?"

She winced to let him know his barbs were drawing blood. "That you'd get hurt, Paul."

In the stark basement light, she couldn't tell if he was smiling or grimacing. "So you're on the lam, now, huh? Cover's blown?"

Her eyes looked sad. "You know, I miss the job. I thought it'd be a relief—no more double life. But I did a lot of good."

"For the sheep, you mean."

"Not everyone can be special."

"Maggie the revolutionary. What happened to all that talk about letting go of things?"

"You let go of what you can't control. You change what you can."

"So why am I here, Maggie?"

She looked at the tips of her shoes. Why'd she wear heels? She hated heels. "You're a valuable asset," she said softly. Heels made her legs look better in a tight skirt, that's why.

"I'm a liability. Why did Armitage go to all the trouble of bringing me back?"

She wanted to dissolve, become someone else, anyone but this stupid, obvious female. She saw his lips twitch as he understood. He leaned back, pressing his palms onto the table.

"*You* did it," he said. "Without permission."

Heat crept into her cheeks. "Yeah, well, you were such a snappy dresser, you know, the way you pulled that hat down over one eye—"

"Maggie."

She was a rube. For all her smarty detachment, she was a tongue-tied teenager. "Don't you love how life throws you those little curves?" she said.

He didn't say anything.

"Wouldn't have worked anyway. A computer program and a dead guy…" The heat was behind her eyes now, and she was shocked to discover that she was on the verge of tears.

"Look, I—" he said.

"Just don't, okay? Just don't."

They sat like that. Somewhere, a water pipe rattled. Donner looked at her miserable face, her furrowed brow. And did the last thing she expected. He snorted a laugh.

"What?" she barked.

"Sorry."

He tried to stop, but his face wouldn't quite straighten.

"Oh great," she said.

"Sorry."

"Make fun of the infatuated smarty."

Another snort.

"You louse!"

"But you're—"

"If you say I'm cute, I'll kill you," she said.

He held it in for a moment, silent.

"Computer program and a dead guy?" he said, and this time Maggie brayed a short laugh in spite of herself.

34

DONNER

Light spilled down the steps from above. I motioned for Maggie to compose herself. Armitage thumped partially down and paused grumpily. "Alright, cut the comedy."

Behind him, Pastor Jonathan wore burgundy vestments. Pulling up the rear were Max and Tippit, stoic in gabardine and gray flannel. The gaggle trouped down and stood there, letting their eyes adjust to the dim light.

"Nice suits," I said, meaning it.

Max adjusted his tie defensively. "Thanks." It sounded like it hurt him to say it.

Armitage pulled his hat off and batted the brim. "Pouring out there," he said. "I swear, the Umbrella Lobby's paying off the damned Blister techs." He shrugged out of his slick trench coat and laid it on a crate. "Ready to continue our conversation?"

I waved at the wooden chairs stacked in the corner. Armitage snapped one open. Jonathan sank cross-legged onto a crate and the Bookend Brothers settled back on their heels. Armitage showed me his palms.

"Let's hear it," he said.

I'd done the math. It might've bruised my ego to get used, but in their shoes I might've done the same thing. As Bart used to say, the stakes call the play. And the stakes here were off the chart. "What's the phrase?" I said. "Necessity makes strange bedfellows?"

Armitage didn't look receptive, but he didn't look hostile either, so I continued. "Let's review," I said. "Crandall's team was working with Shift DNA to develop a drug."

"Two drugs," he said.

"*Two* drugs?"

"Controlled precipitors of the Shift's major effects. Retrozine-A reverses the aging process in normal humans. Retrozine-B revives the dead."

"Guess I'm proof the Retrozine-B works."

"Living proof," said Max. Tippit tried not to giggle.

"Nicole will turn the city upside down," I said. "A monopoly on those drugs is their leverage. They're no good to Surazal if everybody has them."

"Leverage for what?" asked Jonathan, still wiping the moisture from his shaved head.

"These drugs give Surazal control over life and death," said Armitage. "Exclusive control."

The room was suddenly very silent.

Jonathan shivered. "Who do we think we are?"

"The same creatures we've always been," I spat. "Brainy chimps with too much curiosity and not enough humility."

"We're not animals," Jonathan protested. "We're people."

"People," I said. "People who give each other poison-laced Kool-Aid to drink. People who blow each other up or gas each other or shoot their classmates at school. People who eat caviar while their neighbors starve to death three blocks away."

Everybody's eyes were a little too wide, so I shut my clam.

"Imagine you're a banker, a judge, a senator," said Armitage. "A *president*. How often will you cross the only person in the universe who can make you twenty again, forever?"

"How much do they want? They already run New York," said Maggie.

"With her type, there's always more," I said. "Once they've got all the pieces of the pie, they want the bakery."

"Enough sociology," said Armitage. "Someone besides us is working against her. Killing her research team."

"*You* killed Crandall," said Max to me.

"I aimed at Nicole. Lady moves fast for a skirt."

"Hey," said Maggie, bristling. A couple laughs. She realized I'd baited her and shot me a dirty look.

"So who's her enemy?"

"Nicole didn't share."

Armitage pulled his pipe from his coat. The bowl was elaborately carved. It seemed too showy for the man, somehow. He sniffed it. "This adversary of hers could be an ally."

"The enemy of my enemy is my friend?" I said. "Maybe. He's a pro, though. Each murder had a different M.O., and none had witnesses."

"What about the merc, McDermott? Could he be back?"

"Nicole said he died in Bolivia. But that doesn't mean it's true."

"Wait a minute. You said there were no witnesses?" said Maggie. "What about the bottom?"

"Huh?" said Max.

"The submissive, at the hanky-spanky club," I explained. "She was tied up facing the dungeon." To Armitage: "I'd like to talk to her. I don't believe in locked room mysteries."

For some reason, Maggie was plucking nervously at her sleeves.

Armitage clamped the pipe stem between his teeth. "Next order of business. What's this I hear about some connection between you and Nicole Struldbrug from your first life?"

I wasn't sure I was ready to think about this, let alone talk about it. It felt like my first time on the high board at the YMCA as a kid, looking down past my toes at all that empty space between me and the hard water below, the next guy already impatient on the ladder behind me, cutting off any escape. Only one way off.

Sometimes no choice is the best choice.

"There's a small subdivision in the Department of Health and Human Services called the Office of Research Integrity. Used to be, anyway. My wife worked there."

"What does it do?"

"Government oversight of scientific research."

"You mean like that stink over cloning and stem cell research in the early 21st?" said Max. "Much ado about nothing," he sniffed, the expert.

I couldn't help it. I was starting to like the guy. "It's about ethical treatment of test subjects and employing proper scientific methodology. My wife was a an attorney. She'd investigate violations, get injunctions, that kind of thing."

"I thought the FDA did that," said Tippit.

"The FDA's mandate is food and drug safety. The ORI deals with safety and ethics during scientific research and development."

"The process, not the product," said Armitage.

"Exactly."

Armitage pushed a pack of real Marlboros across the table. Roy Rogers grinned at me from its side. I shook one out. "Elise told me that she was investigating a biotech company committing gross research violations. Said the scandal was big enough to lead the nightly news."

Everyone hid a smile. It pissed me off. "What?"

"There hasn't been a 'nightly news' in thirty years," said Jonathan gently.

I lit a cigarette and inhaled, clinging to the smoke like a lifeline. "Okay, here's the crazy part. I have a memory of Nicole, a memory from the day Elise told me about the scandal. I passed Nicole in the hall. *She* was the company rep, going to see my wife. Which means the company was Surazal."

That earned me a robust chorus of disbelief.

"How old was she?" Max asked.

"Early thirties."

"That'd make her over seventy years old now," Jonathan said.

"Look, Nicole confirmed it. She told me that Elise gave her three days to go public on her own and lessen the charges. That's when Nicole had us killed."

"You're saying Nicole Struldbrug, sister of the man who runs the twelfth largest economy in the world, murdered you and your wife forty years ago to cover up illegal scientific research. That since then, she hasn't aged a day. And that after you revived, she hired *you* to find her missing scientist," said Armitage.

"And then dusted you again when you did," added Max.

An animal noise came from my throat. "Kill me once, shame on you. Kill me twice, shame on me."

There was a moment of empty sound.

"Why hire you?" asked Tippit. "Not very prudent."

"She's a classic sociopath. In terms of behavior, they're the hardest to predict because they don't play by a set of rules and they don't think they'll be caught."

"So it's all a game to her? A high wire act?" They looked dubious.

"I know how it sounds," I said.

"Crandall *did* recognize Donner's name," said Maggie. "I heard it." Maggie described Crandall's professing that he'd had nothing to do with Donner's murder.

"Christ," Armitage muttered.

"Is she a reborn?" said Jonathan.

"She's not," I said.

"And you know this how?" said Armitage.

"I've, uh, been close enough to tell." That earned me some snickers. I coughed.

"He's right," said Maggie. "I scanned her DNA. She's a norm."

"The Retrozine-A, then?" said Max. "Could she have used youthed herself back to her thirties?"

Armitage rubbed the stubble on his jaw. "According to you, the drug was unstable until very recently. Melted people into a puddle of cells."

The memory of that room blew dread across my neck. The stuff on the floor that smelled like rotting cheese. How many people had been swept down that drain to satisfy her agenda?

Armitage sucked on his cold pipe, thoughtful.

"You ever gonna light that thing?" I said.

He ignored me, turning to Max and Tippit. "I want background on Surazal. The works."

Max looked pained. "What am I, a librarian?"

"If Nicole's been around since the last century, there's a record."

"I have a link in my quarters," offered Jonathan.

"No, do it from a Conch cafe, or a library," Armitage said. "Somewhere public, in case you're traced."

I ground out my cigarette. "So what's the plan?"

"I'll contact my superiors," he said. "The decision's theirs, but I'll advise them not to go public about Retrozine."

"What?!" said Maggie, her mouth a perfect circle.

"Not until we have hard evidence."

"What do you call Donner? And the formulas?"

"That's not proof of anything illegal, Maggie."

"They killed people testing it!"

"Says you. Look. We have one chance at this. We throw wild accusations we can't prove, we're finished. Adam Struldbrug is the high pillow. His influence is global. In the public's mind, Surazal is the only thing between them and chaos. They're gonna hate hearing that their savior is really a monster. Now, the Cadre has a sympathetic ear in Congress. But this person will not make a stand against Surazal unless we can hand him undeniable proof."

"A smoking gun, you mean," said Maggie, looking at me.

"What makes you think this congressman's going to throw down when the time comes?" I said. "Even with proof, it's David against Goliath."

Armitage applied flame to his pipe. The room filled with the fragrance of his tobacco. "He's a good man, and he's chairman of the right committees. If we give him solid goods, he'll break the story on the floor of the goddamned Senate the same time we flood the Conch with it. There's no way they could avoid an investigation. Once the facts came out, the administration will have to distance itself from Surazal. It would be the first step in getting the public to rethink what's been done here."

I looked at the floor. There was a sticky trap in the corner, full of dead insects. A fresh line of ants was heading for it, lockstep to their doom. "The public watched for a century as multinationals bought governments, cowed the media and chewed up the third world to run their machines. We didn't care what happened as long as we had our SUVs and TV shows and an easy enemy to hate. What makes you think we're going to do the right thing now?"

"Did being a cop made you this cynical?" Armitage asked.

"Being murdered a couple times."

Armitage waved this all away. "The Blister Joining Ceremony is in two weeks. The President will be in Necropolis for the first time. The whole world will be watching Times Square for the ribbon-cutting."

"Great time to go public," I said.

He grinned sideways at me. "Just what I was thinking."

Maggie gaped. "Two *weeks*?"

"My monks are at your disposal," said Jonathan.

"I appreciate that," said Armitage. He turned to me. "About that smoking gun. Think you can handle that, soldier?"

"Why me?"

"You're dead. Off their radar."

Dead. And expendable. "We're talking penetrating Surazal's deepest defenses. "

"You got in once," said Armitage. "The lab, remember?"

"Yeah, that went *real* well."

Max let out a surprised laugh.

"We need evidence they've been snatching people, testing this drug on them, killing them." He stood. "Two weeks."

They all stood. Meeting over.

I waited until they left and it was just Maggie and me.

"Nicole's no fool," I said. "There may *be* no incriminating evidence. Eight thousand people go missing in this city every year. It'll be next to impossible to identify the ones Surazal kidnapped."

"So what do we do?"

I drummed my fingers thoughtfully. An idea had come to me. There was another way. But it was incredibly high-risk. Armitage would never go for it.

I pushed back from the table. "Any clothes in this place?"

"Why?" said Maggie. "You going some place?"

"Yeah," I said. "The morgue."

I pulled out my Beretta and checked the mag.

It was time to play hard.

35

BRIAN

Previously labeled a pussy, Brian now regularly waded into battle with the deadliest kids on campus. He never won, having no size or skill. But his innate fury and refusal to stay down earned grudging admiration from the school badasses. Security now searched him for kinetic knives and such, unaware that his most potent weapon was his hopelessness.

On this day, La-Ron Zellers and Dell Broggorico, the worst J.D.s in school, blocked his way. The flow of kids instantly diverted to avoid the throw-down. Brian still wore the scratches and bite marks from his last encounter. But he fixed the larger boys with dead eyes and the muscles of his forearms knotted into bands. "Well?" he sighed.

The insult that was the cursory precipitant to school fighting (e.g., "outta my way, you punk ass bitch") was surprisingly not flung. Instead, La-Ron, who had a cruel brow and cubic zirconium teeth, grinned. Dell looked like a hyena who'd stumbled across a brokeback hare.

"You fought Bill Markem," La-Ron said.

"So you want to try me, now?" Brian asked in monotone.

La-Ron and Dell exchanged an amused look. "I outweigh you two-to-one."

Brian sighed. "I gotta go."

La-Ron was fidgeting now. This irritated Dell. "You hear of the

205

Devil's Fist?"

There it was. Forget the Crips and Bloods, the Devil's Fist were hardcore gangbangers that redefined hardcore. Their rank-and-file were mostly ex-cons with too much hate and too little future. They were a reeb hunt pack. Over sixty local murders had been attributed to them. They'd get pulled in for questioning once in a while, but the Anti-Gang Task Force mostly turned a blind eye. Reborn rights groups screamed that this amounted to state-sanctioned "reborn cleansing," but the public was apathetic. After all, they only attacked freaks.

An East Side councilman had run on an "anti-hunt pack" platform last year. He was found unconscious in a dumpster on C Street with some fingers missing. He'd dropped from the race, citing family issues.

"Meet us outside Tally's Gym tomorrow at six and we'll show you how to *really* have fun."

Almost despite himself, Brian's lips curled into a grin, as the hatred awoke and uncoiled in his belly.

36

MANUEL / MEDICAL EXAMINER

The guard felt bad for the guy. The man had wandered into the Ambulatory Care Pavilion's glass atrium at the worst possible time: 3:10, precisely when first shifters swarmed from the elevators in a lemming-like exodus. Their work was done, and God help anybody that got in their way. Manuel watched the man get buffeted by the crowd, then waved from his podium.

"Sir! Over here!"

The man surfed his way over.

"Can I help you?"

The man looked at him with a tremulous expression. "They called me. I have to…" His lip trembled. "Someone from the Medical Examiner's office. My brother, he… Oh God."

Shit. Manuel hated this part of the job. Bellevue Hospital was massive, covering multiple blocks along 1st Avenue. He got lots of lost people. He'd direct them to the right block, the right building, floor and unit. Sometimes people were distraught. There was never an easy way to deal with them. But the ones looking for the morgue—they were the worst.

"They called you to identify him?" The man barely moved, a whisper of a nod.

"What's his name?"

207

"Crandall. Morris Crandall."

Manuel punched keys on his monitor and frowned. "He's been here for weeks."

"I was on my boat off the Sound with no cell. They couldn't find me."

Manuel cringed inside. *Lousy bureaucrats.* Now the guy was gonna see what his bro looked like after weeks on ice. "He's in the morgue, lower level. Do you have ID?"

The man buried his face in his hands, and like that, he was sobbing. *Jesus.* People looked over, giving Manuel accusatory scares. People hated security guards.

"Maybe he'll come back," Manuel offered.

The man raised his face hopefully. "You think?"

Manuel typed into his console. A temporary clearance pass popped from a slot. He handed it to the man. "You're in the wrong building, sir. Wave this at any one of the wall panels; they'll direct you to the ME's office."

"Thank you."

Manuel touched his intercom. "I'll announce you."

"Can't I just go over?"

"It's a secure area, sir."

The man's hand was suddenly covering Manuel's. "This is so traumatic. Is there a cafeteria? A place I can get coffee?"

"There are vending machines on Level Two."

"Bless you. I'll come back when I think I can… face it. You can announce me then. Is that okay?"

"Take all the time you need."

The man headed for the elevators, shoulders hunched in grief. Manuel was so relieved to be rid of the guy that he didn't notice when the man diverted to the rear exit.

The porcelain-tiled room stank of disinfectant and worse. The rimmed metal autopsy table had holes for draining fluid and spigots that delivered water from underneath.

A camera drone weaved around in the air, looking for the best angle. The creature annoyed the Assistant ME, but a clear record was essential. Bodies weren't what they used to be. They had a tendency to sit up and scream in the middle of the autopsy.

The AME and two assistants examined an obese sixteen-year-old reeb. He'd been weighed, X-rayed and measured.

The AME held the liver up in the harsh light. Enlarged. He dropped it into a weigh pan. "Name: Belushi, John. Cause of death…" He sighed. "Same as the last time."

A throat cleared behind them. They turned, and were startled to find themselves at the business end of a gun.

"Hi, boys," the man said. "I'm here to pick up a friend."

37

DONNER

"You brought him *here*?"

Veins stitched Armitage's temples. The bare bulbs of the basement made his mottled face look leprous.

"I thought we were in this together," I said, lighting a cigarette.

"How is compromising our security being in this together?"

"We didn't compromise anything," said Maggie hotly. "Nicole thinks Donner's dead, remember? Crandall, too."

"Crandall *is* dead!" Armitage swung his paw towards the tunnel, where the body was sitting in my wheelchair draped with auto deodorizers. "Dead and stinking up the place!"

Twenty or so Enders and Cadre members had formed a rough circle around us, divided by their loyalties. During my recovery, Jonathan's inner circle had taken a shine to me, due to my semi-holy status as a double reborn. It was either that or my sparkling personality. I hadn't cared enough to discourage it, but now I had a following I didn't know if I wanted. Armitage's people were bristling dangerously, sensing a threat to his authority.

"Let's all just calm down," Jonathan said.

"We would've stayed at the safe house on Bleeker, but there was no way to get there. Checkpoints are going up all over the city."

"You got him out of the morgue easy enough."

"Yeah, how'd you do that?" asked Max.

Maggie looked at the ground. "We, uh. We stole a hearse."

"You stole—" Armitage stopped, gaping.

Someone stifled laughter. Armitage looked ready to blow.

"You prefer we took your Silver Wraith?" said Maggie.

"How do you know you weren't tracked here?" he asked.

"Give me some credit, okay?" I said. "I wiped down the hearse with bleach and dumped it in Alphabet City."

"What about the hospital security cameras?"

"Security experienced a cascade failure around the same time as the robbery," smiled Maggie.

Armitage was not appeased. "We don't operate this way."

"You mean we didn't have your permission," Maggie said.

"That's right!" he roared. He gestured to the tense faces. "I'm responsible for these people's safety! This man has his own agenda."

There were unhappy stirrings from the Enders.

"You wanted proof that Surazal is killing people," I said.

"I didn't say break into Bellevue and steal a body!"

"There's no time, remember? We want this to happen in two weeks, we have to take some risks."

"Our savior! We've done alright without you."

I didn't blame the man for feeling like I was a threat. But this wasn't about being elected Class President, it was about survival. So I dropped my gauntlet. "Done alright?" I said. "Living like rats in a hole, hiding from any loud voice? Jamming up the Conch with your little protest messages and managing to get yourself blamed for every violent act some other crazy group commits?"

The tension in the room surged geometrically. There were angry murmurs.

"How *dare* you," breathed Armitage.

"Boss."

It was Max. "Boss," he said. "Donner's right."

Armitage gaped, blindsided. Limbs shifted uneasily.

"We've been surviving, but that's it," said Max. "It ain't enough anymore."

"Surazal is the best-equipped security force in the world! They control the streets, the media, the minds of the public!"

"It don't matter," said Max. "You want to live like this forever? I'd rather die trying for something better."

Armitage fired a molten look at him, but Max puffed his barrel

chest and held his ground. Behind them, there were nods of agreement, vehement "no's", and shuffling indecisive feet. Armitage gog-
gled at the floor, an internal wrestling match playing out for his self-
control.

"If we can revive that guy," said Max, "he's the smoking gun you
were looking for. Donner got him in one clean move."

Sandy and Tippit entered from the tunnel.

"How's the doctor?" I asked.

"His tissues are regenerating," the nurse replied.

"It's pretty gross," added Tippit.

One of Jonathan's monks rushed down the wooden steps from the
church above, sweaty and out of breath. "Jonathan! Checkpoints are
going up all over the city!"

Everyone turned.

"They have barricades, armed squads. I passed three on my way
here. If my ID hadn't held, I would've been detained. They're breaking Manhattan down into enclosed neighborhoods. They say it's security for the President's visit."

"They're looking for *you*," said Armitage to me.

"They're looking for all of us," I said. "This was always just a matter of time."

It showed on his face then, the toll of leading a double life, being responsible for so many people. I'd self-destructed with self-pity
while this man had soldiered on.

"Look," I said, more gently. "I don't know another man who could
have accomplished what you have. But you're not going to be able to
hide much longer. Those of you who still hold jobs will be ferreted
out and arrested. The rest will be firebombed out of existence."

"They can't," a voice insisted weakly from the crowd.

"They're already doing it!" said Maggie with a heat that shocked
me. "Open your eyes! What's after checkpoints? A reborn Warsaw
ghetto? You think the norms will protest?"

Armitage said nothing. His stony blue eyes looked sad.

"Pastor," said an Ender. "What do you think?"

"We're coming to some turning point," said Jonathan. "What it is,
I can't predict. That man in there has a lot of answers, if we can bring
him back. Answers we can use against Surazal. It may be the only way
to end this thing without violence."

Armitage blinked his craggy lids slowly, an ancient turtle.

Somewhere gravity yanked a drop of water from an overhead pipe and killed it on the cement floor.

"You love us," Maggie said. "But you can't protect us and fight a war at the same time."

He finally sighed. Everybody else did as well, in relief.

"It's moot anyway," he said. "But no more going off half-cocked. We figure the next plan out together."

I gave him my eyes, softening them enough to let him see inside. "Okay, boss."

His expression didn't change visibly, but something moved along his mouth. Something that gave me hope we'd edged past the stalemate, maybe to a place where trust could grow.

"Somebody get Donner some food," he said.

"Could I have something, too? I'm famished."

Heads swiveled. Doctor Morris Crandall was peeking from behind the metal cabinet, his hair a fluorescent white.

38

DONNER

The doctor needed a little time to recover, so I decided to interview the witness to Dr. Smythe's murder. Queenie St. Clair, *Acquiesce*'s proprietress, gave me the name. Sharon was a landscape architect who lived/worked out of a converted warehouse in SoHo. On Queenie's recommendation, she agreed to see me.

I took the train. Laid into the walls of the station was artwork composed of hundreds of tiny ceramic tiles. I'd never seen subway art this beautiful before. It said "REBORNS IN REBORN CARS ONLY."

The C Local slid into the station. "This train making all stops!" the speaker screamed. The PA system hadn't improved any in forty years.

Every fourth car was black metal. Reeb cars. The norm cars were sparsely filled, the reeb ones packed body to body. The doors hissed. I cast a longing look at the elbow room next door. A transit bull within caught the look and threw out an arm. I felt like breaking his face, but crammed myself in with the reborn cattle, telling myself I couldn't afford trouble.

Yeah, Donner. That's what they all tell themselves.

On the way, we were boarded by a squad in combat cyberwear. They went down the aisle, checking everyone, more methodical than they used to be. New directives. Cold sweat wormed down my back as I waited for their handheld to approve me. To my relief, my new

Cadre-supplied ID tat survived their scrutiny.

My mobility wouldn't last. Nicole would figure out who stole Crandall's body. I'd be branded. Travel would be impossible. Worse, I'd be a liability to the Cadre instead of an asset. They'd cut me loose and I'd have to go it alone, survive underground with my face splashed across every smartscreen in town. In my day, with my old resources and friends, I might've been able to do it. But Surazal's biometric tech made the city transparent. I'd be easy pickings. A grim scenario.

▼▼

Sharon's loft took up the second floor of the building. It was accessed by a creaky freight elevator that rattled like it had been last serviced during the Reagan administration.

The warehouse was a showcase for industrial chic. The floor was oiled South American hardwood, the brick beautifully re-pointed. Clusters of exotic plants were strategically grouped throughout the space. Ivy garnished the double-hung windows. The air hung heavy with jasmine and bougainvillea.

Polychrome art frames, some empty, some not, floated at different levels throughout. The opaque panels held holomorphs of pain. A mother screaming as her child was torn from her grip. A mass grave with emaciated, half-buried corpses. A metal spike piercing a human triceps. This one didn't hide her taste for the rough stuff.

The loft's southern end had been partitioned into living quarters. Brushed aluminum cabinets peeked around the translucent wall.

Three junior architects were perched at tables of powder-coated steel in the center of the room. They hunched over their smartboards and measured and drew and erased, measured and drew and erased. No one looked up when Sharon ushered me in. They were well-trained.

"Wow," I said.

"It's home."

Sharon was petite—the kind of pixie that didn't intimidate smaller men and didn't interest the gorillas. Her trim figure had a soft edge, one that eschewed the hard-body aesthetic of cardio addicts. She'd feel velvety under your hand. Her eyes were slate. They saw deeply and didn't care if it unnerved you. Her burgundy hair had been left to find its own shape, and she ran her fingers through it every few minutes. Impatient, starved for sensation, or both.

She directed me toward her office. It wasn't exactly a room, since the walls didn't reach the fifteen foot ceilings. But it had a door, so we went through it. There was a work table covered in stone samples and horticulture books. A single orchid, stunningly perfect, sat atop an Art Deco credenza.

She offered me the ottoman and went to a lacquered sideboard. On its door, a samurai was mounting his concubine from behind. They both looked like they had other things on their minds.

"Drink?" she asked.

"No."

"Mind if I have one?"

"No."

She poured some Maker's Mark into a pony glass and returned, curling her bare feet beneath her on the far side of the ottoman. "It's lunch time," she said. "I could order something."

I shook my head.

"You look like a meal would do you good."

"I'm fine."

She raised an eyebrow.

"Been through a lot lately," I said.

She took a sip. "Nothing serious, I hope."

"I wasn't myself for a while."

Her eyes roamed my face. "But you're better now?"

"Yes."

"Good," she said. "If you don't have your health…"

"Someone else has it," I replied. She laughed.

She seemed professional, mature, well put together. Not the sort who hung out at places like *Acquiesce*.

"You're wondering what a successful businesswoman like me is doing tied up in an S&M club," she said.

I tried not to look like she'd just looted my brain pan. "That's a good place to start."

"Have you ever been tied up, Mr. Donner?"

This one didn't beat around the bush. "Not the way you mean," I said.

"How, then?"

The memory pulled my lips down. "It was unpleasant."

"Try me."

"When I was on foot patrol, I responded to a domestic disturbance call. I should have waited for back-up, but I was a rookie and immortal. The apartment door was unlocked. I heard noises of distress, so I went in. The husband cold-cocked me."

Her thick lashes narrowed.

"A roll of nickels in his fist. Old-fashioned but effective. Before my vision could clear, he'd fastened me to the radiator with my own bracelets."

Sharon crossed her legs tighter.

"He resumed beating his wife. Methodically, to within an inch of her life. Then he let me go."

"Why'd he do that?"

"He said he didn't like to leave anything half-finished. Crazy world."

"The world's okay. It's the people that are crazy."

I liked this one. "Tell me about the club."

A little laugh, glitter in those gray eyes. "To survive in this city, as the owner of a business, you have to be a man. If you're a woman, you have to pretend you're a man. Understand?"

I did.

"*Acquiesce* is a place where I can be a woman again."

"Dominated?"

"Yes."

"Gloria Steinem is turning over in her grave."

"Actually, in her bed in Hippieville. And I don't care what she thinks. I know what I am."

"A bottom."

"That's right."

"Who likes to be tied up."

She touched her upper lip with the tip of her tongue. "Have you ever slapped a girl, Mr. Donner? During sex? I don't mean to really hurt her, just playfully."

"For a submissive, you ask a lot of questions."

"I'll stop if you want," she said. The twinkle was back. I knew what she was after. I supposed it was fair trade. "I had a girlfriend who liked to be spanked a little during sex."

Sharon pointed to the sideboard and the picture on it. "Like that? From behind?"

I cleared my throat. "Anything else?"

"Oh, much more. But we don't have time, do we?"

"No."

"Okay," she sighed. "I was tied onto a saltire."

"The X-shaped cross?"

"Yes. St. Andrew the apostle was martyred on such a cross, feeling he was unworthy to be crucified in the same manner as his Lord. The saltire faced the door to the execution chamber. I saw that poor man go in. Dr. Smythe."

"What time was this?"

She wrinkled her nose, looked skyward. "About seven, I think. Before the place got crowded." She smiled. "It really cooks on the weekends."

"He went in alone?"

"That's why I noticed. *Acquiesce* is not a place you go to be alone."

"Anyone else in the room before he entered?"

"No. And the doctor was the only one afterwards."

"How long were you in that position, facing the door?"

She rubbed her wrists as though remembering sweet past pain. "A couple hours."

I couldn't hold back a snort. "This is recreation?"

"I was being softened up. Primed."

"By whom?"

"Vince, one of my partners. He was wearing a hand-tooled leather hood and chaps."

"A boy to bring home to Mom."

"Depends on the mom."

"Did you hear anything from inside the room?"

"Moaning," she said.

"And you didn't tell anyone?"

She laughed. "Mr. Donner. Moaning is to be expected."

"Right."

She shuddered. "Then the shrieking started. That kind of scream-ing, you don't expect. It was horrible."

"Different from what you're used to?"

"Oh god yes." She ran her hand through her hair again. "Mr. Donner, you have to understand, we know where the line is. This is for pleasure. The sickos and the sadists, the ones who are there to do real damage, they're quickly weeded out." A pause. "For the most part."

"But once in a while…"

"When the screaming started, the place emptied in a hurry. We all knew. Someone got past the radar. Someone went too far. No one wanted to be around when the cops showed. Most of us have respectable lives, lucrative careers."

"You were still tied up?"

"No one would stop and untie me. People were freaked."

"What happened then?"

Sharon opened her mouth, then closed it. She carefully placed the drink on the end table and wrapped her hands around her knees. When she spoke, her voice was quieter.

"Queenie and Bumpy ran down the staircase. Queenie released me while Bumpy forced the door open, took a step in, and saw the body."

"Smythe was dead?"

A tight nod. "Bumpy came out looking like he'd seen a ghost. Told Queenie to call the police."

"Did Bumpy ever go deeper into the room? Out of sight?"

"I know what you're thinking, but no. He just stood in the doorway, far enough in to see the electric chair. He couldn't have killed Smythe, not without me seeing it."

"And that's it?"

A pause. Then another tight nod.

She was leaving something out. Her delicate little hands, still clasped, were trembling. She looked at the floor, suddenly unwilling to meet my eyes.

I rubbed my brow, feeling old. "Thanks for talking to me about this. I know how upsetting it can be."

"It didn't happen to me."

"It doesn't matter. Witnessing violence can be as traumatic as being a part of it."

"I just heard screaming."

"While you were bound and helpless. The killer could have come out and seen you…"

"But it didn't, Mr. Donner." The slate eyes were still perusing the hardwood floor, but with a desperation now. Looking for a way out, ready to chew off her own paw.

I cocked my head. "It?"

There was a silent moment. Then she said, "What?"

"You said, 'it didn't.' Not 'he didn't,' or 'she didn't.'"

Her whole body clamped tight, the barricades snapping into place. "I'm not a linguist, Mr. Donner. So if there's nothing else—"

She would have pulled off the terse dismissal. But when she reached for her glass, her hands were still shaking. The drink went off the table and shattered on the floor. Sharon jumped to her feet with a cry. Her architects were well-trained. Nobody rushed in. Sharon bolted to the sideboard, poured another double and drained it in a single motion. I stood, slipping some cushioning into my voice.

"During trauma we can see things that don't make sense. Violence doesn't fit into a neat little box."

"Get out," she said.

But her eyes were desperate, full of need. For guidance. For control.

There was only one way this was going to play out. "Tell me, and I'll help," I said, my voice hardening.

Her lips trembled. "I said leave."

I walked to her. I took a fistful of her hair, forcing her head back until her wide eyes were on mine, her white neck exposed.

"Tell me, Sharon," I said, gravel into my voice. "Now."

A soft moan escaped her. My fist tightened in her hair. "Call me a bitch," she said.

"No."

"Please."

"No."

She let out a noise, somewhere between a sob and a hiccup. "It was a shadow," she said in a whisper. "A shiny shadow."

Her wide eyes searched my face for signs of belief. I didn't have much I could give her. I walked to the sideboard, poured myself some water from a siphon. It tasted metallic.

"So something did come back out."

"Through the door. From inside the chamber."

"You said the door was closed."

"It was."

"You're saying this shadow came *through* the closed door?"

"That's what I said."

"After the shrieking started?"

"Yes." She shuddered.

I'd hoped that whatever she'd been holding back would be relevant, but this? This could be anything. Flotsam, a random spike of imagery from a terrified mind. "Sharon, maybe it was a reflection or something. From all the lights, the strobes."

"No." Her face had drawn together defiantly.

"You'd been tied up for hours. You were exhausted, or in pain, or delirious."

"No!" She was adamant now, angry I didn't believe her.

"Alright," I said, pressing my fingers to my temples. "A shiny shadow. I don't know what that means."

"It was like an oil slick, but in motion."

"A moving oil slick." I had a sudden flashback to my dream and the human-shaped shadow that dragged Elise into the ground.

"You think I'm crazy," she said.

"Maybe," I admitted. "Anything else?"

"It had a human shape." She put her hand over her mouth. The vibrating transferred from her lips to her hands. It looked like she was frantically patting her mouth. "Arms, legs, head. An outline, like a shadow, but not on a surface. It went through the air."

"Like a ghost?"

"No, it—"

"Not like a ghost?"

"I don't know, Jesus! When you picture a ghost, its edges are blurry. This wasn't like that. It was sharp, defined."

Then I remembered Maggie. I'd seen her become translucent. A wrecking ball swung through my ribcage.

"As it went past me, I heard it."

"It made a noise?"

"Like a… whispering chuckle. An awful sound." Bright points of fear silvered her pupils. "It went past me, out. Then the house lights came on."

"No one else saw it?"

Abruptly she started to cry, softly. "No."

I walked back to her, pushed back a lock of her hair, smoothing the burgundy tresses I had pulled. "Sharon. Maybe it's time you found a new hobby."

She sniffled. "Don't I know it."

◢◣

They stood staring at me.

"Probably a drugged-out whacko," said Armitage.

"No."

"C'mon, Donner."

"She wasn't a junkie," I said.

"She believed what she told me. Where that leaves us…"

My spine ached from sleeping on the cot. I never thought I'd be fondly remembering the monstrosity in my Park Slope bedroom.

I drained the tea. I had an abrupt urge to smash the chipped cup. I really wanted a beer. I rolled my neck, listening to the grinding glass. I hadn't thought about booze lately. A radical cure—just die a couple times, ha ha. It was wishful thinking. It wasn't gone, just in remission. Eventually the cravings would jump from their ambuscade and hit me jackhammer hard. And it would be when I was most vulnerable.

Muffled Ender voices drifted from above:

"There are signs so that we may know.

There is time so that we may change.

The dead rise as witness;

Witness the incorruptibility of the spirit.

What proof need you now?

When God's finger moves among us

For all to see?"

Nearby, Max and Tippit were playing cards with two Enders. A tensor lamp cast yellow gloom over the table. It was a strange sight, the shaved monks' heads and deep burgundy robes, sitting across from the Guido suits and craggy jowls. Both jowls and heads had five o'clock shadows. Max, unsurprisingly, had a superb poker face. Not Tippit. Right now, everyone was folding because he looked like the proverbial feline that consumed the canary. I found myself smiling. Then frowning. Attachments were dangerous.

Maggie had been watching the game, too. I flashed her a smirk and indicated Tippit's expression. Instead of returning my amusement, she flinched like she'd been stung by a scorpion. She looked away, suddenly preoccupied with straightening her blouse. What the hell?

I slung a question mark at Armitage, who'd seen the strange reaction, too. He rolled his cuffs down and ambled over to her.

"What's up, Mag?" he asked. "You look like you're about to jump out of your skin."

"Gee, thanks."

"Maggie," he said again. She examined the cracks in the concrete.

"A straight flush!" crowed Tippit.

"Imagine that," muttered Max. He tossed down his cards.

I laid a hand on Maggie's shoulder.

"A shiny shadow," she murmured.

"Sharon's story?" I said. She looked up at me. Her eyes were so wide I could actually see nanoswarms in the irises, like schools of fish seen from below, swirling shapes lit by oceantop sun sparkle.

"I saw something like that."

"What?" said Armitage. "Where?"

"Alvarez's apartment."

My hands tightened the back of the chair. The wood groaned. I knew it! I'd known it back in Red Hook. After Alvarez had gone out the window. Something had been wrong with her story. But I'd never pressed her, had I? I'd let her distract me with talk about impermanence and separation and consciousness. Again, I felt that rustling of dangerous attachments.

"You're saying you've seen this shadow?" said Armitage.

"In the projects. It killed Hector Alvarez."

Armitage sat back down, his hands dead weight on his thighs. "Oh boy."

Something about her resolution changed, a subtle shift in colors, like an adjusted TV aerial. "Donner was searching Alvarez's bedroom. The old man was looking out the window, like his whole life was over. Then all of sudden... this *thing* crossed the room, in a flash, from nowhere. It had a human shape. It was translucent but you could see it shine."

"Jesus," I said.

"It *pushed* at him, like a strong wind. It pushed him straight out the window. It killed him."

I wanted that beer again, bad. "Two independent sightings," I said.

"Boss," said Max. "This thing's real?"

"Sharon's story places this same... phantom... at the Smythe crime scene in the dungeon."

"With a knife?" reminded Armitage. "A ghost with a knife?"

"If it killed Dr. Smythe, then it killed the doc you found in the laundry hamper, too, right? Hakuri?" asked Max. "And faked a break-in and a robbery to cover it up? What kind of ghost does that?"

223

"Worse," I added, "what do Hector Alvarez and the Surazal scientists have in common? They're not connected."

"Except by you," said Maggie.

Tippit sucked in a startled breath. "Oh shit."

"Awfully convenient, Alvarez getting whacked precisely at that moment," said Armitage.

"To keep him from talking? Leading Donner back to Nicole?" said Max.

"It doesn't make sense. Who would protect Nicole but kill her team at the same time?"

"Do ghosts have to make sense?" asked Tippit.

"It wasn't a ghost," I said. "It was a smarty."

Maggie opened her mouth, then snapped it shut. Armitage was staring at her, hard. "Maggie?" he asked. The players had drifted from the table and we stood in a semi-circle around Maggie. "I can't tell you," she whispered.

"You fucking well *can* tell us!" barked her leader.

Her exhalation was measured. She stood and looked at each one of us in turn. "It's never been heard by human beings before. Do you understand?"

"Get on with it," I said.

She licked her lips. "There's a legend. About one of the first of us."

"One of the first AIs?" asked Max.

"Legend's probably not the right word. More like a bed-time story. He's kinda like the smarty boogeyman."

"Why's he so scary?" asked Max.

"Because he kills humans."

A deep shock froze the room. Finally, one of the Enders said what we were all thinking. "No smarty has ever killed a human being. Smarties are pacifists."

"Well, this one wasn't. This one hunted humans as prey, according to the tale. He was called the Lifetaker."

"What happened to him?"

"You have to understand. The UN debate whether to grant us rights as sentient beings was a firestorm. The General Assembly was almost evenly split. The idea of artificial consciousness terrified the shit out of people. Muslims still view us as demons."

"I remember," said Armitage. "Every link in the world was tuned in to the debates that whole summer."

"What finally tipped the balance in our favor was the fact that not one smarty had ever committed a crime. Any crime. Not one petty theft, let alone a violent act. Our ego structure is different. We can't comprehend putting ourselves before another, which is a prerequisite for violence or crime. That, along with our lack of material ambition, convinced people that we'd be harmless. We wouldn't become enemies or competitors, the two things humans fear the most."

"But the Lifetaker—"

"Threatened all that. If you found out a smarty could kill, it'd be over. There'd be nothing left for us except slavery or destruction. So, the story goes, he was banished."

The planes in Armitage's face shifted, but he said nothing.

Maggie said: "I thought he was a cyburban myth."

"But what you saw?"

"It definitely could have been a smarty."

"Who knows more about this Lifetaker?" asked Armitage.

"My old guardian, Jakob," she said. I must've looked lost. "We don't have parents as such. Newborn smarties are put under the tutelage of a more experienced AI. If anyone would know more, it'd be Jakob."

"Contact him," I said. "If this Lifetaker is more than a spook story, then he's back. Maybe we can get an answer to why Hector Alvarez and these dead scientists are connected."

"Well great!" mourned Tippit. "A smarty serial killer. So much for sleeping tonight."

39

NICOLE / MCDERMOTT

Seething, Nicole Struldbrug hung up on her father. The commtat reshaped into its default spider web pattern. She looked through the glass, struggling to get a hold of herself. The reeb in the metal chair looked like a mound of tapioca pudding. Time to send Loretta out again.

Nicole closed her eyes. Her father's voice—so papery and thin, so young, yet so full of dust and years. It made her want to retch.

Previously, he'd been content to fling his criticisms at her from a distance, but now he was clearly suspicious. She could count on a summons from her brother. A calling out on the carpet, and soon. Good. It was time for a reckoning.

The booth door opened, admitting Dr. Gavin and the reborn McDermott, her security chief. They waited diplomatically while she wrangled her loathing back into its box.

She regarded them. The two men couldn't be more opposite ends of the human spectrum. Urbane sophistication and scientific brilliance, next to animal brutality and cunning. The only thing they had in common at the moment was displeasure. It was serious. They never came here.

"Well?" she said.

"Someone found Donner," said McDermott.

"So? Some ghetto rat stumbles across his bones—"

"He's been revived."

It was the first time they'd ever seen her completely blindsided. She seemed to realize her mouth was open and clamped it shut. "How?" she asked. Her voice threatened pain.

"Maggie Chi," said Gavin.

"The smarty bitch who stole our formula?"

"Yes. She must have used it to revive him. A surveillance wasp in the subways took his picture yesterday."

"Where was he going?"

"We don't know," said McDermott. "By the time the biometrics identified him, he was long gone."

Nicole drummed her fingernails on the Plexiglas. McDermott caught a glimpse of leather beneath her sleeve. She carried Japanese Tanto knives in sheaths on each forearm. She could flick her wrists in a certain way and they'd spring forward, ready to do damage. The blades were graphene-tipped—honed to the monomolecular level and capable of slicing through steel. It was whispered that she'd used them on a secretary who'd eavesdropped on her phone call. According to the legend, the only thing that'd kept the woman's head from being completely severed was a single strand of cartilage.

"Donner, Donner," Nicole mused, flashing her teeth. "What a naughty boy you are."

A groan erupted from Gavin. "Didn't *you* bring Donner into all of this?"

McDermott shook his head. *Don't do it, Doctor, don't do it.*

Her brow darkened. "It doesn't matter now, Doctor," she said.

McDermott saw it coming. Men like this—men with huge intellects and even larger egos, men used to having everyone kowtow around them, men who never developed humility or restraint—they eventually went out in a self-destructive tirade when challenged by an inferior mind with superior authority. Gavin's resentments charged into the room like a berserker bull.

"Doesn't matter!? You've endangered everything we've worked for with your games! Hiring him was insane! Now the Retrozine is in the hands of the Cadre!"

"We don't know that."

"Who else could've gotten Donner past our security in the lab? Or on the subway?" Spittle flecked his lips. "It won't take much to figure out what we've been doing."

"You're overreacting, Doctor."

Gavin yanked on the his coattails and actually shrieked at them. "I'll let Adam decide that! I have a feeling he'll be very interested in what's been going on around here."

There was a silent moment. McDermott steeled himself for something ugly.

But Nicole sighed and said softly, "You're right. If I hadn't hired Donner, none of this would have happened."

Gavin opened his mouth, then shut it in confusion. McDermott stifled a smile. Gavin had probably told her off a million times in his head, but now all the verbal barbs and lashes he'd honed to titanium brilliance were useless. She'd taken the wind out of his sails simply by agreeing with him.

"However, if, as you say," she continued, "this is the Cadre at work, they won't go public until they have hard evidence."

McDermott had an epiphany. "The morgue theft! They're going to revive Crandall."

Gavin looked like he was about to suffer an attack of apoplexy. His face turned the color of a fresh bruise. "He knows everything! If they break him—"

Nicole cut him off. "McDermott, find Crandall before he can talk."

McDermott acknowledged her with a jerk of his head. She smiled in dismissal, then paused. "Oh, McDermott." He stopped. "One more thing."

Here it comes.

"Dr. Gavin is going on leave. Exhaustion. Notify the press office."

Gavin whitened. "What—"

"And McD? Be a dear and close the door on your way out."

McDermott exited quickly. He knew he should keep going down that hall without pausing, but he couldn't help himself. He crept back and listened outside the door.

It wasn't very dramatic. A whisking sound, a wet plop. A gasp. Then a large thud a moment later as the body hit the floor.

Eviscerations were the worst. You had whole seconds to watch your purple-gray entrails spill out onto the carpet in front of you before your heart failed.

As McDermott hurried down the corridor, he wondered whether, in the brisk air conditioning, Gavin's guts had been steaming.

40

BRIAN

The Devil's Fist stalked their prey in Battery Park City. More reebs, Dell Broggorico said. Better hunting. Here, it was the 1880s, and the ladies sashayed in hoop skirts and bustles, twirling parasols. The men sported natty herringbone suits. Kids in kneesocks and knickers rolled their kinetic hoops along the sidewalks, annoying shop owners as they interfered with the local power grid.

The residents of BPC had managed, through their jackass of a representative in City Council, to get a permit for equestrian transportation. They'd tried to ban cars outright, but the Mayor had quickly put an end to that nonsense. Consequently, the traffic jams down here were infamous and bizarre, as floater and buckboard jockeyed for position and horses bolted when their manes rose in the vehicles' mag fields. Motorists stayed clear if they could. Horse shit superheated by a EM pylon was an olfactory experience you wanted to avoid.

The hunters dressed to blend in: spats, sweater vests and bow ties, their tats and piercings hidden. Brian didn't get a weapon. That would be earned by his first *bona fide* kill.

Kill. Electric ferocity disrupted his thoughts. Another part of him, however, a part that was slowly growing smaller, murmured with discomfort.

They found a homeless reeb beneath a bridge support. He hummed tunelessly along with the whine of the asynchronous

229

HDVC fuel ribbons. Empty bottles of rotgut stood sentry around him. He was in his re-twenties, but his jaundiced skin hung in elephantine folds, unable to keep pace with the accelerated alcoholic youthing. The men's faces had a predatory shine in the glow of his sterno fire.

The act itself was disappointingly inelegant. They simply dove at the poor fool, punching and stabbing. The pathetic old fuck died much too quickly. Brian managed to get a kick in to the man's groin that elicited a satisfying rasp of pain, but their frenzy didn't leave him much room. They stood, panting, faces blazing, looking down at his broken form.

La-Ron whirled to Brian. "Whaddaya think a that, eh?"

"It was okay, I guess."

Dell guffawed. "Okay? Did you hear that, Yrko?"

Yrko was the scariest of the adult Devil's Fisters. His face carried the history of some ancient conflagration. One eyebrow was missing, and the rest looked melted, the cauterized flesh twisted like putty. Yrko relished the revulsion he inspired. He had a weird Cockney accent. He'd burnt an ear off the last guy who laughed at it. He hauled Brian by his shirt up to his ugliness. "Lad's a goer, eh?" he said. "Maybe we have a job fer ya."

La-Ron bristled. "That was my job!"

Yrko ignored him, studying Brian's fearless face. He understood how dangerous a hollow man could be.

"We got us a… patron," he said. "From time to time, we do work for her. She's looking for a certain few blokes. Deep underground, hard to find. But even worms come up in the sun once in awhile, eh? Now, I got me plenty o' eyes uptown, but I need somebody down here. You up to that, me lad?"

"Right-o, guv'nah," said Brian, and everyone snickered.

Everyone except Yrko.

41

DONNER

My Beretta was in a docker's clutch, the strap digging into my side. I wriggled my shoulders and managed to shift the chafing to another spot. Armitage's shirt was freshly ironed. It didn't matter. He still looked rumpled.

"He'll be hostile. You killed him."

I shrugged. "Brought him back, too. Maybe it'll balance out."

We were in the old rumrunning tunnel. Storage rooms had been carved into the rock. The Cadre had reinforced them with neocrete and metal doors. Now one of them was Crandall's make-shift holding cell.

"Doesn't matter, I guess," he said. "Interrogation techniques have come a long way since your day."

"Yeah?" I said. "No more waterboarding?"

Armitage held up a pneumatic syringe. "Veracity virus."

I shook my head. More bugs.

Maggie came around the curve of the tunnel. "Crandall's got countermeasures."

"Shit."

"You mean biodefenses?" I said

An appreciative smile from Maggie. "You've been studying."

"I was getting tired of being a mark."

"His system's swarming with defense nanites. Probably a standard employee injection."

I rolled up my sleeves. "Guess we'll have to do it the old-fashioned way."

"What does that mean?" asked Maggie.

"We may have to do things in there, Mag. I need to know you're not going to get in the way."

"I don't have much of a choice, do I?"

"No," I said. "You don't."

Crandall had the complexion of a slug, a creature of filthy folds in the earth. The gauntness of his face made his eyes look sunken; he stared into space, slack-jawed and unfocused. His hair was brittle and receding, a crop far past season, ready to blow away at the first strong wind. The long black toenails were better suited to a lizard than a man. Sitting in this dim room of rust and concrete, he seemed totally alien.

Jesus. Armitage and I looked at each other. Maybe this guy was toast.

Then Crandall picked up a cup from the tray beside him and sipped delicately at some tea. The demure act instantly destroyed the frankenimage.

"Mmm. Earl Gray."

He focused his watery eyes on me, amusement on his face. He'd been playacting the shock treatment routine to unnerve us.

I fished a cigarette from my shirt and set fire to it. He was into games? Good. It would spell out my approach.

He glanced at me over his Earl Grey. "Ah. My assassin."

I shrugged. "Want some slippers?"

"No thank you." He blotted his worm lips with a napkin.

Armitage looked him up and down. "Jesus, talk about the cosmetic underclass." He straddled one of the wooden chairs and crammed a piece of gum into his face. He flicked his hips, scraping the chair closer across the cement. Crandall's face screwed up.

"Senses are raw the first couple of days," I said. "Is the light okay? We could dial it down a couple degrees."

I got an iguana stare. "Such concern for my comfort, when I'm about to be interrogated."

"We won't insult your intelligence with clumsy tactics."

"Flattery is a tactic, is it not?"

I looked at Armitage, smiling: "Didn't I tell you?"

Armitage blew a bubble. I didn't know how he was doing it, but there was this masterful vibe of working class resentment simmering below his surface. He'd picked up on Crandall's "my IQ is bigger than your IQ" thing and adopted the heavy-limbed roll of a lowbrow.

"So he's brainy," he said. "Big deal."

"Hardly helpful at the moment. I am in the dark here, quite literally, am I not?"

Armitage snapped his gum.

"Oh, the doctor's figured out plenty already, haven't you?" I said.

I hid from his gingivitis smile in a lungful of tobacco smoke. "I am reborn," he said. "You used the Retrozine. That much is obvious. Now, as to the meeting I glimpsed when I awoke craving sustenance—"

"'Craving sustenance'?" Armitage snorted.

"You can't expect the doctor to talk like street trash," I said.

"I expect him to make himself understood."

"Forgive my erudition." A smile. Taunting.

Armitage snarled, his neck reddening. Crandall looked as if he'd just won a round. Good. Let him build his high tower.

"I suppose he figured out we're Cadre, too," Armitage said.

Crandall's eyes lit up. I bit off an expletive like Armitage had just sold the farm.

"I wasn't sure," Crandall said. "What with that gaggle of misfits up there you could have been anyone. Thank you for clearing that up."

Armitage left his chair murderously. I pushed the wall away and laid a hand on his shoulder. Armitage deflated, glowering, and reinstalled himself in his chair. I continued to the ashtray and ground out my filter. Crandall didn't try to hide his delight. Stupid. We let the silence condense a bit while I lit a fresh one.

"You don't have to be the enemy, Morris," I said.

"Save the bonding routine. And the good-cop-bad cop. It was ancient when you were alive."

"Okay," I said. "Here's what I really think: I think you should join us."

Armitage exploded, "What??"

Crandall's newest smile masked puzzlement. "Why would I do that?"

"Surazal's got the completed formulas now. What do they need you for?"

That got a rise out of him. "Retrozine A and B are only the beginning."

"Not any more. They've announced your death in the media. Called you a traitor. Said you stole secrets."

He paled. "You're lying!"

"C'mon, you know how Nicole works. Once you got dead, you became the perfect scapegoat. Your death covers everything. A deranged, missing scientist. Now believed to have killed his own team members. Turns up hiding in the wall like a rat. Stealing vital Shift research. He gets violent when security confronts him, and *voila*."

I watched it make sense in his eyes. Watched the "after all I've done for them" program run in his head.

Armitage grinned. "You're a fugitive, same as us, pal."

The man twitched at the word. "I only have your word—"

I put a smartscreen in front of him and ran the press highlights. He watched in growing fury as he was portrayed as a greedy, murderous turncoat, trying to sell vital secrets to the highest bidder.

"You'll have to go underground," I said.

"I have friends—"

"Not anymore. Your funds have been frozen. Your body's missing. Nicole's not stupid, Morris. She knows you've revived."

He whitened a little more.

"Oh yeah," said Armitage, his jaw savoring the gum and Crandall's shock in equal measure. "You haven't seen the recent changes in our lovely city. Checkpoints, searches. You're all over the Conch. Enemy of the state."

Crandall's poise had gone the way of the dinosaurs.

"Then there's the wasps," I added. "Thousands of these little walnut-sized things, buzzing the streets doing resonance biometrics of everybody. And they're armed. Three Cadre members were vaporized right on 6th Avenue yesterday."

"In front of their families," spat Armitage.

"Even in this city of a million back rooms and alleys, it's getting damned hard to hide. And let's face it, doc. On the street, the smarts you got? They ain't the kinda smarts you need."

I could almost hear Crandall's processors spinning into overdrive.

"We'll put you in one of our safe houses," I continued. "A

basement somewhere, with blacked-out casement windows. Someone will bring you food, clothes, the necessities. It won't be fun, but you'll survive."

"And in exchange for this assistance?"

"Everything you know. Starting with Struldbrug."

"Which Struldbrug, Mr. Donner?"

"The brother and sister are working together, aren't they?"

The smirk was back. "My information is more valuable than you suspect."

Armitage and I traded eyebrows.

Crandall's eyes clouded in longing for a vanished life. "My work is everything. Can you find me another lab, funding for my experiments? If what you've shown me is true, nothing can bring that back." He raked skeletal fingers across his face. "I do not desire some mole-like existence in this nightmare city. Therefore, I want to leave Necropolis."

Armitage laughed. "Are you fucking nuts?"

Crandall folded his hands. "There is someone beyond this place who may shelter me."

"You'd infect the outside world."

He didn't say anything. But his eyes flicked sideways.

There it was. Fresh information. Information that I knew couldn't be finessed out of him.

Good. I was going to enjoy this.

I let my brow go smooth suddenly. "Fuck." I stood and rolled down my sleeves.

Armitage said, "What?"

"We wasted our time."

Crandall's arrogance faltered. "What? You don't—"

"He's playing us. He's got nothing we need. It's all bullshit."

"I'm—now wait a minute—"

I went into the hall and then returned with a two-meter polyethylene bag stamped "City Morgue." I dropped the pouch at the man's feet.

"Use his body bag," I said to Armitage.

Armitage rose, sneering. I tossed him a roll of duct tape. He caught it and tore a strip free, nice and slow. The rending sound was awful in the room.

"Tape the feet, hands and face," I said. "Put him in the bag, take him to the swamp around LaGuardia. Cut notches in his belly so he doesn't rise when he bloats."

Crandall's composure exploded like the face of Bart's building.

"I *do*—I have information—"

I stared my contempt at him. What he was worth to me. Armitage stepped forward with the tape. Crandall's stink filled the room. He rattled in his wheelchair. Racking gasps hitched from his chest, staccato bursts of terror. "No, no! Anything! Anything!"

Easier than I'd thought. "We'll give you a minute to compose yourself."

In the hall, Maggie stared at me, her eyes a little too wide.

"He's ready," I said.

"You cracked him open like a piñata," said Armitage.

I looked at Jonathan. "Have a novice clean him up."

He nodded. "Terrence. He needs to work on his humility."

Jonathan and Maggie came back in with us. Crandall looked tiny and pathetic in his fresh jammies. Good. I didn't want to lose momentum.

"Alright, Doctor. How did Surazal cause the Shift?"

Everyone in the room gave a little noise of astonishment.

I ticked the points off. Index finger. "Forty years ago, Surazal conducts illegal genetic experiments on humans." Second finger. "My wife, a federal regulator, is killed to prevent an investigation." Third finger. "The Shift occurs. Supposedly an act of bio-terrorism, but no culprit ever identified. The Shift works by modifying and reviving dead human DNA." Fourth finger. "Surazal just happens to be the company that identifies the retroviral carrier of the mutated DNA." Fifth finger, contracting into a fist. "Surazal exploits this to become the power in Necropolis."

"You think the Shift was caused by some accident of ours? That I'm part of some elaborate, forty-year cover up?"

"Surazal *was* conducting genetic experiments."

Crandall looked skyward, asking the heavens for patience. "As were *hundreds* of New York companies in the early 21st century. Any one of them could have been responsible. Genetics was the next trillion-dollar medical frontier. By the 1980s, we'd already sequenced and cloned human genes. Once viruses had been trained to—"

"Trained viruses?" I sighed and turned to Maggie for help. "Okay. Talk to me like a child."

"Retroviruses are the perfect vehicles for genetic modification," she said, "because when they attack the host cell, they introduce their own genetic material into not only the cell but its genome—its DNA. When the cell replicates, it continues making the new DNA. So the desired effect—the manufacture of a necessary protein, for instance— continues for life. The technique originally treated diseases caused by single-gene defects, like cystic fibrosis, muscular dystrophy, hemophilia. Retroviruses could replace the defective gene with a functional one and cure the patient."

"What's wrong with that?"

"Nothing," replied Maggie. "As long as geneticists followed established protocols."

"So what was Surazal doing that was illegal?" I asked Crandall.

He examined his fingers. "Germline therapy."

"Which means what?" asked Armitage, exasperated.

"Human germline therapy is banned," said Maggie. "Unlike the somatic cells of the body, when you modify germline cells—sperm cells, ova, or their stem cell precursors—the genetic changes not only become permanent, they become inheritable."

"Isn't that good?" Armitage asked. "A hemophiliac knowing that his son won't have the disease?"

"Creating an inheritable change is genetic engineering, not gene therapy," said Maggie. "It opens a huge ethical can of worms. Forget the debate about whether we should tamper with God's blueprint. What if we accidentally created some mutation that could wipe out humanity?"

Crandall laughed derisively. "That old saw?"

"Genetic manipulation is difficult and risky," Maggie retorted. "It's hard to prevent undesirable effects. You have to get the virus to infect the correct target cells and ensure the newly inserted gene doesn't disrupt any vital ones already in the genome."

"Sounds like Russian Roulette," I said.

"More like cooking when you don't know how ingredients will interact," said Maggie. "You could produce the tastiest chili in existence or poison sludge."

"Is that what the Shift is?" Armitage said.

"No!" barked Crandall. "Look, the Shift is carried by a retrovirus, I won't deny that. But it's a mutation of a bioweapon, not some experiment that got loose from our lab."

"So you say."

"I don't deny we've capitalized on the event, but Surazal did not cause the Shift!"

I looked at Maggie. At her polygraph eyes. "He's telling the truth," she said. "As he knows it."

"Nicole could've kept him in the dark," said Armitage.

"Okay," I said, "Go back to Surazal in my time. Why would they risk running illegal experiments in the first place?"

"Sheer competitive impatience, probably. Marketable products were at least a decade away. That's ten to fifteen years of very expensive R&D before the first big product comes to market. And faster is not only cheaper: whoever gets there first, well… We're talking about products as world-transforming as the telephone, the light bulb, the personal computer. Remember how long Microsoft had the market cornered?"

"What kind of 'world-transforming' products are we talking about?"

"A gene-therapy drug that produces more intelligent children? More attractive children? Disease-resistant children?"

I'd forgotten Jonathan was here until he spoke. "A world where ignorance, disease and disparity are banished. Where every child is a genius and an athlete. Think of how much we could accomplish."

I shook my head. How could anyone retain that kind of optimism? Was it faith or denial? From wherever it sprang, I'd never feel it. I was built different—I'd come out of my mother wanting to slap the doctor back.

"Drug companies don't just give away billion dollar treatments, Jonathan," said Armitage.

"Neither do insurance companies," said Maggie. "Only the rich would be able to afford them."

"The beginning of a true genetic underclass," I breathed. "The rich could actually become physically and mentally superior to the poor."

"What about longer-lived?" asked Jonathan, getting us back on point.

"Surazal could have been exploring anti-aging," said Crandall. "A bit early for significant research, but… perhaps."

"Logical. Except for the fact that Nicole Struldbrug hasn't aged a day in forty years."

Crandall reeled like I'd struck him. "What are you talking about?"

Could he really not know? I thought back to that cement room. Nicole *had* sent him away before admitting it to me in the cement room. "How long have you known Nicole, doctor?"

"Sixteen years."

"Who ran the company before her brother, Adam?"

"Isodor, their father. It's been family-held since the 1800s."

"Then how did you know I'd been killed?"

"Nicole told me."

"She told you she killed someone?"

"I balked at first when I learned that our team was to use human test subjects. So, as *incentive*, she told me a story about encountering a resistant investigator and what happened to the woman and her husband. She didn't tell me it had happened forty years ago. Then, to make sure I really understood, she brought in McDermott. I took one look at his scarred face and realized I didn't have a choice anymore."

A glacier crept over the surface of my thoughts. "McDermott's dead."

"No, he revived during the Dark Eighteen down in Ecuador or somewhere."

"Bolivia," I hissed.

"When he was shipped to Necropolis, she made him Director of Security."

Yet another lie from Lady Nicole. Alvarez's tattered newspaper clipping rushed back at me. The close-cropped platinum blonde hair, the dead blue eyes... The man who'd blackmailed Hector Alvarez into killing two people...

When I came back a minute later, everyone was looking at me in alarm. Maggie placed her hand on my arm.

"Donner," she said.

My mouth was bone-dry. "I'm okay." I swallowed. "When did Adam become CEO?"

"About fifteen years ago, after Izzy retired." Crandall clicked his tongue. "Tell me why you think Nicole hasn't aged in forty years."

So I gave it to him, the whole thing. Nicole in that hallway forty years ago. The murders. What she said in the cement room. Instead of looking shocked, Crandall quietly nodded to himself. "You don't seem surprised."

"It… explains a few things."

"Like what?"

Crandall's eyes fired in scientific passion. "Nicole provided us with human tissue samples to reverse-engineer. Tissue samples with re-markable properties."

"From where?"

"She wouldn't say. But the cells were resistant to free radicals. Very long telomere chains. And they had a Hayflick limit which was greater than normal by a factor of three."

"Someone translate that, please?" asked Armitage.

"They're factors in aging," I said.

"We assumed it was gen-enged material, stolen from another com-pany. We never dreamed it could be from a real person. Because that would mean that the person could be—"

"Hundreds of years old," whispered Maggie.

Maggie, Armitage, Max and I stood with Jonathan in his office at the rear of the sanctuary. It had been a storeroom for Maury's Deli, but now it housed a couple of gray filing cabinets and a desk salvaged from a defunct insurance company. Since the Shift, life insurance wasn't what it used to be.

Max tossed his smartscreen onto the wall. A graphic flashed up, bathing us in blue sheen. "Surazal began as a chemical manufacturing company in 1879 in Germany. The founder, Abel Struldbrug, was a German Jew. The factory was destroyed during Dresden's firebombing in World War II. Abel's son Abraham got out of Germany and restart-ed the business in New York in 1946. He retired in '83, passing the reigns to son Isodor—Izzy to his friends. By 2005, the company had become a diversified conglomerate. One of the nation's largest drug companies, it had its fingers in a lot of pies. They had subsidiaries that manufactured weapons and provided private security for contractors in the Gulf wars. Combined with their scientific and pharmaceutical divisions, they were perfectly situated to step in when things went to hell."

Max punched a couple keys and the image changed. "Adam Struldbrug took over as CEO from Izzy in 2038. Nicole is Adam's

creator, protector, and destroyer. Which meant it was a Temple vehicle, not some vendor.

The routine was always the same. The truck would turn into the narrow alley, stopping next to the metal doors in the macadam that led to the church's basement.

Brian's mother had told him never to walk across loading doors. He'd dismissed her over-protectiveness, finding the saggy bounce of the metal exciting—

Emotion surged hotly in his throat. He stamped his feet until slivers of hurt shot up his shins. Fuck! Kid's stuff. His old life was never coming back.

Once the loading doors were open, sealed boxes floated on magloaders down into the bowels of the church. But no one was ever there to supervise. Another oddity. Customers still didn't trust automated loaders enough to leave them unattended. Usually there was some Teamster with his butt crack showing. But not here. Just the steady humming flow of those boxes up and down.

Come to think of it... There were as many boxes leaving the Temple as arriving. What would a Temple regularly export in such quantity? It couldn't be garbage. Autocompactors rumbled through the streets twice a week and vacuumed the city's dumpsters. So, what? Pamphlets, newsletters? But these boxes were covered in official-looking government labels, and they were really long, long enough to...

Long enough to smuggle *people* in and out of the building!

People who didn't want to be seen.

Brian smiled.

That night at check-in, he told Yrko. Yrko told Loretta. And Loretta, after receiving her bundle of godsmack, transmitted the information to Nicole.

The complicated events that led a sheltered son of a prominent East Side attorney to report a generic delivery van to his tribe of gangbangers were as ironic as they were unlikely. Brian never realized the part he played in the raid on the Ender Temple and the loss of so many lives, because the next night, Yrko killed him.

Yrko had taken a strong dislike to the bindlepunk. The brat thought he was better than everybody else because he came from money. Fuckers like that had sneered down their noses at him his whole goddamned life. So late that night, Yrko tried to rape Brian, to teach him a lesson. As he himself had been raped in the tombs of a Rikers VCVC Prison Barge in the East River. Yrko had been violated by six men on that awful boat. A lesson he decided to pass along to Brian. Brian, surprisingly, fought back. Yrko lost his temper and broke his neck.

It was four days before Brian's sixteenth birthday.

His father—had he lived—would've been fifteen.

His mother, having lost her entire family to forces unknown, upped her daily consumption of Xanax and wine and was soon another of the city's walking dead.

43

DONNER

We were smuggled out of the temple in a polycomposite crate built to ship dark matter. If anyone looked close enough, they'd see EMD holostickers plastered across the sides. Which was ludicrous, because if someone was looking close enough to verify approval by the Exotic Materials Directorate, they'd almost certainly be wondering why an Ender Temple would need enough juice to power a suborbital. But the box was the right length and shape, so that's what we used.

To me, it was just another coffin.

Dark matter had the helpful characteristic of being almost undetectable. Which gave the delivery driver an excellent excuse when checkpoint scanners couldn't get an accurate image of a crate's contents. And, my God, you couldn't *open* the crates, man! You wanna contaminate the neighborhood? So the only thing the Surazal rent-a-cops could do was check the forged ID and motion us on with irritated jerks of the head. It worked well for the Cadre's little underground railroad. It would keep working until some security ace cross-referenced shipments and discovered that this little church shuffled around twenty times more dark matter than existed on the planet.

I hated taking this risk, but we didn't have much choice. Maggie had been unable to convince Jakob to come to us, and it was dangerous to talk by uplink. So here we were, en route to his place disguised as exotic electrons.

Maggie's heart rested on my belly. My mind drifted back to the extraordinary sensations of being "inside" her in that lab hallway: the half-coalescent awareness of thoughts and feelings. The intimacy stirred a chiaroscuro of fear and comfort. I knew two things: I'd never be able to tolerate so complete a fusion again. And I would forever be smaller and more alone without it.

As I was ruminating on this, Maggie materialized in the crate, half-wrapped around me, her leg thrown across my knees, her left arm resting on my chest, like lovers snuggling after an afternoon tryst. "Cozy," she said.

"Cramped." I tried to neutralize my face as I looked into those limpid epicanthic peepers.

"I had something important to tell you." She played with a button on my shirt.

"Something that couldn't wait until we got there?" I thought about slapping her hand away. For some reason I didn't.

"Nope, sorry."

She smiled. She had me trapped. Too close to even fidget. "What did you need to tell me?" I asked.

"Hmm. I forgot."

"Uh-huh."

"So. Whatcha thinking about?"

I hesitated. "Us," I said.

She stiffened a little. "Care to fill me in?"

"Wish I could, Mag. It's pretty confusing."

"Yeah," she sighed. I felt her breath on my cheek. Another mechanical illusion, to simulate humanity?

I drove the thought away. Down that path lay madness. She lay there, looking into my eyes, all pretense gone, and I suddenly wondered how long I was going to spin my wheels. Who's really ready for what happens next, anyway?

Her lips felt the way I knew they would. I crushed her to me, savoring her warmth, the softness of her skin. She was as real as anyone could ever want. I heard her moan against my mouth.

"Everything okay back there?" said the driver over the intercom. "The temperature just jumped five degrees in your box."

Maggie pulled back, her face flushed. "Watch the road."

▼▼

"You're being emotional," Jakob said.

Maggie's face fell.

A mentor was the closest thing to a parent that a smarty had. Because of their rapid maturation, the relationship usually only lasted six to eight months. But Jakob had maintained a fatherly interest in Maggie. And Daddy had just found out his little cupcake was a radical. He wasn't taking the news well.

"The Cadre! Of all the groups to get involved with! You know our way," he said, his voice gruff and judgmental. "We don't get involved in human affairs."

"We're intimately involved in human affairs every single day."

"You know exactly what I mean."

He ran a hand through a tangle of graying, shoulder-length hair. Jakob had chosen the well-trod look of an Ivy League professor, a man too distracted by great thoughts to focus on his appearance. His jaw hid behind a thicket of beard. A cute pot belly jutted from his cardigan. I'd lay money on the fact that he'd been too preoccupied this morning to manifest matching socks.

The crinkled eyes that peered at us, however, were as unerring as the crosshairs of a plasma rifle. The man had undoubtedly vaporized many a protégé's rebuttal with that withering stare. The academic impression was further enhanced by his library. We were surrounded on all sides by books. Thousands of volumes, reaching to the ceiling, three stories of stories. Balconies and ladders provided access to the upper reaches. The overflow was stacked in piles across the floors, next to high-backed reading chairs, on broad oak tables or propped up on window ledges.

The sight and smell of leather and manuscript made me think of my father's paperbacks. He'd been voracious, tearing through three or four a week. It exasperated my mother because he absolutely refused to part with any of them. Good or bad, pulp escapism or highbrow masterwork, he kept every one. Who knows, maybe to him they were evidence that he had something more going on upstairs than the average civil servant. But up and up they piled, despite my mom's regular fits of ranting, until they filled our little

Brooklyn home.

Until that day. The day when the world caved in. The day I got my first glimpse of the obsidian void that lurks beneath the sunlight.

"A smarty anarchist," Jakob proclaimed, bringing me back to them.

"I'm not an anarchist, and you know it," she objected. "There's a difference."

"Not to *them*," he said, pointing to the world beyond his library. "All they see is black and white. Order and chaos, fear and security. There are no distinctions beyond that anymore."

"Exactly!" she said. "That's how they get away with it! Remind us how scary and complex the world can be! Intone our need for security! When the latest revelations about corruption or torture or surveillance surfaces, replay the Footage, trot out the Horrible Images! Watch the critics subside into grumbles. They can't *afford* to have a backbone, not against all that empty patriotism!"

"Our existence depends on our neutrality," he said. "Who are you to risk that?"

"Who do I have to be, Jakob?" she said. "I won't be paralyzed by the fear of some terrible, hypothetical future. The present is terrible enough."

He threw his hands in the air and turned away. There was a moment where we listened to the metronomic ticks of a case clock in the corner.

Maggie looked heartbroken. But her eyes still held their mettle. Elise had possessed that same resoluteness of will...

Elise...

All at once I was struggling to control surges of guilt that were like trumpet blasts in my head. I cleared my throat, testing the steadiness of my voice. "Can I ask a question?" I said. "Why the books? When you can get everything instantly on the Conch?"

He pivoted, his eyes lustrous with enthusiasm. His annoyance vanished. *Uh-oh.* I'd hit upon a pet topic.

"Instantly, yes. We're so efficient nowadays, aren't we? We get from one place to the next so quickly. Information is plucked from the ether, effortless and immediate. But what's the trade-off? Once, we had to walk. Many roads, many steps, many hills. It took more time and effort. Everything moved slower. But we passed homes and stores, said hello to the shop owners or people on their porches, inquired about their families. Noticed the new buds on the trees. Isn't that important information, too?"

I felt myself kindle to the man. I knew where Maggie got her rebellious streak. He was as much a misanthrope as she was.

"Once we had to read. I mean, really read. Oh, the Conch will give me the words to *Oliver Twist*. But would I see how the volume was bound? Which typeface the printer had carefully chosen? What about the way the previous owner had loved and cared for the book, or how she'd worn down the edges with frequent readings, or how she'd left a chocolate fingerprint right at the point when the Artful Dodger lifts the gentleman's pocketbook?" He picked up the nearest volume. "Would it really be the same if I didn't feel the weight of it in my hand, the smoothness of the paper? Oh, the glorious, smooth paper! Like the inside of a lover's thigh. And its weight—that, my boy, critical information! It conveys the labor that went into its creation. The effort of filling each page, word by word, thought by thought." His face beamed, his cheeks two shiny apples. He lifted a data pebble and rolled it around in his palm. "This piece of gravel contains the complete works of Shakespeare. Doesn't seem like much of an achievement."

"No, it doesn't," I murmured.

He smiled. "You're a reader, Mr. Donner!"

"Once," I said. "My job left little time."

"But you came from a family of readers?"

"My father, when he was alive. My parents were killed when I was nine." That brought a chorus of raised eyebrows. I cleared my throat. "Drunk driver. They were coming to see my basketball game. I was raised in foster care."

Shock reverberated from Maggie. Her expression said: *Why didn't you tell me?*

Jakob shook his head sadly. "Terrible, terrible," he said.

Their eyes were suddenly intrusive, trying to excavate my pain. I fired back an angry look, in default mode, using the mask-shield of rage I'd forged in all those foster homes. Until age sixteen, that is. When I'd bolted again and Children's Services, worn down, hadn't bothered to look for me anymore.

Bart's voice echoed in my head: "Do you know what it's like to lose all your landmarks in a day?" I knew. I knew the gray tension stitched through the fabric of the world. The dread that comes with the night. The noises that turn a child's young mind into a cornered animal.

"Were you… well-treated?" she asked.

I didn't answer. I counted to ten, willing my muscles to uncoil. Maggie and Jakob waited for me, as though they understood. Which they never could.

"Let's talk about the Lifetaker," was what I said.

"The Life—!" Jakob went ballistic. To Maggie: "Are you insane, to tell a human of this?"

"I had no choice, Jakob," she said stoically. "He's returned to Necropolis."

"Impossible!"

"It's true!"

"Even if it were, it would still not be for human ears!"

"We're beyond all that, goddamn it! He's killing Surazal scientists. Do you understand? He's raised the stakes, not us. His existence won't remain hidden much longer, no matter how desperately you desire it."

Jakob stroked his beard furiously, pacing. "He can't be back. Oh God!"

"Tell me what you know." I said.

The room thickened with his anxiety. "I was part of the group that… took action… when his crimes became known to us." If Jakob had been human, the beard would've come away in clumps.

"The banishment?" said Maggie.

"We couldn't destroy him. That would make us as bad as he was. So we changed him. We changed him so that he could not survive contact with sentient beings in any way. If he couldn't be near them, he couldn't destroy them."

"Including us?" asked Maggie. "Oh god, you banished him from smarties as well?"

"We feared he could pollute us somehow with his deviancy."

Outcast. Unclean. The smarty reaction hadn't been much different from humans. "How did you change him?" I asked.

"A fail-safe program in his core DNA. Proximity to another person would create a complete cascade failure," Jakob said. "His mind would fragment, he'd break down and die. To survive, he must remain alone. He cannot even communicate from a distance."

I saw Maggie shudder. Total isolation.

"He killed people!" said Jakob. "For the dark pleasure of it! He was an abomination!"

"Where was he banished to?" I asked.

"The Blasted Heath."

"The wasteland surrounding Necropolis," Maggie explained.

"I remember."

"A corny name, true," said Jakob. "Who would spot a reference to H. P. Lovecraft?"

"Or Shakespeare," I said. They looked at me. "*Macbeth.* 'Upon this blasted heath you stop our way.'"

"Where on earth did you find this man?" Jakob said to Maggie.

"I know."

"Extraordinary."

"I know."

"I'm right *here*," I said.

"Pretentious or not," said Jakob, "it captures the soulless quality of the place."

"What was that poem?" asked Maggie. "Remember? About the Lifetaker? The one you used to recite when I was a kid?"

Jakob nodded, and his eyes went distant.

"Upon the scorched and blasted heath
He stands his post of endless hate
A pallid stain of what's beneath
When Death lays claim to hope and fate.
His cloak of shimmer and of rain
Flows wild in the bleached-out skies
He howls his song of rage and pain
And chaos pours from out his eyes.
Alone he'll stand until you're dust
And laugh aloud at love's dark rot.
He'll watch the turn of worms and rust
For he is one whom Time knows not.
He needs no warmth, he needs no lair
For he is one whose power lies
In every creature's bleak despair
As chaos pours from out his eyes.
Love will rise, and so will fall
He'll gnaw its bones with sharpened teeth
And stand his post as Time claims all
Upon the scorched and blasted heath."

"Delightful," I said.

"He can't have returned," Jakob repeated. "It'd be suicide."

"He's found a way," said Maggie.

With that, Maggie unfolded the tale of the shiny shadow seen by herself and Sharon, and the murder of the scientists who worked on the Retrozine formulas. Jakob dropped weakly into one of the leather armchairs. Without his passion, he looked frail.

"How could this be?"

"More important is why," I said. "What's its agenda?"

Maggie gave me a sharp look. "Please don't say 'it.' Even if he is a monster, he's not an 'it'."

My patience was thin as spandex on a fat hooker. "Alright, why would *he* try to stop the drugs?"

No one had an answer. Jakob shuffled over to Maggie. He put his hands on her shoulders, patting a rhythm of comfort. "You were right to come to me with this. You've done the best you could." He turned to me. "I'll make inquiries. Perhaps someone has heard something. In the meantime, we need a way to track him. A daunting task."

"Why's that?" I asked.

"Well, Mr. Donner," said the old smarty, showing me his gray teeth, "how do you track a shadow?"

44

"JAKOB"

After Donner and Maggie left, Jakob paced for a while with his troubled thoughts, then finally gave up and returned to his vessel to rest and recharge.

It had listened in the shadows.

Now it moved to the far side of the library, to the carved wooden box that sat on a reading table. It lifted the mahogany lid and withdrew Jakob's heart. It rotated the silver orb in the lamp light as though trying to read a crystal ball.

Its eyes closed, and it absorbed everything. Its form changed in a twinkling.

"Thanks for the memories," it said.

And dropped the orb onto the floor, crushing it beneath his heel.

45

MCDERMOTT

The moon undulated beyond the Blister like a dissolving seltzer tablet. Outside the Church of the Holy Epicenter, newspaper skittered across the asphalt. An occasional vehicle hummed overhead on cooling morphinium, but for the most part, the area was as deserted as the Blasted Heath.

A rat scuttled out from a cluster of garbage cans with a prize: a gristly chicken bone. Halfway across the alley it froze, its whiskers twitching. It sensed a new, less empty kind of silence on the street. The rat abandoned its prize and bolted for cover, its tail rigid as a pencil.

It had seen something obscuring graffiti on a far patch of brick. A shadow on top of a shadow. The kind of thing that makes you rub your eyes to clear them, look again harder, then nervously dismiss it as a trick of the light.

It *was* a trick of the light, but it was also real. Real and not wanting to be seen.

The street went back to being dead.

Eventually, the darkness moved, and in its motion resolved into a shape. A human shape. The shape gestured with its hand, two abrupt downward thrusts of an upturned fist. Four more phantoms crept forward out of the gloom. They took equidistant positions around the Church's delivery doors, holding penumbral weapons.

The first shadow adjusted his optical mask, zooming to the shops across the street. He focused on an empty storefront window. Within, an Ender sentry was at his observation post. The shadow couldn't see his own man entering—the team's polymer body armor absorbed light and energy. So he waited for the signal that the sentry had been neutralized.

There. A discreet flash of green. They were go.

Bolt cutters appeared. The lock was cut. The shadows filed silently down into the Church basement, weapons tight against their chests.

The team found him huddled on his cot, his legs tucked under an Indian blanket.

No longer a shadow, McDermott put a hand over the man's mouth and woke him with a nudge from his weapon. The eyes came awake, then alive with panic. McDermott pulled his visor up. He wanted the man to know who he was. The eyes widened farther, the fear deepening into despair. All struggle seemed to have been sucked from the man's bones. The man whimpered and tried to scramble backwards, but there was nowhere to go except the cold stone wall behind him.

McDermott torched him.

Outside, a second team converged on the Transtar Deluxe. A second Cadre sentry slept within. Had he been awake and on duty like he was supposed to have been, things might have been different. But now it was too late. White lightning arced from their weapons. The vehicle shrieked as its frame superheated. It seemed to swell a moment, the atmosphere inside reaching the ignition point, then it erupted. The heat wave roiled out in all directions, catching wood and metal on fire. The sides of the buildings were instantly scorched. Chunks of cement rained down. The little rat, who'd hidden well, became a knot of roasted bones, a gristly prize for the next scavenger.

The men kept moving, their suits absorbing the energy that washed over them, no more hazardous than a summer breeze.

Sounds of battle came from within. The men's ear buds crackled with McDermott's voice: "Packages in place. Subjects are trapped in tunnel. All units, withdraw to primary. Repeat, withdraw to primary."

Within a minute, both squads were back out on the street.

Now, the sounds of explosions. First, muffled deep within the building, then a growing cadence of WHU-WHUMPS that culminated in the eruption of the church's face. Green flame billowed. Blacktop belched upward like a tar bubble, then collapsed in on itself. The loading doors were blasted from their moorings, cartwheeling across the street and through the storefront window. A homeless woman who'd gone unnoticed beneath her newspapers began screaming, her hair on fire.

Then it was over.

Of the Church of the Holy Epicenter, formerly Maury's Deli, there was nothing left but rubble, steam and ash. The only sounds were distant car alarms and the hissing of cooling cement—and a few blocks further, the faint gurgle of the Hudson, which moved serene and uncaring about the violent actions of men.

McDermott stood in the street, the optical mask around his neck, his need for stealth gone. Moonlight glistened on his scar.

"Let's see him come back from that," he said.

46

DONNER

The lake is glassy and still. Our kayak slices through the water. It's overcast—it's been drizzling on and off all morning. To me, it's perfect.

"Look," says Elise, pointing skyward.

A bird wheels above, the only other living thing in sight, graceful on the air currents. It's a bird of prey. I can tell that much from the wingspan.

"Turkey vulture, maybe," Elise says.

It ignores us. We, the narrow human blemishes on an otherwise pristine landscape. It scans the waters in search of dinner.

Elise looks at me over her shoulder, throws me a wink. The weather's made a beautiful mess of her hair. It wreaths her cold-pinched cheeks like a corona. She laughs in abrupt delight, and it echoes across the lake.

I'm glad she talked me into coming. I'd balked at the idea of camping. To a city boy like me, the idea of pitching a tent under the stars with only a composting outhouse and a flashlight as my lifelines to civilization filled me with clichéd fears of becoming a mountain lion's lunch or a hillbilly's new boyfriend.

But Elise had proclaimed it the perfect time to escape Manhattan. The summer houses were all closed up, the RVs in storage. Campsites were closing, except for the few that catered to the lunatic fringe, the polar bear dippers and the Jeremiah Johnsons. Campers would be scarce.

As usual, she'd been right. Out of the eighteen primitive sites in Connecticut's Pachaug State Forest, maybe five were currently occupied. And all by serious campers—no stoned, boom-boxing teens or wailing infants. We'd enjoyed two days of almost eerie quiet, hiking, eating simple campfire food, and snuggling within our double-wide sleeping bag.

At night, with that perfect black around us, I could almost forget the unsolved cases that waited for me back home. The primeval silence could almost blot out the voices whispering for retribution.

Almost.

I'd bought a hip flask at the corner store before leaving. My first. I filled it with Dewer's. In the evenings, before the crackling fire, I'd slip some into my coffee—quietly, to avoid Elise's contracting face.

Somewhere my mind said, hey, buddy, hidden drinking. Not good. Then it said, hell, just a little fortification in the wilderness. What would a campfire be without whiskey?

On the lake, she says: Look. An island.

I peer over her shoulder. The island is small, maybe a couple thousand yards square, dense with scrub and small trees, perfectly framed by the water and the hills of pine beyond.

I marvel at how we can be the only ones here. We could be pioneers in a virginal America of two hundred years ago. The allure of a simple, rustic life pulls at me for a moment, but even as I enjoy it I know it's just a fantasy. The people of that time lived brutal, short lives. Things haven't changed much.

Elise wants to explore the island. I match her strokes as we approach, then hold my oar flat against the current, just as she taught me. The boat turns in the right direction and I feel absurdly proud of myself. Paul Donner, outdoorsman. We glide to the far side. Lily pads with tiny white flowers cluster in granite alcoves.

Hey, I say, let's claim it. We'll move here. Live off the land. Me Tarzan, you Jane.

If I remember right, Jane did the hut work while Tarzan was off having adventures.

Jane big spoil-sport.

She responds by rocking the kayak a little.

Hey!

Dread arcs up my back. I can't swim. I'd never have agreed to join her out here in this plastic lozenge without the life vest around my chest.

What? she says, mock-innocent, and rocks the boat some more. Water splashes over the edge, wetting my jeans.

Not funny. My voice is strangled. The thought of that gray liquid closing over my face…

Then she issues a little yelp from up front and the landscape tilts wildly and suddenly we ARE in the water, really in the water, the kayak on top of us, the ice-shock of the lake instantly piercing clothes and skin.

This isn't happening, I think crazily.

Help me push it off us, she says, but I'm more concerned with keeping my head above water. The icy water grabs at me, looking for ways in, and I sputter out a mouthful. The lilies have complicated roots below the surface, and my kicking feet are tangling in them. Panic shoots through me.

Paul, she says more urgently, we have to get the boat off us.

Okay, I say, and push hard on my end. It flips over, right side up again on the water. I clutch its side, grappling for the raised lip of the seat, looking for anything to hold onto.

Damn, we lost the oars, I hear her say beyond the thundering of my heart. Sure enough, they've floated beyond our reach.

Then she's next to me in the water, holding me.

It's okay, she says. You're doing okay. Let the vest do the work. Kick your legs a little.

That's what I AM doing, I reply, alarmed by the panic in my own voice. How do we get back in the boat?

We don't, she says.

She's right. Remounting the kayak would be impossible from the water. It'll be easier to just hang on and kick ourselves back to shore. I look at the shoreline, so far away, then back to her. She gives me a buoyant smile, but somewhere beneath, something else is going on.

Suddenly, I'm struck with the strangest thought.

Elise… you didn't capsize us on purpose, did you?

A laugh. Of course not. There was a rock.

I look deeper into her eyes for reassurance, but there's this passive-aggressive enjoyment of my panic bleeding from the corners of her face.

And now I'm aware of her arms around me, her hands on my chest, a moment before so supportive, now hovering too close to the Velcro straps of my life preserver. One tug and those straps will rip right open. I'll drop like a stone from within, down, down, into the black darkness, while the turkey vulture wheels above, watching me grow smaller and smaller until...

Elise's eyes are dark and shiny now, like a doll's eyes.

How long, she says, her breath misting over the water's surface, did you think I was going to wait for you to get your shit together?

I came out of one nightmare into another.

One of men dying.

A face loomed over me, an alien face of glass and plastic. It jerked backward as my eyes opened. The muzzle of a plasma rifled hurried around to point at my chest.

I grabbed the barrel out of instinct. We both froze. All he had to do was pull the trigger, but he didn't. He was green, surprised. It saved me. I torqued up out of my cot. My attacker struggled back to keep his rifle, which pulled me right to my feet. I twisted it in his hands. He cried out and it ripped free.

We stood like that, me in T-shirt and jeans, he in assault gear.

Small-arms fire rattled from the sanctuary above. Flashes of plasma strobed around the stairwell door. Splintering wood. Cursing. Screaming. Dying.

A raid. A Surazal raid, the worst of all worst-case scenarios.

My assailant grabbed for his sidearm. I fired point-blank at him. The shock wave drove him three feet back, down onto one knee. His suit glowed, managing somehow to absorb the energy. A neat trick. And bad news for me.

He cursed, smoke curling off him. He reached for his dropped pistol.

I jumped over the cot. My Beretta was on the milk crate I'd used as a bedside table. Before my assailant could sight his weapon I put three slugs into his chest. His body armor didn't absorb these nearly as well. He went down, permanently.

I popped the Beretta's clip, checked my rounds, snapped it back into place, and moved for the base of the stairs.

And hesitated.

Tactically, I was screwed. Running blind up those steps would be crazy without knowing what was beyond the door. But my only alternatives were to remain here and defend the room or retreat down the tunnel, past the power substation, to the other exit I knew existed.

I couldn't do either. Not while my friends were up there, fighting and dying.

It wasn't the first time I'd picked the crazy play.

I grabbed the extra clips from my milk crate, then gave the dead soldier another look. Maybe I could help my odds. I ripped off his cyberwear and wrestled the camo jacket on over my T-shirt. Shoved my feet into his largish boots. When I put the helmet on, voices crackled to life in my ear.

"Delta Foxtrot, check your nine!"

"Kitchen is clear." "Bathrooms are clear."

"Proceed to secondary targets."

I thought briefly about how, by sheltering me, Jonathan and his Enders had brought this down on themselves. Then I launched above into the house of God to do some killing.

The sanctuary was thick with the fog of phosphorous grenades. Forms moved through this blue-white landscape in crouched stances, tracking targets in their optics, firing controlled bursts. Most of the monks were already down, their bodies reduced to angular heaps. Some Cadre members had gotten to their weapons and were returning fire from behind overturned desks and pews. An eighteen-year-old kid who'd served me the best chili I'd ever tasted was torn in two when he raised himself too far over the barricade to fire.

Don't lose it. Tight, stay tight. Use the element of surprise.

A couple soldiers swung toward me, then turned back to their grisly work. My disguise was working. I scuttled over to the nearest heap of bodies. The first charred face I turned over was Jonathan's. His left eye was blue and full of wonder. His right eye was boiled in its socket.

I welcomed the fury, letting it cloak me, its icicles shattering my indecision and fear. I passed more bodies, the bodies of people I had eaten with, shared laughs with, made plans with…

Mourn them later.

I didn't bother to crouch. I moved steadily, sighting, firing. I dropped three, then four men. They all shared the same perplexed look as tiny holes in their armor spurted their life's blood. After my fifth, the voices in my head let me know they'd figured out that one of their own had gone rogue.

I leapt up to the main platform where Jonathan had held services. Behind the toppled lectern, there was an baptismal pool cut into the floor, framed by a thick oak balustrade. I threw myself behind it just as shots blasted past and set a row of drapes on fire. More plasma fire hit the balustrade, singing and cracking the thick wood. Miraculously, it held.

Someone moved in my peripherals. I turned too late. A leg lashed out, catching me in the face. I hit back hard, but a forearm like iron deflected the blow. Another leg swept me from my feet and I tumbled down into the empty baptismal. My gun clattered away down the drain. Knees came down hard on either side of my chest, pinning my arms. A rifle butt cracked me across the jaw. The pain was unholy, threatening to take me all the way to black. I heard a growl of murderous rage.

A familiar growl.

"Max!" I cried through blood. I tried to flip my visor up with furious shakes of my head. "It's Donner—don't cook me, pal!"

Max grunted in recognition. He slid off me. "Their body armor—"

"I know."

I snatched up my Beretta, saying a little prayer of thanks that the drain's grill had been in place. We heard more screams, more thuds as flesh hit the ground. Four or five soldiers fired from behind two doorframes leading into the main corridor.

"We can't win this," I said.

"Downstairs, the tunnel," Max said. "The hidden exit, past the substation."

Past the power juncture that Armitage had converted into his anachronistic little office, the Cadre had extended the original tunnel through to the next building, an accountant's office. It led to a hidden trap door in a utility closet. That meant going back to the basement. But the cellar door was fifteen feet across the sanctuary with nothing between it and us except folding chairs.

Max pointed to a ten-foot bureau that held racks of devotional candles. "Some of our people are behind that thing."

"Maggie?" I said.

"Don't know," he said. He put fingers in his mouth and whistled at them. "Firing cover, my direction," he barked to me. "I'll take the right door, you take the left."

We threw lead and plasma across the sanctuary at the hallway. The soldiers retreated. "Now!" Max screamed. I saw forms launch themselves out from behind the bureau into the mist.

A moment later, Maggie and Tippit were at our sides behind the balustrade. I was never so happy in my entire life.

"Hey," I said.

"Thank god," she breathed.

"Time to leave," I said. Max and I laid down a second volley of cover fire, forcing the soldiers back again. Then we all got up and ran for the basement door.

It was the longest four seconds of my life.

Maggie, Max and I went through the basement door, with Tippit pulling up the rear. I was allowing myself to be amazed that we'd made it out clean when Tippit caught one. His right side dissolved into a brilliant swarm of fireflies. Maggie froze as what remained of him dropped into the stairwell. She started screaming. I pushed her down the steps, slamming the door shut behind us. As I threw the door's pathetic little sliding bolt, I realized what I was doing and let out a hysterical laugh.

We had maybe two minutes. One for them to realize we weren't in the sanctuary anymore and another to tactically clear the room before coming after us.

I grabbed the dead soldier's plasma rifle and incinerated the staircase. In my headset, I could hear organizing commands. We ran to the metal cabinet that opened onto the tunnel.

There was a surreal sense of déjà vu as we ran that tunnel, the lights strobing on and off as they had during my first visit a millennia ago.

We reached Crandall's cell and paused. I pushed the door open with a finger.

He lay on his cot, fried to a crisp.

"Jesus," said Maggie.

"Someone's been down here already," said Max.

Which meant our exit was probably blown. But we couldn't go back.

"Oh no." Foreboding contorted Maggie's face. She pushed past us and ran pell-mell down the tunnel.

"Maggie!"

She disappeared into the substation. Max and I followed, but paused at the hatch as noises came from further down the tunnel. From the other exit, to the accountancy.

"There must be another squad, holding there, waiting for the sanctuary team to flush us toward them."

"Then our exit's blown. What about in here?" I motioned to the substation.

"This door's the only way in or out."

"Fuck!" So there it was. Cut off from both ends. Nothing to do but make a stand and take as many of the bastards with us as we could. We went through the hatch.

Time slowed as I saw it.

I wanted to turn my head, but for some reason it wouldn't cooperate.

Maggie had thrown herself across his lap, weeping. He sat at his cherry law desk, the unlit pipe still in his mouth, a half-smile on his face.

There was mayo on his tie.

Something wanted to tear free from me then. I beat it back, wouldn't let it loose. I needed the pain to get me through. I closed the hatch and Max ripped some metal bracketing from the wall. He wedged it through the handle, a pathetic finger in the dike, but something, at least. I crossed to Maggie and held her shoulders while she shook.

"Who?" she sobbed. "Who?"

I kicked over Armitage's desk. His chess board toppled and the little marble pieces scattered, the pawns running for the dark corners of the room. *Good for you. Let the kings fight their own fucking war.* I toppled the file cabinet as well and shoved it next to the desk, trying to create some kind of barricade.

"Donner," said Max quietly.

I pulled the Beretta and my spare clips from the jacket. "You're a better shot than me," I said, "so I'll take the plasma rifle. This is a Beretta 9 x 19 Parabellum caliber. Fifteen rounds." I popped the mag and showed him the action of the Brigadier slide.

"Donner," he said again.

"It's not over," I said.

He looked at our pathetic bulwark, but nodded.

I motioned again to the gun. "The rounds are Teflon-coated. They penetrate the body armor, so forget the head. Put them right into the chest."

"You sprayed your bullets with Teflon?"

"Modern gear is designed for energy weapons. It's not effective against lead."

"You were expecting a gunfight with soldiers?"

"It's a hard-knock life." I handed him the gun and turned to Maggie. "Time to go, Mag."

"Can't." She looked at Armitage's fried smartscreen. "My exit's blown, too."

I surveyed the room. "We'll hide your heart under the rubble. Once they're gone, you can rematerialize and get the hell out of here."

"No." Armitage's desk lamp made her tears shine like diamonds.

"Catch a plasma burst when you're fully formed, and it'll be over for good, Maggie," said Max. "Real death."

"I don't care."

"There's no other way!"

"I don't care."

"How admirable," came a sudden voice from behind us. It issued from the shadows of the relay junction, behind the frozen displays. We whirled, weapons raised.

Jakob stepped into the light. Maggie extended a shaking finger, beyond shock.

"What the fuck?" barked Max.

Maggie threw herself into Jakob's arms, before I could tell her to wait. Before I could I tell her it wasn't possible that this man could be here, now.

"How did you—?"

"There's another way out of this room," he said to us. He gestured to a steel pipe that ran from the wall to the junction box. It was maybe a meter in diameter, painted and galvanized.

"That's no good," said Max. "It's full of wiring."

"There's no time," said Jakob. He pointed to the walls, and for the first time we noticed small rectangles stuck to them at regular intervals. Rectangles with glowing red lights.

It didn't take a rocket scientist.

Max hissed. "FOX-7. The whole place is wired."

"That's why they haven't come in yet. They're just going to fall back outside and bring the whole place down on our heads."

"As I said, no time," said Jakob. He went to the conduit where it joined the box. He wrapped his frail academic's arms around the pipe. What the hell was he thinking?

"It's welded," I said. "You'll never—"

There was an agonized groan of metal as the weld tore. The pipe came away from the juncture in a shower of sparks, exposing the end, full of torn cables and wiring. Maggie was staring at Jakob like he'd sprouted an extra head.

"Old weld," muttered Max.

Jakob reached his gnarled hands within, wrapping his fingers around the wiring. I couldn't see past his blue cardigan. There was no way his tiny hands could get a grip on all that conduit, and besides, it would take a metric ton of force—

Then his back was rippling and he was pulling and there was a tremendous wrenching sound, and impossibly, long lengths of wiring and cables came free in his hands. He passed the bundle ends off to us, bucket-brigade style, and we dragged a good twenty feet's worth clear of the trunk line before we finally came to their jagged ends.

"Should be enough to get us through to the next juncture," said Jakob.

"Who are you?" I said. "You're sure as hell not Jakob."

He pulled idly at his beard. "I'm your only way out."

"You're the Lifetaker."

He merely looked at me.

Maggie, her voice thick as syrup, said, "What?"

"You killed Jakob. Impersonated him," I said.

"My price," he said.

"Price?"

"For saving your worthless lives. Now come with me, or die. I don't care which."

Maggie threw herself at him before we could even react. He caught her clawed hands and held them while she twisted and spat. I watched his resolution shimmer, watched him go shiny and transparent for a moment. Then he was Jakob again. Maggie seemed to run out of steam, sagging. He released her and she collapsed sobbing into my arms.

"Let's go," I said. "First we survive. The rest later."

"I can't do this," said Maggie.

"Maggie," said Max. "Your memory—of the lab, Crandall's interrogation, this raid. You have to survive so that you can upload it to the Conch. It's all we have left to fight them with." Max put a hand against her cheek. "Too many of my friends have died today," he said.

She blinked back the moisture in her eyes and turned them with pure hate to the Lifetaker.

"Alright," she said. "Lead on, you miserable piece of shit."

47

DONNER

The next few hours were a jumble of cement tunnels, dank air, stumbling and heavy breathing. The Lifetaker led us through the pipe into an empty chamber beyond. From there it was deeper into the bowels of the city and away from the battle.

We heard the church go. Down here, it sounded like the world ending. Maybe it was.

When the explosions faded, Max pulled me aside. "This thing killed the Surazal doctors! And Hector Alvarez! And *Jakob*!" he whispered. "Why the hell are we trusting it?"

"We don't trust it, Max," I replied. "We follow it."

"We should destroy it now!"

"You know how to get out of here, do you?"

The others walked back to us. "Is there a problem?" it asked.

"Where the fuck are you taking us?" said Max.

"Beyond the Blister."

"That's impossible. We're infectious!"

"You pose no risk to the world."

"You kill people for fun," barked Max. "We're supposed to take your word for it?"

The Lifetaker shimmered. "I shall scout the tunnel ahead. You have two minutes."

"Like hell," I said. "I want some answers. Now."

"Your questions will be answered, but not by me," it replied. "For now, your choice is to hold your miserable tongues and do what I say or I will kill you right here."

I had the feeling that this thing could do exactly what it said.

Maggie reddened. "Stop manifesting as Jakob."

Its face contorted into the rictus of a grin. "No. It causes you pain."

I wanted to knock that smirk off its synthetic mug. "We don't move until you drop the charade."

It sighed. And like the snap of a finger, Jakob was gone and the Lifetaker appeared in its true form. It undulated in the air like a floating oil slick, its shape vaguely human. Rough amalgams of eyes, nose and mouth flowed incompletely across its "head," but they were constantly changing, constantly in motion. Its "feet" brushed the surface of the ground without touching it. The thing moved with an obscene ripple that raised my hackles and churned a wave of nausea in my gut. I had never seen anything so completely *wrong*. In the dim tunnel, it was truly monstrous.

"Two minutes," it said, its voice no longer close to human. It moved off down the tunnel.

Maggie whirled to me, her eyes wild. "Kill him, Donner! We'll take our chances!"

For some reason, in a day filled with horrors, her sudden bloodthirstiness hurt the worst. I'd come to rely on Maggie's pacifism to balance my ever-present desire to lash out in rage. What an ironic symbol of this counterclockwise world—that an artificial person should become the anchor for my humanity.

"Armitage, Jonathan... they're gone," I said. "We won't last ten minutes out there with Nicole's patrols and biometric wasps. This thing is our only chance right now. Besides, we need to get some questions answered. The thing has as much as admitted that it's only helping us because it's under orders. I very much want to find out whose orders those are."

"You really think we can leave Necropolis?" asked Max. "Safely?"

I rubbed sweat from my eyes. "Crandall said we could leave Necropolis too, remember?"

Max cracked his walnut-sized knuckles. They sounded like gunshots in the tunnel. "Big risk to take with the whole world," he said. "You wanna carry that freight?"

"Screw the world," I said.

"Donner!" Maggie gasped.

"The Shift virus isn't a weapon of mass destruction. It doesn't *kill anything*. Worst case scenario, more dead people come back. The world's precious status quo gets upset again. You know what? Maybe it's time the world learned to live with it."

They were silent. The Lifetaker flowed back, solidifying into a six-foot amoeba. I could barely keep my eyes on it. It offended every animal instinct I had.

"Have we a verdict?"

"Yeah," I said. "Go fuck yourself. In the meantime, we'll keep following."

It seemed to find amusement in that.

We made our way uptown through a maze of auxiliary corridors and service tunnels. We kept a good distance from human activity. Occasionally I could hear the rumble of the subway, and once I caught the *dee-ding!* of its doors opening, but down here, with all the echoes, it could have been three feet or a million miles away.

At a junction, the Lifetaker produced some flashlights from a cached bag. We used the beams to explore our subterranean surroundings. The corridors were narrow and utilitarian, empty except for the mesh-covered corpses of light bulbs or rusted metal drains. Water trickled past our feet, carrying the occasional candy wrapper or soda can. On the street this morning, the wind had blown fresh and cold, but down here it tasted stagnant and worn out. My face was caked with grime. I was coated with cobwebs, crushed insects and worse, but there was nothing clean with which I could wipe my face. My T-shirt had been a hand-me-down from Armitage. I could smell his pipe on it. It made me want to scream.

By the time we'd covered three or four miles, my arms were quivering. The shakes. A massive amount of adrenaline had dumped into my system during the fight, and now I was paying for it.

I was getting flashes from the battle—little mental instant replays. Dead monks, limbs askew. Jonathan, who'd nursed me from the brink of madness with saint-like patience. Armitage, light leaking through his eyes from the hole in the back of his head. My mind was trying to process what had happened. I couldn't let it. As long as my emotions stayed in deep freeze, I could function. But when they started to thaw, things would get bad. Real bad.

Minutes later we hit a dead end. The tunnel simply ended in a blank wall of cement.

"Uh…" said Max.

The Lifetaker pointed to a jagged crack at its base. Water and time had fissured open a hole. It was maybe just big enough for a body to squeeze through. Maybe.

"You want us to crawl through *that*?" asked Max.

The Lifetaker slipped into it like grease poured down a drain, but sideways.

"Nice to have a choice," Max mumbled.

I gripped my flashlight in my teeth and wriggled into the adit. Using my elbows, I pushed deeper, measuring progress in inches, straining with my toes against the sides, working hard to focus on moving forward and not on what would happen if I got wedged in this spelunker's nightmare.

Max grunted behind me, having more trouble with his Grand Canyon shoulders. At one point he sounded stuck, but a mighty thrust cleared him. It brought a shower of dirt down on us.

"Careful, buddy," I said. "Suck it up."

"Too many goddamned slices," he grumbled. I smiled, wondering if anybody but a New Yorker would know he was talking about pizza.

Finally we were clear, standing on a ledge of some sort. Maggie half-crawled, half-flowed out of the hole beside us. I pushed away how similar her movement was to the Lifetaker's.

"What," breathed Max, "the hell is this?"

The space that stretched before us was more like the interior of an aircraft hangar than a tunnel—an enormous steel and concrete superstructure around a pair of railroad tracks. It had to be seventy feet wide and thirty feet high. I looked down, and realized that we were standing on the top of a cement wall that dropped another ten feet down to the gravel of the track bed.

Here, there was no noise at all. Only sepulchral silence. The feeling of having stepped into some ancient catacomb was overwhelming.

"What is this place?" whispered Maggie.

"Riverside Park Tunnel," said the Lifetaker.

Recognition in Max's eyes. "The Mole People Tunnel!"

I turned to him. "The what?"

"I read about this place," he said. "It started as part of Vanderbilt's New York Railroad in the 1850s," he said. "Runs north-south along the Hudson, along the West Side Highway and under Riverside Park from around 72nd to up in Harlem somewhere."

"123rd Street," said the Lifetaker.

"New Yorkers hated the tracks… they were ugly, plus they blocked access to the river, so in the 1930s they were encased in cement and the park landscaped around it. Can you believe it? That ceiling up there is the floor of a pedestrian plaza."

I tried to imagine people walking their dogs and playing Frisbee over our heads.

"There was actually a thriving homeless community down here. The Mole People."

"I thought that was a myth," said Maggie.

"This place is full of utility rooms, sheds and recessed nooks that got turned into homes."

I thought of H.G. Wells' *The Time Machine*. The Eloi and the Morlocks. The above and below people. Stockbrokers making million-dollar deals on their cell phones during a morning stroll in the park, while down here these people ate dumpster food.

"Most of 'em got kicked out when Amtrak started using the tracks again in the early '90s."

"Looks abandoned now."

"Since the Blister, no more trains across the Harlem River."

"No wonder my legs are killing me," I said. "We've gone over ninety blocks."

"More," said Max. "It sure as hell hasn't been a straight route."

The Lifetaker flowed down to the track bed. Max squatted on his haunches and found a handful of broken cables bolted into the cement. He gave them a couple hearty tugs. "Bombs away." He swung over the edge and lowered himself to the ground with surprising agility. Maggie and I followed, hitting the gravel with streaks of rust on our hands.

A few dozen feet down the tracks we again stopped in astonishment. The space had become an art gallery. Twenty foot murals burst dazzling color under our flashlight beams. Recreations of famous art were rendered with incredible skill, like a ten-foot tall Mona Lisa and a melting Salvador Dali clock. Further down, there were newer works by another artist, trying to emulate the earlier master. Sad faces with golden eyes. Reborns.

"Unbelievable," said Maggie. "After all these years, they're mostly intact."

"The taggers leave them alone, out of respect."

"If the art appreciation class is over," said the Lifetaker, "may we continue?"

Max gave him half a peace sign. On we went.

"Look at this," Maggie said. Stone pillars cut in the sides had created niches and galleries. Inside one of them was a cot, a battered dresser, tattered paperbacks, a pile of clothing. Someone's living quarters.

All of it dust-free.

Our flashlights revealed more galleries, maybe dozens of similar rooms full of scavenged possessions. Well cared for. And finally, we came across a table loaded with food.

Bread. Fruit. Half a salami.

Max lowered his nose for a sniff. Fresh. His face reflected my own sudden foreboding. "Maybe we better pick up the pace."

But it was already too late.

They coalesced from the galleries, more than thirty of them, surrounding us. Their gold eyes shone with feral luminescence beneath dreadlocked white hair. Some had filed their teeth to points. Some had the young-old look of rapid youthing. They brandished shivs made from spikes and spoons.

Several of them fired torches, casting the scene in flutters of stark orange. They pushed closer. We'd instinctively formed a circle, our backs to each other. Max and I clicked off our safeties.

"Follow my lead," I whispered. "Don't fire until I do."

Max nodded grimly. Even with his plasma rifle, it would be Custer's last stand.

The Lifetaker spoke. "Which of you is Alexander?"

Hesitation. One of them stepped forward. He wore filth-encrusted jeans, a mesh vest and a canvas utility belt. The locks of his hair were porcupine quills. Nose and lips were laced with scars. "I am Alexander," the boy-man said.

"You know who I am," said the Lifetaker. "Why do you approach us this way?"

The gold eyes all riveted on Alexander. He drew himself up. "I claim these"—he pointed to us—"as spoils."

This evoked a barrage of chanting and *root-root-rooting* from the assembly, accompanied by waving fists and weapons. Maggie flinched as a soda can hit her shoulder. They wanted to tear us to pieces. The only thing that held them back was their obedience to Alexander.

I touched Max's arm. It was like granite. "Wait," I said.

"I won't go out like this," he said, his finger tightening on the trigger.

"Wait," I repeated.

The Lifetaker's face had become more human. There was something awful about a smile from a mouth with no lips. "Bold words. Your pack is strong, to have such a *sachem*." Alexander puffed up a little. "How sad that such boldness should be displayed now. When I could kill you all in the blink of an eye."

I watched the group's bravado waver in shock, then shatter. Lowered eyes, shuffling feet. They knew, alright. Without a doubt, they knew.

I knew that kind of terror as well. Once a child feels it, it's a tattoo he can never remove. The terror of trapped prey.

"These people are under my master's protection. You've been told this."

I felt Max's eyes flick toward me. Master?

"In return," it continued, "I have ceased to hunt you."

Jesus. They'd lived down here in the twilight like animals, listening to screams in the night as their friends were dragged away by this synthetic demon.

"You wish to return to the old ways? You would rather take these worthless trophies and suffer again?"

More shuffling, murmurs, a cry of outright despair. Alexander's defiant eyes had fallen. "No," he said. "We'll honor the pact."

The Lifetaker looked almost disappointed. "We need transportation and safe passage to the Heath."

Alexander summoned a lieutenant with a strange whistle. They conferred while the Lifetaker drifted to us. "It will take them an hour," he said. "They will bring you food and drink. You may rest."

We exchanged a look. Rest. Right...

◣◣

How can I describe the journey which followed? A journey that seemed designed to take me farther and farther from all references of the world I knew?

It's pitiable when a man learns exactly how much he relies on his environment to define himself. The million daily sonar pings that not only illuminate his place in the world, but his character. Coffee at Starbucks. Ping! Put off that big cleaning job. Ping! Take a pen from work, nobody'll notice. Ping! Let the old lady have the cab. Ping! Vote Republican. Ping! Vote Democrat. Ping! Earn that key to the executive washroom. Ping! Leave your wife. Ping! Take that drink. Ping!

Then, one day, the sonar goes out and returns indecipherable. Suddenly, there's nothing out there that you recognize. At first, you rally yourself. You remind yourself of all the things you are (or ought to be). Faithful husband, dutiful employee, helpful neighbor, whatever. But as those pulses keep going out and returning with unfamiliar shapes and unwelcome images, as the void deepens around you, your boundaries falter. Your once so well-defined framework softens, become permeable. For better or worse, you start having a lot of "did I just do that?" moments. Even your memory becomes suspect, because when you look back to your life, you begin to see that these new parts of yourself aren't really new at all. You just hadn't noticed them before. And the slippery sense of disorientation widens as you come to understand that you weren't really all that good a husband, or a very hardworking employee; you never even knew your neighbors. You come to understand that you saw yourself as you wanted to be, not as you were. All those sonar pings went out and came back filtered, *interpreted*, didn't they? Selectively designed to reinforce the fragile identity of a fictional man.

And when those things are removed, when only the emptiness calls back from your shouts, when you tremble and stumble and wonder whether your hand still exists if you can't see it in front of your face, when you can't color inside the lines anymore because your edges have melted to smudges, when your past is a bruise and your future a burning coal, you are not only faced with a crisis but with a fresh chance.

A fresh choice.

Did I ever expect to be in the back of a cart, resting on a bed of straw, next to an artificial woman I might be in love with? Did I think I'd ever be pulled by a sway-back horse through a tunnel *under* the Hudson River? Could I have predicted my reaction when we came above ground and turned, gasping, at the sight of the arching magnetic spine of the Blister over Manhattan in the distance? Or continued on through towns that were once called North Bergen and Secaucus but now were a desolate landscape of crumbling buildings and empty streets? Where nothing, not even weeds, grew?

I had been reborn twice. Each time, I'd clung violently to many false pieces of myself, even as they were torn away.

The first time I'd come back, I'd tried to play Philip Marlowe in their little retro fantasy world, because I needed a place to fit in, a new identity. The second time, I'd turned into some kind of half-assed Che Guevara. Neither role suited me.

The source of my rage had seemed obvious. A family had been taken from me, a wife, a life. But the suspicion grew, as we ferried across the Hackensack on a pontoon barge made of planks and plastic barrels, that perhaps it rose not so much from my lost life as from my lost illusions. Perhaps denial had been my most jealously-guarded possession.

But it, like everything else, had been stripped away.

I had not been a good husband. I was an alcoholic. I had not become a detective to serve justice. I had put those people behind bars to hurt them, as revenge for a crushed childhood.

My wife had come second to this vendetta, something it had not taken her long to figure out. I had given her a home, but I had not given her myself. The innermost parts of myself I had withheld. How could I not? They had been wrapped in chains of terror.

We passed beneath a highway interchange, broad loops of road that curled back on themselves into knots of cement. The upper levels had collapsed. It looked like a Roman ruin, a thousand year-old Ozymandian toe-tag for some dead civilization.

Beyond, where the Meadowlands Sports Complex had once stood, the ground became barren. Mile after mile of nothing, stretching to the horizon. Everything had been razed and cleared. Nothing, not so much as a broken bottle or a rusted fender. Nothing but fissured earth and bloated sky.

The Blasted Heath. Deliberate desolation.

The horse did not like this lifelessness. It stomped at the ground, its nostrils flaring.

"The animal will not cross into this place," said the Lifetaker. "We must walk."

"Walk to where?" said Max.

He got no reply. We climbed off the buckboard, flexed our stiff legs. Without a word, Alexander's man turned the buckboard around and head back for the city.

As we marched across the parched clay, I made a promise to myself. Whatever lay ahead, I would try to encounter it with more honesty than I had in the past. If I could accept the world for what it was and not what I wanted it to be, perhaps there was still a chance for me.

Whatever lay ahead, perhaps there was still a chance.

It started as a black blip on the horizon. A trick of the light, a mirage. As we got closer, it resolved itself into an impossible thing, just as I knew it would be.

"Welcome," said the Lifetaker, "to Arg-é Bam."

PART THREE:

UNICORN HUNT

Dead men are heavier than broken hearts.
—Raymond Chandler, *The Big Sleep*

48

DONNER

A fortress in New Jersey.

Well, I came back from the big one, so what did I know?

I turned and caught Max actually rubbing his eyes, sure he was viewing a mirage. I knew how he felt. It was a scene out of the *Arabian Nights*: the vast, cracked plain sweeping away from us, rising in the distance into a hillock on which rested the castle.

No, not a castle. A castle-city, with the keep forming the highest point, overlooking everything. Ancient. And so out of place that every time you looked away and then swung your eyes back to it, you expected it to be gone. But there it was, as real as—

As real as it gets, baby.

"You gonna explain this to us?" I asked the Lifetaker. Its reply was to continue forward across the dead ground. Max and Maggie pulled close. "What did he call it?" I asked.

"Arg-é Bam. Which is impossible," she said.

"Why?"

"Arg-é Bam was an ancient Persian citadel," said Maggie.

"Persian?" said Max. "As in Middle East?"

"Pre-Islamic Iran," said Maggie. "Supposed to have been built before 500 BC."

"What's it doing *here*?" asked Max.

"This has to be a re-creation. The real Arg-é Bam was destroyed by

281

an earthquake in 2003. Before its destruction it was the largest adobe structure in the world."

"Adobe?" said Max. "You mean clay?" He blinked at it again. "It's *miles* in diameter! You can't build a whole city out of clay... can you?"

Maggie narrowed her eyes in a way that told me a lecture was coming. "Anglo-centric Americans! Iranian architecture and urban planning go back ten thousand years. They were among the first to use mathematics, geometry and astronomy. In the Middle Ages, while your European forefathers were scratching in the mud with sticks, Persian empires had libraries and universities. Persian doctors performed brain surgery. They rediscovered the great works of the Greeks and Romans long before you had your Renaissance."

"Okay," I said. "We're arrogant bastards. That doesn't explain why a destroyed Iranian castle—"

"Citadel," said Maggie.

"—*citadel* is sitting where the Meadowlands used to be."

The Lifetaker shimmered in scorn. "Your questions will be answered in—"

"In time. Yeah, I got that the first time. Okay, I'll shut up and enjoy the scenery."

It took two more hours of walking to reach the base of the complex. Irrigation ditches ran past groves of evergreen palm and citrus trees.

"I thought nothing could grow out here," I said to Maggie.

"Nothing's supposed to. The ground was salted with an enzyme that suppresses organic growth. It's to keep anyone from living here if they somehow escape Necropolis. When the Blister's finished and reborn containment is 100%, they'll neutralize the enzyme and resettle the area."

"So what are date trees doing here?"

"You got me."

"Curiouser and curiouser," muttered Max, sounding disgusted. I knew how he felt. These bizarre sights filled me not with wonder but leaden resentment. Someone was playing a vast, arrogant game. I doubted the purpose was to make us squeal in childish delight.

We crossed over an empty moat. The entrance to Arg-é Bam was a narrow gatehouse at the top of an incline. We were panting by the time we reached its summit. As we stopped to catch our breath, we looked back. I still couldn't quite accept the miles of emptiness stretching away to the corpses of Jersey towns and industrial plants. Further still was the Blister. From here, it looked like a table of snow globes someone had taken a flamethrower to.

"Not much farther," said the Lifetaker.

"Thank God," whispered Max. "I'm out of gas."

I craned back to look at the walls in front of me. They had to be thirty feet high and were crenellated at the tops. The structure was rectangular, but unlike a European castle, its corners were rounded. Even the battlements were rounded, with notches rising like little half-moons from the tops. Watch towers rose from each corner. Near their tops were holes for sentry watch or weapons fire.

We passed through an octagonal gatehouse into the main complex. As I passed, I noticed that the walls were five feet thick. Adobe nor not, it would take artillery to pierce that depth.

We stood in a vast bazaar. Twisting lanes ran off from the central space, with shops on each side. The buildings were brick and clay mortar. "This place is huge," I said.

The Lifetaker surprised me by speaking. "Two million square feet. It was a completely self-contained community—over 400 houses, from small hovels to mansions. Schools, shops, public baths, a gymnasium, a mosque, wells, gardens, cattle and sheep stalls. If the ruler was under siege, the gates could be closed and the inhabitants could live through a very lengthy isolation while they were defended by the sixty towers above." I guess even a Lifetaker could be proud of his home.

We twisted up a roofed lane. Our footfalls on the stone rang hollow and mocking. No one anywhere. Deserted. Our corridor exited into a columned plaza. At the far end, a building with arched windows sat hunkered down. It was topped with domes of ornamental masonry.

"The caravansary," said the Lifetaker. "An inn where caravans, traveling the Silk Road, could stable their animals."

"It's breathtaking," said Maggie.

The Lifetaker again gestured us forward. Halfway across the courtyard we were accosted by a delightfully cool breath of wind. It ruffled our clothing. "Oh, that's nice," sighed Maggie, lifting her hair off the back of her neck.

"It is the *badgir*."

"The whosit?"

"Special towers designed to catch the wind. The air passes over troughs of water to cool it and then funneled down into the inner buildings."

"Three thousand year-old air conditioning," mused Max.

The Lifetaker led us into the inn. The "lobby" area was filled with low couches and enormous silk pillows on the floor. Compared to the sand-colored outer areas, this room was an explosion of color: rich maroons, blues, aquamarine and yellows.

A corridor led us to two adjoining bedrooms. The rooms were divided by a beaded curtain and furnished with simple wooden pieces. The table held a water pitcher and a bowl of figs, dates and nuts.

"Refresh yourselves," said the Lifetaker. "There is a bathroom with modern plumbing down the hall. I will return at seven o'clock, when you will meet the Master of Arg-é Bam."

I gave him a pained look. "Please tell me we're not having dinner with Dracula."

"There is nothing supernatural about this place or its occupant, I assure you."

"Yeah, silly me," I said. "Besides, vampires are so Eastern Europe. This place is more suited to, what… ?" I looked pointedly at the Lifetaker's form. "Genies?"

"Donner…" said Maggie.

The Lifetaker cocked its head. "I have been called many things. Perhaps a *djinn* is most appropriate." With that, it flowed out the door and down the hall.

"Keep riding him," said Max. "He may just decide to ice you."

"He isn't allowed."

"Yet," said Max.

I blinked. "Good point."

"I'm taking the other room," he said. "You two have fun. But don't be loud. I plan to have a nice scrub, a couple pieces of fruit, and a nap."

"Don't be loud?" Maggie said. "What did he think we were going to do?"

I stared out the window. With their ornamental blue windows and geometric designs, the stables and barracks were the most elegant I'd ever seen. Had the main structure been the stable or the barracks? Who'd gotten the best housing? His men or his horses?

I grabbed the sill suddenly. Dizzy.

"You're dehydrated," said Maggie, rushing over with a cup of water. "Drink this."

"Just tired." It was the sweetest water I'd ever tasted.

"Exhausted," she corrected. "Fighting a battle and then walking over twenty miles… I can't believe you're still on your feet."

Maggie refilled my cup and I gulped it. Some splashed onto my hand. I looked at my wet fingers.

Maggie soaked a hand towel in the water. She tried to lay it over my face to cool me.

Water, water over my head…

"No!" I said, snatching the towel from my face.

Her hand on the Velcro straps of my life vest.

But that didn't really happen.

How long did you think I was going to wait for you to get your shit together?

"Donner? Hey, shamus."

I felt her hand on my arm. "What's wrong?" she said.

"What isn't wrong?"

"Donner."

I didn't answer until I had forced three deep breaths into me. "It's nothing. A nightmare I had about my wife."

Maggie sat on the edge of the bed. "What was she like?"

"Smart, beautiful, accomplished. And tough. To be a prosecutor in New York, you have to be."

"Sounds hard."

"We met about when I got my detective's shield. I was the hot young Turk on the force, you know. An up-and-comer."

She grinned. "I'd have loved to have seen you back then."

"One of the best records in the Division. They were grooming me for division head."

"Elise must've been proud."

My face started to get hot. "Oh, yeah, she…"

I realized I was clenching Maggie's hand. I dropped it.

"What?"

"All I cared about was putting bad guys behind bars. I sometimes did… unpopular things, wouldn't let go of things…"

"She didn't approve?" Maggie was silent. Waiting.

I looked at the ceiling. "Ever see that movie, *A Star Is Born*? That's what happened with us. When I met Elise, she was talented but insecure. I encouraged her to dream, backed her up, helped her see that she could believe in herself, to see what she could achieve. And she did it. But somehow, along the way, things… flipped. I was the one who needed support, I was getting more depressed, drinking more, blowing it, and she was rising higher…"

"Passing you by?"

"It's one of the most awful feelings in the world. She was patient for a long time. I thought she owed me for all the support I'd given her. Her point of view was more… practical."

"The nightmare, Donner?"

"Yeah?"

"What happened in it?"

I pulled her to me. "It was just a dream, angel. This is real."

"So I'm real, now?"

"Baby, you're the realest thing in my whole sad life."

She blinked those limpid eyes, misting. "Detective," she whispered, "that's the most beautiful thing anyone's ever said to me."

"Donner," Maggie whispered, "Donner."

Maggie's clothes melted away. Our bodies merged effortlessly. I was making love to a magical creature, more tangible than the firmest flesh yet liquid and flowing at the perfect moments. Her fingers pulled at the straining muscles of my back, her legs tightened around me and pulled me in deeper, grasping, breath washing past my ear.

"Oh my God," I heard her say, "Oh God."

Fireflies of thought swarmed through me again, as they had in the lab, her love and passion coaxing my synapses into song. This time I didn't fight it but welcomed her thoughts and let her have my deepest mind. We were inside each other, no way to tell where one left off and the other began, vibrating together, rising in a crescendo of wind and electricity. I tasted her sweat and felt her rising heat, moving with me in a precision beyond human yet with an animal need that was almost scary.

Then we were lost, igniting like phoenixes, consumed yet intact, dying yet reborn, fled to someplace else for a time, a blessed momentary reprieve from the terror of our lives.

She cried for a long time. In those moments, she'd seen inside me as far as I'd seen into her.

"In those foster homes. What they did to you..."

The thing I could never look at, that squirmed out of the corner of my vision, that hid behind my barricades. Somehow she'd made it possible to face.

"Yes," I said.

49

NICOLE

She upgraded Donner to a knight and put him back on the board. "It won't make any difference," she said to herself.

Her smartscreen beeped. "What?" she said.

The face of the woman who appeared was shrunken in anxiety. "Everything's ready. All the packages have been delivered."

"Keep worrying," said Nicole. "And those tiny wrinkles around your eyes will be gone in a week."

"You're not nervous? With what we're about to do?"

"No."

The woman shook her head, bit her bud-like mouth. "I'm not like you."

"Clearly." Nicole took a sip of wine. It was a Californian pinot noir that managed to astonish her every time with its oaky smoothness. She'd bought the winery. "How's the public handling the church incident?"

"Incident? Is that how you think of it? It was a massacre."

"Don't let your personal feelings intrude, sweetie." Whoops. The look on the woman's face told Nicole that she's been too glib with a sensitive subject. "Look, I understand. To go through losing someone twice… well, it's more than a person should have to handle."

"You could have warned me," the woman said, her voice trembling.

"To what end? What would you have done? Asked me to stop?"

The woman's eyes lowered in guilt. "I'm not sure."

"Which is why you are you and I am me," said Nicole. "Now quit sulking like a dumped schoolgirl and brief me on the President's visit."

50

DONNER

Beneath the Great Hall's vaulted ceiling, sunlight canted through spade-shaped windows, making the turquoise-tiled floor glow. Some of the tile patterns on the wall were maze-like; others embodied floral motifs. They were bordered by a broad band of calligraphy. It was an elegant, flowing script, as much art as language. I hoped the sentiments were as beautiful as their expression and not the Persian equivalent of "reborns in reborn cars only."

The Lifetaker ushered us past a series of seven tapestries. Each had to be thirteen, fourteen feet high and almost as wide.

I'd seen these before. At the Cloisters, that medieval monastery *cum* museum some bored rich guy had shipped from France and re-assembled in Washington Heights. Elise and I had gone one sunny Sunday and spent the whole day there.

The tapestries depicted a story about a unicorn hunt. Elise had called them a "medieval comic book," since each panel advanced the tale.

Now, somehow, they gave me the creeps.

At the far side of the room, silk pillows were laid out on a Kashan rug, covered in arabesques.

The Lifetaker pointed at Max and Maggie. "You two will remain here."

Max swelled. "Like hell."

"He will only see Donner, for now."

"It's okay." Max's face went into "Are you fucking kidding?" mode. "Fill you in when I get back." Maggie opened her mouth to protest. I closed her down with a look.

The Lifetaker motioned me up narrow stone steps to a final door.

I entered alone. I expected this new room to be more of the same—more palatial Arabian castle—but it was not.

It was a New York City bar.

▼▼

"What'll you have?"

I stared at the woman behind the bar. She'd been slicing lemons and limes. Now she was looking at me, waiting for my order.

It could've been any working class bar. Dark and low-slung. No pre-Islamic tiles, just curlicues of neon and cheap malt liquor mirrors. At the far end, past the row of two-seater tables, a jukebox blasted out Stevie Ray Vaughn. In the back, the room turned at a right angle like an upside down L. There was just enough space for a pool table. Back there the walls held more neon, all promising the same thing: hops-induced oblivion. In a recess off the tip of the L, signs in a rodeo font directed "stallions" and "fillies" to their respective stalls.

"Whiskey man, aren't you?"

The man was leaning on the pool table. There was a quarter laid on its rail, reserving it for another game. Which was a stitch, since the nearest pool players were far, far away.

The man smiled, the stick resting behind his neck, his forearms dangling over the ends. Waiting.

He was slim and not too old—thirty-five, maybe. Hair so black it had blue highlights, like Superman's in the comics. Taffy apple skin. The eyes were protuberant and enormous, their owlishness mitigated only by stunning speckled irises and the fact that they were currently brimming with relaxed amusement.

He wore a turtleneck of oxblood and cream—the thick kind that only beanpoles can pull off. Tan slacks and faun loafers with tassels completed the ensemble. The very model of a middle-class, middle-aged, Middle-Eastern man. Not what I'd expected. But then I'd begun to expect what I hadn't been expecting.

A throat cleared to starboard. The bartender was leaning on her palms, letting me know she was ready to get irritated.

"A Coke," I said.

Her ire congealed, but the man laughed. "You heard him."

He slid the stick off his shoulder blades and motioned me closer with it. When I approached he thrust his hand out at me, grinning like he was my new prowl car partner and not some impossible potentate who lived in an impossible citadel.

I took his hand, feeling like an idiot. He pumped it heartily.

"Izzy Struldbrug, how are ya," he said.

"Izzy," I said. "Short for Isodor. Adam and Nicole's father," I said. "You're the Master?"

He gave me my hand back. "I'm a little excited, I have to admit. I've waited a long time to meet you."

The bartender laid my Coke on the rail with a neat little napkin beneath it. She faded back to her fruit.

"Did you know Coke had cocaine in it until 1903?" Struldbrug said.

"Yeah," I said. "Everybody knows that."

"But did you know they still flavor it with coca leaves? There's only one plant authorized to grow them, right here in Jersey for the Coca-Cola Company. They claim they're 'spent,' of course. But in truth you can't process out the alkaloids completely. To this day, Coke still has minute traces of cocaine in it."

"No wonder it's so refreshing."

"It was originally sold as a patent medicine. They claimed it could cure morphine addiction, dyspepsia, neurasthenia, headaches, impotence…" He chuckled. "Back then, there was no FDA to make sure they couldn't lie."

"And no Department of Research Integrity," I said.

He grinned like he hadn't heard me. "Listen to me. Once a chemist, always a chemist. Just don't spill your Coke." He ran a reverential hand across the surface of the table. "It'd be hard to replace my billiard cloth out here."

"What is it?" I said, playing his game. "Felt?"

He gave me the look of benevolent patience reserved by experts for amateurs. "Bar tables are usually covered in a wool and nylon blend called baize. This is worsted wool. It's a napless weave. Gives the ball a little more speed. You a player, Mr. Donner?"

"I've dabbled. Mostly when drunk," I replied.

"Oh my. An honest one."

"Don't give me any medals yet."

"Get yourself a cue. We'll see what you're made of."

"I was mostly a rats and mice man."

"Sorry, no craps table. But I'll go easy on you."

I didn't move. "Is this for my benefit? This bar?"

He smiled. "Why on earth would you think that?"

"Doesn't match your castle."

His smile broadened. "I'm eclectic—sue me."

I went to the rack on the wall, stared at the cues.

"They're all good, Mr. Donner. Hard rock maple. Just grab one that strikes your fancy."

I did. He was at the other end of the table, racking the balls. "Eight-ball, American rules okay?" he said, sighting down the plastic triangle.

I'd reached my limit. "I didn't come here to play pool."

He carefully extricated the rack from around the balls. "I know that, Mr. Donner. You've waited a long time for answers. A few more minutes won't kill you." He straightened, twirling the rack on a finger. "And besides, if my banter gets too exasperating, you can always 'stick your roscoe in my mug and threaten to squirt metal if I don't spill.'"

I picked my cue back up. "I'll keep that in mind."

"Very good," he said. "You may break."

I had a nice solid break, sinking the nine in the right corner. I dispatched another couple stripes and was almost feeling confident when I used too much english and missed an easy bank with the fourteen.

"You're better than you let on," said Struldbrug, rousing from his stool to survey his options. "A relaxed stroke. And you know the physics. With practice, you'd be formidable."

"The story of my life."

He polished off the table with astonishing speed.

"Eight ball in left corner pocket, please," he said. He sunk it, leaving the cue ball spinning calmly on the lip of the pocket, to show his finesse. He pulled a quarter from his pocket. "Another?"

I curled my lips. "If that's what it takes."

He rolled those large eyes of his and grabbed the rack. "Alright, Mr. Donner, fire away."

I pulled a couple balls from the nearest pocket and rolled them at him. "You say you're Nicole's father, but you don't look a day over thirty."

"That's right. And I never will."

Okay, that stopped me dead.

Almost like it was orchestrated, the jukebox went silent. I looked back. The bartender had vanished. I swung back to Struldbrug. He smiled, waiting.

"You're a reborn," I said.

He shook his head.

I rotated the pool cue in my hands. Whatever this was, I didn't want it. I really didn't want it. "Then you're taking the Retrozine."

"C'mon, Mr. Donner," he said.

I'd gotten good at knowing when I was about to get blindsided. It wasn't exactly a premonition—more like when you're a boxer on the canvas and you see your opponent's shoulder drop and his weight shift, you know a right cross is coming.

I was about to get knocked out.

"The math's simple," he said. "You just won't accept it."

Connected, but not connected. An impossibly young father, an impossibly young daughter. Working on a fountain of youth drug, derived from mysterious DNA…

The jukebox lurched back into life, and Louie Armstrong started lying about what a wonderful world it was.

Connected, but not connected. Impossibly young, *before* there was Shift, *before* there was a drug to take. Before, and after.

Connected.

I watched the cue vibrate. An earthquake, out here?

But not connected.

It wasn't an earthquake. It was my hands.

"Sure you don't want something stronger?" he teased. "I've got some eighty-year old Scotch…"

"This place," I croaked.

"Arg-é Bam? I was feeling homesick. Of course, Persopolis was nice, too. Back then, I went by Achaemenes. It means, 'Friendly By Nature.'"

I sank onto the stool, my lungs shrink-wrapped in plastic.

"Do you know these revisionist historians are trying to say that Cyrus the Great, his son, *made up* Achaemenes? To legitimize his reign?"

I hitched in a breath. I sounded tubercular.

"Of course, I was Cyrus, too. Now I couldn't very well make myself up, could I?"

I dropped my head, worked on getting oxygen.

"I know," he said, "You're hung up by the Struldbrug thing. Your research said the family that founded Surazal were German Jews from Dresden. How could I be a Jew if I'm an Arab?" He leaned in to me, like he was being confidential. "Let me tell you something. It gets *boring* being one thing. Along the way, I've been Muslim, Jewish, Christian… even a Hindu for a while. That was fun. Their deities are so colorful."

"Immortal," I said. "You're immortal."

His eyebrows went up another notch.

"God," I said. "Jesus God."

"Take it easy," he said. "Have another Coke. Dottie!"

The bartender appeared, and he pointed at me. She cracked another can, poured, and then messily dropped in some ice cubes.

This was worse even than that first awful day when I saw my gold eyes and my white hair and they told me what had happened to the world. Where was Walter Winchell and his adenoidal rap to help me through? "Good evening, Mr. and Mrs. America and all you ships at sea—let's go to press! So you're sitting next to someone who'll never die. This reporter says: don't be a pantywaist!"

"Immortal," I said again.

"I prefer the term 'ageless.'" he said.

He took the stool next to me, still all casualness. Just two buddies talking. Dottie put a fresh Coke under a fresh napkin and went back to her holding position.

"Actually, there's no such thing. Accident, murder, suicide, severe physical trauma—poof. I've been very lucky. And very careful."

I couldn't get my mind around it. It was like looking up at the walls of the Grand Canyon after mule-riding to the bottom. All you got was all that looming oppressive rock. No big picture, just your vision crowded by immensity.

I said it again. "Immortal."

His brow darkened. "What are you, a parrot? Yes, immortal—

eternal, unceasing, perpetual, everlasting, imperishable, ceaseless, incorruptible, amaranthine—"

"Stop."

He went to the table and finished racking the balls. His break was like a thunderclap. He bowed his head for a couple seconds, marshalling himself.

"I apologize," he said. "For some reason, this always irritates me. The going into shock routine, the denial. Somehow it gets me more than outright disbelief. It's easier when they just think you're crazy."

Louie Armstrong finished "Wonderful World". They say when he came back, he refused to ever sing it again.

"How?" I said, trying to find the words. "I mean, this happened, uh, naturally?" I asked.

"If by natural, you mean without the aid of any outside force, yes. But I am the furthest thing from natural, Mr. Donner. I am a one-in-a-zillion freak. A creature so beyond the laws of probability, there has never been another like me."

"Gavin… Gavin told me about aging…"

"Ah, yes. All the different processes and events that combine to make immortality impossible. Programmed cell death, apoptosis. The Hayflick limit. Telomeres. Environmental damage. Each one of which would have to be accounted for, and corrected, in an ageless being."

I looked at his skin, his face, his hair. "And you—"

He shrugged. "Like I said, a fluke. A cosmic joke. The perfect collection of mutations, all at the same time, working together in perfect synchronicity. Infinite, faultless cell reproduction. Massive production of telomerase, which replenishes my telomeres. A unique internal antioxidant process. Blah blah blah. The result is a perfectly self-repairing organism." He smiled. "Although I do try to stay out of the sun."

"This is impossible, isn't it?"

"Nothing is impossible, Donner, only improbable. I am living proof of that statistical truth. In actuality, given enough time and enough couplings, enough re-shufflings of our genes, enough random mutations, an ageless human would have eventually happened a couple billion years down the pike. The weird thing is that it occurred so early in the history of our race. But here I stand, having arrived at the party far too early."

I must've started looking stunned again, because he said, "Oh no. Am I going to need to provide evidence to support my wild claim? Let's see, what can I pony up? Hmm. A Gutenberg Bible, signed by Gutenberg?" He mimed opening a book. "To Izzy; thanks for the printing press idea.'" He laughed.

"No," I said. "I believe you."

He seemed impressed. "And why is that, Mr. Donner?"

"It explains Nicole, all those years ago. She's like you."

"You haven't been listening. Another anomaly like me is as about likely as all the stars in the Universe going nova at the same time."

I ran a hand down my face, looked at the Coke. "I could use a cigarette."

A suede sports coat was slung over some chairs. He pulled a pack out from a pocket. "Menthol okay?"

A laugh burst out of me, too hard, the semi-hysterical kind. "You *smoke*?" I said.

"Why not?"

Why not, indeed?

He shook out a pair, fired both from a match and handed me one. "Tobacco's stale, sorry. I don't get deliveries often enough."

I blew a storm cloud over my head. "Nicole's mother—?"

"Normal."

"Then how—"

"Nicole inherited *some* of my traits, Mr. Donner. She's what you would call a hybrid. She and her brother Adam are unusually long-lived. They age, but very slowly. They will die. Eventually."

I flashed back to Crandall's interrogation. "The tissue samples that Nicole gave Crandall's team, back in the beginning—the ones with the strange DNA that they used to develop the Retrozine. Yours?"

"Hers."

"But your DNA—passed down to her—it's still the basis for Retrozine."

"Yes."

Something clicked in my head. The big question, finally answered. Now it seemed so obvious.

"Uh oh," he said. "I just saw a light bulb go off."

"We couldn't figure out who would kill Nicole's scientists to thwart her, yet would also kill Alvarez to protect her from me. Didn't make sense."

"But…"

"But a father would do something like that. Protecting her from others and herself at the same time."

He went back to the table. He sunk two balls and perfectly positioned the next shot. "My daughter sees these drugs as a means to unlimited power. But doling out immortality to the highest bidder is a very bad idea."

"Living forever's not all it's cracked up to be?"

He gave me a weary look. "Everyone thinks they know what it would be like," he said.

Two of my balls were in the way of his shot. If he struck his ball into a pocket with one of mine, it would be a fault. Struldbrug elevated the end of his stick to a severe angle, scoping down its shaft. "The Flying Dutchman, doomed to sail around the Cape of Good Hope forever. Tolkien, Borges, Swift, Rice. An immortal would grow weary of life. After centuries of living, life would become a burden. Everyone you knew and loved has faded and died, blah blah blah."

He struck the cue ball from this high angle. It reversed direction and swerved backwards around the obstruction to nudge his thirteen into the pocket. A trick shot, done perfunctorily and without fanfare.

"Mr. Donner, I've been alive for six thousand, four hundred and twenty-seven years. I've done pretty much everything a human being can do on this earth. I've been rich and I've been poor, a king and a slave. And I have never wanted to go on living more than I do right now, today. So let's dispense with the crap about what a curse immortality would be."

"Then why not share? Just don't want the other kids playing in your sandbox?"

He sunk the eight ball. Game over. "You think I prefer the charade? I do this for you. One immortal, weaving his way through the ages, keeping his nature hidden, does not disrupt humanity. But a hundred, a thousand, ten thousand of our most powerful and wealthy rulers, suddenly ageless?" He shook his head. "Do you think the masses would ever stand for it? For having to grow old and die, when their neighbor *doesn't*?" He went to the rack and put up his stick. "It would be anarchy, rioting in the streets. And if they did get what they wanted—if everyone received the gift, what then? Can this earth sustain nine billion immortals, with billions more on the way?"

"And that's the scenario Nicole is creating?"

Struldbrug took a leatherette tarp from a bureau. He threw an end at me and we worked to cover the table with it.

"Not intentionally, Mr. Donner. She sees the Retrozine as a means of control, for seizing greater power. She intends to very carefully dole it out. But it is too powerful a thing for anyone to control for very long."

"She's done okay so far," I said quietly. "I mean, creating and managing the Shift."

He smoothed the spruce-colored vinyl where it had bunched. His fingers were tapered and well cared for. Almost delicate.

"Or did *you* do that," I pressed, "before your 'retirement?'"

He turned and walked to the jukebox. I followed him across the room, pretending not to notice the bartender pretending not to watch us.

"I've engendered hundreds of offspring. I didn't tell a single one about my gift, always leaving before they noticed my agelessness. But Nicole and Adam were different. They were the first to inherit some of my longevity. I thought they would be stronger. Adam is a rock, but he is not very ambitious or imaginative, because he already has everything he could want. But Nicole... Nicole is uniquely... *unquiet.* The reservoir of hate that fuels her ambition is bottomless."

"She's nuts," I said.

He looked at me, startled. "Why, yes, she is, in a sense." He tapped the glass of the jukebox. "I made a mistake with Nicole. The children of famous people often crash and burn. How could they not, living in that kind of shadow? After all, it is the parent's job to eventually fade to the preeminence of the child, the new generation. But how can you, when you're a President or a Chairman or a billionaire or the discoverer of the cure for cancer? Some children, the strong ones, find their own identity and use the benefits of a powerful father to their advantage. But what if you're not smart or beautiful or talented? What if you're a movie star's kid and you can't act your way out of a wet paper bag? What if Dad won the Pulitzer for fiction and your prose sounds like the back of a cereal box? How could you not feel 'less than' and resent that?

"Nicole's hatred of this world has little to do with my parenting skills. Although I admit to failings there. It is simply because I am immortal and she is not. It doesn't matter to her that she has a gift shared by only one other person on the planet. It doesn't matter that

I handed her an empire and stepped aside into self-imposed exile so she could rise. All that matters to her is that she cannot supersede me, ever. She will die and I will remain. And there's not a thing I can do about it."

"You could die," I offered.

"Kill myself?" He chuckled. "One thing about immortality, Mr. Donner—it makes you selfish. Why should I die just so my daughter can brush a chip off her shoulder?"

"So she hates Daddy. What has she got against the rest of us?"

"Every time she looks at you, she is reminded that she has more in common, in her eventual death, with you, than with me."

"So creating the Shift—that was her revenge?"

"Is that what you think?"

Then I had him bent backwards over the jukebox, my Beretta in his mouth, my hand around his throat, before I even knew I was moving. He gagged around the metal. I pulled it from between his gums and pressed it against his right eye.

"I think an immortal might not like going through eternity blind."

The eyes narrowed in defiance. I cocked the hammer. They flew wide again.

I caught a liquid motion out of the corner of my vision. I stepped back as fast as possible, hands up, the gun dangling from my forefinger.

"Stop!" choked Struldbrug.

Dottie made it all the way over the bar and across the space in the time it took me to step back. She shimmered in homicidal rage a foot away. If I hadn't been ready for it, I'd be lying on the floor in smoking pieces. She lashed out, batting the pistol out from my hand. It was like slamming into dry ice, so cold it burned. My wrist was instantly on fire.

"I said, stop!"

Struldbrug righted himself, rubbing his throat, coughing.

Dottie/The Lifetaker just glared at me. "Smarter than you look," it said in that unholy voice.

"Real bartenders fill the glass with ice first, then pour the drink," I said. "So it doesn't splash."

"You're the expert," it sneered.

"That's enough," said Struldbrug. "Get him a bandage."

It hated that idea, but obeyed and flowed out of the room.

I sat at the nearest deuce, my face covered in sweat. "You need a shorter leash for your dog."

He took the other chair across from me. "He and I have a great deal in common. Both outcasts."

He picked up the box of matches from the table. The cover said "The Blue Rose." He rotated the box in his fingers.

"I *was* tired, Donner. Not ready to jump off a bridge tired, but I wanted a rest. I'd been Abel Struldbrug, then his son Abraham, then his son Isodor. When the twins came along, I welcomed the chance to turn over the company to them. I was sick of humanity. The endless repeating of the same mistakes. So I went back to my old haunts. Babylon. Mesopotamia."

He suddenly looked all of his six thousand years. It was something haggard in his expression, some sheen of age on his olive skin.

"The Shift," I insisted.

"Yes," he sighed. "Nicole caused it."

So there it was, at long last. Confirmation.

There was no feeling of pride at having the answer. No relief, no elation. Nothing but a knot of fear at the base of my spine.

"Containment protocols at the lab failed, she said. The retroviral agent escaped. When the Shift started, she seemed as horrified as we were. She promised us—Adam and me—that she would make it right."

"Necropolis? That's how she made it right?"

"She wasn't running things, then. A lot of decisions were made by a lot of people."

"She *fucking caused it*, Izzy! All this horror, it's her fault, because she was trying to develop her fucking Retrozine and get even with Daddy! She killed me and my wife *forty years ago* so nothing would slow her down!"

"I didn't know then, of course," he said mildly. "I was in Iran. When the Shift happened, I took it as a sign and came here, to this manmade desert, and rebuilt my beloved citadel. To continue my retirement, but be a little closer to Nicole, just in case."

"So you just watched from afar as she built her little magnetic gulag across the river."

"I don't expect you to understand being a parent," he sighed. "If you step in every time they make a mistake, how will they ever learn?"

I gaped.

"Then I discovered it hadn't been an accident after all."

I gaped harder. He walked over to the bar and ran a long finger over the wood. "She... she did it on purpose. She deliberately seeded the Shift virus all over the world."

I could feel myself not wanting to believe. It was too extreme, even for this world. I could buy Nicole exploiting an accident, creating a police state, murdering thousands... but deliberately unleashing it in the first place was beyond monstrous.

"Izzy..." I said, "That's like... that's like setting off a couple nukes in your backyard to see what the radiation would do."

Struldbrug knew as well. He was as unburdened by conscience as men come, but even he looked at his hands in shame. "She believes in the illusion of her control. You see... she's deliberately continuing its effects."

"What do you mean?"

"The Shift naturally dissipates over time. This concept of containing it within the Blister, this bill of goods that she sold to the world—it's a shell game. The Blister has nothing to do with containing it. The virus naturally disappeared everywhere else. She's still keeping it going artificially in Necropolis, regularly re-seeding the virus. The Blister is for an entirely different reason."

Elvis Costello came onto the juke box. "What's So Funny About Peace, Love and Understanding?" I felt like crying.

"You knew Nicole was deliberately continuing the Shift and you did nothing!"

"I am only one man, Mr. Donner. And Nicole had become very powerful indeed. Plus, there was a trade-off." He gestured to our surroundings. "How do you think this place goes undetected? How did I get the technology to create my little oasis, reverse the sterility in the ground? Nicole. I remained comfortable and alive, as long as *I didn't get involved.*"

He saw the disgust on my face and chuckled, unfazed.

"And the Lifetaker?" I asked.

"I found him out there wandering, half-insane. I took him in, undid his programming."

"And started killing the scientists to thwart her without being discovered."

"Yes."

"But you didn't kill her."

"That would make me a monster as well, to kill my own daughter."

"So what's changed? Why intercede, bring us here?"

"I now know Nicole's plans for the city. She's given me no choice. I have to stop her."

The Lifetaker was back with a bandage and a tube of burn ointment. It dropped them onto the table and roiled away.

I zeroed in on Struldbrug's buggy baby browns. "What does she have planned, Izzy?"

"It's madness. Beyond madness."

"Be a little more specific," I growled.

He sighed, and then he told me.

51

DONNER

"We have to go back to Necropolis," I said.

Maggie and Max both started yelling. It even startled the Lifetaker, who briefly lost cohesion and resembled a splattered tomato in mid-air. I gave them time to squawk, then held up my hands.

The sun was clouded behind the Blister. Standing on Bam's parapets, the pale conjoined geodesics suddenly looked like their name: a bubbling, festering wound on the skin of the earth, swelled with disease.

I put the device on the edge of the battlement and turned it on.

TRANS00\INTERCEPT\GEOSAT231\121754\PRIORITY05-32\CLASS5EYESONLY

WEBSQUIRT INTERCEPT AS FOLLOWS:

(NAMES AND OTHER IDENTIFYING INFORMATION HAVE BEEN DELETED PER NSA REG 1037459324)

1: McDermott.
2: Madame Struldbrug.
1: Are the preparations in order?
2: Two hundred thousand wasps have been loaded with aerosolized

Retrozine-C. They will be released during the Joining Ceremony.

1: What about the President's biofilter suit?

2: It will fail at precisely the right moment.

1: How long will it take?

2: Probably fifteen minutes or so for complete saturation of the atmosphere within the Blister. Then, five minutes or so for everyone to succumb.

1: The world will see the whole thing happen?

2: The human camera crews will die, but the AI drones will continue recording. The whole world will watch millions of people, norms and reborns alike, youthe into nothingness in front of their eyes.

1: What about your men?

2: They only know what I've told them.

1: And the Vice President in Washington? He's still on board?

2: As soon as he's sworn in as President, he will launch an investigation that will prove without doubt that the Cadre are responsible for the terrorism. You and I escaped because we were pursuing Cadre terrorists in the Blasted Heath at the time of the attack, so we miraculously survived. Your brother Adam will not be so lucky. The new President, as is his right, will appoint you Vice President in honor of your heroic service. The two of you will preside over the resettlement of New York, now that the Shift has been eradicated.

1: And if the President is a good boy, I may let him live forever.

(RECORDING IS INTERRUPTED AT THIS POINT.)

END END END END TRANS00\INTERCEPT\GEOSAT231\DATE END END END END

When it was done, for a long time there was only the rasp of wind in the throats of the *bagdir*.

Finally, Max bellowed, "That's fucking crazy! That's the craziest thing I ever heard!"

Maggie looked weak. "How could she think that would work?"

"How did Hitler think he could conquer a continent and exterminate an entire race? The reason tyrants keep getting away with it is because the rest of us think it's too crazy for anyone to actually try."

"Surely someone will object—"

"With the wasps doing most of the work, she'll have to tell a remarkably small group of people. And she's got no shortage of fanatics. She's been preparing them for years."

"It's beyond belief. She's tricked the whole world into building the Blister. And they don't know it's not to keep the Shift *out*, it's to keep the aerolized Retrozine *in*."

Maggie said, "Why hasn't Struldbrug warned his own son that he's about to be killed?"

"Nicole has Adam bugged. Struldbrug can't warn his son without tipping her off. The same logic goes for letting Washington know. Her spies and electronics are everywhere. If she knows she's been compromised, Nicole will just unleash the wasps early."

"Yeah, but—"

I cut her off. "Look, it doesn't matter! It's the hand we've been dealt! There's no time for why-didn't-he's and if-only's. This guy Struldbrug, I don't like him and I don't trust him, but I believe him. The rest doesn't mean squat until Nicole is stopped."

"Yeah, but why does it have to be *you*?" cried Maggie.

"Because it is what he was born to do," said Struldbrug, cresting the steps behind us.

He wore a jewel-encrusted turban. The ceremonial *madîl* was wound into an ellipsoid, like a fat Indian plum. The biggest solitaire diamond I'd ever seen was centered on his forehead. Beneath his flowing robes was a short-sleeved tunic with triangular notches at the sleeve. The robes were white linen brocaded with golden thread. A girdle sash held a curved scabbard and his hand rested lightly on its pommel. His draw-string pants billowed in the breeze, framing his strong legs.

Behold Achaemenes, founder of empires.

"What the hell does that mean?" asked Max.

"It means it is his destiny. Donner is the only one who can stop her. He is the only one who ever could."

The sapphires in his headdress caught the morning sun. They almost matched the smolder beneath his brow.

"It is the reason I brought him back from the dead in the first place."

52

DONNER

Struldbrug and I walked alone through the Great Hall. The place was too big. I felt like a bug waiting to be stepped on. We stopped at the first of the medieval tapestries.

"Do you like them?" he asked.

"I like the detail," I replied. "Why'd you steal them?"

He chuckled. "I merely reclaimed them. They were woven for me in Brussels, in 1495. As a wedding present." His face darkened. "A beautiful bride. She died of plague in 1510." He looked at my hair, my eyes. "Is it really so bad, Mr. Donner? Having a second chance at life?"

I lit one of the cigarettes he'd given me. Watched the smoke fan out in the light. "Maybe in a different place, a different time. I don't know." I blew twin plumes from my nose. "Did Crandall know about this final solution?"

"No. She has not trusted anyone except McDermott."

I squeezed the cigarette ember dead. Put the butt in my pocket. "I don't know. The way people can convince themselves that mass murder is righteous… Maybe this universe would be better off without us."

Struldbrug steepled his fingers. They were wrapped in rings of precious stones. "You don't really believe that."

I whirled on him. "Don't get too sure about what I believe! You

307

wanna tell yourself you're doing this to save those people, fine. But like everything you've done, it's to protect your own ass." I spit on his precious gold floor. His fingers curled into fists. "So you've made me your boy. I get to take your risks for you. Alright, I accept that, because—as my murdered partner used to say—the stakes call the play. But riddle time is over."

"What would you like to know?" he said tightly.

"What'd you mean about bringing me back?"

"You thought Nicole was kidnapping those people to stabilize her youthing drug, but in fact she was trying to perfect the 'unstable' version—Retrozine-C—an accelerated youthing drug that would kill in minutes. She wasn't trying to *stop* its effects. She was trying to *speed them up*."

"Yeah, I got that."

"Crandall perfected the original revival version of the drug—Retrozine A—many months ago. The Lifetaker stole the formula. I'm a chemist, remember? I synthesized a batch and sent the Lifetaker with it to Maple Grove Cemetery. October 31, to be exact. Halloween."

He must have seen my eyes ignite as I understood, because he took a step back. "Oh, Mr. Donner, you're not going to attack me again, are you?"

"It wasn't the Shift? You used the Retrozine to bring me back the first time?"

"Revivals don't occur outside the Blister anymore."

My skin felt so tight I thought my face would burst open. "Why? Why me? What is it—what is it you think I am?" The pain in my own voice was shocking. "I'm not special. I'm just a— Before I died, I was flushing my life down the toilet. Since I've been back, I haven't done much better."

"Yes," he said with bland gentleness. "My daughter had you murdered. One small wrong I could right. But the real reason is that I need you. You are particularly suited to help me."

"*Why?*"

Struldbrug turned back to the tapestries. "The unicorn's horn is a symbol of rejuvenation. In this first panel, the hunt begins. In the second, they come upon the unicorn dipping its horn into a poison stream, purifying it. In the third panel, they attack, and in the fourth, the unicorn defends itself. They fail, of course. The unicorn is elemental, untamable. He can't be defeated through conventional means."

I nodded, mind thundering, trying to follow him. We walked to the fifth panel. The unicorn was now sitting at the feet of a beautiful young woman.

"But he can be captured through deceit."

There was thrumming in my temples.

"He comes eagerly to the lap of a maid and surrenders his fierceness to her."

The maid had one arm raised. She seemed to be looking lovingly at the unicorn and yet also signaling the hunters to take him. She looked torn.

The look was familiar.

"She then gives him over to be slain. In the next panel, the unicorn's flesh is torn by spears."

All the warmth in my body was bleeding into the gold tiles of the floor. I started to shiver. What was happening to me?

"In the last panel, the unicorn is reborn in captivity."

My mouth opened. *Reborn in captivity—*

Something burst in my mind, a flash of insight, a door opening—

—bright slivers of memory—

"The tapestry is an allusion to marriage as an entrapment for the bridegroom."

The bodega.

—like the shards from a broken mirror—

Alvarez behind the counter, looking startled when I walk in.

"Men seek to benefit from the unicorn's death. When it cannot be killed, they attempt to contain it. What the maiden does not understand is that, although it can be temporarily lulled, its true nature will eventually reassert itself."

—a mirror, not shattering, but being once shattered, coming together again—

I see him recognize me—how can that be?

"For the unicorn is a warrior creature."

—whole but not whole—

My heart was beating itself apart. The dread was shaking me to pieces.

"*You* are the unicorn, Mr. Donner."

Alvarez tries to pull the piece from under the counter, but he's too slow. I've seen the panic in his eyes, I know something's wrong. My hand punches the gun away from him, and his eyes dart behind us—

—Behind us?—

—I turn, already too late, and see, a millisecond before the muzzle flash whites out my vision and the stink of cordite fills my nostrils. Thundering in my ears I hear the words from my nightmare, those acid words—

—I see—

—I see—

I sank to my knees then. I screamed at the sky, battered at the floor.

Struldbrug walked to the windows. When the worst of it had subsided, he returned. I looked at him through a haze of red.

"You remember, finally? You understand now?" he said.

I replied from the dark side of the moon, where there would never be light or warmth.

"Yes."

53

MAGGIE

That night they rode in a helicopter. Maggie could feel Donner's warmth through the flight suit, but his eyes were fixed on worlds beyond her scope.

After a shock, a man's hair can go white overnight. With reborns, it was no less extreme. Donner had dropped five years since he'd gone into that room with Struldbrug. The web of worry lines around his eyes and mouth—lines that had been her hachures and waymarks in a world whose topography was inconstant—were gone. Erased as simply as a sculptor smoothing over wet clay. He didn't look better now, just like an incomplete version of himself. Not refurbished. Unfinished.

Donner had endured what would have sent a yeoman to the loony bin or the bottom of the East River. And yet here he was, en route to Queens aboard Struldbrug's radar-invisible helicopter.

It wasn't fair!

There should be some elite government force flying in from Washington right now, men of Teflon and secret weapons. Not some feckless rush into the heart of darkness by an exhausted reeb and his smarty sidekick.

It defied reason, this trip. But Donner had thrown in with Struldbrug. And whatever he'd been told in that room, he'd come out of it blasted into youthfulness, baked young by horror. Just how much and in what ways, only time would tell.

If they had time.

Time, the betrayer.

Except for Struldbrug. Even smarties had lifespans. But not Struldbrug. She loathed him. He represented everything detestable in the human blueprint—vainglorious, selfish, myopically unable to take responsibility for his actions. He'd had *years* to stop Nicole. Yet here they were in a last-minute gambit that the retros would called "a mug's game."

Donner's forehead was pressed to the glass of the window, watching the landscape evaporate past at 180 miles per hour.

Wouldn't he ever be allowed to have a life? Wouldn't they ever be allowed to explore the rare thing that had risen between them?

The craft bucked against a thermal, bringing Maggie out of her ruminations.

They'd unloaded weapons and surveillance equipment to make room for themselves. It was cramped. Maggie could adjusted her physical parameters to compensate, but like a schoolgirl hiding a blemish from her boyfriend, she didn't want to remind Donner how alien she was. The Lifetaker had no such compunction. Disgusted at being this close to humans, he'd retreated to his orb. Thanks for small blessings.

Max was next to Struldbrug, in the copilot seat. He wore a matching helmet with VR display. Under different circumstances, she would have laughed. She doubted he'd ever been up in a helicopter in his life. But now he was quietly nodding as Struldbrug briefed him over their comm line, pointing out the displays, the night vision systems and infrared-jamming countermeasures.

He was looking pretty overwhelmed, so she decided to interrupt the avionics lesson.

"Would it be too much to ask why we're going to Queens?"

Struldbrug swiveled. The tinted glass of the VR display magnified his already-large eyes and Maggie had the sudden flash of a praying mantis. He hit a switch, globalizing his intercom.

"For her plan to work, Nicole needs to be outside the Blister, but still close by. So I monitored all Surazal's former property holdings in the Heath."

"Property?" said Max. "There's still property?"

"Only the outermost western and northern parts were razed. Anyone who might escape the Blister and flee east into Queens and Long Island has nowhere to go—they're surrounded by water. The shorelines are mined and patrolled. Even harder to cross than the western desert."

Maggie remembered the blasting. The obliterating of cities and roads and schools and factories. Scarsdale, Mt. Vernon, Jersey City, Staten Island... Endless bombing runs, the night banished by fireballs, the new rhythm of life become the muted thump of impacts. The generals couldn't quite mask their glee. They were allowed to use everything except nukes. It didn't matter that it was their own country. They were kids told they could smash all of mom's fine china and still have dessert, and that's exactly what they did.

"There was activity in only one place," said Struldbrug. "This mansion in Kew Gardens."

He flashed a holo map from a pen-like emitter.

Maggie startled. "That's right across the street from Maple Grove Cemetery."

"So?" asked Max.

"So Donner was buried there."

"Across the street from Nicole's property?" said Max. "That couldn't be a coincidence."

Struldbrug turned back to his displays, saying nothing.

Great. More cloak-and-dagger. "What's at this mansion?"

"Nicole has constructed a computer center there, transferred her command structure. The only possible reason is that she will conduct the attack from that location."

"The wasps will be controlled from there?" asked Max.

"Yes."

"So, destroy the computer, stop the attack."

"It's not that simple. This isn't an ordinary mansion."

"Of course not," said Maggie.

Struldbrug ignored her sarcasm. "During the Cold War, it was transported from Baltimore, much as the Cloisters were, stone by stone, by a munitions manufacturer. It is much older than the town. The residents thought it was a vanity project for a millionaire, but actually the relocation effort masked the construction of a secret military communications center. It's got an underground bunker hardened against nuclear attack. If New York Command thought the city was about to be hit, this was one of the places they could evacuate their top brass to and ride out the attack."

"Lovely," Maggie sighed. "So do we have any mansion-bunker-busters on this crate?"

"Negative," said the Lifetaker, from his ball.

"Jesus!" cried Max, startled at the disembodied voice.

The Lifetaker's voice floated up from its orb. "The RAH-99 carries seven Hellfire anti-tank missiles, fourteen Stinger anti-aircraft missiles, twenty-three Hydra air-to-ground rockets, and an XM301 twenty-millimeter cannon."

Struldbrug said, "No, we can't penetrate the bunker. Our purpose is to get Donner as close as possible to Nicole's position, and that's it."

Maggie wanted to say, *but that's insane!* but she bit her tongue. Donner had signed off on the plan, even if he was now brooding out the window. "How?" she finally managed. "Nicole's going to have the place defended."

"Yes," said Struldbrug. He gestured to the helo's interior with a gloved hand. "Hence the Comanche."

"RAH-99 Comanche Reconnaissance/Attack Helicopter," said the Lifetaker.

"A second-stage prototype of the RAH-66," said Struldbrug, "developed by Boeing and Sikorsky for the US Army. The order for the helicopters was discontinued in 2004, reinstated in 2009, and cancelled again a year later."

"They couldn't decide whether they wanted it or not?"

"They wanted it, alright," said Struldbrug. "They couldn't afford it after invading Iraq broke the bank."

"We're in a forty-year old helicopter?" asked Max, glancing around the cockpit.

"Its age is precisely why we'll get in undetected. McDermott's defense grid is set to detect modern stealth craft, which are based on an entirely different technology."

"So it'll get us close without being detected."

"Close enough."

"Then Donner goes in and blows the computer mainframe."

"No," said Struldbrug. "He has no chance of doing that."

"Then what the fuck!" said Max.

Struldbrug clicked his holo pen and beamed another image into the air in front of them. The image was of a simple aluminum tube with a cap. "Nicole has a remote control on her person." In the animation, the cap swung back, revealing a single red button. "It's the only way the wasps can be activated."

"Wait a minute. That little button is the only possible way to launch the Retrozine-C? That's so…James Bond."

He looked grim. "She always did have a sense of the dramatic. Along with a healthy dose of paranoia."

"No one else can do it in case she's taken out?"

"No."

"So destroy the remote, and you stop the attack."

"No. Nicole may be a control freak, but she's not stupid. Should the remote be destroyed or its signal interrupted, the attack will be triggered automatically. Donner must separate the remote from Nicole so that she cannot press the button."

"And exactly how is he going to do that?"

"Ask him." Struldbrug nodded toward Donner, then swiveled and took the craft back to manual.

Ask him.

But she couldn't ask him. Because things had changed. *He* had changed, in that room. All illusion had been burned out of Donner. He had a job to do. It didn't matter to him if he got killed doing it. He was beyond self-preservation now, beyond revenge, even beyond his own heartbreak. Her job was to help him.

She'd grieve later.

54

DONNER

We came in low and quiet. Struldbrug was remarkably agile with the helo. He hovered over a fire-destroyed house, and we rappelled from its belly through a carbonized cross-hatch of timber into the open foundations of the basement. Then he was arcing off back to Necropolis for his part of the mission.

In the cellar, water nipped at our ankles, swamp-thick with rot and debris. It was so foul I had to will myself not to retch.

I tapped my headset and the three of us brought our VR online. The setup was much cruder than the wetwiring in our opposition. Nicole's soldiers didn't need cyberwear, not with their Nike corneas and the quantum nanolace spiderwebbed through their brains. Their combat programming and cybernetic enhancement could almost double their speed, agility and reaction time.

Maggie and the Lifetaker could match their abilities naturally. Max and I, on the other hand, were running on Workahol. Jazz juice, as it was known on the street. It wasn't popular with the junkies or steroiders because the downside was too steep, even for them. It boosted adrenaline and endorphin production to an insane level. We'd be fast, clearheaded and pain-resistant for hours. After that came the crash and complete agony for days.

I hoped we lived long enough to experience it.

Struldbrug had been reluctant to give me the drug. My reborn metabolism might process it differently, he said. But after the fire-fight in the church and the trek here, I was already on my last legs. No way I could go into this without major help. So far, it worked fine.

"Keep an eye out for rats," I said.

We waded through the muck to a set of cement steps that were crumbling around their rebar skeleton.

Kew Gardens. Maybe half the buildings were intact. Many had been looted and burned during the forced resettlement. Others had simply caved in under time's weight.

Maggie had been right about permanence. It was an illusion—a psychic bulwark against the entropy that was always behind the scenes, patiently pressing, probing, working new cracks, bleeding through as relentlessly as a cockroach.

We had three blocks to cover on foot.

We stayed tight against the sides of buildings. Our smartskins adjusted their camo scheme every millisecond to match our surroundings. They were pretty astonishing in their accuracy. Had Max's GPS blip not been flashing in my VR, I might not have even known he was there.

Getting in undetected would be the easy part, though.

We were betting everything on how I'd perform.

These weren't the snow-shrouded December streets I'd grown up with. The temperature was above freezing, even this late. If those clouds overhead congealed, we'd be treated to nasty cold rain.

We moved single file through Kew Gardens' commercial district. The faux-Tudor buildings would've been quaint if not for the rusted fire escapes plastered across their faces. Add the garish, primary-colored awnings that crested the nail emporiums, chicken shacks and bail bondsmen, and this community neatly homogenized itself into the rest of Queens.

The Gardens had started in the 1900s as a Greenwich Village wannabe, attracting artists like George Gershwin, Dorothy Parker and Charlie Chaplin. But it didn't lived up to its bohemian infancy. In the 1960s it had been home to Kitty Genovese, the murder victim whose cries for help went unanswered by over twenty witnesses. Whose name became the symbol of a nation's slide from Mayberry to mayhem.

Now the Kew Convenience Mart was a fire-gutted tomb and the washers and dryers of the Super Size Laundromat were trash-buried monoliths for future archeologists to puzzle over. Our clothing briefly held their images as we moved silently past.

I held up my fist when we reached the end of Lefferts Boulevard. Struldbrug blinked into my periphery via the uplink.

"Take a right at the intersection onto Kew Gardens Road. The mansion is two blocks down on your side of the street."

Across the road, the cemetery took up the next eight blocks to our right. A stanchioned metal plaque held the cemetery's name. The stems of the M, P and Y were elongated by rust drippings, nature's own creepy Halloween font. Weeds had claimed the spaces between the gate and fencing before they'd died.

Home sweet home.

In the city, selling "pre-owned" burial plots had become a needed source of revenue for mortuary owners, ever since they'd gone from landscapers to landlords. Hence, used graves. The open plots awaiting resale were covered with holograms of lawn. It was cheaper than moving dirt.

But not in this place. Whatever holes had been empty at the time of the Shift would never be filled, except by nature.

Maybe.

Back at the citadel, when Struldbrug told me where we were going—and its significance to me—I did a Conch search. Now I pulled out a piece of paper from a pocket and dialed up my optics to read what I'd copied down.

"Something wrong?" asked Maggie.

I folded the paper away. "Not a thing."

Another half-block down the street, the brick wall at our sides became the Lifetaker.

"Our advance man," said Max with revulsion.

"Well?" I said.

"They have a slaved AI working their antiviral security."

"Slaved?" Even through her camo routine I saw Maggie whiten.

"I couldn't get past the firewalls."

"Pretty much what we thought," said Struldbrug in my ear. "What about security?"

"Two guards on the lot, both out front. In the mansion: three downstairs, two upstairs with McDermott. Only one is out back in the carriage house, with our target."

"What about the bunker?" I asked.

"Couldn't risk getting in to see. The AI would've caught my scent. But by process of elimination, that's where Nicole is. The bunker."

"Wait a sec. You said Nicole was in the carriage house," said Maggie.

"I said the *target* was in the carriage house," said the Lifetaker.

She blinked. "Nicole's not the target?"

I gave her a "hold all questions" look. She didn't like it.

"Why doesn't she have a whole platoon guarding the place?" I asked Struldbrug.

"It won't mesh with her story after the attack. Besides, she has faith in McDermott's tech," said the Lifetaker.

"So what," said Maggie. "If *you* can't get in there, we sure as hell won't be able to."

"Nicole will come to us," I said.

Maggie looked again but said nothing.

"Did you divert the sensors?" asked Struldbrug.

"Masked," replied the Lifetaker, which I took for an affirmative. "We're clear until we reach the live security."

We moved on, hugging the wall.

55

CONCH BEAM

** WEBSQUIRT/LIVE FEED/INSERT PEBBLE/NOW FOR/ACCESS THANK/YOU **

Perfect glowing female smarty face:
>Wow, Kinner, Times Square hasn't looked this good in fifty years!<
Perfect rugged male smarty jawline:
>I'll say, Mala! They really pulled out all the stops for this one!<
>Reminds me of the old flatflicks of New Year's Eve!<
>Hey, yeah, that's right! When the silver ball dropped!<
>Well, tonight's event should be a lot glitzier than that!<
> Hellfire yes, Kinner! Hey, speaking of, guess who'll be with us later
   for commentary?<
>Who, Mala?>
>Dick Clark!<
>No way!<
>Yes way!<
>That reeb doesn't look a day over twenty!<
> Well, he could youthe a year when the Blister goes online tonight!
   It'll be SPECTATOR-TACULAR!<
>Ha ha! Good one, Mala! Hey, good ole Broadway looks filled to
   capacity! Must be hundreds of thousands of onlookers, all jostling
   to get a look at our Commander-in-Beef!<
>President Hawkins and Adam Struldbrug, President of Surazal, of

320

course, will be speaking to the world from the lounge platform on the 8th floor of the Marriott Marquis!<

>Yes, Mala, when that EM disc floats out from the eighth floor, we'll get our first ever realtime live view of these famous men! If I had skin, I'd have goose bumps!<

>Yuck! Keep your piloerections to yourself, Kinner!"

>Haw haw!<

56

ADAM

Adam Struldbrug loathed public ceremonies. He was always more comfortable working behind the scenes, so much so that, other than his entourage and vast army of employees, no more than a handful of Necropolitans would have recognized him on the street.

That was not the case for the man he was currently beside.

"What a remarkable day," said the President of the United States.

Adam nodded.

He didn't like the President and the President didn't like him. The President was a man for whom aggression, necessary in his world, had become a reflexive, blunt tool instead of a fine-edged weapon to be used only in time of necessity. He no longer crushed enemies—both actual and perceived—because he had to, but because he had developed a taste for blood. Because of that, he was not a true predator of nature, like Adam was. Adam killed only when necessary. He had recognized the same quality in the man Donner. Both were skilled and lethal, but had developed control and restraint. The President had the insatiable air of a buffalo hunter who killed and killed and killed and then took only the hides, leaving whole herds to rot under the hot sun.

Adam believed this bloodlust, and the fact that the President had never in his life lost a contest (either political or personal) made the man too comfortable in his preeminence. He had forgotten, as Adam had not, that there was always another wolf below planning to make his move to the alpha position.

But politics made strange bedfellows, so here they were behind protective glass high above Times Square, smiling and waving down at the churning throngs below, their holoimages splashed across every building in the area.

Far above them, technicians were waiting for their cue to connect the last fibers of buckypaper, completing the inner skin of the Blister domes and bringing the monolithic structure finally and completely online.

It was just for show, of course, like the golden spike that had been hammered into the last tie plate of the Transcontinental Railroad almost two hundred years. But symbols were important.

Hence his presence today.

The tops of the thousands of wasps that hovered over the crowd caught the sun. From his higher position, they made it look like the crowd was covered by shimmering fireflies of gold. Nicole had insisted on the protective measure, which had surprised him, because she didn't care about anyone. When she explained it was an opportunity to show off the new technology to potential customers all over the world, he'd demurred.

He wished that they could just get this thing over with so he could make his short speech, turn the show over to the President, and get out of this monkey suit.

The Secret Service agent closest to the President touched the dermal implant at his temple, listening. Adam had been wondering whether the man's mouth was just for show, merely a line drawn in granite, so immobile had it been, but now it curved downward into a scowl.

"Mr. President, Mr. Struldbrug's personal assistant insists on seeing him."

The President turned to Adam, waiting for him to dismiss the intrusion. But Roberts would never dare interrupt them unless it was an absolute emergency.

"It must be serious," he said.

The President sighed, but nodded.

Roberts was ushered onto the observation platform flanked by more agents.

Roberts looked as though he'd seen a ghost.

57

DONNER

The Victorian mansion was as conspicuous as a stockbroker on skid row. It was a Second Empire anachronism, the only free-standing house on the block. The government hadn't cared. They'd just needed something intimidating the locals would stay away from. Hadn't worked of course. Its Virginia brick face had been tagged and scrubbed more times than a call girl's.

I scanned the mansard roof, the dormer windows. It was four stories, narrow and high. Two guards stood post on the dead lawn between the steps and the sidewalk, in front of the left and right quoins, twenty feet apart.

"Can't take them out," Max streamed in my ear. "With their wetwiring, any changes in body function will be noticed."

"I'll have to neutralize the guard in the back house—no choice," I said. "That's as much as we can risk. One man down could be a glitch, trigger a diagnostic instead of an alarm, but three? We'd hear the sirens from here. So we wait 'til break time and then camo past."

Twenty minutes later I was beginning to think the guards were really scarecrows. Then the one nearest to us yawned elaborately and ambled away to his partner in front of the far bay window. They lit cigarettes. Their lighters almost overloaded my night optics.

"Breathe shallowly," I subvocalized as we moved.

I felt like the Invisible Man, slinking slowly, softly, step by silent step up the driveway to the porte-cochere, where we'd be beyond their sight. It took forever. Finally we were beyond the edge of the building. We passed blacked-out casement windows in the foundation. The basement was a lie. Beneath it was the real basement—the secret fall-out shelter. The driveway was empty.

When we reached the rear corner of the mansion, I held up my hand. I felt Maggie press lightly against my back, her breath on my collar. Max held the rear, backpedaling, his rifle trained on the sidewalk in case our guard was a speed-smoker.

There were no guards between the mansion and the carriage house, some fifteen feet arrears. Just empty lawn. McDermott was relying solely on his sensors, which the Lifetaker had masked.

I hoped.

I looked at our objective, the two-story carriage house. Lights glowed dully through the mullioned windows of the kitchen and parlor. The building had been converted into what Bart would've called a "mother-in-law" cottage.

We moved quickly now, double-timing across the backyard to the carriage house door. Maggie and Max took up positions on each corner, becoming part of the walls.

I went up to the kitchen door and gently tried it. Unlocked.

I stepped inside. The guard glanced up from his sandwich, mayo on his face.

"Man," I said. "Don't you worry about cholesterol?"

58

CONCH BEAM

Perfect glowing female smarty face:
>Kinner, have you noticed all the wasps?<
Perfect rugged male smarty jaw line:
>Yes, Mala! They're Surazal's newest security device, and boy, are they impressive! At six ounces apiece, and with a length of only an inch-and-a-half, you wouldn't think they could do much, but they pack state of the art punch!<
>Guess we don't have to worry about terrorists today, do we, Kinner?<
>No, Mala! With two hundred thousand of these babies patrolling our streets today, we're totally SAFE!<

59

STRULDBRUG

It was the hotel's largest ballroom—fifty thousand square feet—and it was ready for a hell of a party. After the joining was complete, four thousand VIPS would swarm into this place and ooh and ah over the tens of millions of dollars that had been spent: the food, the booze, the body-painted aerialists moving in complex rhythms over their heads, the 1:50 scale replica of the Blister rendered in glow-ice, the serotonin gas wafting from the air system that produced a mild but clear-headed euphoria. It had been electronically swept and re-swept for all manner of nastiness. Up until a moment ago it had been under the capable watch of the President's personal safety detail.

Now, it was empty. Except for one man, sitting at the nearest table, fiddling with a Blister keychain party favor.

His son, Adam.

Struldbrug had to give him credit. Adam was able to suppress the shock of seeing him almost completely.

"You would pick today," Adam sighed.

"Hello, Adam."

Adam dropped the keychain onto an ivory plate and the noise galloped across the room. "I suppose this is meant to be some kind of punishment."

"No."

"How the hell did you get into the city? Here, into this building?"

Struldbrug shook his head and wondered why, in this day and age, people insisted on linking age with declining ability. "I got into the Holy of Holies during the siege of Jerusalem, remember? Got back out with a couple important items that couldn't be allowed to fall into the hands of the Babylonians. This, in comparison, is child's play."

Adam shook his head. Struldbrug knew that there was nothing more tedious to his son than being reminded of his father's ancient exploits. It was kind of like some singer who'd had a hit song thirty years ago and was now playing the local state fair. "I don't have much time, so get to it."

"You're right," his father said, pulling up a chair and sitting beside him. "You don't."

He laid the player on the table and turned it on.

60

DONNER

I found her in the parlor, sitting in a Queen Anne chair, sipping a cup of tea. She looked up and froze as solid as Lot's wife.

"Hey, baby," I said.

She seemed to realize her cup was fixed halfway between lap and mouth and put it carefully back in the saucer on the sideboard. To her credit, her hand shook only a little.

"Paul," she said.

Nobody called me Paul. Nobody but her.

I looked around. Pocket doors, the heavy kind that rolled on tracks into the walls, were closed at the left. Behind her was a fireplace with a floor-to-ceiling mantle, ornamented with beveled mirrors. Its ledge held wax flowers under glass domes. Fake life under glass. Appropriate.

"You look great," I said.

"God, you're so young," she replied softly.

"Guess we're both full of surprises."

She straightened her back, clasping her hands in front of her. The lamp on the sideboard made her russet hair gleam. I knew exactly how it would feel.

"Let's go through it, shall we?" I said. "For the record?"

"Is that necessary?"

"Humor me."

She flicked a wrist toward the other chair, but I chose the American Empire sofa. It was comfortable as a pile of rocks. I laid the Beretta on the coffee table. Within reach of both of us.

"My case is unusual," I started. "Usually the memories don't come back."

"When did you remember?"

"It first started surfacing in fragments, blended into dreams and other memories. But, with a little prodding from someone, it came back clearly yesterday."

"You're holding up pretty well, then. I doubt I'd have."

I canted my head noncommittally.

"Where should I start?" she said with a tremor.

The funny thing was, I really hated putting her through this. Wasn't that funny?

"The first time you met Nicole."

"Such a long time ago."

"Seems like yesterday."

She expelled a puff of air through her nose that I couldn't interpret. That delicate nose. "Well, you'd just left my office after your visit with the roses."

"Yeah, you loved roses."

Her eyes flickered. "Actually," she said, apologetic, "not really. But you took such pleasure from giving them to me..."

"Huh," I said, unable to summon more.

"Anyway, that day, I was getting ready to read this Struldbrug woman the riot act. But before I could get a head of steam going, she told me something that took my breath away."

"About her and her father."

An impressed widening of the eyes. "Still a detective. Yeah. About their peculiar... gift."

"She came right out and told you?"

"I had her 'by the short hairs,' as you used to be fond of saying."

She'd hated my gutter talk. Except in bed.

"I thought she was crazy, of course. I was ready to call security, but she'd come with evidence. She kept laying it out: pictures, drawings, files, and then finally the research."

"That's what swayed you? The science?"

"It was my job to know fake science from real science," she replied.

"What was her pitch?"

"It was simple. If I turned her in, the government would shut her down, confiscate her research, and pretty much do to their family what Hitler would've done—dissect them. There wasn't a government on Earth that would act any differently."

"But she offered you an alternative."

"She said her team would crack her father's secret in my lifetime. Of all the generations that had come and gone, I'd been born at precisely the right time to be the first to take advantage of their gift."

"And that gave you pause."

"It would give *anyone* pause, Paul."

"Eternal youth. And all you had to do was keep your mouth shut."

She looked at me evenly. "No. I never deluded myself about that. The price would be high. It would mean violating my oath to my country, betraying my coworkers, lying to my friends and family, and…"

Her face wrestled with itself for a moment. The mask of composure reasserted itself.

"Why'd she make the offer? It'd be safer to kill you."

"That's what she said. Which gave me a whole different kind of *pause*. But she felt, with my background, I could be useful. If she could flip me to her side, with my knowledge and expertise, I could help her avoid any future governmental entanglements. That was very valuable to her. So she offered me the carrot and the stick."

"Live forever or die right now," I mused. "She gave me the same extreme choice."

She picked the cup up, took a sip, grimaced, and put it down again. "Tea. It's the loveliest thing in the world," she said softly. "Unless it's gone cold. Then it's the worst." *Kind of like you, Paul*, her eyes said. "Her scientists answered my questions, showed me the data. I had three days to come to a decision."

"How'd she know you wouldn't turn her in?"

"I was under surveillance. She could have killed me any time, I suppose." She shifted, re-crossed her legs. Every familiar movement was a spike through my chest. "I went home that night like I was drifting through a dream. I don't even remember the train. I was beyond confused, beyond upset, beyond…" Anguish distorted her alabaster poise. "And then I found you passed out on the couch."

My vision went grainy.

"It got very clear then. Despite the endless promises, you weren't going to change. You were going to flush your potential down the toilet, along with mine."

I expected the taste of hot tears. The Workahol must have been keeping me numb.

"I'd married a drunk, just like my mom. I just couldn't bear repeating that future." She tossed back her hair. Her lowermost locks sank into the darkness beyond the range of the candelabra. Her eyes flicked to the gun. "You're giving them a lot of time, sitting here chatting."

"It's alright. Keep going."

Her lips shrank into a perfect rose. "You believed in that ''til death do us part' fiction. Your parents never split up. But I came from a different world, Paul. I had three stepfathers. It wasn't a mortal sin to cut your losses."

"Yeah," I said. "For you, leaving was the right choice."

That shocked her. For the first time she made real eye contact with me, searching. *You haven't actually changed, have you?*

"A divorce, at least, I could have lived through."

"Nicole was convinced you'd never accept it. You'd start digging and eventually find out about her. Nothing ever could stop you, once you'd made up your mind. You were like one of those left-behind dogs that find their owners three thousand miles away. There was no way around you."

"So you had me killed."

Her eyes widened. "God, no! How could you—?" She looked actually hurt. "Is *that* what you thought?"

I rubbed my brow. "Then what *was* the plan?"

"The only solution was for me to disappear. I had to die, but right in front of your eyes, so you'd believe it, accept it."

"A dangerous game."

"Yeah. With your training, your experience? It had to go perfectly. Which it didn't."

I shook my head. "You were going to let me think you'd died. I was supposed to go through the rest of my life grieving for you—"

"Nicole wanted to kill you, Paul! This was the only way I could save your life, understand?" She looked at the plaster decorations on the ceiling, working very hard not to meet my eyes. "If we had one of our famous fights, you'd offer to take me some place nice to make up, a show, a four-star restaurant. It was—what do you guys call it?—

your *modus operandi.*"

My throat tightened. "Yes."

"So we had a fight. Remember? A real doozy. And you came up with *Don Giovanni*, like clockwork. All I had to do was get you into that bodega. There'd be a stick-up gone bad. Wrong place at the wrong time. And you'd become a widower."

Regained memories…

Lincoln Center. The spotlighted fountain shoots streams of water into the air—

"I knew you'd want a smoke before you went in, to hold you through the performance. So I emptied your pack before we left."

Me: "Listen, if I'm going to sit through three hours of this Don Corleone thing—"

"I steered you to the bodega."

Elise nods in the direction of Korean grocery across from the subway. "We'll go to that one. It's cheaper."

I'd been so easy to maneuver.

Anger clouded her eyes. "Nicole spun this elaborate tale about how some 'robber' would run into the store and 'shoot' me right in front of you. They had me rigged up with blood squibs, just like the movies. Then Alvarez would shoot you with a stun gun or some tranquilizer or something. You'd wake up in the hospital a week later, a widower, your wife already buried." She shook her head. "I was an idiot."

"It wasn't exactly your area of expertise."

"Please," she said, her voice hardening. "Don't be nice."

"So how'd it really play out?"

"Nicole never had any intention of letting you live. McDermott told Alvarez to kill you the moment we walked in."

More memories…

—Alvarez behind the counter, looking startled when I walk in—

—I see him recognize me—how can that be?—

"But he froze. And that gave you all the time you needed."

—Alvarez tries to pull the piece from under the counter, but he's too slow. I've seen the panic in his eyes, I know something's wrong. My hand punches the gun away from him, and his eyes dart behind us—

—Behind us?—

"Nicole gave me a backup weapon, just in case. She said it was a tranq gun. If things went wrong, I was supposed to sedate you. So when you disarmed Alvarez, I… I…"

—I turn, already too late, and see—

—I see—

Elise pointing the gun at me, face screwed tight like rose petals crushed by a boot heel.

—Thundering I hear the words from my dream, those acid words—

"How long," she says in a shredded voice, "did you think I was going to wait for you to get your shit together?"

And then the muzzle flash whites out my vision and the stink of cordite fills my nostrils—

The broken mirror, its shards re-laid. But still broken.

"When I saw the blood, I knew…"

She sat there, crying softly, hands fluttering in her lap. "Oh my. I thought it'd be easier, after all this time."

"It never gets easier," I offered. "It just goes to sleep for a while."

She sniffled. "From then on, I was her creature. I did Nicole's bidding, helped keep the feds off her back. A second, empty grave was placed next to yours. And I grew old without you. I was seventy-five years old when they finally perfected the Retrozine. I'd given up hope they'd have the breakthrough in my lifetime. Talk about a bitter old woman. To my mind, I'd been the victim of the longest long con in history."

"But then Crandall actually had his breakthrough."

"Yeah. True to her word, Nicole made sure I was the first normal human to be youthed."

"Betting both teams, as usual. You'd be an ally for eternity if the drug worked. Or a tied-up loose end if it didn't."

"But it did work." She gestured to herself. "Courtesy, in part, of that horrible, horrible accident."

"What accident?"

"The Shift, of course."

I stood. She tensed. All I did was go to her, sitting in the other chair. I took her hand, felt the delicate bones beneath the translucent skin. Her pulse thrummed, fast and faintly blue.

"Elise. The Shift wasn't an accident. Nicole did it on purpose."

She took her hand back. It was like an eclipse. "What are you talking about?"

"How's it coming, chief?" It was Max, in my VR. I tilted my head away, seeing him in my left contact lens.

"Slower than expected," I replied.

"Pick up the pace," Max said. "We're running out of time." He blinked away.

Max was right. But convincing Elise was the cornerstone. I turned back to her. "We don't have much time, sweetheart—"

She winced. "Please don't call me that."

Habits die harder than men.

I laid the player on the coffee table and turned it on.

She listened to the recording, like we had. Listened to Nicole's voice, laying it out. Insanity made to sound reasonable.

Elise shut the player off.

The tall case clock thundered in the corner.

After an eternity, she looked at me. "I'm the reason Struldbrug brought you back, aren't I? For this very moment."

I nodded. "Nicole trusts you—a very rare thing. You're the only one in her inner circle who can make this work. And he thought I was the only person who could convince you to do it."

It broke my heart, there was such sadness in her eyes. "God, Paul. There's never been a moment, through this whole thing, when we haven't been manipulated, has there?"

"It doesn't matter. We still can make this come out right."

She looked out the window. "What do you want me to do?"

61

BUNKER

Nicole watched the President's speech over the Times Square websquirt.

"Look at that asshole," she said. "Making a big show of being in Necropolis. He's wearing a triple-redundant filter field to protect himself!"

McDermott looked at his watch. "Sadly, that field will fail in about ten minutes."

There was a chime on the tech's console. Elise was signaling from the carriage house.

"Pull up the feed from the parlor," she said.

The tech, Marco, complied. Display Two resolved into a pale, red-headed beauty, standing in the middle of the empty room, looking up at the camera drone.

"I'm busy," snapped Nicole.

Elise held up a cell phone. Marco smirked. What a Luddite. She was obviously the type that feared implants.

"It's Adam," the woman said. "He's suspicious."

Nicole's whole manner slowed down, focused. She lifted her veil, securing it to her hat with a long and dangerous pin. "He's on the phone now? He's calling you from the Ceremony?"

"I have him on hold," Elise stammered. "He wants to know why we're not there."

"Why is he calling *you*?"

"He couldn't reach you."

"If he's calling from his implant, there's no reception in the bunker," explained Marco. "It's lead-lined, hardened against nukes."

Nicole gave him a life-sapping glare. To Elise: "Tell him what we rehearsed, you idiot. We're tracking a potential Ender attack uptown."

"He doesn't believe me! He's demanding we get up there now."

Nicole swore. "Hold for a minute." Marco paused the feed. Elise could be seen talking on the phone again.

The titanium door to the bunker hissed open and McDermott strode to her side. "I told you she was a lousy liar," he said.

Nicole flicked a dark nail at Marco to restore the feed. "Transfer the call here," she said to Elise.

Marco said, "We'd lose reception in the bunker. Same as if she physically brings the phone to us."

"Then have Adam call me here directly from a land line!" she snapped.

Before he could reply, Elise put the call on her cell's speakerphone. You could hear Adam's fury all the way into the bunker. "Nicole!" he thundered. "I want to talk to you NOW or this ceremony is OVER!"

Elise clicked off the speaker and covered the phone with her hand. "He wants to know something about the security wasps," she whispered up at them.

"Jesus Christ." She clenched her fists. To McDermott: "You have a man in the house?"

McDermott looked to Marco, who checked his data. "He's offline," said the tech.

"What?"

"It's probably a glitch. The AI's running a diagnostic as we speak."

McDermott scowled. "Bring up the kitchen feed."

Marco's fingers flew across the board. Display Three lit. McDermott's offline guard was shoving a sandwich into his face, his mouth smeared with mayonnaise.

"Jennings! Get your ass on post!"

Jennings looked to the camera drone, cheeks and eyes bulging. He nodded, swallowing something far bigger than his esophagus could handle. Several gulps of milk later, he was able to choke out, "Roger that."

"Ms. Struldbrug is coming out to talk to Elise."

"Roger."

McDermott spoke into his own uplink. "All posts, check in."

The men out front and upstairs all confirmed that everything was quiet.

"Alright," said Nicole.

McDermott laid a hand on her forearm. "Maybe you should leave it here," he said. His eyes drifted to the pocket where she'd tucked the remote control device. "Just to be safe."

She shook off his hand like he was leprous. "'Just to be safe' is the reason I had it made." She went to a cabinet and opened it, revealing a mounted row of pneumatic syringes, glowing with orange liquid. She stuffed a syringe into her pocket. "If that bitch is lying to me, I'm going to youthe her back to diapers."

"I thought you trusted her," said McDermott.

She looked at him like he was a small child. "You're so cute sometimes."

62

STRULDBRUG

"**S**he's coming," Adam told him. Into the phone: "You did a convincing job, young lady." He listened, then turned to his father. "Why is she laughing that I called her young lady?"

Adam hadn't protested, hadn't demanded further proof or claimed that the recording must be fake. He hadn't bombarded Struldbrug with any of the millions of questions or objections one might raise when told that their twin sister was about to murder millions of people, themselves and the President of the United States included.

He had simply turned off the recorder and gazed down at his father. His father who suddenly looked so old and tired.

"I have an environmentally-sealed suite in this building," Adam now said. "You can wait there until this is over."

Struldbrug shook his head. "The inhabitants of this city don't have protection, do they? I'm needed out here."

Adam snorted. "When did you become such a concerned citizen? You'd risk eternity for them?"

Struldbrug's large eyes flicked downward. Adam couldn't place the look on his father's face—he'd never seen it before. Then he realized what it was. Shame. "Donner," Struldbrug said. "The way he looked at me. With pity. He didn't think me a monster for all that I've done, he just thought me pathetic. Me, pathetic, a king of kings.

And I realized that was exactly what I had become." He looked up at his son. "I was a great man once. A warrior. An empire-builder. Once, the thought of hiding from the world in a make-believe castle would never have entered my mind. But somewhere along those centuries…" The chandeliers made his irises deepen to the color of rich, dark loam. "Maybe it's not power that corrupts. Maybe it's time. Too much time to grow afraid." He stood and shrugged. "I cannot live that way."

Adam looked thoughtful. "Donner and his friends. You trust them?"

"Yes."

"Alright. I've already seen to the President's safety." He pointed at the phone. "I will finish this little ruse, and then we shall wait. When we know that the threat has passed, I'll take you to the main Blister Control Center and we'll end this fucking nightmare together."

63

NICOLE

The guard had removed all traces of his meal. Wise. He snapped to attention as she entered the kitchen. "You're with me," she said, not slowing.

She pushed at the pocket doors. Heavy as they were, they slid effortlessly into the walls. Elise was sitting in a high-backed chair. She held the cell phone like it was a inscrutable alien artifact.

Nicole took two steps toward it and stopped dead as the cold metal of a pistol was pressed against her skull.

"Not a muscle, Miss Nicole," said the voice.

Oh man.

She had to smile. She couldn't help herself.

One in a million, this fucking guy.

"Donner! Baby!" she said. "If I had a soft spot, it'd be for you."

She tensed as he patted her down for weapons. But his reborn inexperience betrayed him. His fingers were probing for the weapons of his day, so he missed the wafer-thin nanoblades through her thick sleeves. Her smile broadened.

Then she felt him take the Retrozine-C and the remote from her skirt pocket, and that was it for smiling.

"You can turn around now," he said.

When she turned, she expected to see the kitchen guard sneaking up behind Donner. The guard was behind him alright, but he was

341

undulating, becoming amorphous. Then his edges blurred and he turned into something else. Something horrifying.

"Thanks," said Donner to the thing.

It bled away into the floor.

So. Doubly betrayed. "Daddy's little helper. You've made some new friends since we last talked," she said.

Donner leveled the antique pistol at her. "On the couch. Hands in your lap."

She complied. Jesus, it was uncomfortable. She smiled reproachfully over at Elise, just to watch the color bleed from her cheeks.

"*E tu*, Elise?"

Two more people resolved out of the fruity wallpaper. Their smartskin camouflage cycled off. Little Maggie Mannequin was unarmed, but a fireplug of a man she didn't recognize held a plasma rifle.

She curled her hands in her lap, letting her thumbs drift toward tiny tattoos, the ones below the first joints of her forefingers.

The ones that would trigger her blades.

Donner jammed his pistol into a holster and examined the remote.

"I'd be careful with that, if I were you," she said. "If its power source is interrupted, it triggers a default response in the mainframe that launches the wasps."

"So I can't destroy it," Donner said. He flicked the top off the tube and stared at the simple red trigger. "We make destruction so easy." His voice was marinated in disgust. "It always comes down to a red button."

Donner pulled a silver box from a pocket in his smartskin. He slipped the remote into the box and tapped a code on the side of the rectangle, then angled it so Nicole could see. Clear morphinium flowed around the device like molasses, encasing it completely, filling the box.

"No back-ups, right?" he said.

Her stomach lurched in a premonition of disaster.

He keyed another sequence and the morphinium solidified. The remote now looked like a dragonfly trapped in amber. Donner turned the box upside down and the square clattered out onto the ground, functional as a paperweight. "The signal's still going out. But that button will never get pushed," Donner said.

Nicole held back a howl that would've split the Earth in two. A muscle popped in her neck.

"Simple as that," said Donner.

"Getting out of here won't be," she replied hoarsely.

"Doesn't matter," he said sadly. "Got what I came for."

She arched an eyebrow at Elise. "Guess so."

Maggie's resolution wavered.

How interesting.

"You've been a naughty little sociopath," he said

"Poo." She looked up at the camera drone, batting around the ceiling like a confused fly. "McDermott, in case you didn't figure it out, kill these motherfuckers!"

64

MCDERMOTT

McDermott had problems of his own. Currently he was watching his men being decimated by a six-foot-long grease stain.

Three minutes before, Marco lost the feed to the house. McDermott paced the cement floor while the tech and his pet AI nailed down the problem. When the screen finally flared back to life, his blood ran cold. A man he thought he'd killed several times was in the process of turning Nicole's all-important remote control into a doorstop.

"Intruder alert! Carriage house!" he screamed in his link, but there was no response. Then the lights flickered. He hauled Marco out of his chair. "What the fuck is going on?"

"I-I don't know!" Marco stammered. "My systems are going haywire! I think the AI just crashed!"

McDermott pulled his pistol and turned the incompetent technician into two hundred pounds of rare roast beef. The other techs, a man and a woman, screamed in unison. He kicked at the man-shaped charcoal briquette, cursing, then realized something. The flesh stunk worse than it should have. Which meant the oxygen scrubbers were offline. He'd have to evacuate the bunker before the air ran out.

God damn it! Things were going to shit fast.

Somewhere on the news feed in the background, Maya and Kinner were explaining that the President had cut short his address and left the platform. An explanation was apparently to be forthcoming.

McDermott's breath stopped short upon hearing that. "I'm going to the carriage house. I want these systems up in five minutes. And I want another way to activate the wasps."

The male tech paled behind his Coke bottle glasses. "There is no other way! That was the whole point!"

McDermott pressed his weapon under the man's chin. The tech screamed as his goatee was singed by the hot muzzle.

"If I can't control those wasps in ten minutes, you're dead. Is that clear enough?"

Then his two guards started firing at the door, and he whirled to confront a sight that made his mind hiccup and his insides turn to liquid.

65

NICOLE

"You really think there's only one way to launch the attack?" she asked, crossing her arms.

"You're a control freak, Nicole," said Donner. "It finally bit you in the ass."

"Such language," she purred. She coughed to cover the click as she flicked open the metal clasps on the harnesses under her blouse. If she triggered the knives now, they'd fire as projectiles.

Donner turned to Max. "Sit rep?"

"The Lifetaker has engaged McDermott in the bunker. I'm hearing weapons fire."

"That'll do them a lot of good," said Maggie.

Elise said, "What now?"

Elise, the traitor. She'd been an idiot to let her live.

"Yeah," Maggie repeated, looking between Elise and Donner. "What now?" The question carried multiple meanings, deeper inquiries.

Donner's features were an unreadable mask. "Now we get the hell out of here."

"W-we?" Elise's eyes were saucers.

He reddened, like she'd misinterpreted him. "This isn't charity, Elise. You were part of this. We'll do what we can, but it'll be up to the authorities what happens to you."

"Damn, that's cold," said Nicole. "This is what you left me for?"

Elise slowly nodded at Donner.

"Oh, don't look so stricken," said Nicole. "Prison's so much more fun when you're young."

Elise stared at the carpet as though inertia was the only thing keeping her on her feet. Nicole could read her mind. *How'd I get here?* she was thinking. *How'd I get to this place?*

Max to Donner: "You're not planning to leave this witch alive, are you?" Meaning her.

"That was the deal with Struldbrug."

"What deal?"

"In exchange for his help, I said I wouldn't kill her. Unless I had to."

"Dear old dad," sighed Nicole. "Makes me all misty." She blinked twice in rapid succession to bring the targeting system in her veil online.

"She killed you! Twice! She'll kill us all if she gets the chance."

"Her squad and her comm systems are down. By the time she gets back to her people in Necropolis, we'll be safely ensconced at Arg-é Bam and the Conch and the President both will have the story. There's a big world out there that ain't gonna be thrilled she played it for a sucker."

Then, out of the blue, Donner's smile dropped from his face like he'd been sucker-punched. For a moment, she thought he'd decided to break his promise to Daddy and kill her. Then he rocked on his feet and raised his hand against his forehead, looking gray. "Whoa," he stammered.

"What's wrong?" said Maggie.

"The Workahol," he said. "It just cut out."

"Shit," said the smarty, grabbing his arm. "Your reborn system metabolized it faster than normal."

"Poor angel," said Nicole. "That's gotta hurt."

And fired.

66

MCDERMOTT

The Lifetaker reacted before the eye could blink, dematerializing enough to let the energy pulses pass right through it. It wrapped one of McDermott's men into itself like a shroud, suffocating him while it continued to fight the other two.

McDermott and the techs backed up against the dead environmental controls.

They all heard the second guard's spine snap. The female tech fainted, unable to stomach another serving of reality. She was lucky; she got to miss the Lifetaker thrust an appendage *into* the third guard and squeeze his lungs until they burst. Gray cottage cheese spilled from the dead man's lips. The Lifetaker dropped the bodies and swung around to them.

"Fucking demon from hell!" McDermott shrieked.

It cocked its head protrusion. "Nothing supernatural about me, boss. I'm just your garden-variety smarty." It started forward, issuing a screeching metal-on-metal laugh that threatened McDermott's shaky composure.

Wait a minute—

The male tech howled, his sanity deserting him, and tried to scramble up the wall.

A smarty—a machine! That was it!

He pulled the EMP grenade from his belt. It was the last thing he ever thought he'd need. But it paid to be prepared.

Thank you, God, he thought, as he pulled the pin.

67

DONNER

It happened all at once and very slowly.

My adrenals failed beneath an avalanche of lactic acid, muscles swamped by a kind of pain and fatigue I'd never known before. There was fur in my throat, cotton in my head.

Maggie strode to me in alarm. Elise took a step back, confusion in her eyes, a clementine blush on her cheeks.

"Poor angel," said Nicole. "That must hurt."

She flung her arms out at us, palms upturned. Two blades fired from her sleeves, shooting across the room, quicksilver flashes too fast for me to react to.

Max leapt sideways, but even jazzed he wasn't fast enough. The projectile caught him across the right triceps, severing muscles and tendons, turning his arm into dead weight. Blood drenched his side in arterial paroxysms.

Elise stumbled back into me. In that instant, there were a million things I wanted to cry out. But all I could do was watch. I tried to lift my arms, but they were underwater, wrapped in chains. She was at my side just as the blade arrived. It sliced through my Beretta. Then it passed through her midsection as if she was made of gossamer and not flesh and I had time to register her puff of air across my cheek, her familiar scent filling my nostrils, her look of shock and satisfaction burning into my mind.

Then she fell, hair flowing. She seemed to meet the ground lightly, like petals strewn from a careless hand. I screamed, dropping down beside her, watching her blood flowing too fast and too thick into the carpet beneath, clamping my hands to the top of my head in horror.

She grasped my elbow, patting it, and then she closed her eyes and let herself slide down to the place she'd hidden from all these years.

Before I could even moan out a denial, a concussion boomed from somewhere outside.

Maggie cried out. I looked up to see her sizzle and jerk like she'd stepped on a live wire. She burned nova bright for an instant and flashed out of existence with a pop, like an old flashcube. Her orb dropped to the carpet, smoking.

Darkness claimed all.

68

DONNER

Somewhere a generator cleared its throat. Emergency lights snapped on, bathing us in white shafts.

I looked around.

Nicole had fled, taking one of the blades with her.

Max struggled over to Elise, but I knew she was dead. I was violently sea-sick. My jinxed equilibrium sent me reeling sideways, arms flailing. Somehow I managed to stay on my feet.

"What was that?" I grunted.

"EMP grenade," Max said, his teeth clenched. He fell back on his haunches, his good hand clamped around his shoulder, blood leaking around his nails. "Someone in the bunker must've used it to kill the Lifetaker."

"Is Maggie dead?"

"Don't know. Those things have a limited range. Maybe she's just temporarily offline."

I tore a piece of material from my smartskin sleeve. "Let's get a tourniquet on that arm."

He put a hand against my chest, stopping me. "Forget me, I'm okay. Get that bitch."

I stood. Struldbrug was going to regret ever bringing me back.

My Beretta was in pieces. The blade that had pierced it was lying on the carpet, dull with blood. It had ricocheted through a metal bust of Sophocles, taking his eyes with it.

I picked it up by its hilt and ran outside.

McDermott came out of the bunker just as I stumbled onto the driveway. He pointed his plasma pistol at me and tried to fire, but its insides had been fried by the EMP. He tossed it down, grinning, flexing his arms. "Good," he said. "As it should be. You and me."

"You watch too many holos," I said.

I put all my energy into one move.

I threw myself forward, tucked into a ball. I came out of the roll low, my arm extended, the blade deep in his abdomen. His mouth formed a perfect "o" of shock, his golden irises ringed in wide surprised white.

"Sorry," I said. "No time for a showdown."

I yanked the blade sideways. It tore through his obliques and came free in a spray of blood and tissue. McDermott fell to the cement, dead as love.

Pain shrieked up my limbs like screech beetles, biting and tearing. Only the thought of Nicole escaping got me to my feet. I moved to the front of the house, fighting nausea, shaking my head to clear the black spots from my vision.

Nicole stood on the hillock behind the cemetery's fence. She must have paused in her flight to watch me kill McDermott. Now I saw her whirl and disappear down its far slope.

There was a crack of thunder and the heavens opened up, drenching me in an instant, making my camo and my night optics useless.

I tore the headpiece off and ran toward the cemetery.

69

DONNER

The rain beat at me like a living opponent, every drop lancing through my tattered nervous system like a blow. The screech beetles had turned into locusts, devouring my muscles and tendons, consuming my strength in a million tiny bites.

I stumbled twice before I even reached the fence. When I hauled myself over it, I lost my footing. For a second I thought it was all going to end there with me impaled on the iron gate. Somehow I avoided the worst of the spikes and barbed wire and got myself across the top. But I slipped on the way down and hit the ground hard, on my back. The concussion sent so much torment through me that I blacked out for a minute.

I picked myself up. Blood ran out of my mouth—somewhere along the line I'd bitten my tongue. Part of my mind, my lower reptile brain, screamed at me for rest, telling me to curl into a ball under one of the big oaks, just drift into an exhausted stupor and forget everything. But I had one more job to do.

Sometimes no choice was the best choice.

Lightning tore holes in the sky, revealing purple-black clouds that looked insane with rage. The trees were dead, their trunks serving as their own grave markers, their twisted arms reaching to the sky for a reprieve that never came. They had resisted the elements for as long as they could, but now chunks of bark and wood hurled down with every fresh slash of water.

The weeds that overgrew the place were a sickly white-gray. Somehow they'd survived the enzyme, but only barely. Matted and dense, they clutched at my ankles, trying to snare me. Hidden beneath their chaos was an obstacle course of markers, rocks and roots.

I went down three more times, the last one an ungainly pitch headfirst against a headstone that made me see sparklers and hear brass bells.

Behind me, over the storm, I thought I heard voices calling my name.

I really hoped that it was Maggie. I didn't know what I would do if she wasn't okay.

I staggered forward through the headstones.

The place was enormous. So many lives. When I was tiny my dad had taken me to a cemetery; I'd seen the headstones and asked him how they got them to grow out of the ground that way. He'd laughed himself silly. The question didn't seem childish now. God did grow headstones for us. And our epitaphs were already written.

Ten feet further I almost fell into an open plot that had been half-filled with leaves and debris. Only a sizzle of lightning revealed it in time. Arms pinwheeling, I staggered back onto my ass, cursing.

The lightning and thunder went to their corners for a round break. The rain took the opportunity to redouble its efforts. It was so gelid that my fingers were numb around the knife.

Then, without warning, the Blister went out.

One minute its electromagnetic discharges were sparking into the sky, crimsons and maroons splashing the firmament. Then, nothing. I could still faintly make out the shape of the domes, reflecting the city lights below, but they themselves were off-line.

Struldbrug had promised to fly back and find Adam and the President, tell them everything: how the Shift was a farce, that neither reborns and norms were infectious to the world, that the Blister hadn't been designed to keep the Shift in but to contain her deadly Retrozine-C while it destroyed everyone. Them included.

I guess they believed him.

Somewhere I heard a howl. Nicole had seen it, too.

Without sky flash and Blister, it was terribly dark now.

Onward.

The thunder uttered a growl and the rain increased its pummeling. I stopped, disoriented. The darkness of solid objects was indistinguishable from the black canvas before me. The rain blanketed all sounds.

This was hopeless. I couldn't track Nicole in this void. She could be anywhere, far away by now.

Then the lightning returned with a vengeance, sundering a tree maybe three hundred feet distant. The wood literally screamed. In the flare of its illumination, I saw her. She'd ducked out from behind a mausoleum when the electricity struck. She froze for a second and we saw each other, our eyes locking over the distance. Then she sprinted over a hillock.

I ran after, determined not to lose her again.

When I staggered to the top, she was gone. Water spattered the stones ahead of me, but she was nowhere.

How had she—?

Too late I realized she'd been baiting me. She'd let herself be seen deliberately, to lure me forward to this position. Perched there like I was, at the top of the rise, I'd stand out clear as day when the next lightning bolt hit. A perfect target. She would double back around.

I turned in alarm, my feet tangling in the thick vegetation. Jesus, this couldn't be happening.

My knife, where was my knife?

The next bolt of lightning struck, and there she was, just a few yards below me, her arm already raised to throw.

I fumbled my own blade up with insensate fingers, but the hilt slipped from my grasp to tumble into the dark grass.

Find it, where did it—

Her dagger took me in the chest. I felt it pierce my breastbone, but its blade was so finely honed I didn't know it had penetrated deeper until I felt my heart try to beat around the metal. And shudder.

Then I was falling backwards, down the hill toward an empty mawing mouth. Just like she'd planned. The sides of the earth opened up and swallowed me, black walls rushing toward the sky around me. I hit the bottom of the empty grave with barely a gasp.

It got quiet. Just the rain. Water turned by gravity into a weapon. It kept me conscious, smacking me in the face. Lying there in the grave, I was too tired to laugh at the absurdity of it.

The sky lightened a little bit, dark blue struggling against black.

A foot planted itself at the edge and Nicole peered down at me.

"Damn, can't stay away from holes in the ground, can ya?"

She squatted closer. My heart was spasming in violent arrhythmia. It would fail soon. Couldn't pull out the blade—I'd bleed to death. My hand fumbled at my sides, searching.

She looked out at the offline Blister. "You really screwed things up," she said with a sigh. "But don't think I can't get out of this. By morning, my spinsters will have made me the hero of Necropolis, and you, the worst terrorist of the last fifty years. How does that sound?"

Sense of touch was almost gone. Muscle control nonexistent. Hands like slabs of meat. Darkness. Crowding. My. Vision.

Hang on… hang…

"First I'm going back to the house," she said. "Anyone who's still alive, I'm going to kill. Then I'm going to crush that smarty's globe into fucking dust. What do you think about that?"

Dead fingers smacked. Against a shaft. Hanging from left pocket. Hadn't. Lost it.

Get it out, get it out…

"Sorry about your wife," she said. "I'll bury her next to you."

My arm flopped back over my head. Nicole saw the glint. "What've you got there?"

Please, guide my hand.

I threw. The pneumatic syringe sailed up through the rain. Straight into Nicole's neck. Before she could bat it away, it had autoinjected its entire ampoule of Retrozine C.

She yanked it out of her flesh and stared at it. "What the fuck?"

Then she realized what it was. Dropped the syringe. Spasmed as she felt it begin.

She turned and ran. I was forgotten.

Run all you want.

Nowhere to go.

70

MAGGIE

Maggie watched Nicole stagger through the tombstones.

She crashed into one, leaning over its cement cross, gasping, twenty-five years old now, her face young and gorgeous and filled with mortal terror. She pushed back, kept staggering forward.

Twenty years old now.

Cursing, screaming, as the rain abruptly stopped and the skies softened. A strong wind began herding the storm front away from them.

Nicole stumbled against a tree, clinging to a low branch, her hands thinning, shortening until the branch was too thick to hold onto.

Now sixteen, now twelve, her clothes falling away as she shrank, her face dissolving and reforming, then dissolving again.

She saw Maggie. She ran toward her, begging in a voice strangled by shrinking vocal chords. A gold ring dropped from her too-tiny hands into too-large shoes. She stumbled out of them. Her stockings swam around skinny pre-adolescent legs.

Her knife sheathes slipped off her forearms into a tangle of weeds. Her veil fell to the earth, forever discarded.

Four years old, naked, Nicole finally dropped to her knees, threw her head back and screamed at the sky. But it was a child's scream, without power, without even understanding anymore.

Then she disappeared behind a low monument.

Maggie walked over. A tiny fetus lay in a puddle of rainwater. It twitched, its pathetic limbs grasping, moving, its bird-eye blinking against the last drops of rain.

Maggie turned away in revulsion. When she looked back a moment later, all that was left was a glob of indistinct cells, a wad of flesh, shrinking, shrinking...

Dissolving...

Then nothing but the sound of wind.

Struldbrug landed the chopper in the street beyond the fence. The mansion was burning, casting a wicked yellow light down the embankment. Three dark forms climbed from the vehicle.

The moon slinked out, full and bright. Where it had been hiding during the storm, she didn't know. But now it added its preternatural glow to the sky, sparking off the wet marble like angel fire.

In the distance, she could hear more choppers coming, probably tactical dragonflies ordered up by the President.

The figures were clear now. Struldbrug. Max, a long coat thrown around his shoulders, teeth gritted in pain.

And then Armitage, his hat on his head and that damned pipe in his mouth, his hair a fluorescent white, his eyes golden.

She uttered a bleat of astonishment and ran to him. Her hands drifted over the craggy surface of his face. He gave her a wry frown. "A funny thing happened on the way to the morgue."

She threw herself into his arms.

Maggie slipped into the grave next to Donner.

There was a piece of paper clasped in his hand.

She was about to tell him they'd get him out of there, he'd be okay, they'd radio for paramedics, but before the first syllable had passed her lips, he said, "Shh."

She clamped her mouth shut, eyes brimming with tears. She leaned forward and he whispered into her ear.

She nodded. "The scientists are dead. I'll make sure their research disappears, too. I'll make sure it ends."

He smiled that crooked smile at her. The one only he could make work.

He tried to say something else, but death took him first.

She knew what he'd been trying to say, so it was alright. Three little words, words that transformed a cold cosmos into a place of hope.

She climbed out and opened the paper. She read what he'd written. Max and Struldbrug walked over to her.

"My daughter?" said the immortal.

She shook her head. He wavered, but then nodded. It was as though he'd always known, despite his best efforts, the inevitability of this outcome.

"I've flooded the Conch with the news," he said. "The origins of the Shift, and its inevitable end now that Nicole is gone. There will be some revivals for a while, but Shift will fade of its own accord. The reborns alive now will be the last. There will be a generation, not very long from now, that will read about them like creatures from a fairy tale."

Armitage looked like he couldn't quite believe it.

Max eyed the paper. "What's that?" he asked Maggie.

"A newspaper clipping Donner pulled off the Conch." She cleared her throat. "From the *Long Island Democrat*, September 30, 1890: 'Frule Eklund, a Frenchman, aged 52 years, who has been engaged as grave digger and general assistant in the Maple Grove Cemetery, dug a grave in one of the rear plots last Thursday, unbeknown to his keeper. It was not discovered until Saturday morning, and not until after Eklund had been found sick with fever in his bed in the barn. He died on Saturday night, but just before he breathed his last told of the grave which he opened for the receptacle of his own body, in which he was buried yesterday, as desired.'"

Max chewed it over for few seconds. "What's it mean?"

"Donner's telling us he dug his own grave. He doesn't want us to bring him back," said Struldbrug.

Manhattan's aeries were glowing red with the rising sun. The day would be its own color now, not enhanced by the Blister. It would be cold but clear.

Maggie was staring at Armitage's fedora. She snatched it from his head put it on her own. "Hey," he said, surprised.

She fished the cigarette—the one she'd snatched out of Nicole's hands in the parlor—out of her pocket.

"Damn shame," said Max solemnly, looking at the grave. "I was starting to like the guy."

"Not to worry," Maggie said. They looked at her in a triple take of surprise.

She pulled the brim down aslant over one eye and grinned. They were all gaping now. She lit the cigarette with a burst of plasma from her fingertip. She drew in the smoke and held it in her holographic lungs, relishing its feel. She released it into the rain-fresh air and treated them to a perfectly arched eyebrow.

"After all—"

She raised the syringe that had fallen from Nicole, and twirled it.

"—You can't keep a good man dead."

THE END

ACKNOWLEDGMENTS

First and foremost, thanks to my friend Scott Fishkind, who had a seriously cool idea that started me down the long road to this book. I am deeply indebted to him.

To my agent, Sandy Lu of L. Perkins Agency, for rescuing me from the slush pile.

To Dina Waters, Eric Kibler, Craig Snay, Mark Frost, Hilda Speicher and Xavier Amador for their active support and insightful comments on this manuscript. To Scott Sutton, who read this book on his tiny Blackberry screen at least ten times (and counting), and always managed to find a new typo.

Thanks also to fellow Youngstown natives Greg Smith and Chris Barzak (a talented novelist—check him out!); and especially TV writer/producer Jack LoGiudice, who took me under his wing in the wilds of LA and helped me become a professional TV writer. To my former TV agents Nancy Jones and Sue Naegle, to Peter Tolan, and to comedy titan Chuck Lorre, for taking a chance on a green NY playwright.

To Tracee Patterson, for her love and support. You too, Nathan and Lindsay!

Special heartfelt thanks to my brother, John, for the countless hours we spent in the basement creating worlds out of teddy bears, cardboard and imagination, setting us both on the path to writing careers. And for his support and advice, in good times and bad. We may not share the same genes, but you could not be more my brother, John.

To the fifth-grade teacher (I wish I could remember her name) who was my first publisher. She took my short story, typed and bound it, and put it in the class library next to all the other books. That was all it took to make me writer. Teachers are more precious than gold. It's a shame we don't treat them that way.

And finally, to the memory of Michael Bennahum, my first manager and agent, who never gave up on me, even when I screwed up. I still miss you, Michael.

Night Shade Books is an Independent Publisher of Quality Science-Fiction, Fantasy and Horror

ISBN: 978-1-59780-323-6 ◖ $24.99 ◖ Look for it in e-Book

It's the dawn of the 22nd century, and the world has fallen apart. Decades of war and resource depletion have toppled governments. The ecosystem has collapsed. A new dust bowl sweeps the American West. The United States has become a nation of migrants--starving masses of nomads roaming across wastelands and encamped outside government seed distribution warehouses.

In this new world, there is a new power: Satori. More than just a corporation, Satori is an intelligent, living city risen from the ruins of the heartland. She manufactures climate-resistant seed to feed humanity, and bio-engineers her own perfected castes of post-humans Designers, Advocates and Laborers. What remains of the United States government now exists solely to distribute Satori product; a defeated American military doles out bar-coded, single-use seed to the nation's hungry citizens.

Secret Service Agent Sienna Doss has watched her world collapse. Once an Army Ranger fighting wars across the globe, she now spends her days protecting glorified warlords and gangsters. As her country slides further into chaos, Doss feels her own life slipping into ruin.

When a Satori Designer goes rogue, Doss is tasked with hunting down the scientist-savant, and as events spin out of control, Sienna Doss and Brood find themselves at the heart of Satori, where an explosive finale promises to reshape the future of the world.

Night Shade Books is an Independent Publisher of Quality Science-Fiction, Fantasy and Horror

ISBN: 978-1-59780-232-1 ❦ $15.99 ❦ Look for it in e-Book

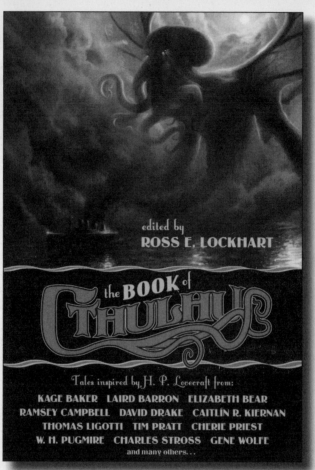

edited by
ROSS E. LOCKHART

the BOOK of CTHULHU

Tales inspired by H. P. Lovecraft from:

KAGE BAKER LAIRD BARRON ELIZABETH BEAR
RAMSEY CAMPBELL DAVID DRAKE CAITLÍN R. KIERNAN
THOMAS LIGOTTI TIM PRATT CHERIE PRIEST
W. H. PUGMIRE CHARLES STROSS GENE WOLFE
and many others...

Ia! Ia! Cthulhu Fhtagn!

First described by visionary author H. P. Lovecraft, the Cthulhu mythos encompass a pantheon of truly existential cosmic horror: Eldritch, uncaring, alien god-things, beyond mankind's deepest imaginings, drawing ever nearer, insatiably hungry, until one day, when the stars are right....

As that dread day, hinted at within the moldering pages of the fabled Necronomicon, draws nigh, tales of the Great Old Ones: Cthulhu, Yog-Sothoth, Hastur, Azathoth, Nyarlathotep, and the weird cults that worship them have cross-pollinated, drawing authors and other dreamers to imagine the strange dark aeons ahead, when the dead-but-dreaming gods return.

Now, intrepid anthologist Ross E. Lockhart has delved deep into the Cthulhu canon, selecting from myriad mind-wracking tomes the best sanity-shattering stories of cosmic terror. Featuring fiction by many of today's masters of the menacing, macabre, and monstrous, *The Book of Cthulhu* goes where no collection of Cthulhu mythos tales has before: to the very edge of madness... and beyond!

Do you dare open *The Book of Cthulhu*? Do you dare heed the call?

Night Shade Books is an Independent Publisher of Quality Science-Fiction, Fantasy and Horror

ISBN: 978-1-59780-285-7 ❆ $14.99 ❆ Look for it in e-Book

"*Southern Gods* is scary, smart, and effective both as Lovecraftian fiction and as a Southern Regional novel set in 1951."
— DAVID DRAKE, author of *Balefires*

SOUTHERN GODS

JOHN HORNOR JACOBS

Recent World War II veteran Bull Ingram is working as muscle when a Memphis DJ hires him to find Ramblin' John Hastur. The mysterious blues man's dark, driving music—broadcast at ever-shifting frequencies by a phantom radio station—is said to make living men insane and dead men rise.

Disturbed and enraged by the bootleg recording the DJ plays for him, Ingram follows Hastur's trail into the strange, uncivilized backwoods of Arkansas, where he hears rumors the musician has sold his soul to the Devil.

But as Ingram closes in on Hastur and those who have crossed his path, he'll learn there are forces much more malevolent than the Devil and reckonings more painful than Hell . . .

In a masterful debut of Lovecraftian horror and Southern gothic menace, John Hornor Jacobs reveals the fragility of free will, the dangerous power of sacrifice, and the insidious strength of blood.

ABOUT THE AUTHOR

Michael Dempsey is a novelist, actor, playwright and theatre direc-tor. Michael wrote for network television in the mid-'90s. *Necropolis* is his first novel and the result of a lifetime's passion for crime and speculative fiction. He lives in northeastern Ohio with his family, where he is working on his next novel.